BRIAN LUMLEY

BOB EGGLETON

THE TAINT AND OTHER NOVELLAS

THE TAINT AND OTHER NOVELLAS

Best Mythos Tales, Volume One

BRIAN LUMLEY

Subterranean Press 2007

"The Horror at Oakdeene," from the collection of the same name,
Arkham House, 1977.
"Born of the Winds," from *F&SF No. 295*, December, 1975.
"The Fairground Horror," from *The Disciples of Cthulhu*, DAW Books, 1975.
"The Taint," from *Weird Shadows Over Innsmouth*, Fedogan & Bremer, 2005.
"Rising With Surtsey," from *Dark Things*, Arkham House, 1971.
"Lord of the Worms," from *Weirdbook No. 17*, 1983.
"The House of the Temple," from *Kadath No. 3*, 1980.

First Edition

ISBN
978-1-59606-125-5

Subterranean Press
PO Box 190106
Burton, MI 48519

www.subterraneanpress.com

CONTENTS

INTRODUCTION

The Cthulhu Mythos.

Just three words, yet somehow fascinating in themselves. Just imagine someone stumbling across them for the first time; better still, try to remember when *you* first came across them in a book of macabre fiction. For even if you had never heard of Howard Phillips Lovecraft, or his biggest fan and publisher August Derleth, or Arkham House, *Weird Tales*, or indeed any of the original Lovecraft Circle or later imitators, or "literary disciples," of HPL, still in all likelihood you were struck by those words—if only because they caused you to wonder, "The Cthulhu Mythos? Now what the *hell* is that!?"

And how might one describe or explain to such a newcomer to weird fiction—for you could hardly be anything other than a newcomer—the pronunciation of that dreaded *Name* central to this unheard of mythology, Cthulhu? (What, in all seriousness, you should be informed that one whistles or burbles it?)

No, I am not going to try to offer a detailed explanation of the Cthulhu Mythos in this brief introduction; many and various authorities have already done that in as many articles and books, and it's likely you would not have bought this volume if you didn't already know at least something of H. P. Lovecraft's literary legacy. But if after reading these novellas the Mythos is still a mystery to you—which I most sincerely hope is not the case—then I would refer you to the master himself: to H. P. Lovecraft, and Clark Ashton Smith, Robert E. Howard, August Derleth (of course), and to Colin Wilson, Ramsey Campbell, and a veritable host of other writers, including many Arkham House authors and even Stephen King (the latter in his notable story, *Crouch End.)* For at one time or another they've all "had a go" at the Cthulhu Mythos—as, I might add, have many dozens and perhaps even hundreds of others, most frequently amateurs whose outpourings of Mythos dross still haven't managed to remove all of the gloss and mystique from the original concept.

Ah, but what was or is this concept? Well, actually, it's not only a horror theme but very much a Science Fictional sort of thing, too—which states, but in a great many more words:

That this Earth and its neighbouring "dimensions" conceal centuried (aeonian?) prisoned, slumbering or hibernating alien creatures of vast evil (or total indifference?) whose telepathic dreams infest the minds of certain artistic, sensitive, and often mentally "fragile" human beings, to the extent that they are caused to meddle with seals real and metaphysical that confine these Great Old Ones in their various forgotten (drowned, buried, or extradimensional) tombs or "houses."

As for Cthulhu: no better description of Him can be discovered than in HPL's own *The Call of Cthulhu*, and any horror fan who hasn't yet discovered Him should do so now, at once!

Myself, I came across the Mythos when I was just thirteen or fourteen in a story by Robert Bloch of *Psycho* fame, (though *Psycho* was only one of that superb writer's achievements). The short story was called *Notebook Found in a Deserted House*. And from then on, for the next seven or eight years, I would keep stumbling across various hints in the weird fiction I was reading that suggested an interconnected thread or threads; a very intricate literary theme, like a web woven from oddly similar stories by a handful of disparate authors. This was, of course, the very fabric or skein of the Cthulhu Mythos, though at that time I failed to make a solid connection. (Another connection I failed to make, which was pointed out to me by Donald A. Wollheim of DAW Books fame, was that I was born on the 2nd December 1937, just nine months after Lovecraft's death. Wollheim found the chronology or synchronicity interesting; I find it entirely coincidental.)

But then, as a young soldier taken in the draft and based in Germany—upon finding an entire book by Lovecraft, entitled *Cry Horror!* (the British title of a volume originally published by Arkham House in the USA)—suddenly all of these vague hints and allusions coalesced in my mind into this single, remarkable literary concept, this fictional phenomenon called The Cthulhu Mythos! But—

—I wasn't yet an author "in my own write," and it would be some time, several years in fact, before I was seduced onto the strands of that web myself...

In one of his introductions August Derleth described me as "A *young* British author": my italics. Well I wasn't *that* young. I was twenty-nine when—having by then collected almost all of the available Lovecraft material—I wrote to Derleth at Arkham House to order books. Along with monies, I sent some "extracts" from a handful of dubiously titled "black books," the survivors of antique, now extinct civilizations that either worshipped or shunned the variously imaged "gods" and "demons" of the Cthulhu Cycle. These forbidden volumes were of my own invention (following in the footsteps of HPL and others) and Derleth seemed much taken by them; he hinted that I might like to "try my hand" at writing "something solid in the Mythos" for an anthology he was going to call *Tales of the Cthulhu Mythos*. Of course I attended to that immediately!

So, why hadn't I tried my hand prior to this invitation? But I had! As a boy of twelve or thirteen I had, er, "composed" a Science Fiction yarn and read it to my coalminer father. And he, a knowledgeable but very down to earth man, had commented, "Aye, all very nice, lad—but there's no money in words." He simply couldn't conceive of anyone making a satisfactory living writing fiction. And it has to be conceded that at that time a large majority of writers weren't at all well paid.

All that aside, now (or then) at the age of twenty-nine, I began to write for Derleth at Arkham House, and of course I did so very much in the mode of Lovecraft; those early stories were steeped in the fantastical, fictional lore of the Cthulhu Mythos. So, that is where most of the stories in this book had their beginnings. I should point out, however, that not all of my Mythos stories read like HPL; they're not all slavish pastiches, such as Derleth's own supposedly Lovecraft "collaborations." For despite that it narrates Lovecraftian themes, still my voice is my own.

My work in this vein has two distinct forms: novellas and short (or shorter) stories. The book you hold in your hands is from the first of two companion volumes; it contains the novellas. Volume Two will have most of my Mythos short stories that in my opinion are worthy of this sort of hardcover collection. The stories here presented are not in chronological order, but for readers who are curious about such matters I have included, as a preface to each novella, brief details of the when, where, and the why of its writing.

But there, enough from me; now I'll let the Cthulhu Mythos more properly explain itself...

—Brian Lumley

THE HORROR AT OAKDEENE

My first stories were published by August Derleth in 1968, so I was still a relative beginner in the first half of 1970 when I sent him this novella. I was also still in the British Army: a recruiting sergeant, of all things, in the city of Leicester. The story was published (eventually) by Derleth's Arkham House, but I had to wait all of seven years to see it in print in the hardcover collection of the same name, a book which is now long out of print. The Horror at Oakdeene—quite obviously the work of a beginner and very heavily influenced by Lovecraft—is one of a quite small handful of stories that has not been reprinted until now...

In the summer of 1935 Martin Spellman went to work as a trainee mental nurse at Oakdeene Sanatorium. He was twenty-four years old and already dedicated—but not to nursing. Spellman's one ambition since his early teens had been to be an author; and since a rather odd and macabre turn of mind had dictated for his first projected work a compilation of rare or outstanding mental cases, he had decided that the best way to gain a first-hand insight on his subject—the *feel*, as it were, of asylums—would be to work in such an institute.

Of course, Spellman's real intention in applying for training was kept well hidden, but that did not mean that he was not going to try his best in the job to which he was committing himself. The minimum contract period was one year, with a further year of full-time nursing, and Martin cheerfully agreed to these terms in the furtherance of his project.

His colleagues and superior officers alike were quite astonished at the unaccustomed zeal with which young Spellman threw himself into his work, and every night that he was not on duty saw the light in his room burning well into the early hours. Martin had allotted his time off-duty in the following manner: for three hours he would study the theory of mental nursing, for five hours he would work on his book. This would leave him at least six hours for sleeping in any given twenty-four hour period. At those times when night-duty came around—once or twice each week—he would alter his schedule so as to spend the same amount of time in these aforementioned tasks.

Often Martin's immediate superior and tutor, Dr. Welford, caught him in the late summer and early autumn of the year working on his manuscripts; but who could complain about a student mental nurse writing a series of "theses" or correlations on the stranger, more complex cases of his calling? If anything Martin was to be congratulated on his studious attention to all details of his sanatorium routine.

In fact Spellman soon discovered that he did not like his work at the institute; his night-duties were an especial abomination, when on occasion he had of necessity to wander those lower corridors of Oakdeene wherein the worst patients were held resident. His harder, more stoic colleagues called the basement ward "Hell," and Martin Spellman would not have contested this seemingly harsh appellation. It *was* hell down there, with the corridor lights starkly illuminating the heavy doors with their little barred spy-holes and their labels bearing brief, typed case histories of the occupants of the cells. Behind those doors, separated from Martin by only the thickness of the oak panels and battens and the rubbery warm panels within, many of Britain's most terrible lunatics dwelt in the perpetual horror of their own madness, and Martin Spellman made sure when on night-duty that his hourly tours of Hell were undertaken with a thoroughly efficient but speedy dispatch.

One of Spellman's so-called "colleagues" at the sanatorium, Alan Barstowe (an ugly, squat-bodied, fully-trained nurse of some thirty-five years), was able on occasion to help the trainee out with his dread of the ward known as Hell. Barstowe, it seemed, had no fear of that part of night-duty whatever; indeed, in the eerie atmosphere of the nighted asylum, he appeared to welcome the hourly visits to the lower ward. He would often exchange duties with Spellman, saying that he did not mind working nights—that in fact he preferred such duties to those of the daylight hours. Every man to his own tastes!

Spellman's room at the institute was on the ground floor—one of four bed-living-room combinations—separated from the two mental wards on the same floor by reinforced, soundproofed walls. With the recruiting of nurses at Oakdeene going badly, two of the four "living-in" rooms were empty. The other occupied room belonged to one Harold Moody, a fully-trained, middle-aged mental nurse whose partial deafness was certainly no handicap in living directly above Hell; the flooring of the ground-floor quarters was definitely *not* soundproof! Not that the sounds from below bothered Spellman often, but he did notice that Hell's inmates were always exceptionally vociferous whenever Alan Barstowe was on night-duty; and at those times the screams, moans, and gibberings from the basement ward seemed to penetrate the stone floor beneath his bed with an insistence that bothered him inwardly as well as keeping him physically awake often until four and five in the morning.

Eventually there came a time when the student and Barstowe were detailed for night-duty together, and frankly the younger man was not at all happy with the arrangement. For all Barstowe's apparent amicability, and quite apart from the contours of his face and body, there was something ugly about the man. And yet the evening shift started quite normally at 9:00 P.M., with nothing in Barstowe's manner to substantiate Spellman's feelings or cause him any untoward concern.

The orders for night-duty included the stipulation that each ward would be visited—each cell, room, and occupant checked and, as far as possible, inspected once every hour. Martin Spellman had been detailed for duty in the lower wards and Hell, while Barstowe had the upper wards and the rooms of the quieter, less permanent inmates. At 11:00 P.M., when the student nurse was about to descend for the second time to the dreaded basement ward with its padding-muted gibberings, curses and moans, he was hailed from above as he stood at the top of the stone steps.

"Young Spellman! Hold on a minute," the guttural voice of the froggish Barstowe came down to him. Looking up towards the first-floor landing, the trainee saw the squat man making his way quickly down the stairs. In his hand Barstowe carried what looked like a black stick, about eighteen inches long and with a silver tip.

As he descended, the nurse saw Spellman staring at his weapon and held it closer to his body, concealing it as best he could. "Come prepared, I always say," he muttered with a strained grin as he came to a halt beside the trainee. "Look, Martin," he quickly changed the subject, "I know you don't care much for the lower wards and Hell—so if you fancy I'll stay down here and you can carry on upstairs. I was just about to do Ward Four—so if you'd care to—"

"Ward Four? I wouldn't mind—but what's *that* for, Barstowe?" Spellman pointedly indicated the stick which the older man had almost managed to hide in the clinical white folds of his smock. "I mean, it's not as though they were about to break out!"

"No," Barstowe answered, turning his eyes down and away, "it's just that I feel more…more comfortable down there with a stick. You never know, do you?"

As Spellman climbed the stairs he retained in his mind's eye a mental picture of that stick of Barstowe's. If one of the officers got to know of the weapon, Barstowe would be in serious trouble. Not that the squat nurse could do the inmates any harm with the thing—if threatened through the bars of a spy-hole, an occupant would. only have to move to the back of his cell to be out of harms's way—no, obviously it was as Barstowe had explained; his stick was simply a comforter.

Nonetheless, Spellman could not help but remember those screams he listened to deep into the night whenever Barstowe was on duty in the basement ward. The funny thing was that later that night—even on the second floor, in the open rooms of the more trusted patients and in the corridors between those comparatively homely billets—the trainee nurse could *still* hear those muted, tortured echoes from Hell….

Towards the end of October Martin Spellman's reading and studying for his book had taken a turn toward rather more specialized cases: in particular aberrations apparently influenced by imaginary or hallucinatory "outside" forces. He had seen definite connections in a fair number of reasonably well authenticated cases—connections which were especially interesting inso far as they depicted almost carbon-copy fancies, dreams, and delusions in the afflicted parties.

There was for instance the very well documented case of Joe Slater, the Catskill Mountains trapper, whose lunatic actions in 1900-01 had seemed governed not by the moon but rather by the influence of a point or object in the heavens much farther out than the orbit of Earth's satellite. The authenticity of this case, however, seemed to Spellman spoiled by its chronicler's insistence that Slater was in fact inhabited by the mind of an alien being. Then there was the German Baron, Ernst Kant, who, before his hideous and inexplicable death in a Westphalian Bedlam, had believed his every insane action controlled by a creature he called Yibb-Tstll; described as being "huge and black with writhing breasts and an anus within its forehead, a black-blooded *thing* whose brains feed upon its own wastes…."

More recently there was Dr. David Stephenson's recorded observations of one J. M. Freeth, a female zoophagous maniac whose declared intention was to *absorb* as many lives as she could. This she set about, like Bram Stoker's Renfield, by feeding flies to spiders, spiders to sparrows, and finally by devouring the sparrows herself! She, too, as with the maniac in Stoker's story, had been refused a cat once her intentions were quite clear! Her odd fancies had been part and parcel of her belief that she had watching over her a supernatural "God-creature" who would eventually come to release her. Miss Freeth's obsessions and her "life-devouring" mania were far from unique, and the student collected and recorded a number of similar cases.

Again, this time from the records of a certain Canton madhouse in America, Spellman culled the horrible story of an innate who had been, before his escape and subsequent disappearance some seven years previously in 1928, completely sure of his immortality and of the fact that he would "dwell in Y'hanthlei amidst wonder and glory forever…." His destiny (he was righteous in his self-assurance) was governed by "the Deep Ones, Dagon, and Lord Cthulhu"—with the former of which he would serve in the worship and glorification of the latter—whoever or whatever these names were supposed. to signify! There was, though, a clue to this last poor unfortunate's aberrations. He was pronouncedly ichthyic in appearance, with protuberant eyes and scaly skin, and it was believed that these physical abnormalities had led him to dwell too often and too long over certain obscure myths and legends involving oceanic deities. In this connection it seemed likely that his "Dagon" was that same fish-god of the Philistines and Phoenicians, sometimes known as Oannes.

So Spellman's studies grew more specific as the weeks passed, but he little dreamed that in a certain cell in Hell there resided a man whose case was as odd as any he had so far collected for his book….

In mid-November, knowing something of the new direction his pupil's studies were taking, Dr. Welford invited Spellman to read the case-file of Wilfred Larner, usually one of the quieter residents of Hell but a man who could swiftly turn from a reasonably controlled individual to a raging, savage animal. Larner's case, too, seemed to have had its genesis in those "outside" regions which so fascinated the student nurse.

Thus it happened that in his room above the basement ward Martin Spellman first came into close contact with Larner's file, and from the first he became absorbed with the thing; particularly with those mentions of a certain "Black Book"—a thing called the *Cthaat Aquadingen*—purported to relate to the raising of water- and ocean-elementals and other "demons" of more obscure origins. Apparently this book was one of the main causes of Larner's rapid mental decline some ten years previously; and, according to the file, its hints, suggestions, and the occasional blatantly blasphemous "revelation" could scarcely be considered safe reading for any man with a delicately balanced mind.

Spellman could hardly be blamed for not recognizing the title: *Cthaat Aquadingen,* for the book was known only to a scattered handful of men, most of them erudite antiquarians or students of rare and ancient works, some of them students of darker things: the occult sciences! Indeed, only five copies of the work in various forms existed in the whole world at that time; one in the private library of a London collector; one under lack and key—along with the *Necronomicon,* the *G'harne Fragments,* the *Pnakotic Manuscripts,* the *Liber Ivonis,* the dread *Cultes des Goules,* and the *Revelations of Glaaki*—in the British Museum, and two of the others in even more obscure and inaccessible places. The fifth copy: that one was soon to fall into Spellman's unwitting hands.

But this book aside, during his decline and before his sister committed him to the institute's care, Larner had also assembled something of a Fortean collection of cuttings from newspapers all over the world; cuttings which, especially if considered as from the often narrow viewpoint of a disordered psyche, might take on all sorts of disturbing aspects.

Spellman wondered just where the institute had gained its often detailed information regarding the events leading to Larner's confinement; and in this he was lucky, for enquiries with Dr. Welford the next morning led him to discover that Larner's sister had placed *all* documents relevant to her brother's derangement in the hands of the institute's alienists. Both Larner's cuttings-file and his "*Cthaat Aguadingen*" (a great sheaf of stapled foolscap pages in Larner's own handwriting; presumably copied from some other work) were still safely stored in a cupboard in Oakdeene's spacious administrative offices—and Dr. Welford was not adverse to the idea of placing them, for a few days at least, at Spellman's disposal.

Of the great manuscript in Larner's hand the student could make very little; there were too many inconsistencies in its strange contents—odd juxtapositions in sentence-structure and so on—that seemed to point to its being a translation from some other language, possibly German, and done by a man none too well versed in the tongue, perhaps Larner himself. On the other hand, Larner could have copied his work from some other translated version; and then again, it was just possible that the entire work was his own, but that seemed hardly likely. There were lurid descriptions of rites—hideous magical ceremonies involving human and animal sacrifices—which, even suffering as they did through poor translation, were more than sufficient to convince the student nurse that the study of this work had indeed gone far to helping Larner on his way to the institute's basement ward. Having a very well balanced mind himself, and therefore seeing no point in wading through three or four hundred pages of such material, Spellman passed quickly on to the cuttings-file.

Now this was something one could get one's teeth into and what a bonus for Spellman's book! Why, the cuttings-file was crammed full of stuff he was sure he could use. There were cuttings from sources scattered throughout the globe, from London, Edinburgh, and Dublin; from the Americas, Haiti, and Africa; from France, India, and Malta; from the Troodos Mountains of Cyprus, the Australian Outback, and the Teutoburger Wald in West Germany; and the great majority of them involved the actions of persons—both singularly and in groups or "cults"—allegedly influenced by alien or "outside" forces!

They covered a period from early February 1925 to mid-1926—detailing cases of panic, mania, and weird eccentricity—and as Spellman read he quickly spotted connecting links in what at first had seemed dissociated stories. Two columns of the *News of the World* had been given over to coverage of the case of the man who uttered a hideous cry before leaping from a fourth-storey window to his death. His room showed proof on investigation that the suicide had been involved with some sort of magical rite; a pentacle had been chalked on the floor and the walls were painted with a crude representation of the blasphemous *Nyhargo Code*. In Africa missionary outposts had reported ominous mutterings from little-known desert and jungle tribes, and it was shown in one cutting how human sacrifices had been made to an earth-elemental called Shudmell. Spellman was quick to tie this report in with the fantastic and still unexplained disappearance of Sir Amery Wendy-Smith and his nephew in Yorkshire in 1933; they, too, had seemed obsessed by the conviction that they were doomed to death at the devices of a similar "deity," one Shudde-M'ell, "of gigantic, rubbery, snakelike, and tentacled appearance." In California an entire theosophist colony donned white robes for a "glorious fulfillment" that never arrived, and in Northern Ireland white-robed youths sacked and burned three churches in outlying districts to make way for "the Temples of a greater Lord." In the Philippines American officers had found certain tribes extremely bothersome throughout the entire period, and in Australia sixty percent of Aboriginal settlements had shut themselves off completely from contact with whites. Secret cults and societies all over the world had brought themselves into the open for the first time, admitting allegiance to various gods and forces and declaring that the vision of their faiths, an "ultimate resurrection," was about to take place. Troubles in insane asylums were legion, and Spellman wondered at the stoicism of medical fraternities that they had not noted the parallelisms or drawn anything other than the most mundane conclusions.

On the first night of his serious study of the file, Spellman did not get to his bed until very late, leaving it at a correspondingly late hour in the morning. This was a rare indulgence for him; indeed, feeling somehow lethargic the whole day, he did not bother to study or even to work on his book. That evening, when the time came around for his late shift, he still felt sleepy and dull, and it was only then that he discovered he had been detailed once more for the abhorrent lower wards and Hell. Again Barstowe shared the night shift with the student nurse, and Spellman guessed that before midnight the froggish man would come down to make his usual offer.

At eleven he was in the basement ward, beginning his first hurried tour of the morbid place, when he was startled to hear his name called from the small barred spy-hole in the door of the second cell on the left. This was Larner's cell, and apparently the man was in one of his more lucid states. This suited the student very well, for he had intended to talk to Larner at the first opportunity. Now he saw he had his chance.

"How are you, Larner?" he carefully enquired, moving over to peer at the white face framed in the tiny square spy-hole. "You certainly seem in good spirits."

"I am, I am—and I trust you'll help me stay that way…."

"Oh? And how might I be of service?"

"Tell me," Larner secretively asked, "who is on duty with you tonight?"

"Nurse Barstowe," Spellman answered. "Why do you ask?"

But Larner had scurried back away from the door on hearing Barstowe's name spoken, so that Spellman had to peer in through the spy-hole to see him.

"What's wrong, Larner? Don't you get on with Barstowe, then?"

"Larner is a trouble-maker, Spellman—didn't you know?" Barstowe's guttural, strangely menacing voice came suddenly from close behind. Spellman jumped, startled by the unexpected sound, turning to face the squat nurse who must have crept up on him quiet as a mouse. "And anyway—" the ugly man continued, "since when is it your practice to discuss senior personnel with the inmates? Very odd behavior, that, Spellman."

But the student was not a man to be easily intimidated, and the instinctive fear Barstowe's appearance had aroused in him quickly turned to anger when he heard the veiled threat in the older man's question. "You're out of bounds, Barstowe—" he harshly answered, "—and what do you mean by sneaking about down here? If you're thinking of changing duties with me you can forget it—I don't like the way these people behave when you're on duty!" Spellman made his oblique accusation and watched Barstowe's reaction.

The fully-trained nurse had gone gray on hearing Spellman "tick him off," and he was plainly at a loss as to how to answer. When he did speak he had dropped his "Spellman" attitude: "I—I—what are you getting at, Martin? Why! I only came down here to do you a service. I'm not blind, you know. It's plain you don't *like* it down here. But you've done yourself now, Martin. I won't be offering to help you out again—you can bet your life on that."

"That suits me fine, Barstowe—but hadn't you better be getting back upstairs? By now half the inmates could be out running about the grounds— or are they too afraid of that stick of yours to try it?" Barstowe's gray color took on an even lighter shade, and beneath the folds of his smock his right hand jerked involuntarily at mention of his stick. "Got it with you, have you?" Spellman pointedly stared at the tell-tale bulge in the froggish man's clinical attire. "I shouldn't have bothered if I were you. You won't be needing it tonight—not down here at any rate."

At that Barstowe seemed to shrink into himself, the color leaving his face completely, and he turned without another word and almost ran along the corridor and up the stone steps. For the first time, as the squat nurse hurriedly climbed those steps, Spellman noticed that all the spy-holes in the doors lining the corridor were occupied. Faces—in various stages of agitation or animation—with eyes all fixed on the retreating figure of the ugly man, were framed in those tiny barred openings. And Spellman shuddered at the positive *hatred* those mad faces and eyes reflected.

On his next visit to Hell one hour later, Martin Spellman tried to talk to the basement ward's three or four occasionally articulate inmates; to no avail. Even Larner would have nothing to do with him. And yet the student nurse seemed somehow to detect an air of satisfaction; a peculiar feeling of *security* flowed out quite tangibly from behind those locked doors and padded walls....

For at least a week after the incident with Barstowe, Spellman felt tempted to mention the man's odd ways to Dr. Welford; and yet he did not wish to cause Barstowe any real harm. After all, he had no genuine proof that the man was not carrying out his duties in anything other than a proper manner, and the fact that he carried a stick with him whenever he visited the basement ward could hardly be called conclusive evidence of any unprofessional intent; there was no way at all in which Barstowe could put his weapon to any use. It seemed purely and simply that the man was a rather nasty coward and nothing more—someone to be avoided and ignored, certainly, but not really worth bothering oneself about.

Beside, things were bad at that time; Spellman did not want a jobless Barstowe on his conscience. He did ask one or two discreet questions of the other nurses, however, and while it appeared that none of them particularly cared much for Barstowe, it was likewise evident that no one considered him especially evil or even a bad nurse. And so Spellman dismissed the matter....

Towards the end of November Spellman first heard the news of Barstowe's projected move into "living-in" quarters; apparently the landlady with whom the squat man lodged was expecting her son home from abroad and needed Barstowe's room. Only a few days later the unpleasant possibility became reality when the oddly offensive nurse did indeed move into one of the four ground-floor flatlets; and he had hardly settled in when, at the very end of a month, the first hint of the horror came to Oakdeene.

It happened in the small hours of the morning following one of those rare evenings when, unable to endure his surroundings for another night without a break of some sort, Martin Spellman had allowed himself to be persuaded by Harold Moody to go down into Oakdeene village for a drink. Martin was not a drinking man and his limit was usually only three or four beers, but that night he felt "in the mood," and the result was that when he and Moody got back to the sanatorium just before midnight he was more than amply prepared for his bed.

It was, too, the beer that saved Martin Spellman from possible involvement when the horror came, for at any other time the hideous screams and demented shrieks from the basement ward would most certainly have shocked him from sleep. As it was, he missed all the "excitement," as Harold Moody had it the next morning when he went into the student's room to shake him awake.

The "excitement" was that four hours earlier, at about three in the morning, one of Hell's worst inhabitants had died after throwing a particularly horrible fit. During his attack the man, one Gordon Merritt, a hopeless lunatic for twenty years, had somehow contrived to gouge out one of his own eyes!

It was only later that Spellman thought to enquire which of the nurses had been unfortunate enough to be on duty when Merritt took his last, fatal fit; and an almost subconscious tremor of strange apprehension went through him when he was told that it had been Barstowe!

✥ ✥ ✥

For the two weeks following Merritt's death Barstowe kept very much to himself; much more than ever before, and he had never been much of a mixer. In fact, had he not known better, Spellman might never have suspected that Barstowe was "living-in" at all. The truth was that the directors of Oakdeene had been far from happy at the enquiry, and it was thought that the squat nurse had been given a sound dressing down—something about his responses to the situation on the night of the incident being inefficient and altogether too slow. The general belief seemed to be that Merritt's seizure might well have been avoided if Barstowe had been a bit "quicker off the mark"....

On the 13th December Spellman again found himself on nightduty, and once more it was his hourly lot to have to patrol the ward called Hell. Until that time he had never realized that there existed in his subconscious the slightest intention of trying to discover more details of the facts surrounding Merritt's death—he only knew that something had been bothering him for far too long and that there were certain things he would like to know—and yet, on his first visit to the basement ward, he went straight to Larner's cell and called the man to the spy-hole.

The cells were constructed in such a way as to make every interior corner visible from those small, barred windows; that is to say that each cell was wedge-shaped, with the "sharp" end of the wedge formed by the door itself. Larner had been lying on his bed at the far end of the cell staring silently at the ceiling when Spellman called out to him, but he quickly got up and went to the door on identifying his caller.

"Larner," Spellman quietly questioned as soon as the other had greeted him, "—what happened to Merritt? Was it—was it the way they say, or—? Tell me what happened, will you?"

"Nurse Spellman, would you do me a great favor?" Larner apparently had not heard the student's question—or perhaps, Spellman thought, he had simply chosen to ignore it!

"A favor? If I can, Larner—what is it you want me to do?"

"There is a matter of *justice* to be attended to!" the lunatic suddenly blurted out, so suddenly, with such urgency—with something so very akin to fervor in his voice—that the young nurse took a quick step back from the cell door.

"Justice, Larner ? Whatever do you mean?"

"Justice, yes!" The man peered out at Spellman through the bars, blinking rapidly, nervously as he spoke. And then, in the manner of certain lunatics, he abruptly changed the subject. "Dr. Welford has mentioned how you find the *Cthaat Aquadingen* of interest. I, too, once found it a very interesting work—but for a long time now the book has not been available to me. I suppose they believe its contents to be…well, 'not in my best interests.' Perhaps they're right, I'm not sure. It's true that the *Cthaat Aquadingen* put me in here. Oh, that's true—quite definitely—yes, that's why I'm here. I read the Sixth Sathlatta far too often, you see? I almost broke down the barrier completely. I mean, it's all very well to see Yibb-Tstll in dreams— you can stand that much at least—*but to have him breaking through the barrier!*…Ah! There's a monstrous thought. To have him breaking through—*uncontrolled!*"

As Larner spoke, something he said rang a bell in the student's mind. Spellman had glimpsed in his brief scanning of the contents of the madman's book a passage or two containing certain chants or invocations, the Sathlat-tae, and he made a mental note that later he must go back to that strange volume and discover whatever he could of them…and also of this— creature?—Yibb-Tstll.

But then, speaking again, Larner broke into his thoughts; and again the lunatic's expression had changed, his eyes being wide and steady now in his white face. "Well, nurse Spellman, would it be possible for you to—to do me a little harmless service?"

"You'll have to say what it is first."

"Quite simply—I'd like you to make me a copy of the Sixth Sathlatta from the *Cthaat Aquadingen*, and bring it to me. No harm in that, is there?"

Spellman frowned: "But haven't you just this moment blamed your being here on that very book?"

"Ah!" Larner made to explain. "But then I didn't know what I was doing. It's different now—except I can't remember how the thing goes: the Sixth Sathlatta, I mean. It's been almost ten years…."

"Well, I really don't know," Spellman carefully considered. "But see here, Larner, favors work two ways, you know? You still haven't answered my question. I might be able to do as you ask, but are you willing to tell me what happened the night Merritt died?"

Larner's eyes, however, had gone furtive, nervous again. He turned his face away. "We'll handle it ourselves, Spellman, no matter the price," he muttered. Then he glanced sharply back at the face of the student framed in the barred window, and again Spellman was amazed at the mercurial property of the man's character. Now his eyes were penetrating, almost sane. "Nothing happened. Merritt took a fit, that's all. He was a madman—you know?" Again Larner turned away, this time to walk over to his bed and lie down in his former position.

Spellman, knowing that their "chat" was over, continued slowly down the stark corridor, peering in at the barred spy-holes as he went.

The remainder of that night, despite the fact that he knew all was in order, Martin Spellman could not rid his subconscious of distant alarm bells, and as he walked the nighted halls he found himself occasionally glancing nervously over his shoulder.

Spellman had the next weekend free of duty, and he used his Saturday to track down Larner's strange references in the *Cthaat Aquadingen*. He eventually found a decidedly alien-looking—chant?—hidden away in one of the manuscript's four coded sections under the legible heading "Sixth Sathlatta." Almost without knowing, he copied the weirdly jumbled letters down onto a sheet of paper, attempting a tongue-twisting pronounciation as he did so:

> "Ghe 'phnglui, mglw'ngh ghee'yh, Yibb-Tstll,
> Fhtagn mglw y'tlette ngh'wgah, Yibb-Tstll,
> Ghe'phnglui mglw-ngh ahkobhg'shg, Yibb-Tstll,
> THABAITE!—YIBB-TSTLL, YIBB-TSTLL, YIBB-TSTLL!"

Then, before searching for further references to Yibb-Tstll, the young nurse spent a few more minutes vainly trying to make something of what he had written down. Finally he gave up the hopeless task, moving on eventually to find the notes he sought—crowded marginalia apparently deciphered from the coded pages, so-called methods of evocation—in another of the book's sections. To clarify the "message" of these notes, and to make of them something of a readable passage, again, as with the Sixth Sathlatta, he neatly copied the words down onto paper:

(1) TO CALL THE BLACK:
This method involves a wafer, of (flour?) and water composition—printed with the Sixth Sathlatta in the *original* symbols—handed to the victim with the summoning chant (Necronomicon, p. 224, under heading *Hoy-Dhin*) called out aloud within the said victim's hearing. This will not produce Yibb-Tstll but his Black Blood, which has the property of being able to live apart from Him; called from a universe so alien that it is known only

to Yibb-Tstll and Yog-Sothoth, conterminous with all spaces and times. The victim is taken when the Black Blood settles like a mantle about him and smothers him. Then the juice of Yibb-Tstll returns with the soul of the victim to the body of The Drowner in His own continuum....

(2) TO SEE YIBB-TSTLL IN DREAMS:
...& the Sixth Sathlatta may be used...that one might scry in Dreams the Form of The Drowner, Yibb-Tstll, who walks in all Times & Spaces. It must however be observed that the Chant should be used sparingly—*once only*—before each Sleep wherein the Scrying is to be done, lest the Seer impart into That on which he gazes a Perception of the Gate of his Mind; & that, in using this Gate to enter from Outside, & in returning thither through this same Gate, Yibb-Tstll may *burn out* the Mind & Gate & all in His coming & going...for the Agony is great & Death certain. Nor, in such a visitation, would His Actions in this Sphere be controlled; The Drowner's Appetite was well known to the Adepts of old....

(3) TO CALL YIBB-TSTLL:
This method again involves the use of the Sixth Sathlatta: called out three times by thirteen adepts in unison at midnight of any First Day. Note: *any* thirteen callers will find the ritual as described answered, provided at least one amongst them is an adept; but unless at least *seven* of the callers are adepts—and unless, on the night before the midnight of a calling, they first seal their souls with the Naach-Tith Barrier—they may well suffer hideous reversals and penalties!

There was a note here in red ink, added by Larner to the foregoing marginalia: "Must try to find the remainder of the words to raise the barrier of Naach-Tith...." Obviously, Spellman thought, at the time the man in the ward called Hell had written that last cryptic note, he had already been well along the strange paths of insanity.

For the rest of the afternoon Spellman left the pages of his rapidly shaping manuscript alone and turned to his studies, only making a break for a meal at about six and returning to his textbooks immediately after. At eight he brewed a pot of coffee, which, rather than giving him a lift, seemed to make him somewhat weary so that he lay down on his bed for a few minutes. He had been more tired than he thought, however, waking up cramped and chilly some three hours later when a nightmare—the nature of which he could not remember—shocked him from his sleep.

He turned on his gas fire then, brewing another cup of coffee before taking out his manuscript to make a few small alterations and further notes. He worked solidly until two in the morning, only undressing and climbing into bed when he was satisfied that the current chapter of his book was going well. But before sleeping he took up the loose sheets of paper bearing those notes copied earlier from the *Cthaat Aquadingen*.

Again, out loud, he commenced to attempt a pronounciation of that weird jumble of letters entitled the Sixth Sathlatta, fancying that his low utterances this time sounded more nearly like they should. But before reaching the end of the second line, when he felt a strange dread welling up inside him, he paused. An involuntary shudder ran the length of his spine.

What was it he had read of this so-called "invocation"? Yes, there it was, just as he had copied it down: "…& the Sixth Sathlatta may be used…that one night scry in Dreams the Form of The Drowner, Yibb-Tstll, who walks in all Times & Spaces."

An odd dizziness seemed to come over him and he shook his head to clear it; but though this steadied him somewhat, nonetheless he put away his papers and settled himself down in bed. Something was wrong with his nerves, that was plain. It must be this place and its inmates. He would have to get himself down into Oakdeene village more often with Harold Moody.

Again Spellman dropped quickly off to sleep, and once more his dreams were of a nightmarish nature….

There were weird scenes of alien herbage and evil-looking monochrome flowers. Jungles of darkly exotic ferns stretched writhing fronds toward starless, dark green skies through which fantastic birds slid on veined and pulsating wings. There was a clearing close by in the hellish tangle of unknown growths, towards which Spellman's subconscious spirit seemed drawn in some inexplicable fashion. Fungoid shrubs drew back from him as he moved toward the clearing, and huge insects buzzed evilly as they burst from the bells of poisonous-looking blooms at his approach. He realized that he was the alien in this monstrous dimension of dream, and that the reluctance of its denizens was such as his own might be were the roles reversed.

Soon he reached the clearing, a great scabrous area of bleached and sterile earth stretching for at least a mile before the jungle took up again on the other side. In the center of this hideous expanse The Thing stood, and at that distance Spellman judged It to be at least three times as tall as a man. As he drew closer across the crumbling and scabby ground he saw that The Thing was turning, slowly turning about on feet hidden from his view by a great green cloak, a cloak that bulged and jerked and writhed as it fell from just beneath the—head?—to the corroded and powdery surface on which it stood. Drawing still closer, the dream-Spellman felt a scream welling in his throat as the great figure turned towards him and he saw the face clearly for the first time. Had the terrible shape not gone on turning—had those eyes noticed him for a single moment—Martin Spellman knew he must shriek out loud, but no, The Thing in Green continued Its apparently aimless turning, and Its voluminous cloak was alive with uncanny motion....

When Spellman was very close to the giant, no more than a score of paces away, his movement towards It ceased. The Thing had still been turning away from him, but, as he came to a halt, Its motion also faltered.

Then The Thing stopped turning altogether!

For a moment the scene seemed frozen, the only movement being the fantastic billowing of the green cloak, then, slowly but inexorably, the monstrous form began to turn back towards the paralyzed dreamer.

Soon the great figure halted again, facing squarely in Spellman's direction, and he screamed voicelessly as the blasphemous cloak billowed out more violently than ever, parting to permit the dreamer one mad glimpse beneath its green folds. There, about the pulsating black body of the Ancient One, hugely winged reptilian creatures without faces cluttered and clutched at a multitude of blackly writhing, pendulous breasts!

This much Martin Spellman saw—

—And the next thing he knew was that he was being roughly shaken and slapped awake!

Harold Moody, pleasantly drunk, having just returned on foot from Oakdeene village, had "dropped in" to see if Martin fancied a brew of coffee; he knew that Martin often worked quite late. But he had found his young friend in the throes of nightmare. Never was a man—half inebriated or not and despite the hour—more welcome than Harold Moody; for, even realizing now that he had only been dreaming, Spellman sat and shivered uncontrollably on his bed while has late visitor brewed hot coffee. He could remember his nightmare clearly, and what he remembered was quite the most hellish thing he had ever known.

The monstrous dream-jungle had been bad enough...and the blossom-bloated insects...and the clearing of dead and crumbling earth. Worse still had been the membranous, blind, winged creatures beneath the sickening green cloak of the giant. But worst of all had been the eyes in the head of that slowly turning colossus....

❖ ❖ ❖

The next morning, despite an odd listlessness against which he had to fight very hard, Spellman set himself to the long task of searching diligently through the *Cthaat Aquadingen*. The dream of the previous night had been so real—and yet for his life he could not remember having seen in Larner's "Black Book" a description of anything remotely like the nightmare vision he had experienced. Even in broad daylight, with a weak December sun shining in through his window facing the exercise yard, Spellman shuddered as he recalled The Thing of his dream. Other than Ernst Kant's description of "a thing with black breasts and an anus within its forehead"—not from the *Cthaat Aquadingen* but a comparatively modern work on singular foreign mental cases, similar to the book Spellman was trying to write—there was nothing. From where, then, had his subconscious conjured up the monster of the dream?

Spellman realized that he must after all have a mind far more open to suggestion than he would ever have formerly believed. He had, of course, dreamed of The Thing after reading of the supposed method of "scrying Yibb-Tstll in Dreams." Ridiculous though it all was, the idea had strongly influenced his subconscious, and the nightmare had been the result....

For the next ten days and through Christmas, Spellman's time was taken up in the main with matters far less to his liking than the work he had thus far been doing. In short, while he was free most nights, his day-duties included being instructed in methods of keeping the more dangerous inmates "neat and tidy." He had to learn how to feed and bathe violent patients, and how to clean out the cells of those disposed to animal-like habits. He was glad when the lessons had passed, when he could settle once more to his old routine.

It was the 27th December before Spellman found himself on night-duty again, and as the fates would have it his name appeared on the roster opposite that especially offensive duty: the lower wards, and particularly the one called Hell.

That night, on his very first visit to Hell, Spellman found Larner waiting for him at the spy-hole of his cell.

"Nurse Spellman—at last, it's you! Did you...did you...?" Eagerly he peered out through the bars.

"Did I what, Larner?"

"I asked you to copy down the Sixth Sathlatta—from the *Cthaat Aquadingen*. Did you forget?"

"No, I didn't forget, Larner,"—though in fact, he had—"but tell me—what do you intend to do with…with the, er, Sixth Sathlatta?"

"Do with it? Why!—it's—it's an *experiment!* Yes, that's it, an experiment. In fact, Nurse Spellman, you might like to help us out with it?"

"*Us*, Larner?"

"Me—I meant me—you might like to help *me* with it!"

"In what way?" Spellman found himself interested, and despite the circumstances he was impressed with the lunatic's apparent lucidity.

"I'll let you know later—but you'll have to let me have the Sixth Sathlatta soon—and a few sheets of paper and a pencil…."

"A pencil, Larner?" Spellman frowned suspiciously. "You know I can't give you a pencil."

"A crayon, then," the man in the cell begged in seeming desperation. "Surely I can't do any harm with a crayon?"

"No, I don't suppose so. A crayon would be all right, I should think."

"Good! Then you will—" The madman let the question hang.

"I can't promise, Larner—but I'll think about it." It would be interesting, though, Spellman told himself, his hideous dream of a fortnight gone dim now in his memory, to see just what Larner would do with the Sixth Sathlatta.

"Well, all right—but think quickly!" the man's voice cut into his thoughts. "I'll have to have the things I need well before the end of the month. If I don't—well, the experiment would be no good—not for another year, at any rate."

Then Larner's eyes quickly went wide and vacant, his positive expression altering until his features seemed vague and weak. He turned and walked slowly over to his bed with his hands behind his back.

"I'll see what I can do for you, Larner," Spellman spoke to the man's back. "Probably tonight." But Larner had apparently lost all interest in their conversation.

It was the same later, when Spellman returned to the basement ward after a quick visit to his room. He spoke to Larner, passing through the bars a crayon, blank paper, and that sheet with the Sixth Sathlatta copied from Larner's book, but the lunatic sat on his bed and made no attempt to answer. Spellman had to let the articles the man had requested fall to the floor within the cell, and even then Larner showed not the slightest flicker of interest.

Toward morning, however, when the stain of approaching dawn was already making itself known through the snow-laden clouds to the east, the young nurse noticed that Larner was busy writing; working furiously with his crayon and paper, but as before he ignored all of Spellman's efforts at communication.

It happened two days later that after his mid-morning break Spellman went down to his room for one of his rare cigarettes before beginning his afternoon duties. As he pulled at the cigarette he peered contemplatively out through the bars of his window (Harold Moody had once jovially explained that the bars were not to keep him in—no one doubted *his* sanity—but to keep exercising madmen *out!*) at the dozen inmates of Hell as they walked or shambled up and down the high-walled yard. The worst of them were shackled at the feet, so that their movements were restricted and much slowed down, but at least half of them knew no physical restrictions whatever—except the watchful vigilance of their half-dozen white-clad warders.

The latter seemed especially lethargic that day, or so it appeared to the curious observer, for from his vantage point it was plain to him that Larner was up to something. Spellman saw that every time Larner came within speaking distance of another inmate he would say something, and that then his hand would stray suspiciously close to that of the other. It looked for all the world as though he was passing something around. But what? Spellman believed he knew.

He also realized that it was his duty to warn the warders in the yard that something was up—and yet he did not do so. It was quite possible that, should he bring Larner's activities to the attention of the others, he would in the end be causing trouble for himself; for he believed Larner to be passing around copies of the Sixth Sathlatta! Spellman smiled. No doubt the madman intended making an attempt at raising Yibb-Tstll. How the lunatic mind contradicts itself, he thought, turning away from the window. Why! You could hardy call the twelve creatures in the the exercise-yard "adepts," now could you? And in any case, Larner was one man short!

At 4:00 P.M. Spellman was required to go down to the yard with five other warders to stand guard over Hell's inmates as they took their second and last exercise of the day. One of the other five was Barstowe, looking extremely nervous and uncomfortable, but he kept well away from the younger man. Spellman had noticed before how when Barstowe was in the exercise-yard the madmen were always exceptionally subdued—and yet now, for the first time, there seemed to be an indefinable attitude of quiet defiance about them—quite as though they had an "ace," as it were, up their collective sleeve. Barstowe had noticed it too, and his interest picked up when Larner went over to Spellman to talk to him.

"Not long now, Nurse Spellman," Larner quietly said after exchanging reasonable greetings.

"Oh?" Spellman smiled. "Is that right, Larner? I saw you today, you know, passing round those copies you made."

Larner's face fell immediately. "You didn't tell anyone, did you?"

"No, I didn't tell anyone. When are you going to tell me what it's all about?"

"Soon, soon—but isn't it a pity I don't know the Naach-Tith formula?"

"Er—a pity, yes," Spellman agreed, wondering what on Earth the fellow was rambling on about now. Then he remembered seeing that mention of a so-called "Naach-Tith Barrier" in Larner's notes in the *Cthaat Aquadingen*. "Will it spoil the experiment?"

"No, but...but it's *you* I'm really sorry for...."

"Me?" Spellman frowned. "How do you mean, Larner?"

"It's not for myself, you understand," the madman quickly went on, "what happens to me can't much matter in a place like this—and the others are as badly off. Not much hope for them here. Why! Some of them might even benefit from the reversals! But it's you, Spellman, it's *you*—and I'm really sorry for that...."

Spellman considered his next question carefully. "Is the—*formula*—is it so important then?" If only he could get through to the man, discover the twisted circles in which his mind moved.

But Larner was suddenly frowning. "You haven't read the *Cthaat Aquadingen*, have you?" He made the question an accusation.

"Yes, yes of course I have—but it's very difficult, and I'm no—" Spellman searched for the word: "I'm no *adept!*"

Larner nodded his head, the frown vanishing from his face: "That's it exactly: you're no adept. There should be seven but I'm the only one. The Naach-Tith Formula would help, of course, but even then—" Suddenly Larner caught sight of Barstowe edging closer. "*Lethiktros Themiel, phitrith-te klep-thos!*" he instantly muttered under his breath, then turned back to Spellman: "But I don't know the rest of it, you see, Spellman? And even if I did—it's not designed to keep *his* sort of evil away...."

The next day, on the one occasion Spellman snatched to watch the inmates of Hell through his barred window, he again noticed the odd camaraderie between them. He also noticed a thin red welt, absent the previous day, on Larner's face, and wondered how the madman had come by such an injury. On a whim, not knowing exactly just why he did so, he checked the roster to find out who had been on duty the night before. And then he knew it had been no whim at all but a horrible suspicion—for Barstowe had been on duty the previous night, and in his mind's eye Spellman pictured the squat, ugly nurse with his stick! And the old unease welled up in his heart as he thought again of the welt on Larner's face, and of that other inmate who had somehow contrived to gouge out one of his own eyes in "a fatal lunatic fit...."

That night, late on New Year's Eve—after a day of very limited festivities, marred for Spellman by his growing unease—he received what should have been his first definite warning of the horror soon to come. As it happened he paid little attention: he was off duty and working on his book, but after all the shouting had died down in the ward beneath, Harold Moody, on duty, came to his room to tell him about it.

"Never saw anything like *that* before!" he told Spellman after settling himself nervously on the younger man's bed. "Did you hear it?"

"I heard some shouting, yes. What was it all about?" Spellman was not really interested; his book was coming well and he wanted to get on with it.

"Eh?" Moody cocked his good ear in his friend's direction. "Shouting, did you say? *Chanting*, more like it—all of 'em together, at the top of their voices, so loud as to almost deafen me completely. Not words, mind you, Martin—at least not recognizable words—but gibberish! Utter gibberish!"

"Gibberish?" Spellman got up immediately, crossing his small room to be closer to the shaken Moody. "What sort of—gibberish?"

"Well, I really don't know. I mean—"

"Was it like this—" Spellman cut him off, taking out the *Cthaat Aquadingen* from his bedside locker and flipping its pages until he found the one he wanted.

> "Ghe 'phnglui, mglw'ngh ghee'yh, Yibb-Tstll,
> Fbtagn mglw y'tlette ngh'wgah, Yibb-Tstll,
> Ghe'phnglui...."

He stopped abruptly, realizing that he did not *need* to read the thing from the book, that of a sudden it was imprinted indelibly on his mind! "Did it—did what they were chanting go like—like that?"

"Eh? No, no it was different from that—harsher syllables—not so guttural. And that Larner chap—my God, he's a real case, that one! Kept ranting on about 'not knowing the ending'!"

Moody got up to go. "Anyhow, it's all over now—"

As Moody reached the door Spellman's alarm clock began to clamor. The young nurse had set the mechanism to go off at midnight, simply so that he would know when to welcome in the New Year. Now he remembered and said "Happy New Year, Harold!" Then, as his friend answered in kind and closed the door behind him, he again took up the *Cthaat Aquadingen*.

New Year's Eve—the night before the First Day of the year! So, Spellman silently mused, Larner had attempted to build the "Barrier of Naach-Tith"—but of course, he had not known all of the words. Spellman pondered, too, the odd fact that he was able to remember, without any effort worth mentioning, the Sixth Sathlatta; and that the weird consonants of those diseased lines seemed somehow clearer in his mind and on his tongue.

Well, all right—given that he had allowed himself a folly or two with Larner, that was over now—it was time the madman's weird experiment came to an end. But for his foolish pandering to the lunatic's crazed fancies the disturbance in the ward known as Hell would not have happened. And what of tomorrow night? In another twenty-four hours, would the inmates of Hell use the thrice-repeated Sixth Sathlatta in an attempt to call forth the dread Yibb-Tstll? Spellman thought so, and (damn the cunning of the lunatic mind), Larner had attempted to draw him into the—coven?

Not that Spellman believed for a single moment that any sort of harm, supernatural or other, could come from the concerted mouthings of madmen; but a repeat performance of this night's disturbance might well alert the sanatorium's hierarchy to his decidedly illegal dealings with Larner. He would then certainly find himself in some sort of trouble, if not actual hot water, and he did not want to damage the atmosphere between himself, Dr. Welford, and one or two others of his superiors. He was on duty in the upper wards in the morning, finishing at 4:00 P.M., but before he finished he would find a way to get down to see Larner. Perhaps a gentle word with the lunatic would do the trick.

In his bed before sleeping, Spellman thought again on his puzzling ability to recall in detail the chaotic Sixth Sathlatta, and no sooner had he pictured the thing in his mind than it was on his lips. Amazed at his unsuspected fluency he whispered the words through in the darkness of his room, and almost immediately fell into a deep sleep.

—He was back in the alien forest beneath dark green, weirdly populated skies. Again, far stronger than before, his dream-spirit felt the pull of The Thing in the scabrous clearing: Yibb-Tstll, huge and potent, turning inexorably, almost stupidly about His own axis, with His cloak billowing monstrously as

the night-gaunts beneath its folds flapped and clung in blind horror to the black and writhing multiple breasts.

This time, as soon as Spellman drifted (his dream-motion was as eerie as the drift of weeds in some outré Sargasso morass) into the crumble-earthed clearing, the vast obscenity at its center stopped Its turning, and as he wafted closer he saw Its eyes full upon him....

The utter horror of the occurrence which followed as he drew closer to the loathsome Ancient One shocked Martin Spellman from his sleep, and if anything its simplicity only went toward heightening that horror. The wonder was that Spellman had been able to recognize the—*writhings*—of those hellish features for what they were!

"It smiled—*the Thing smiled at me!*" he screamed, sitting bolt upright and flinging the bedclothes from him. For a long moment he simply sat, staring about wide-eyed in the darkness of his room; then, limbs trembling and with a sick feeling in the pit of his stomach, he got up and shakily brewed coffee.

Two hours later, at about 4:00 A.M., with dawn still some way off, he managed with some trepidation to get back to sleep. For the remainder of the night his slumbers were mercifully undisturbed....

When Martin Spellman awoke on the morning of New Year's Day, 1936, he had no time to pause in consideration of the occurrences of the previous night; he had slept late, was on duty soon, and the time was flying by. Spellman was not to know it but that day was to be the most eventful since his arrival at Oakdeene—and at the end of the day....

At ten-thirty in the morning he managed to find a way to get down to the basement ward, and once there in Hell he went straight to Larner's cell. Through the barred spy-hole he saw that his mission was useless. Larner, frothing at the mouth, was flinging himself in a silent fit from wall to padded wall, his eyes bulging and his teeth bared through the foam of his madness in gnashing frenzy. The student left the ward and found the nurse whose duty it was to attend the lower wards. He made Larner's silent raging known and then returned to his duties.

Toward the end of the lunch-break, after missing Spellman at the dinner table, Harold Moody found the young nurse prowling worriedly back and forth across the restricted but private floor of his room. Spellman would say nothing of what was on his mind. In fact, he did not himself know what was bothering him, except that he had feelings of an impending—something. Feelings which were somehow relieved a little when Moody delivered his news that Alan Barstowe had quit his job at the sanatorium. No one, it transpired, knew for sure why the squat nurse was throwing up his job; but apparently there had been rumors about his nerves for some time. Moody stated that in his opinion the place and the inmates must have been "getting on top" of the man....

Later, after finishing duty for the day, Spellman—still inordinately pleased at the news of Barstowe's imminent departure, feeling more himself and easier in his mind by the minute—ate a quick meal before returning to his room and getting out his manuscripts. By nine in the evening, however, discovering that with the encroachment of the dark outside his queasy uneasiness had returned at the expense of his concentration, he put away his book and simply lay on his bed for a while. He spent some time in trying to detect unusual sounds from Hell, finding himself no happier to discover that all seemed very quiet down there. A few minutes later, catching himself beginning to nod, he got up and smoked a cigarette. He did not want to sleep; his aim was to stay awake until midnight, to see if the inhabitants of the basement ward would get up to any more Larner-inspired tricks.

By ten a powerful desire had taken hold of Spellman to read through the *Cthaat Aquadingen* again—particularly the Sixth Sathlatta—and he actually got the book out before managing to fight down the urge. For his life he could not see just what there might be in Larner's "Black Book" to interest him now. He was feeling very tired, though, natural enough considering the disturbances of the previous night, and he had something of a headache coming on. But even following a hastily brewed cup of coffee and an aspirin, Spellman's weariness and the pain behind his temples increased until he was forced to lie on his bed. He glanced at his watch, seeing that it was ten-fifty; and then, before he knew it—

—Someone, somewhere—a well-known voice—was muttering the chaotic words of the Sixth Sathlatta, and even as he fell into a deep sleep Spellman knew that the voice was his own!

He was at the edge of the poisoned clearing again, under dark-green skies and with the evil jungle already behind him; and to his front, in the center of the clearing, Yibb-Tstll waited, turning inexorably as ever on His own axis. Spellman wanted to turn and run, to get away from The Thing that waited in Its great green billowing cloak; and he fought—pitting all the strength of his subconscious mind and will against the awful magnetism radiating from the revolting, revolving monstrosity before him—fought and almost won....But not quite! Slowly, agonizingly slowly, with his sleeping mind squeezed to a tiny ball of concentration, Martin Spellman was pulled forward across the leprous earth. And as he pitted himself against the horror of the Ancient One, he could feel Its anger, could sense the urgency It engendered now in this hideous dream-region's atmosphere.

For what seemed like hours Spellman fought his losing battle, and then Yibb-Tstll—tiring of the game and aware of the shortness of time—tried a different tactic. While he had yet a good distance to go to the center of the clearing, Spellman saw The Thing stop Its turning; and then, without warning, the horror threw back its cloak to release the hellish "pets" beneath!

Spellman could only fight one thing at a time, and Yibb-Tstll was not going to allow him to escape this time into wakefulness. Even knowing he was dreaming Spellman was at the mercy of his dream. He screamed voicelessly, lashing out at the flapping, blank-faced, vile-bodied night-gaunts as they buffeted him with skin-and-bone wings and tried to shove him off his feet. Finally they won and he fell, cowering down and wrapping his arms about his head as he felt himself swiftly borne forward on his nightmare's ghost-drift. When the noisome activity about him ceased, he fearfully looked up—and found himself at the feet of the colossal Thing in the green cloak!

Again those awful eyes—those red eyes that were not fixed in their places—the eyes that moved quickly, independently—sliding with vile viscosity over the whole rotten surface of Yibb-Tstll's pulpy, glistening head!

Mercifully distracted from the horror before him, he saw suddenly that he was not alone. There were others with him—twelve of them—and even in the dream the features and shapes of some of the twelve were twisted, and some of them slavered and their eyes were strange, making their identities obvious.

Larner!—and the rest of Hell's inmates—a complete coven, now, come to worship at the feet of a lunatic "God," the loathly Yibb-Tstll!

Still kneeling, sickly turning his face away, Spellman saw a book lying open before him on the rotting ground. The Cthaat Aquadingen, *Larner's copy, and open at the Sixth Sathlatta!*

"No—oh, no!" Spellman screamed voicelessly in sudden understanding. Why?—to what end should this—Thing—be allowed to walk upon Earth?

Larner got down beside him: "You know, *in your heart, Nurse Spellman. You* know!*"

"But—"

"No time," Larner cut off his protest. "Midnight is almost here! You'll join us in The Calling?"

"No, damn you—no!" Spellman cried his mental denial.

"YOU WILL!" answered a booming, alien voice in his head, "NOW!" And Yibb-Tstll reached out from under His cloak a green and black thing that might have been an arm, with a hand and fingers of sorts, pushing the tips into Spellman's mouth and ears and nostrils—deep into his mind—searching and squeezing in certain places....

When the great Ancient One withdrew his slimy fingers Spellman's eyes were very vacant and his mouth, trickling saliva, hung slack. Only then, at midnight—as if at a spoken command though none was given, simultaneously and in perfect unison—did the coven begin the invocation; with Spellman sitting bolt upright in his bed, and with the others below in their cells.

It was early February before the furor at Oakdeene died down, by which time the events of the night of 1st January 1936 had been carefully examined—as best they could be—and chronicled for future reference in various reports. By then, too, Dr. Welford had resigned; he had been unfortunate enough to be Duty Officer of the night in question; and while it was generally recognized that the responsibility had in no way been his, his resignation seemed to appease directors, newspapers and the relatives of many of the inmates alike.

Certainly, had Dr. Welford been a man without scruple, he might have turned at least part of the result of that night's happenings to his advantage; for in the following month five of Hell's inhabitants—three of them previously "hopeless" maniacs—were released as perfectly responsible citizens! Alas, five others, of which one was Larner, had been found dead in their cells shortly after the midnight disturbance—the victims of "frantic lunatic convulsions." The remaining two—*survived*—but in states of deep and constant catatonia.

Such had been the upheaval at Oakdeene on the morning of the 2nd January, that at first it was believed Barstowe's ghastly death on the lonely road between the sanatorium and Oakdeene village had been brought about by a madman escaped in the confusion. For some reason the squat nurse had not waited until morning to leave—perhaps he had some premonition of the horror to come—but had departed on foot with his case shortly after eleven that very night. Apparently Barstowe had tried to fight back before succumbing to his attacker: a black telescopic stick with a silver tip—an instrument that could be opened out to make a pointed weapon some nine feet long—was found near his body, but his efforts had been of no avail.

As soon as Barstowe's body was discovered, a count of Oakdeene's inmates, living and dead, served to put down any rumors that might have arisen in respect of the institute's security; but certainly the squat nurse *had* suffered some sort of maniacal attack. No sane man, not even any ordinary sort of animal, could have savaged him so and chewed away half his head and brain!

In all, the occurrences of the night of the 1st-2nd January 1936 could have filled a whole chapter in Spellman's book—had he ever finished that book. He did not finish it, nor will he ever. Having suffered a terrible *reversal*, Martin Spellman, now in late middle-age, still occupies the second cell on the left in Hell; and because, even in his more lucid moments, he only babbles and drools and screams, for the most part he is kept under sedation....

BORN OF THE WINDS

In late 1972, early '73, I wrote BOTW. Agented in America by Kirby McCauley, at 25,000 words it was too long for Ed Ferman's "Fantasy & Science Fiction" and had to be reduced by some 5,000 words. By the time I had completed the work on it I was a Staff Sergeant serving in Celle in Germany, writing evenings or whenever I could find some spare time. This novella first saw light of day in the December 1975 issue of "F&SF," and at once earned itself a World Fantasy Award nomination—I suspect for its originality. Alas that it didn't win the award! Reprinted two years later, in "The Horror at Oakdeene," and having twice seen print in the quarter century gone by since then, it remains one of my personal favourites...

I

Consider: I am, or was, a meteorologist of some note— a man whose interests and leanings have always been away from fantasy and the so-called "supernatural"and yet now I believe in a wind that blows between the worlds, and in a Being that inhabits that wind, striding in feathery cirrus and shrieking lightning storm alike across icy Arctic heavens.

Just how such an utter *contradiction* of beliefs could come about I will now attempt to explain, for I alone possess all of the facts. If I am wrong in what I more than suspect—if what has gone before has been nothing but a monstrous chain of coincidence confused by horrific hallucination—then with luck I might yet return out of this white wilderness to the sanity of the world I knew. But if I am right, and I fear that I am horribly right, then I am done for, and this manuscript will stand as my testimonial of a hitherto all but unrecognized plane of existence…and of its *inhabitant*, whose like may only be found in legends whose sources date back geological eons into Earth's dim and terrible infancy.

My involvement with this thing has come about all in the space of a few months, for it was just over two months ago, fairly early in August, that I first came to Navissa, Manitoba, on what was to have been a holiday of convalescence following a debilitating chest complaint.

Since meteorology serves me both as hobby and means of support, naturally I brought some of my "work" with me; not physically, for my books and instruments are many, but locked in my head were a score of little problems beloved of the meteorologist. I brought certain of my notebooks, too, in which to make jottings or scribble observations on the almost Arctic conditions of the region as the mood might take me. Canada offers a wealth of interest to one whose life revolves about the weather: the wind and rain, the clouds, and the storms that seem to spring from them.

In Manitoba on a clear night, not only is the air sweet, fresh, sharp, and conducive to the strengthening of weakened lungs, but the stars stare down in such crystal clarity that at times a man might try to pluck them out of the firmament. It is just such a night now—though the glass is far down, and I fear that soon it may snow—but warm as I am in myself before my stove, still my fingers feel the awesome cold of the night outside, for I have removed my gloves to write.

Navissa, until fairly recently, was nothing more than a trail camp, one of many to expand out of humble beginnings as a trading post into a full-blown town. Lying not far off the old Olassie Trail, Navissa is quite close to deserted, ill-fated Stillwater; but more of Stillwater later….

I stayed at the Judge's house, a handsome brick affair with a raised log porch and chalet-style roof, one of Navissa's few truly modern buildings, standing on that side of the town toward the neighboring hills. Judge Andrews is a retired New Yorker of independent means, an old friend of my father, a widower whose habits in the later years of his life have inclined toward the reclusive; being self-sufficient, he bothers no one, and in turn he is left to his own devices. Something of a professional anthropologist all his life, the Judge now studies the more obscure aspects of that science here in the thinly populated North. It was Judge Andrews himself, on learning of my recent illness, who so kindly invited me to spend this period of convalescence with him in Navissa, though by then I was already well on the way to recovery.

Not that his invitation gave me license to intrude upon the Judge's privacy. It did not. I would do with myself what I would, keeping out of his way as much as possible. Of course, no such arrangement was specified, but I was aware that this was the way the Judge would want it.

I had free run of the house, including the old gentleman's library, and it was there one afternoon early in the final fortnight of my stay that I found the several works of Samuel R. Bridgeman, an English professor of anthropology whose mysterious death had occurred only a few dozen miles or so north of Navissa.

Normally such a discovery would have meant little to me, but I had heard that certain of Bridgeman's theories had made him something of an outcast among others of his profession; there had been among his beliefs some that belonged in no way to the scientific. Knowing Judge Andrews to be a man who liked his facts straight on the line, undistorted by whim or fancy, I wondered what there could be in the eccentric Bridgeman's works that prompted him to display them upon his shelves.

In order to ask him this very question, I was on my way from the small library room to Judge Andrews's study when I saw, letting herself out of the house, a distinguished-looking though patently nervous woman whose age seemed rather difficult to gauge. Despite the trimness of her figure and the comparative youthfulness of her skin, her hair was quite grey. She had plainly been very attractive, perhaps even beautiful, in youth. She did not see me, or if she did glimpse me where I stood, then her agitated condition did not admit of it. I heard her car pull away.

In the doorway of the Judge's study I formed my question concerning Bridgeman's books.

"Bridgeman?" the old man repeated me, glancing up sharply from where he sat at his desk.

"Just those books of his, in the library," I answered, entering the room proper. "I shouldn't have thought that there'd be much for you, Judge, in Bridgeman's work."

"Oh? I didn't know you were interested in anthropology, David?"

"Well, no, I'm not really. It's just that I remember hearing a thing or two about this Bridgeman, that's all."

"Are you sure that's all?"

"Eh? Why, certainly! Should there be more?"

"Hmm," he mused. "No, nothing much—coincidence. You see, the lady who left a few moments ago was Lucille Bridgeman, Sam's widow. She's staying at the Nelson."

"Sam?" I was immediately interested. "You knew him then?"

"I did, fairly intimately, though that was many years ago. More recently I've read his books. Did you know that he died quite close by here?"

I nodded. "Yes, in peculiar circumstances, I gather?"

"That's so, yes." He frowned again, moving in his chair in what I took to be agitation.

I waited for a moment, and then when it appeared that the Judge intended to say no more, I asked, "And now?"

"Hmm?" His eyes were far away even though they looked at me. They quickly focused. "Now—nothing…and I'm rather busy!" He put on his spectacles and turned his attention to a book.

I grinned ruefully, inclined my head, and nodded. Being fairly intimate with the old man's moods, I knew what his taciturn, rather abrupt dismissal had meant: "If you want to know more, then you must find out for yourself!" And what better way to discover more of this little mystery, at least initially, than to read Samuel R. Bridgeman's books? That way I should at least learn something of the man.

As I turned away, the Judge called to me: "Oh, and David—I don't know what preconceptions you may have formed of Sam Bridgeman and his work, but as for myself…near the end of a lifetime, I'm no closer now than I was fifty years ago to being able to say what *is* and what *isn't*. At least Sam had the courage of his convictions!"

What was I to make of that?—and how to answer it? I simply nodded and went out of the room, leaving the Judge alone with his books and his thoughts….

That same afternoon found me again in the library, with a volume of Bridgeman's on my lap. There were three of his books in all, and I had discovered that they contained many references to Arctic and near-Arctic regions, to their people, their gods, superstitions, and legends. Still pondering what little I knew of the English professor, these were the passages that primarily drew my attention: Bridgeman had written of these northern parts, and he had died here—mysteriously! No less mysterious, his widow was here now, twenty years after his demise, in a highly nervous if not actually distraught state. Moreover, that kindly old family friend Judge Andrews seemed singularly reticent with regard to the English anthropologist, and apparently the Judge did not entirely disagree with Bridgeman's controversial theories.

But what were those theories? If my memory served me well, then they had to do with certain Indian and Eskimo legends concerning a god of the Arctic winds.

At first glance there seemed to be little in the professor's books to show more than a normally lively and entertaining anthropological and ethnic interest in such legends, though the author seemed to dwell at unnecessary length on Gaoh and Hotoru, air-elementals of the Iroquois and Pawnee respectively, and particularly upon Negafok, the Eskimo cold-weather spirit. I could see that he was trying to tie such myths in with the little-known legend of the Wendigo, of which he seemed to deal far too positively.

"The Wendigo," Bridgeman wrote, "is the avatar of a Power come down the ages from forgotten gulfs of immemorial lore; this great *Tornasuk* is none other than Ithaqua Himself, the Wind-Walker, and the very sight of Him means a freezing and inescapable death for the unfortunate observer. Lord Ithaqua, perhaps the very greatest of the mythical air-elementals, made war against the Elder Gods in the Beginning; for which ultimate treason He was banished to frozen Arctic and interplanetary heavens to 'Walk the Winds Forever' through fantastic cycles of time and to fill the *Esquimaux* with dread, eventually earning His terrified worship and His sacrifices. None but such worshipers may look upon Ithaqua—for others to see Him is certain death! He is as a dark outline against the sky, anthropomorphic, a manlike yet bestial silhouette, striding both in low icy mists and high stratocumulus, gazing down upon the affairs of men with carmine stars for eyes!"

Bridgeman's treatment of the more conventional mythological figures was less romantic; he remained solidly within the framework of accepted anthropology. For example:

"The Babylonian storm-god, Enlil, was designated 'Lord of the Winds.' Mischievous and mercurial in temperament, he was seen by the superstitious peoples of the land to walk in hurricanes and sand-devils...." Or, in yet more traditional legend: "Teuton mythology shows Thor as being the god of thunder; when thunderstorms boiled and the heavens roared, people knew that what they heard was the sound of Thor's war-chariot clattering through the vaults of heaven."

Again, I could not help but find it noticeable that while the author here poked a sort of fun at these classical figures of mythology, he had *not* done so when he wrote of Ithaqua. Similarly, he was completely dry and matter-of-fact in his descriptive treatment of an illustration portraying the Hittite god-of-the-storm, Tha-thka, photographed from his carved representation upon a baked clay tablet excavated in the Toros Mountains of Turkey. More, he compared Tha-thka with Ithaqua of the Snows, declaring that he found parallels in the two deities other than the merely phonetical similarity of their names.

Ithaqua, he pointed out, had left webbed tracks in the Arctic snows, tracks that the old *Esquimaux* tribes feared to cross; and Tha-thka (carved in a fashion very similar to the so-called "Amarna style" of Egypt, to mix ethnic art groups) was shown in the photograph as having star-shaped eyes of a rare, dark carnelian...and webbed feet! Professor Bridgeman's argument for connection here seemed valid, even sound, yet I could see how such an argument might very well anger established anthropologists of "the Old School." How, for instance, might one equate a god of the ancient Hittites with a deity of comparatively modern Eskimos? Unless of course one was to remember that in a certain rather fanciful mythology Ithaqua had only been banished to the North following an abortive rebellion against the Elder Gods. Could it be that *before* that rebellion the Wind-Walker strode the high currents and tides of atmospheric air over Ur of the Chaldees and ancient Khem, perhaps even prior to those lands being named by their first inhabitants? Here I laughed at my own fancies, conjured by what the writer had written with such assumed authority, and yet my laughter was more than a trifle strained, for I found a certain cold logic in Bridgeman that made even his wildest statement seem merely a calm, studied exposition....

And there were, certainly, wild statements.

The slimmest of the three books was full of them, and I knew after reading only its first few pages that this must be the source of those flights of fancy that had caused Bridgeman's erstwhile colleagues to desert him. Yet without a doubt the book was by far the most interesting of the three, written almost in a fervor of mystical allusion with an abundance—a *plethora*—of obscure hints suggestive of half-discernible worlds of awe, wonder, and horror bordering and occasionally impinging upon our very own.

I found myself completely enthralled. It seemed plain to me that behind all the hocus-pocus there was a great mystery here—one that, like an iceberg, showed only its tip—and I determined not to be satisfied with anything less than a complete verification of the facts concerning what I had started to think of as "the Bridgeman case." After all, I seemed to be ideally situated to conduct such an investigation: this was where the professor had died, the borderland of that region in which he had alleged at least one of his mythological beings to exist; and Judge Andrews, provided I could get him to talk, must be something of an authority on the man; and, possibly my best line of research yet, Bridgeman's widow herself was here now in this very town.

Just why this determination to dabble should have so enthused me I still cannot say; unless it was the way that Tha-thka, which Being Bridgeman had equated with Ithaqua, was shown upon the Toros Mountains tablet as walking splayfooted through a curious mixture of cumulonimbus and nimbo-stratus—cloud formations that invariably presage snow and violent thunderstorms! The ancient sculptor of that tablet had certainly gauged the Wind-Walker's domain well, giving the mythical creature something of solidarity in my mind, though it was still far easier for me to accept those peculiar clouds of ill omen than the Being striding among them....

II

It was something of a shock for me to discover, when finally I thought to look at my wristwatch, that Bridgeman's books had kept me busy all through the afternoon and it was now well into evening. I found that my eyes had started to ache with the strain of reading as it grew darker in the small library room. I put on the light and would have returned to the books yet again but for hearing, at the outer door of the house, a gentle knocking. The library door was slightly ajar so that I could hear the Judge answering the knocking and his gruff welcome. I was sure that the voice that answered him was that of Bridgeman's widow, for it was vibrant with a nervous agitation as the visitor entered the house and went with the Judge to his study. Well, I had desired to meet her; this seemed the perfect opportunity to introduce myself.

Yet at the open door to the Judge's study I paused, then quickly stepped back out of sight. It seemed that my host and his visitor were engaged in some sort of argument. He had just answered to some unheard question: "Not *me*, my dear, that is out of the question....But if you insist upon this folly, then I'm sure I can find someone to help you. God knows I'd come with you myself—even on this wild-goose chase you propose, and despite the forecast of heavy snow—but...my dear, I'm an old man. My eyes are no good anymore; my limbs are no longer as strong as they used to be. I'm afraid that this old body might let you down at the worst possible time. It's bad country north of here when the snows come."

"Is it simply that, Jason," she answered him in her nervous voice, "or is it really that you believe I'm a madwoman? That's what you as good as called me when I was here earlier."

"You must forgive me for that, Lucille, but let's face it—that story you tell is simply…*fantastic!* There's no positive proof that the boy headed this way at all, just this premonition of yours."

"The story I told you was the truth, Jason! As for my 'premonition,' well, I've brought you proof! Look at this—"

There was a pause before the Judge spoke again. Quietly he asked, "But what is this thing, Lucille? Let me get my glass. Hmm—I can see that it depicts—"

"No!" Her cry, shrill and loud, cut him off. "No, don't mention *Them*, and please don't say His name!" The hysterical emphasis she placed on certain words was obvious, but she sounded calmer when, a few seconds later, she continued: "As for what it is—" I heard a metallic clinking, like a coin dropped on the tabletop, "just keep it here in the house. You will see for yourself. It was discovered clenched in Sam's right hand when they—when they found his poor, broken body."

"All that was twenty years ago—" the Judge said, then paused again before asking: "Is it gold?"

"Yes, but of unknown manufacture. I've shown it to three or four experts over the years, and always the same answer. It is a very ancient thing, but from no known or recognizable culture. Only the fact that it is made of gold saves it from being completely alien! And even the gold is…not quite right. Kirby has one, too."

"Oh?" I could hear the surprise in the Judge's voice. "And where did he get it? Why, just looking at this thing under the glass, I should have taken it for granted—even knowing nothing of it—that it's as rare as it's old!"

"I believe they are very rare indeed, surviving from an age before all earthly ages. Feel how cold it is. It has a chill like the ocean floor, and if you try to warm it…but try it for yourself. I can tell you now, though, that it will not *stay* warm. And I know what that means.…

"Kirby received his in the mail some months ago, in the summer. We were at home in Mérida, in Yucatán. As you know, I settled there after—after—"

"Yes, yes I know. But who would want to send the boy such a thing—and why?"

"I believe it was meant as—as a *reminder*, that's all—as a means to awaken in him all I have worked to keep dormant. I've already told you about…about Kirby, about his strange ways even as a baby. I thought they would leave him as he grew older. I was wrong. That last month before he vanished was the worst. It was after he received the talisman through the mail. Then, three weeks ago, he—he just packed a few things and—" She paused for a moment, I believed to compose herself, for an emotional catch had developed in her voice. I felt strangely moved.

"—As to who sent it to him, that's something I can't say. I can only guess, but the package carried the Navissa postmark! That's why I'm here."

"The Navissa—" The Judge seemed astounded. "But who would there be here to remember something that happened twenty years ago? And who, in any case, would want to make a gift of such a rare and expensive item to a complete stranger?"

The answer when it came was so low that I had difficulty making it out:

"There must have been *others*, Jason! Those people in Stillwater weren't the only ones who called Him master. Those worshipers of His—they still exist—they must! I believe it was one of them, carrying out his master's orders. As for where it came from in the first place, why, where else but—"

"No, Lucille, that's quite impossible," the Judge cut her off. "Something I really can't allow myself to believe. If such things could be—"

"A madness the world could not face?"

"Yes, exactly!"

"Sam used to say the same thing. Nonetheless he sought the horror out, and brought me here with him, and then—"

"Yes, Lucille, I know what you believe happened then, but—"

"No buts, Jason—I want my son back. Help me, if you will, or don't help me. It makes no difference. I'm determined to find him, and I'll find him here, somewhere, I know it. If I have to, then I'll search him out alone, by myself, before it's too late!" Her voice had risen again, hysterically.

"No, there's no need for that," the old man cut in placatingly. "First thing tomorrow I'll find someone to help you. And we can get the Mounties from Nelson in on the job, too. They have a winter camp at Fir Valley only a few miles out of Navissa. I'll be able to get them on the telephone first thing in the morning. I'll need to, for the telephone will probably go out with the first bad snow."

"And you'll definitely find someone to help me personally—someone trustworthy?"

"That's my word. In fact I already know of one young man who might be willing. Of a very good family—and he's staying with me right now. You can meet him tomorrow—"

At this point I heard the scrape of chairs and pictured the two rising to their feet. Suddenly ashamed of myself to be standing there eavesdropping, I quickly returned to the library and pulled the door shut behind me. After some little time, during which the lady departed, I went again to Judge Andrews's study, this time tapping at the shut door and entering at his word. I found the old man worriedly pacing the floor.

He stopped pacing as I entered. "Ah, David. Sit down, please, there's something I would like to ask you." He seated himself, shuffling awkwardly in his chair. "It's difficult to know where to begin—"

"Begin with Samuel R. Bridgeman," I answered. "I've had time to read his books now. Frankly, I find myself very interested."

"But how did you know—?"

Thinking back on my eavesdropping, I blushed a little as I answered, "I've just seen Mrs. Bridgeman leaving. I'm guessing that it's her husband, or perhaps the lady herself, you want to talk to me about."

He nodded, picking up from his desk a golden medallion some two inches across its face, fingering its bas-relief work before answering. "Yes, you're right, but—"

"Yes?"

He sighed heavily in answer, then said, "Ah, well, I suppose I'll have to tell you the whole story, or what I know of it—that's the least I can do if I'm to expect your help." He shook his head. "That poor, demented woman!"

"Is she not quite…*right*, then?"

"Nothing like that at all," he answered hastily, gruffly. "She's as sane as I am. It's just that she's a little, well, *disturbed.*"

He then told me the whole of the thing, a story that lasted well into the night. I reproduce here what I can remember of his words. They formed an almost unbroken narrative that I listened to in silence to its end, a narrative that only served to strengthen that resolution of mine to follow this mystery down to a workable conclusion.

"As you are aware," the Judge began, "I was a friend of Sam Bridgeman's in our younger days. How this friendship came about is unimportant, but I also knew Lucille before they married, and that is why she now approaches me for help after all these years. It is pure coincidence that I live now in Navissa, so close to where Sam died.

"Even in those early days Sam was a bit of a rebel. Of the orthodox sciences, including anthropology and enthnology, few interested Sam in their accepted forms. Dead and mythological cities, lands with exotic names, and strange gods were ever his passion. I remember how he would sit and dream—of Atlantis and Mu, Ephiroth and Khurdisan, G'harne and lost Leng, R'lyeh and Theem'hdra, forgotten worlds of antique legend and myth— when by rights he should have been studying and working hard toward his future. And yet…that future came to nothing in the end.

"Twenty-six years ago he married Lucille, and because he was fairly well-to-do by then, having inherited a sizable fortune, he was able to escape a working life as we know it to turn his full attention to those ideas and ideals most dear to him. In writing his books, particularly his last book, he alienated himself utterly from colleagues and acknowledged authorities alike in those specific sciences upon which he lavished his 'imagination.' That was how they saw his—fantasies?—as the product of a wild imagination set free to wreak havoc among all established orders, scientific and theological included.

"Eventually he became looked upon as a fool, a naïve clown who based his crazed arguments in Blavatsky, in the absurd theories of Scott-Elliot, in the insane epistles of Eibon, and the warped translations of Harold Hadley Copeland, rather than in prosaic but proven historians and scientists....

"When exactly, or why, Sam became interested in the theogony of these northern parts—particularly in certain beliefs of the Indians and half-breeds, and in Eskimo legends of yet more northerly regions—I do not know, but in the end he himself began to *believe* them. He was especially interested in the legend of the snow- or wind-god, Ithaqua, variously called 'Wind-Walker,' 'Death-Walker,' 'Strider in the Star-Spaces,' and others, a being who supposedly walks in the freezing boreal winds and in the turbulent atmospheric currents of far northern lands and adjacent waters.

"As fortune—or misfortune—would have it, his decision to pay this region a visit coincided with problems of an internal nature in some few of the villages around here. There were strange undercurrents at work. Secret semireligious groups had moved into the area, in many cases apparently vagrant, here to witness and worship at a 'Great Coming!' Strange, certainly, but can you show me any single region of this Earth of ours that does not have its crackpot organizations, religious or otherwise? Mind you, there has always been a problem with that sort of thing here....

"Well, a number of the members of these so-called esoteric groups were generally somewhat more intelligent than the average Indian, half-breed, or Eskimo; they were mainly New Englanders, from such decadent Massachusetts towns as Arkham, Dunwich, and Innsmouth.

"The Mounties at Nelson saw no threat, however, for this sort of thing was common here; one might almost say that over the years there has been a surfeit of it. On this occasion it was believed that certain occurrences in and about Stillwater and Navissa had drawn these rather polyglot visitors, for five years earlier there had indeed occurred a very large number of peculiar and still unsolved disappearances, to say nothing of a handful of inexplicable deaths at the same time.

"I've done a little research myself into just what happened, though I'm still very uncertain, but conjecture aside, hard figures and facts are—surprising?—no, they are downright disturbing!

"For instance, the *entire population* of one town, Stillwater, vanished overnight! You need not take my word for it—research it for yourself. The newspapers were full of it.

"Well, now, add to a background like this a handful of tales concerning giant webbed footprints in the snow, stories of strange altars to forbidden gods in the woods, and a creature that comes on the wings of the winds to accept living sacrifices—and remember, please, that all such appear time and again in the history and legends of these parts—and you'll agree it's little wonder that the area has attracted so many weird types over the years.

"Not that I remember Sam Bridgeman as being a 'weird type,' you understand; but it was exactly this sort of thing that brought him here when, after five years of quiet, the cycle of hysterical superstition and strange worship was again at its height. That was how things stood when he arrived here, and he brought his wife with him….

"The snow was already deep to the north when they came, but that did nothing at all to deter Sam; he was here to probe the old legends, and he would never be satisfied until he had done just that. He hired a pair of French-Canadian guides, swarthy characters of doubtful backgrounds, to take him and Lucille in search of…of what? Dreams and myths, fairy tales and ghost stories?

"They trekked north, and despite the uncouth looks of the guides, Sam soon decided that his choice of these two men had been a good one; they seemed to know the region quite well. Indeed, they appeared to be somehow, well, cowed out in the snows, different again from when Sam had found them, drunk and fighting in a Navissa bar. But then again, in all truth, he had had little choice but to hire these two, for with the five-year cycle of strangeness at its peak few of Navissa's regular inhabitants would have ventured far from their homes. And indeed, when Sam asked his guides why they seemed so nervous, they told him it was all to do with 'the season.' Not, they explained, the winter season, but that of the strange myth-cycle. Beyond that they would say nothing, which only excited Sam's curiosity all the more—particularly since he had noticed that their restlessness grew apace the farther north they trekked.

"Then, one calm white night, with the tents pitched and a bright wood fire kindled, one of the guides asked Sam just what it was that he sought in the snow. Sam told him, mentioning the stories of Ithaqua the Snow-Thing, but got no further; for upon hearing the Wind-Walker's name spoken, the

French-Canadian simply refused to listen anymore. Instead, he went off early to his tent where he was soon overheard muttering and arguing in a frightened and urgent voice with his companion. The next morning, when Sam roused himself, he discovered to his horror that he and his wife were alone, that the guides had run off and deserted them! Not only this, but they had taken all the provisions with them. The Bridgemans had only their tent, the clothing they stood in, their sleeping bags, and personal effects. They had not even a box of matches with which to light a fire.

"Still, their case did not appear to be completely hopeless. They had had fair weather so far, and they were only three days and nights out from Navissa. But their trail had been anything but a straight one, so that when they set about making a return journey it was pure guesswork on Sam's part the correct direction in which to head. He knew something of the stars, however; and when the cold night came down, he was able to say with some certainty that they headed south.

"And yet lonely and vulnerable though they now felt, they had been aware even on the first day that they were not truly alone. On occasion they had crossed strange tracks, freshly made by furtive figures that melted away into the firs or banks of snow whenever Sam called out to them across the wintry wastes. On the second morning, soon after setting out from their camp in the lee of tall pines, they came upon the bodies of their erstwhile guides; they had been horribly tortured and mutilated before dying. In the pockets of one of the bodies Sam found matches, and that night—though by now they knew the pangs of hunger—they at least had the warmth of a fire to comfort them. But ever in the flickering shadows, just outside the field of vision afforded by the leaping flames, there were those furtive figures, silent in the snow, watching and…waiting?

"They talked, Sam and Lucille, huddled together in the door of their tent before the warming fire, whispering of the dead guides and how and why those men had come to such terrible ends; and they shivered at the surrounding shadows and the shapes that shifted within them. This country, Sam reasoned, must indeed be the territory of Ithaqua the Wind-Walker. At times, when the influence of old rites and mysteries was strongest, then the snow-god's worshipers—the Indians, half-breeds, and perhaps others less obvious and from farther parts—would gather here to attend His ceremonies. To the outsider, the unbeliever, this entire area must be forbidden, taboo! The guides had been outsiders…Sam and Lucille were outsiders, too….

"It must have been about this time that Lucille's nerves began to go, which would surely be understandable. The intense cold and the white wastes stretching out in all directions, broken only very infrequently by the boles and snow-laden branches of firs and pines—the hunger eating at her insides now—those half-seen figures lurking ever on the perimeter of her vision and consciousness—the terrible knowledge that what had happened to the guides could easily happen again—and the fact, no longer hidden by her husband, that she and Sam were—lost! Though they were making south, who could say that Navissa lay in their path, or even that they would ever have the strength to make it back to the town?

"Yes, I think that at that stage she must have become for the most part delirious, for certainly the things she 'remembers' as happening from that time onward were delusion inspired, despite their detail. And God knows that poor Sam must have been in a similar condition. At any rate, on the third night, unable to light a fire because the matches had somehow got damp, events took an even stranger turn.

"They had managed to pitch the tent, and Sam had gone inside to do whatever he could toward making it comfortable. Lucille, as the night came down more fully, was outside moving about to keep warm. She suddenly cried out to Sam that she could see distant fires at the four points of the compass. Then, in another moment, she screamed, and there came a rushing wind that filled the tent and brought an intense, instantaneous drop in temperature. Stiffly, and yet as quickly as he could, Sam stumbled out of the tent to find Lucille fallen to the snow. She could not tell him what had happened, could only mumble incoherently of 'something in the sky!'

"…God only knows how they lived through that night. Lucille's recollections are blurred and indistinct; she believes now that she was in any case more dead than alive. Three days and nights in that terrible white waste, wholly without food and for the greater part of the time without even the warmth of a fire. But on the morning of the next day—

"Amazingly everything had changed for the better overnight. Apparently their fears—that if they did not first perish from exposure they would die at the hands of the unknown murderers of the two guides—had been unfounded. Perhaps, Sam conjectured, they had somehow managed to pass out of the forbidden territory; and now that they were no longer trespassers, as it were, they were eligible for whatever help Ithaqua's furtive worshipers could give them. Certainly that was the way things seemed to be, for in the snow beside their tent they found tinned soups, matches, a kerosene cooker similar to the one stolen by the unfortunate guides, a pile of branches, and finally, a cryptic note that said, simply: 'Navissa lies seven miles to the southeast.' It was as if Lucille's vision of the foregone night had been an omen of good fortune, as if Ithaqua Himself had looked down and decided that the two lost and desperate human beings deserved another chance....

"By midday, with hot soup inside them, warmed and rested, having slept the morning through beside a fire, they were ready to complete their return journey to Navissa—or so they thought!

"Shortly after they set out, a light storm sprang up through which they pressed on until they came to a range of low, pinecovered hills. Navissa, Sam reckoned, must lie just beyond the hills. Despite the strengthening storm and falling temperature, they decided to fight on while they had the strength for it, but no sooner had they started to climb than nature seemed to set all her elements against them. I have checked the records and that night was one of the worst this region had known in many years.

"It soon became obvious that they could not go on through the teeth of the storm but must wait it out. Just as Sam had made up his mind to pitch camp, they entered a wood of thick firs and pines; and since this made the going easier, they pressed on a little longer. Soon, however, the storm picked up to such an unprecedented pitch that they knew they must take shelter there and then. In these circumstances they came across that which seemed a veritable haven from the storm.

"At first, seen through the whipping trees and blinding snow, the thing looked like a huge squat cabin, but as they approached it they could see that it was in fact a great raised platform of sorts, sturdily built of logs. The snow, having drifted up deeply on three sides of this edifice, had given it the appearance of a flat-roofed cabin. The fourth side being free of snow, the whole formed a perfect shelter into which they crept out of the blast. There, beneath that huge log platform whose purpose they were too weary even to guess at, Sam lit the kerosene stove and warmed some soup. They felt cheered by the timely discovery of this refuge, and since after some hours the storm seemed in no way about to abate, they made down their sleeping bags and settled themselves in for the night. Both of them fell instantly asleep.

"And it was later that night that disaster struck. How, in what manner Sam died, must always remain a matter for conjecture; but I believe that Lucille saw him die, and the sight of it must have temporarily broken her already badly weakened nerves. Certainly the things that she *believes* she saw, and one thing in particular that she believes happened that night, never could have been. God forbid!

"That part of Lucille's story, anyway, is composed of fragmentary mental images hard to define and even harder to put into common words. She has spoken of beacon fires burning in the night, of a 'congregation at Ithaqua's altar,' of an evil, ancient Eskimo chant issuing from a hundred adulatory throats—and of that which *answered* that chant, drawn down from the skies by the call of its worshipers....

"I will go into no details of what she 'remembers' except to repeat that Sam died, and that then, as I see it, his poor wife's tortured mind must finally have broken. It seems certain, though, that even after the...horror...she must have received help from someone; she could not possibly have covered even a handful of miles in her condition on foot and alone—and yet she was found *here*, near Navissa, by certain of the town's inhabitants.

"She was taken to a local doctor, who was frankly astounded that, frozen to the marrow as she was, she had not died of exposure in the wastes. It was a number of weeks before she was well enough to be told of Sam, how he had been found dead, a block of human ice out in the snows.

"And when she pressed them, then it came out about the condition of his body, how strangely torn and mangled it had been, as if ravaged by savage beasts, or as if it had fallen from a great height, or perhaps a combination of both. The official verdict was that he must have stumbled over some high cliff onto sharp rocks, and that his body had subsequently been dragged for some distance over the snow by wolves. This latter fitted with the fact that while his body showed all the signs of a great fall, there were no high places in the immediate vicinity. Why the wolves did not devour him remains unknown."

Thus ended the Judge's narrative, and though I sat for some three minutes waiting for him to continue, he did not do so. In the end I said, "And she believes that her husband was killed by?..."

"That Ithaqua killed him?—Yes, and she believes in rather worse things, if you can imagine that." Hurriedly then he went on, giving me no opportunity to question his meaning.

"One or two other things: First, Lucille's temperature. It has never been quite normal since that time. She tells me medical men are astounded that her body temperature never rises above a level that would be death to anyone else. They say it must be a symptom of severe nervous disorder but are at a loss to reconcile this with her otherwise fairly normal physical condition. And finally this." He held out the medallion for my inspection.

"I want you to keep it for now. It was found on Sam's broken body; in fact it was clenched in his hand. Lucille got it with his other effects. She tells me there is—something strange about it. If any, well, phenomena really do attach to it, you should notice them...."

I took the medallion and looked at it—at its loathsome bas-relief work, scenes of a battle between monstrous beings that only some genius artist in the throes of madness might conceive—before asking, "And is that all?"

"Yes, I think so—no, wait. There is something else, of course there is. Lucille's boy, Kirby. He…well, in many ways it seems he is like Sam: impetuous, with a love of strange and esoteric lore and legend, a wanderer at heart, I suspect; but his mother has always kept him down, Earthbound. At any rate, he's now run off. Lucille believes that he's come north. She thinks perhaps that he intends to visit those regions where his father died. Don't ask me why; I think Kirby must be something of a neurotic where his father is concerned. This may well have come down to him from his mother.

"Anyway, she intends to follow and find him and take him home again away from here. Of course, if no evidence comes to light to show him positively to be in these parts, then there will be nothing for you to do. But if he really is here somewhere, then it would be a great personal favor to me if you would go with Lucille and look after her when she decides to search him out. Goodness only knows how it might affect her to go again into the snows, with so many bad memories."

"I'll certainly do as you ask, Judge, and gladly," I answered immediately. "Frankly, the more I learn of Bridgeman, the more the mystery fascinates me. There *is* a mystery, you would agree, despite all rationalizations?"

"A mystery?" He pondered my question. "The snows are strange, David, and too much snow and privation can bring fantastic illusions—like the mirages of the desert. In the snow, men may dream while yet awake. And there again, there is that weird five-year cycle of strangeness that definitely affects this region. Myself, I suspect that it all has some quite simple explanation. A mystery?—I say the world is full of mysteries…."

III

That night I experienced my first taste of the weird, the inexplicable, the outré. And that night I further learned that I, too, must be susceptible to the five-year cycle of strangeness; either that, or I had eaten too well before taking to my bed!

There was first the dream of cyclopean submarine cities of mad angles and proportions, which melted into vague but frightful glimpses of the spaces between the stars, through which I seemed to walk or float at speeds many times that of light. Nebulae floated by like bubbles in wine, and strange constellations expanded before me and dwindled in my wake as I passed through them. This floating, or walking, was accompanied by the sounds of a tremendous striding, like the world-shaking footsteps of some ponderous giant, and there was (of all things) an ether wind that blew about me the scent of stars and shards of shattered planets.

Finally all of these impressions faded to a nothingness, and I was as a mote lost in the darkness of dead eons. Then there came another wind—not the wind that carried the odor of outer immensities or the pollen of blossoming planets—a tangible, shrieking gale wind that whirled me about and around until I was sick and dizzy and in dread of being dashed to pieces. And I awoke.

I awoke and thought I knew why I had dreamed such a strange dream, a nightmare totally outside anything I had previously known. For out in the night it raged and blew, a storm that filled my room with its roaring until I could almost feel the tiles being lifted from the roof above.

I got out of bed and went to the window, drawing the curtains cautiously and looking out—before stumbling back with my eyes popping and my mouth agape in an exclamation of utter amazement and disbelief. *Outside, the night was as calm as any I ever saw, with the stars gleaming clear and bright and not even a breeze to stir the small firs in the Judge's garden!*

As I recoiled—amidst the rush and roar of winds that seemed to have their origin in my very room, even though I could feel no motion of the air and while nothing visibly stirred—I knocked down the golden medallion from where I had left it upon my window ledge. On the instant, as the dull yellow thing clattered to the smooth pine floor, the roaring of the wind was cut off, leaving a silence that made my head spin with its suddenness. The cacophony of mad winds had not "died away"—quite literally it had been *cut off!*

Shakily I bent to pick the medallion up, noticing that despite the warmth of my room it bore a chill that must have been near to freezing. On impulse I put the thing to my ear. It seemed that just for a second, receding, I could hear as in a sounding shell the rush and roar and hum of winds far, far away, winds blowing beyond the rim of the world!

In the morning, of course, I realized that it had all been a dream, not merely the fantastic submarine and interspatial sequences but also those occurrences following immediately upon my "awakening." Nevertheless, I questioned the Judge as to whether he had heard anything odd during the night. He had not, and I was strangely relieved....

Three days later, when it was beginning to look like Lucille Bridgeman's suspicions regarding her son were without basis—this despite all her efforts, and the Judge's, to prove the positive presence of Kirby Bridgeman in the vicinity of Navissa—then came word from the Mounties at Fir Valley that a young man answering Kirby's description had indeed been seen. He had been with a mixed crowd of seemingly destitute outsiders and local layabouts camping in crumbling Stillwater. Observers—two aging but inveterate gold-grubbers, out on their last prospecting trip of the year before the bad weather set in—had mentioned seeing him. Though these gnarled prospectors had by no means been made welcome in Stillwater, nonetheless they had noted that this particular young man had appeared to be in a sort of trance or daze, and that the others with him had seemed to hold him in some kind of reverence; they had been tending to his needs and generally looking after him.

It was this description of the boy's condition (which made it sound rather as if he were not quite right in his head) that determined me to inquire tactfully of his mother about him as soon as the opportunity presented itself. For the last two days, though, I had been studying the handling and maintenance of a vehicle that the Judge termed a "snow cat": a fairly large, motorized sledge of very modern design that he had hired for Mrs. Bridgeman from a friend of his in the town. The vehicle seemed a fairly economical affair, capable in suitable conditions of carrying two adults and provisions over snow at a speed of up to twenty miles per hour. It was capable, too, of a somewhat slower speed over more normal terrain. With such a vehicle two people might easily travel 150 miles without refueling, in comparative comfort at that, and over country no automobile could possibly challenge.

The next morning saw us setting out aboard the snow cat. Though we planned on returning to Navissa every second or third day to refuel, we had sufficient supplies aboard for at least a week. First we headed for Stillwater.

Following a fall of snow during the night, the trail that led us to the ghost town was mainly buried beneath a white carpet almost a foot deep, but even so, it was plain that this barely fourth-class road (in places a mere track) was in extremely poor repair. I recalled the Judge telling me that very few people went to Stillwater now, following the strange affair of twenty years gone, and doubtless this accounted for the track's derelict appearance in those places where the wind had blown its surface clean.

In Stillwater we found a constable of the Mounties just preparing to leave the place for camp at Fir Valley. He had gone to the ghost town specifically to check out the story of the two old prospectors. Introducing himself as Constable McCauley, the Mountie showed us round the town.

Originally the place had been built of stout timbers, with stores and houses and one very ramshackle "saloon" bordering a main street and with lesser huts and habitations set back behind the street facades. Now, however, the main street was grown with grass and weeds beneath the snow, and even the stoutest buildings were quickly falling into dilapidation. The shacks and lesser houses to the rear leaned like old men with the weight of years, and rotten doorposts with their paint long flaked away sagged on every hand, threatening at any moment to collapse and bring down the edifices framing them into the snow. Here and there one or two windows remained, but warped and twisting frames had long since claimed by far the greater number, so that now sharp shards of glass stood up in broken rows from sills like grinning teeth in blackly leering mouths. A stained, tattered curtain flapped moldering threads in the chill midday breeze. Even though the day was fairly bright, there was a definite gloominess about Stillwater, an aura of something *not quite right*, of strange menace, seeming to brood like a mantle of evil about the place.

Overall, and ignoring the fact that twenty years had passed since last it knew habitation, the town seemed to be falling far too quickly into decay, almost as if some elder magic had blighted the place in an effort to return it to its origins. Saplings already stood tall through the snow in the main street; grass and weeds proliferated on window ledges, along facades, and in the black gaps where boards had fallen from the lower stories of the crumbling buildings.

Mrs. Bridgeman seemed to notice none of this, only that her son was no longer in the town…if he had ever been there.

In the largest standing building, a tavern that seemed to have fared better in its battle against decay than the rest of the town, we brewed coffee and heated soups. There, too we found signs of recent, if temporary, habitation, for the floor in one of the rooms was fairly littered with freshly empty cans and bottles. This debris, plus the blackened ashes of a fire built on stones in one corner, stood as plain testimony that the building had been used by that group of unknown persons whose presence the prospectors had reported.

The Mountie mentioned how chill the place was, and at his remark it dawned on me that indeed the tavern seemed colder inside (where by all rights it ought to have been at least marginally warmer) than out in the raw air of the derelict streets. I was about to voice this thought when Mrs. Bridgeman, suddenly paler by far than usual, put down her coffee and stood up from where she sat upon a rickety chair.

She looked first at me—a queer, piercing glance—then at McCauley. "My son was here," she abruptly said, as if she knew it quite definitely. "Kirby was here!"

The Mountie looked hard at her, then stared about the room in mystification. "There's some sign that your boy was here, Mrs. Bridgeman?"

She had turned away and for a moment did not answer. She seemed to be listening intently for something far off. "Can't you hear it?"

Constable McCauley looked at me out of the corner of his eye. He frowned. The room was very still. "Hear what, Mrs. Bridgeman? What is it?"

"Why, the wind!" she answered, her eyes clouded and distant. "The wind blowing way out between the worlds!"

Half an hour later we were ready to move again. The Mountie in the meantime had taken me to one side, to ask me if I didn't think the search we planned was just a little bit hazardous considering Mrs. Bridgeman's condition. Plainly he thought she was a bit touched. Perhaps she was! God knows, if what the Judge told me was true, the poor woman had enough reason. Being ignorant of her real problem at that time, however, I shrugged her strangeness off, mentioning her relationship with her son as being obsessive out of all proportion to reality. In truth, this was the impression I had already half formed—but it did not explain the *other* thing.

I made no mention of it to the Mountie. For one thing, it was none of his business; and for another, I hardly wanted him thinking that perhaps I, too, was "a bit touched." It was simply this: in the derelict tavern—when Mrs. Bridgeman had asked, "Can't you hear it?"—I had in fact heard something. At the exact moment of her inquiry, I had put my hand into a pocket of my parka for a pack of cigarettes. My hand had come into contact with that strange golden medallion, and as my fingers closed upon the chill shape, I had felt a thrill as of weird energies, an electric tingle that seemed to energize all my senses simultaneously. I felt the cold of the spaces between the stars; I smelled again, as in my dreams, the scents of unknown worlds; for the merest fraction of a second there opened before me reeling vistas, incredible eons flashing by in a twinkling; and I, too, heard a wind—a howling *sentience* from far beyond the universe we know!

It had been so momentary, this—vision?—that I thought little more of it. Doubtless my mind, as I touched the medallion, had conjured in connection with the thing parts of that dream in which it had featured so strongly. That was the only explanation....

I calculate that by 5:00 P.M. we must have been something like fifty miles directly north of Stillwater. It was there, in the lee of a low hill covered by tall conifers whose snow-laden branches bowed almost to the ground, that Mrs. Bridgeman called a halt for the night. Freezing, the snow already had a thin, crisp crust. I set up our two tiny bivouacs beneath a pine whose white branches formed in themselves something of a tent, and there I lit our stove and prepared a meal.

I had decided that it was time tactfully to approach Mrs. Bridgeman regarding those many facets of her story of which I was still ignorant; but then, as if there were not enough of mystery. I was witness to that which brought vividly back to me what the Judge had told me of the widow's body temperature.

We had finished our meal, and I had prepared my bivouac for the night, spreading my sleeping bag and packing snow close to the lower outside walls of the tiny tent against freezing drafts. I offered to do the same for Mrs. Bridgeman, but she assured me that she could attend to that herself. For the moment she wanted "a breath of fresh air." That turn of phrase in itself might have been enough to puzzle me (the air could hardly have been fresher!) but in addition she then cast off her parka, standing only in sweater and slacks, before stepping out from under the lowered branches into the subzero temperatures of falling night.

Heavily wrapped, still I shivered as I watched her from the sanctuary of our hideaway beneath the tree. For half an hour she simply wandered to and fro over the snow, occasionally glancing at the sky and then again into the darkening distance. Finally, as I suddenly realized that I was quickly drawing close to freezing while waiting for her to come back to camp, I went stiffly out to her with her parka. She must by now, I believed, be very close to suffering from exposure. Blaming myself that I had not recognized sooner how terrifically cold it was, I came up to her and threw her parka about her shoulders. Imagine my astonishment when she turned with a questioning look, completely at ease and plainly quite comfortable, immensely surprised at my concern!

She must have seen immediately how cold I was. Chiding me that I had not taken greater care to keep warm, she hurried back with me to the bivouacs beneath the tree. There she quickly boiled water and made coffee. She drank none of the hot, reviving fluid herself, however, and I was so astounded at her apparent immunity to the cold that I forgot all about those questions I had intended to ask. Since Mrs. Bridgeman now plainly intended to retire and since my own sleeping bag lay warm and inviting inside my bivouac, I simply finished off the coffee, turned down the stove and lay down for the night.

I was suddenly tired, and the last thing I saw before sleeping was a patch of sky through the branches, illumined by brightly twinkling stars. Perhaps that picture of the heavens, imprinted upon my mind's eye as I fell asleep, colored my dreams. Certainly I dreamed of stars all night long, but they were uneasy dreams. The stars I saw were particularly sentient and paired like strange eyes; they glowed carmine against a moving black background of hideously suggestive design and immense proportions....

In the morning over breakfast—cheese and tomato sandwiches, followed by coffee and fruit juice—I briefly mentioned Mrs. Bridgeman's apparent immunity to the cold, at which she looked at me with a very wry expression and said, "You may believe me, Mr. Lawton, when I tell you that I would give all of what little I have just once to feel the cold. It is this—*affliction*— of mine, an extremely rare condition that I contracted here in the north. And it has come out in—"

"In Kirby?" I hazarded the guess.

"Yes." She looked at me again, shrewdly this time. "How much did Judge Andrews tell you?"

I could not conceal my embarrassment. "He—he told me of your husband's death, and—"

"What did he say of my son?"

"Very little. He is not the kind of man to gossip idly, Mrs. Bridgeman, and—"

"And you suspect that there might be much to gossip about?" She was suddenly angry.

"I only know that I'm here, helping a woman look for her son, following her instincts and whims without question, as a favor to an old man. To be absolutely truthful, I suspect that there is a great mystery here; and I admit that I am addicted to mysteries, as curious as a cat. But my curiosity is without malice, you must believe that, and my only desire is to help you."

She turned away from me for a moment or two, and I thought she was still angry, but when she turned back her face was much more composed.

"And did the Judge not warn you that there would be—danger?"

"Danger? Heavy snow is due, certainly—"

"No, the snow is nothing—I didn't mean the snow. The Judge has Sam's books; have you read them?"

"Yes, but what danger can there be in mythology and folklore?" In fact, I guessed what she was getting at, but better to hear it from her own lips, as she "believed" it and as her husband had "believed" it before her.

"What danger in myths and legends, you ask?" She smiled mirthlessly. "I asked the same question of Sam when he wanted to leave me in Navissa. God, that I'd listened to him! What danger in folklore? I can't tell you directly—not without you thinking me a madwoman, as I'm sure the Judge must more than half believe—but I'll tell you this: today we return to Navissa. On the way you can teach me how to drive the snow cat. I won't take you to horrors you can't conceive."

I tried to argue the point but she would say no more. We decamped in silence, packed the bivouacs and camp utensils aboard the cat, and then, despite a last effort on my part to dissuade her, she demanded that we head directly for Navissa.

For half an hour, traveling fairly slowly, we followed the course of a frozen stream between brooding fir forests whose dark interiors were made darker still by the shrouding snow that covered the upper branches. It was as I turned the snow cat away from the stream, around a smaller copse of trees to head more nearly south, that I accidentally came upon that which should have gone far toward substantiating Mrs. Bridgeman's hints of terrible dangers.

It was a large depression in the snow, to which I had to react quickly in order to avoid a spill, when we might easily have tumbled directly into it. I halted our machine, and we stepped down to take a closer look at this strangely sunken place in the snow.

Here the drift was deeper, perhaps three or four feet, but in the center of the depression it had been compacted almost to the earth beneath, as if some great weight had rested there. The size of this concavity must have been almost twenty feet long by seven or eight feet wide, and its shape was something like—

Abruptly the Judge's words came back to me—what he had mentioned of the various manifestations of Ithaqua, the Wind-Walker—*and particularly of giant, webbed footprints in the snow!*

But of course that was ridiculous. And yet…

I began to walk round the perimeter of the fantastic depression, only turning when I heard Mrs. Bridgeman cry out behind me. Paler than I had ever seen her before, now she leaned dizzily against the snow cat, her hand to her throat. I went quickly to her.

"Mrs. Bridgeman?"

"He—*He was here!*" she spoke in a horrified whisper.

"Your son?"

"No, not Kirby—*Him!*" She pointed, staring wide-eyed at the compacted snow of the depression. "Ithaqua, the Wind-Walker—that is His sign. And that means that I may already be too late!"

"Mrs. Bridgeman," I made a halfhearted attempt to reason with her, "plainly this depression marks the spot where a number of animals rested during the night. The snow must have drifted about them, leaving this peculiar shape."

"There was no snow last night, Mr. Lawton," she answered, more composed now, "but in any case your explanation is quite impossible. Why, if there had been a number of animals here, surely they would have left tracks in the snow when they moved. Look about you. There are no tracks here! No, this is the footprint of the fiend. The horror was here—and somewhere, at this very moment, my son is trying to search Him out, helped on by those poor devils that worship Him!"

I saw my chance then to avoid an early return to Navissa. If we went back now, I might never learn the whole story, and I would never be able to face the Judge, having let him down. "Mrs. Bridgeman, it's plain that if we go south now we're only wasting time. I for one am willing to face whatever danger there may be, though I still can see no such danger. However, if some peril does face Kirby, then we won't be helping him any by returning to Navissa. It would help, though, if I knew the background story. Some of it I know already, but there must be a lot you can tell me. Now listen, we have enough fuel for about 120 miles more. This is my proposition: that we carry on looking for your son to the north. If we have not found him by the time our fuel reserves are halved, then we head back in a direct line for Navissa. Furthermore, I swear here and now that I'll never divulge anything you may tell me or anything I may see while you live. Now, then—we're wasting time. What do you say?"

She hesitated, turning my proposition over in her mind, and as she did so, I saw to the north the spreading of a cloud sheet across the sky and sensed that peculiar change of atmosphere that ever precedes bad weather. Again I prompted her: "The sky is growing more sullen all the time. We're in for plenty of snow—probably tonight. We really can't afford to waste time if we want to find Kirby before the worst of the weather sets in. Soon the glass will begin to fall, and—"

"The cold won't bother Kirby, Mr. Lawton—but you're right, there's no time to waste. From now on our breaks must be shorter, and we must try to travel faster. Later today I'll tell you what I can of…of everything. Believe what you will, it makes little difference, but for the last time I warn you—if we find Kirby, then in all probability we shall also find the utmost horror!"

IV

With regard to the weather, I was right. Having turned again to the north, skirting dense fir forests and crossing frozen streams and low hills, by 10:30 A.M. we were driving through fairly heavy snow. The glass was far down, though mercifully there was little wind. All this time—despite a certainty in my heart that there would be none—nevertheless, I found myself watching out for more of those strange and inexplicable hollows in the snow.

A dense copse where the upper branches interlaced, forming a dark umbrella to hold up a roof of snow, served us for a midday camp. There, while we prepared a hot meal and as we ate, Mrs. Bridgeman began to tell me about her son, about his remarkable childhood and his strange leanings as he grew into a man. Her first revelation, however, was the most fantastic, and plainly the Judge had been quite right to suspect that the events of twenty years gone had turned her mind, at least as far as her son was concerned.

"Kirby," she started without preamble, "is not Sam's son. I love Kirby, naturally, but he is in no wise a child of love. He was born of the winds. No, don't interrupt me, I want no rationalizations.

"Can you understand me, Mr. Lawton? I suppose not. Indeed, at first I, too, thought that I was mad, that the whole thing had been a nightmare. I thought so right until the time—until Kirby was born. Then, as he grew up from a baby, I became less sure. Now I know that I was never mad. It was no nightmare that came to me here in the snow but a monstrous fact! And why not? Are not the oldest religions and legends known to man full of stories of gods lusting after the daughters of men? There *were* giants in the olden times, Mr. Lawton. There still are.

"Do you recall the Wendy-Smith expedition of '33? What do you suppose he found, that poor man, in the fastnesses of Africa? What prompted him to say these words, which I know by heart: 'There are fabulous legends of star-born creatures who inhabited this Earth many millions of years before Man appeared and who were still here, in certain black places, when he eventually evolved. They are, I am sure, to an extent here even now.'

"Wendy-Smith was sure, and so am I. In 1913 two monsters were born in Dunwich to a degenerate half-wit of a woman. They are both dead now, but there are still whispers in Dunwich of the affair, and of the father who is hinted to have been other than human. Oh, there are many examples of survivals from olden times, of beings and forces that have reached godlike proportions in the minds of men, and who is to deny that at least some of them could be real?

"And where Ithaqua is concerned—why!—there are elementals of the air mentioned in every mythology known to man. Rightly so, for even today, and other than this Ithaqua of the Snows, there are strange winds that blow madness and horror into the minds of men. I mean winds like the *Foehn*, the south wind of Alpine valleys. And what of the piping winds of subterranean caverns, like that of the Calabrian Caves, which has been known to leave stout cavers white-haired, babbling wrecks? What do we understand of such forces?

"Our human race is a colony of ants, Mr. Lawton, inhabiting an anthill at the edge of a limitless chasm called infinity. All things may happen in infinity, and who knows what might come out of it? What do we know of *the facts* of anything, in our little corner of a never-ending universe, in this transient revolution in the space-time continuum? Seeping down from the stars at the beginning of time there were giants—beings who walked or flew across the spaces between the worlds, inhabiting and using entire systems at their will—and some of them still remain. What would the race of man be to creatures such as these? I'll tell you—we are the plankton of the seas of space and time!

"But there, I'm going on a bit, away from the point. The facts are these: that before I came to Navissa with Sam, he had already been told that he was sterile, and that after I left—after that horror had killed my husband—well, then I was pregnant.

"Of course, at first I believed that the doctors were wrong, that Sam had not been sterile at all, and this seemed to be borne out when my baby was born just within eight months of Sam's death. Obviously, in the normal scale of reckoning, Kirby was conceived before we came to Navissa. And yet it was a difficult pregnancy, and as a newborn baby he was a weedy, strange little thing—frail and dreamy and far too quiet—so that even without knowing much of children I nevertheless found myself thinking of his birth as having been…premature!

"His feet were large even for a boy, and his toes were webbed with a pink stretching of skin that thickened and lengthened as he grew. Understand, please, that my boy was in no way a freak—not visibly. Many people have this webbing between their toes; some have it between their fingers too. In all other respects he seemed to be completely normal. Well, perhaps not completely…

"Long before he could walk, he was talking—baby talk, you know—but not to me. Always it was when he was alone in his cot, and always when there was a wind. He could hear the wind, and he used to talk to it. But that was nothing really remarkable; grown children often talk to invisible playmates, people and creatures that only they can see; except that I used to listen to Kirby, and sometimes—

"Sometimes I could swear that the winds talked back to him!

"You may laugh if you wish, Mr. Lawton, and I don't suppose I could blame you, but there always seemed to be a wind about our home, when everywhere else the air was still….

"As Kirby grew older this didn't seem to happen so frequently, or perhaps I simply grew used to it, I really don't know. But when he should have been starting school, well, that was out of the question. He was such a dreamer, in no way slow or backward, you understand, but he constantly lived in a kind of dreamworld. And always—though he seemed later to have given up his strange conversations with drafts and breezes—he had this fascination with the wind.

"One summer night when he was seven, a wind came up that threatened to blow the very house down. It came from the sea, a north wind off the Gulf of Mexico—or perhaps it came from farther away than that, who can say? At any rate, I was frightened, as were most of the families in the area where we lived. Such was the fury of that demon wind, and it reminded me so of…of another wind I had known. Kirby sensed my fear. It was the strangest thing, but he threw open a window and he shouted. He shouted right into the teeth of that howling, banshee storm. Can you imagine that? A small child, teeth bared and hair streaming, shouting at a wind that might have lifted him right off the face of the Earth!

"And yet in another minute the worst of the storm was over, leaving Kirby scolding and snapping at the smaller gusts of air that yet remained, until the night was as still as any other summer night….

"At ten he became interested in model airplanes, and one of his private tutors helped him and encouraged him to design and build his own. You see, he was far ahead of other children his own age. One of his models created a lot of excitement when it was shown at an exhibition of flying models at a local club. It had a very strange shape; its underside was all rippled and warped. It worked on a gliding principle of my son's own invention, having no motor but relying upon what Kirby called his 'rippled-air principle.' I remember he took it to the gliding club that day, and that the other members—children and adults alike—laughed at his model and said it couldn't possibly fly. Kirby flew it for them for an hour, and they all marveled while it seemingly defied gravity in a fantastic series of flights. Then, because they had laughed at him, he smashed the model down to its balsa wood and tissue paper components to strew them like confetti at the feet of the spectators.

That was his pride working, even as a child. I wasn't there myself, but I'm told that a designer from one of the big model companies cried when Kirby destroyed his glider....

"He loved kites, too—he always had a kite. He would sit for hours and simply watch his kite standing on the air at the end of its string.

"When he was thirteen he wanted binoculars so that he could study the birds in flight. Hawks were of particular interest to him—the way they hover, motionless except for the rapid beating of their wings. They, too, seem almost to walk on the wind.

"Then came the day when a more serious and worrying aspect of Kirby's fascination with the air and flight came to light. For a long time I had been worried about him, about his constant restlessness and moodiness and his ominous obsession.

"We were visiting Chichén Itzá, a trip I hoped would take Kirby's mind off other things. In fact the trip had a twofold purpose; the other was that I had been to Chichén Itzá before with Sam, and this was my way of remembering how it had been. Every now and then I would visit a place where we had been happy before...before his death.

"There were, however, a number of things I had not taken into account. There is often a wind playing among those ancient ruins, and the ruins themselves—with their aura of antiquity, their strange glyphs, their history of bloody worship and nighted gods—can be...disturbing.

"I had forgotten, too, that the Mayas had their own god of the air; Quetzalcoatl, the plumed serpent, and I suspect that this was almost my undoing.

"Kirby had been quiet and moody during the outward trip, and he stayed that way even after freshening up and while we began to explore the ancient buildings and temples. It was while I was admiring other ruins that Kirby climbed the high, hideously adorned Temple of the Warriors, with its facade of plumed serpents, their mouths fanged and tails rampant.

"He was seen to fall—or jump—by at least two dozen people, mainly Mexicans, but later they all told the same story: how the wind had seemed almost to buoy him up; how he had seemed to fall in slow motion; how he had uttered an eerie cry before stepping into space, like a call to strange gods for assistance. And after that terrible fall, onto ancient stone flags and from such a great height?...

"It was a miracle, people said, that Kirby was unhurt.

"Well, eventually I was able to convince the authorities at the site that Kirby must have fallen, and I was able to get him away before he came out of his faint. Oh, yes, he had fainted. A fall like that, and the only result a swoon!

"But though I had explained away the incident as best I could, I don't suppose I could ever have explained the look on Kirby's face as I carried him away—that smile of triumph or strange satisfaction.

"Now all this happened not long after his fourteenth birthday, at a time when here in the north the five-year cycle of so-called 'superstitious belief and mass hysteria' was once more at its height, just as it is now. So far as I was concerned, there was an undeniable connection.

"Since then—and I blame myself that I've only recently discovered this—Kirby has been a secret saver, hoarding away whatever money he could lay his hands on toward some future purpose or ambition; and now of course I know that this was his journey north. All his life, you see, he had followed the trail of his destiny, and I don't suppose that there was anything I could have done to change it.

"A short time ago something happened to clinch it, something that drew Kirby north like a magnet. Now—I don't know what the end will be, *but I must see it*—I must find out, one way or the other, once and for all...."

V

By 1:30 P.M. we were once again mobile, our vehicle driving through occasional flurries of snow, fortunately with a light tail wind to boost us on our way. And it was not long before we came upon signs that warned of the presence of others there in that white waste, fresh snowshoe tracks that crossed our path at a tangent and moved in the direction of low hills. We followed these tracks—apparently belonging to a group of at least three persons—until they converged with others atop one of the low bald hills. Here I halted the snow cat and dismounted, peering out at the wilderness around and discovering that from here, between flurries of snow, I could roughly make out the site of our last camp. It dawned on me at once that this would have been a wonderful vantage point from which to keep us under observation.

Then Mrs. Bridgeman tugged at the sleeve of my parka, pointing away to the north where finally I made out a group of black dots against the pure white background straggling toward a distant pine forest.

"We must follow them," she declared. "They will be members of His order, on their way to the ceremonies. Kirby may even be with them!" At the thought her voice took on a feverish excitement.

"Quickly—we mustn't lose them!"

But lose them we did.

By the time we reached that stretch of open ground where first Mrs. Bridgeman had spied the unknown group, its members had already disappeared into the darkness of the trees some hundreds of yards away. At the edge of the forest I again brought our vehicle to a halt, and though we might easily have followed the tracks through the trees—which was my not-so-delicate companion's immediate and instinctive desire—that would have meant abandoning the snow cat.

Instead, I argued that we should skirt the forest, find a vantage point on its northern fringe, and there await the emergence of whichever persons they were who chose to wander these wastes at the onset of winter. To this seemingly sound proposal Mrs. Bridgeman readily enough agreed, and within the hour we were hidden away in a cluster of pines beyond the forest proper. There we took turns to watch the fringe of the forest, and while I took first watch, Mrs. Bridgeman made a pot of coffee. We had only unpacked our stove, deeming it unwise to make ourselves too comfortable in case we should need to be on the move in a hurry.

After only twenty minutes at my post I would have been willing to swear that the sky had snowed itself out for the day. Indeed I made just such a comment to my pale companion when she brought me a cup of coffee. The leaden heavens had cleared—there was hardly a cloud in sight in the afternoon sky—and then, as if from nowhere, there came the wind!

Instantly the temperature dropped, and I felt the hairs in my nostrils stiffening and cracking with each sniff of icy air. The remaining half cup of coffee in my hand froze in a matter of seconds, and a rime of frost sprang up on my eyebrows. Heavily wrapped as I was, still I felt the cold striking through, and I drew back into the comparative shelter of the trees. In all my meteorological experience I have never known or heard of anything like it before. The storm that came with the wind and the cold, rising up in the space of the next half hour, took me totally by surprise.

Looking up, through gaps in the snow-laden branches, I could plainly see the angry boiling up of clouds into a strange mixture of cumulonimbus and nimbostratus, where only moments before there had been no clouds at all! If the sky had seemed leaden earlier in the day, now it positively glowered. The atmosphere pressed down with an almost tangible weight upon our heads.

And finally it snowed.

Mercifully, and despite the fact that all the symptoms warned of a tremendous storm to come, the wind remained only moderate, but by comparison the snow came down as if it had never snowed before. The *husshh* of settling snow was quite audible as the huge flakes fell in gust-driven, spiraling myriads to the ground.

Plainly my watch on the forest was no longer necessary, indeed impossible, for such was the curtain of falling snow that visibility was down to no more than a few feet. We were stuck, but surely no more so than that suspicious band of wanderers in the forest—members of "His order," as Mrs. Bridgeman would have it. We would have to wait the weather out, and so would they.

For the next two hours, until about 5:00 P.M., I busied myself making a windbreak of fallen branches and packed snow until even the moderate wind was shut out of our hideaway. Then I built a small fire in the center of this sheltered area close to the snow cat. Whatever happened, I did not want the works of that machine put out of order by freezing temperatures.

During all this time Mrs. Bridgeman simply sat and brooded, plainly unconcerned with the cold. She was frustrated, I imagined, by our inability to get on with the search. In the same period, busy as I was with my hands, nevertheless I was able to ponder much of what had passed, drawing what half-formed conclusions I could in the circumstances.

The truth of the matter was that there did seem to be too many coincidences here for comfort, and personally I had already experienced a number of things previously unknown to me or alien to my nature. I could no longer keep from my mind memories of that strange dream of mine; similarly the odd sensations I had felt on contact with or in proximity to the yellow medallion of gold and obscure alloys.

Then there was the simple, quite definite fact—bolstered both by the Judge and the widow Bridgeman alike, and by McCauley the Mountie—that a freakish five-year cycle of strange excitement, morbid worship, and curious cult activity did actually exist in these parts. And dwelling on thoughts such as these, I found myself wondering once again just what had happened here twenty years gone, that its echoes should so involve me here and now.

Patently it had not been—could not possibly have been—as Mrs. Bridgeman "remembered" it. And yet, apart from her previous nervousness and one or two forgivable lapses under emotional stress since then, she had seemed to me to be as normal as most women....

Or had she?

I found myself in two minds. What of this fantastic immunity of hers to subzero temperatures? Even now she sat there, peering out into the falling snow, pale and distant and impervious still to the frost that rimed her forehead and dusted her clothes, perfectly comfortable despite the fact that she had once again shed her heavy parka. No, I was wrong, and it amazed me that I had fooled myself for so long. There was very little about this woman that was normal. She had known—*something*. Some experience to set her both mentally and physically aside from mundane mankind.

But could that experience possibly have been the horror she "remembered"? Even then I could not quite bring myself to believe.

And yet…what of that shape we had stumbled across in the snow, that deep imprint as of a huge webbed foot? My mind flashed back to our first night out from Navissa, when I had dreamed of a colossal shape in the sky, a shape with carmine stars for eyes!

—But this was no good. Why!—here I was, nervous as a cat, starting at the slightest flurry of snow out there beyond the heavy branches. I laughed at my own fancies, albeit shakily, because just for a second as I had turned from the bright fire I had imagined that a shadow moved out in the snow, a furtive figure that shifted just beyond my periphery of vision.

"I saw you jump, Mr. Lawton," my companion suddenly spoke up. "Did you see something?"

"I don't think so," I briskly answered, my voice louder than necessary. "Just a shadow in the snow."

"He has been there for five minutes now. We are under observation!"

"What? You mean there's someone out there?"

"Yes, one of His worshipers, I imagine, sent by the others to see what we're up to. We're outsiders, you know. But I don't think they'll try to do us any harm. Kirby would never allow that."

She was right. Suddenly I saw him, limned darkly against the white background as the whirling snow flurried to one side. Eskimo or Indian, I could not tell which, but I believe his face was impassive. He was merely—watching.

From that time on the storm strengthened, with the wind building up to a steady blast that drove the snow through the trees in an impenetrable icy wall. Behind my barrier of branches and snow we were comfortable enough, for I had extended the shelter until its wall lay open only in a narrow gap to the south; the wind was from the north. The snow on the outside of the shelter had long since formed a frozen crust, so that no wind came through, and the ice-stiffened branches of the surrounding trees gave protection from above. My fire blazed and roared in subdued imitation of the wind, for I had braved half a dozen brief excursions beyond the shelter to bring back armfuls of fallen branches. Their trimmed ends burning, Indian fashion, where they met like the spokes of a wheel to form the center of the fire, these branches now warmed our small enclosure and gave it light. They had burned thus all through the afternoon and into the night.

It was about 10:00 P.M., pitch-black beyond the wall of the shelter and still snowing hard, when we became aware of our second visitor; the first had silently left us some hours earlier. Mrs. Bridgeman saw him first, grabbing my elbow so that I started to my feet and turned toward the open end of our sanctuary. There, framed in the firelight, white with snow from head to foot, stood a man.

A white man, he came forward shaking the snow from his clothes. He paused before the fire and tipped back the hood of his fur jacket, then shed his gloves and held his hands out to the flames. His eyebrows were black, meeting across his nose. He was very tall. After a while, ignoring me, he turned to Mrs. Bridgeman. He had a strong New England accent when he said, "It is Kirby's wish that you go back to Navissa. He does not want you to be hurt. He says you should return now to Navissa—both of you—and that you should then go home. He knows everything now. He knows why he is here, and he wants to stay. His destiny is the glory of the spaces between the worlds, the knowledge and mysteries of the Ancient Ones who were here before man, godship over the icy winds of Earth and space with his Lord and Master. You have had him for almost twenty years. Now he wants to be free."

I was on the point of questioning his authority and tone when Mrs. Bridgeman cut me short. "Free? What kind of freedom? To stay here in the ice; to wander the icy wastes until any attempt to return to the world of men would mean certain death? To learn the alien lore of monsters spawned in black pits beyond time and space?"

Her voice rose hysterically. "To know no woman's love but sate his lust with strangers, leaving them for dead and worse in a manner that *only his loathsome father could ever teach him?*"

The stranger lifted his hand in sudden anger. "You dare to speak of Him like—" I sprang between them, but it was immediately apparent that I was not needed.

The change in Mrs. Bridgeman was almost frightening. She had been near to hysterics only seconds ago; now her eyes blazed with anger in her white face, and she stood so straight and regal as to make our unknown visitor draw back, his raised arm falling quickly to his side.

"Do *I* dare?" Her voice was as chill as the wind. "I am Kirby's mother! Yes, I dare—but what *you* have dared!...You would raise your hand to me?"

"I…it was only…I was angry." The man stumbled over his words before finding his former composure. "But all this makes no difference. Stay if you wish; you will not be able to enter the area of the ceremonies, for there will be a watch out. If you did get by the watch unseen—then the result would be upon your own heads. On the other hand, if you go back now, I can promise you fair weather all the way to Navissa. But only if you go now, at once."

My white-faced companion frowned and turned away to stare at the dying fire.

No doubt believing that she was weakening, the stranger offered his final inducement: "Think, Mrs. Bridgeman, and think well. There can only be one conclusion, one end, if you stay here—for you have looked upon Ithaqua!"

She turned back to him, desperate questions spilling from her lips. "Must we go tonight? May I not see my son just once? Will he be—?"

"He will not be harmed." She was cut off. "His destiny is—*great!* Yes, you must go tonight; he does not wish to see you, and there is so little—" He paused, almost visibly biting his tongue, but it seemed that Mrs. Bridgeman had not noticed his gaffe. Plainly he had been about to say "there is so little time."

My companion sighed and her shoulders slumped. "If I agree—we will need fair weather. That can be…arranged?"

The visitor eagerly nodded (though to me the idea that he might somehow contrive to control the weather seemed utterly ridiculous) and answered, "From now until midnight, the snow will lessen, the winds will die away. After that—" He shrugged. "But you will be well away from here before then."

She nodded, apparently in defeat. "Then we'll go. We need only sufficient time to break camp. A few minutes. But—"

"No buts, Mrs. Bridgeman. There was a Mountie here. He did not want to go away either. Now—" Again he shrugged, the movement of his shoulders speaking volumes.

"McCauley!" I gasped.

"That was not the Mountie's name," he answered me, "but whoever he was, he too was looking for this lady's son." He was obviously talking about some other Mountie from Fir Valley camp, and I remembered McCauley having mentioned another policeman who set out to search the wastes at the same time as he himself had headed for Stillwater.

"What have you done to him, to this man?" I asked.

He ignored me and, pulling on his gloves, again addressed Mrs. Bridgeman: "I will wait until you go." He pulled the hood of his jacket over his head, then stepped back out into the snow.

The conversation, what little there had been, had completely astounded me. In fact my astonishment had grown apace with what I had heard. Quite apart from openly admitting to what could only be murder, our strange visitor had agreed with—indeed, if my ears had not deceived me, he had *confirmed*—the wildest possible nightmares, horrors that until now, so far as I was aware or concerned, had only manifested themselves in the works of Samuel Bridgeman and others who had worked the same vein before him, and in the disturbed imagination of his widow. Surely this must be the final, utmost proof positive of the effect of the morbid five-year cycle on the minds of men? Could it be anything else?

Finally I turned to the widow to ask, "Are we actually going back to Navissa, after all your efforts? And now, when we're so close?"

First glancing cautiously out into the falling snow, she hurriedly shook her head, putting a warning finger to her lips. No, it was as I suspected; her almost docile concurrence, following that blazing, regal display of defiance, had merely been a ruse. She in no way intended to desert her son, whether he wished it or not. "Quickly—let's get packed up," she whispered. "He was right. The ceremony is tonight, it must be, and we haven't much time."

VI

From then on my mind was given little time to dwell on anything; I simply followed Mrs. Bridgeman's directions to the letter, questioning nothing. In any case it was obvious that her game must now be played to outwit the enemy (I had come to think of the strange worshipers as "the enemy"), not to defeat them physically or to talk them down. That was plainly out of the question. If indeed they had resorted to murder in order to do whatever they intended to do, they would surely not let a mere woman stop them now.

So it was that when we set of south aboard the snow cat, in a direction roughly that of Navissa, I knew that it would not be long before we were doubling back on our tracks. And sure enough, within the half hour, at about 11:00 P.M., as we came over a low hill in the then very light snow, there Mrs. Bridgeman ordered a wide swing to the west.

We held this westward course for ten more minutes, then turned sharply to our right flank, bringing the snow cat once again onto a northerly course. For a further twenty minutes we drove through the light snow, which, now that it had the slackening north wind behind it, stung a little on my face. Then, again at Mrs. Bridgeman's direction, we climbed a thinly wooded slope to fetch a halt at the top not twenty minutes distant from our starting point. At the speed we had traveled, and given that the enemy had no machine comparable to our snow cat, we could not possibly have been followed; and here, sheltered by the thin trees and the still lightly falling snow, we should be quite invisible to the enemy somewhere to our front.

Now, while we paused for a moment, I once more found questions forming in my mind for which I had no answers, and I had no sooner decided to voice them than my pale companion pointed suddenly out through the thin branches of the trees on the summit of the hill in the direction of a great black forested area some half mile to the north.

It was that same forest into which the enemy had vanished earlier in the day when we had been trailing them. Now at its four cardinal points, up sprang great fires of leaping red flame; and now too, coming to us on the wings of the north wind, faint and uneven we heard massed voices raised in a chilling ritual—the Rites of Ithaqua:

> *"Iä! Iä!—Ithaqua! Ithaqua!*
> *Ai! Ai! Ai!—Ithaqua!*
> *Ce-fyak vulg-t'uhm—*
> *Ithaqua fhtagn!*
> *Ugh! Iä! Iä!—Ai! Ai! Ai!"*

Again and again, repeatedly the wind carried that utterly alien chorus to our ears, and inside me it seemed suddenly that my blood froze. It was not only this abhorrent chanting with its guttural tones, but also the *precision* of the—singing?—and the obvious familiarity of the voices with the song. This was no blind, parrotlike repetition of obscure vocal forms but a combination of a hundred or more perfectly synchronized voices whose soul-rending interpretation of a hideous alien liturgy had transformed it into this present awesome cacophony—a cacophony whose horror might indeed breach the voids between the worlds! Suddenly I knew that if there was an Ithaqua, then he must surely hear and answer the voices of his worshipers.

"Very little time now," my companion muttered, more to herself than to me. "The place of the ceremony must be central in that forest—and that's where Kirby is!"

I stared hard through the snow, which again was beginning to fall heavier, seeing that the nearest and most southerly of the four fires blazed some distance to the northeast of our position. The westerly fire was about a half a mile southwest of us.

"If we head directly between those two fires," I said, "entering the woods and heading straight for the most northerly fire, on the far side, then we should come pretty close to the center of the forest. We can take the snow cat to the edge of the trees, but from there we must go on foot. If we can grab Kirby and make a run for it—well, perhaps the cat can take three, at a push."

"Yes," she answered, "it's worth a try. If the worse comes to the worst…then at least I'll know what the end of it was…."

With that I started up the cat's motor again, thankful that the wind was in our favor and knowing that under cover of the continuous chanting we stood a fair chance of driving right to the edge of the forest without being heard.

As we headed out across the white expanse of snow to the forest's edge, I could see in the heavens the glow of the fires reflected from the base of towering, strangely roiling nimbostratus. I knew then, instinctively, that we were in for a storm to end all storms.

At the edge of the forest, undetected so far, we dismounted and left the snow cat hidden in the lower branches of a great pine, making our way on foot through the forest's dark depths.

The going was of necessity very slow, and of course we dared show no light, but having progressed only a few hundred yards, we found that we could see in the distance the fires of individual torches, and the chanting came much louder and clearer. If there were guards, then we must have passed them by without attracting attention. The chanting was tinged now with a certain hysteria, a frenzy that built steadily toward a crescendo, charging the frosty air with unseen and menacing energies.

Abruptly, we came to the perimeter of a great cleared area where the trees had been cut down to be built into a huge platform in the center. All about this platform a mongrel congregation of fur- and parka-clad men and women stood, their faces showing ruddy and wild-eyed in the light of numerous torches. There were Eskimos, Indians, Negroes, and whites—people from backgrounds as varied as their colors and races—over one hundred and fifty of them at a guess.

The time by then was rapidly approaching midnight, and the deafening, dreadful chanting had now reached such an intensity as to make any increase seem almost impossible. Nevertheless there was an increase, at which, with one final convulsive shriek, the entire crowd about the pyramidal platform prostrated themselves facedown in the snow—all bar one!

"Kirby!" I heard Mrs. Bridgeman gasp, as that one upright man, proud and straight backed, naked except for his trousers, commenced a slow and measured climb up the log steps of the platform.

"Kirby!" She shouted his name this time, starting forward and avoiding the arms I held out to restrain her.

"He comes! He comes!" The cry went out in a hiss of rapture from one hundred and fifty throats—drowning Lucille Bridgeman's shout—and suddenly I felt the expectancy in the air.

The prostrate figures were silent now, waiting; the slight wind had disappeared; the snow no longer fell. Only Mrs. Bridgeman's running figure disturbed the stillness, that and the flickering of torches where they stood up from the snow; only her feet on the ice-crusted surface broke the silence.

Kirby had reached the top of the pyramid, and his mother was running between the outermost of the encircling, prostrate figures when it happened. She stopped suddenly and cast a terrified glance at the night sky, then lifted a hand to her open mouth. I, too, looked up, craning my neck to see—and something moved high in the roiling clouds!

"He comes! He comes!" The vast sigh went up again.

Many things happened then, all in the space of a few seconds, comprising a total and a culmination beyond belief. And still I pray that what I heard and saw at that time, that everything I experienced, was an illusion engendered of too great a proximity to the mass lunacy of those who obey the call of the five-year cycle.

How best to describe it?

I remember running forward a few paces, into the clearing proper, before my eyes followed Mrs. Bridgeman's gaze to the boiling heavens where at first I saw nothing but the madly whirling clouds. I recall, however, a picture in my memory of the man called Kirby standing wide legged atop the great pyramid of logs, his arms and hands reaching in a gesture of expectancy or welcome up and outward, his hair streaming in a wind which sprang up suddenly *from above* to blow slantingly down from the skies. And then there is the vision that burns even now in my mind's eye of a *darkness* that fell out of the clouds like a black meteorite, a darkness grotesquely shaped like a man with carmine stars for eyes in its bloated blot of a head, and my ears still ring to the pealing screams of mortal fear and loathing that went up in that same instant from the poor, paralyzed woman who now saw and recognized the horror from the skies.

The Beast-God came striding down the wind, descending more slowly now than at first but still speeding like some great bird of prey to Earth, its fantastic splayfooted strides carrying it as if down some giant, winding, invisible staircase straight to the waiting figure atop the pyramid, until the huge black head turned and, from high above the trees, the thing called the

Wind-Walker saw the hysterically screaming woman where she stood amid the prostrate forms of its worshipers—saw and *knew* her!

In midair the Being came to an abrupt, impossible halt—and then the great carmine eyes grew larger still, and the blackly outlined arms lifted to the skies in what was clearly an attitude of rage! One monstrous hand reached to the rushing clouds, and through them, to emerge but a split second later and hurl something huge and round to Earth. Still Mrs. Bridgeman screamed—loud, clear, and horrifically—as the unerringly hurled thing smashed down upon her with a roar of tortured air, flattening her instantly to the frozen ground and splintering into a mad bomb burst of exploding shards of—ice!

The scene about the log pyramid at that hellish moment must have been chaos. I myself was thrown in the rush of pressured air back into the trees, but in the next moment when I looked out again upon the clearing, all I could see was…blood!

The ice-torn, mangled bodies of a wide segment of worshipers were still tumbling outward from the blasted area where Mrs. Bridgeman had stood— a number of bloodied bodies still fell, lazily almost, like red leaves through the howling air; logs were beginning to burst outward from the base of the pyramid where flying chunks of ice had crashed with the force of grenades.

Nor was Ithaqua finished!

It seemed almost as if I could read this horror's thoughts as it towered raging in the sky: *Were these not His worshipers?—and had they not betrayed their faith in this matter, which was to have been His first meeting with His son on Earth? Well, they would pay for this error, for allowing this Daughter of Man, the mother of His son, to interfere with the ceremony!*

In the space of a few more seconds huge balls of ice were flung to Earth like a scattering of hailstones—but with far more devastating effect. When the last of them had hurled its ice-knife shards far and wide about the clearing, the snow was red with spouting blood; the screams of the torn and dying rose even above the howling devil-wind that Ithaqua had brought with Him from the star-spaces. The trees bent outward now from the clearing with the fury of that fiendish storm, and logs snapped and popped like matchsticks from the base of the platform at the crimson clearing's center.

But a change had taken place in the attitude of the lone figure standing wild and windblown at the top of the tottering pyramid.

While the gigantic, anthropomorphic figure in the sky had raged and ravaged, raining down death and destruction in the form of ice-globes frozen in his hands and snatched down out of the heavens, so the man-god-child, now grown to strange adulthood, had watched from his vantage point above the clearing all that transpired. He had seen his mother ruthlessly crushed to a raw, red pulp; he had watched the demoniac destruction of many, perhaps all of those deluded followers of his monstrous father. Still, in a dazed bewilderment, he gazed down upon the awful aftermath in the clearing—and then he laid back his head and screamed in a composite agony of frustration, horror, despair, and rapidly waxing rage!

And in that monumental agony his hellish heritage told. For all the winds screamed with him, roaring, howling, shrieking in a circular chase about the platform that lifted logs and tossed them as twigs in a whirlpool round and about in an impossible spiraling whirl. Even the clouds above rushed and clashed the faster for Kirby's rage, until at last his Father knew the anger of His son for what it was—but did He understand?

Down through the sky the Wind-Walker came again, striding on great webbed feet through the currents of crazed air, arms reaching as a father reaches for his son—

—And at last, battered and bruised as I was and half unconscious from the wind's screaming and buffeting, I saw that which proved to me beyond all else that I had indeed succumbed to the five-year cycle of legend-inspired lunacy and mass hysteria.

For as the Ancient One descended, so His son rose up to meet Him—Kirby, racing up the wind in surefooted bounds and leaps, roaring with a hurricane voice that tore the sky asunder and blasted the clouds back across the heavens in panic flight—Kirby, expanding, exploding outward until his outline, limned against the frightened sky, became as great as that of his alien Sire—Kirby, Son of Ithaqua, whose clawing hands now reached in a raging blood lust, whose snarling, bestial, darkening features demanded revenge!

For a moment, perhaps astounded, the Wind-Walker stood off—and there were two darkly towering figures in that tortured sky, two great heads in which twin pairs of carmine stars glared—and these figures rushed suddenly together in such a display of aerial fury that for a moment I could make out nothing of the battle but the flash of lightning and roar of thunder.

I shook my head and wiped the frost and frozen blood droplets from my forehead, and when next I dared look at the sky, I could see only the fleeing clouds racing madly away—the clouds and high, high above them, two dark dots that fought and tore and dwindled against a familiar but now leering background of stars and constellations....

❖ ❖ ❖

Almost twenty-four hours have passed. How I lived through the horrors of last night I shall never know; but I did, and physically unscathed, though I fear that my mind may be permanently damaged. If I attempt to rationalize the thing, then I can say that there was a storm of tremendous and devastating fury, during the course of which I lost my mind. I can say, too, that Mrs. Bridgeman is lost in the snow, even that she must now be dead despite her amazing invulnerability to the cold. But of the rest?…

And on the other hand, if I forego all rationalizations and listen only to the little winds whispering among themselves behind my flimsy shelter?…Can I deny my own senses?

I remember only snatches of what followed the terrible carnage and the onset of the aerial battle—my return to the snow cat and how that machine broke down less than half an hour later in a blinding snowstorm; my frozen, stumbling fight against great white drifts with various items of equipment dragging me down; my bruising fall into a frozen hole in the snow whose *outlines* sent me in a renewed frenzy of gibbering terror across the wastes—until, exhausted, I collapsed here between these sheltering trees. I remember knowing that if I remained still where I had fallen, then I must die; and I recall the slow agony of setting up my shelter, packing the walls solid, and lighting the stove. There is nothing more, however, until I awakened around noon.

The cold roused me. The stove had long since burned itself out, but empty soup cans told me that somehow I had managed to feed myself before giving in to my absolute fatigue. I opened the reservoir of fuel in the stove's body and fired it again, once more attending to my hunger before drying out and warming my clothes item by item. Then, fortified and almost warm, heartened by a slight rise in the outside temperature, I set about the strengthening of this, my last refuge; for I knew by then that this was as far as I could hope to go.

At about 4:00 P.M. the sky told me that soon it must storm again, and it was then that I thought to search out the snow cat and fetch precious fuel for my stove. I almost lost myself when the snow began to fall again, but by 6:00 P.M. I was back in my shelter having recovered almost a gallon of fuel from the crippled cat. I had spent at least fifteen futile minutes trying to restart the vehicle, which still lies where I found it less than half a mile from my refuge. It was then, knowing that I could live only a few days more at the outside, that I began to write this record. This is no mere foreboding, this grimly leering doom from which there can be no escape. I have given it some thought: I am too far from Navissa to stand even the slightest chance of making it on foot. I have food and fuel for three days at the most. Here…I can live for a few days more, and perhaps someone will find me. Outside, in some futile attempt to reach Navissa in the coming storm…I might last a day or even two, but I could never hope to cover all those miles in the snow.

It is about four in the morning. My wristwatch has stopped and I can no longer tell the time accurately. The storm, which I mistakenly thought had passed me by some miles to the north, has started outside. It was the roaring of the wind that roused me. I must have fallen asleep at my writing about midnight.

This is strange: the wind howls and roars, but through an opening in the canvas I can see the snow falling *steadily* against the black of the night, not hurried and hustled by the wind! And my shelter is too steady; it does not tremble in the gale. What does this mean?

I have discovered the truth. I am betrayed by the golden medallion, which, when I discovered the howling thing still in my pocket, I hurled out into a drift. There it lies now, outside in the snow, shrieking and screaming with the eternal crying of the winds that roar between the worlds.

To leave my shelter now would be certain death. And to stay?…

I must be quick with this, for He has come! Called by the demon howling of the medallion, He is here. No illusion this, no figment of my imagination but hideous fact. *He squats without, even now!*

I dare not look out into His great eyes; I do not know what I might see in those carmine depths. But I do know now how I will die. It will be quick.

All is silence now. The falling snow muffles all. The black thing waits outside like a huge hunched blot on the snow. The temperature falls, drops, plummets. I cannot get close enough to my stove. This is how I am to pass from the world of the living, in the icy tomb of my tent, for I have gazed upon Ithaqua!

It is the end…frost forms on my brow…my lips crack…my blood freezes…I cannot breathe the air…my fingers are as white as the snow… the cold…

NAVISSA DAILY
The Snows Claim a Fresh Victim!

Just before the Christmas season, bad news has come out of Fir Valley camp where members of the Royal Canadian North-West Mounted Police have winter residence. During the recent lull in the weather, Constables McCauley and Sterling have been out in the wastes north of Navissa searching for traces of their former companion, Constable Jeffrey, who disappeared on routine investigations in October. The Mounties found no trace of Constable Jeffrey, but they did discover the body of Mr. David Lawton, an American meteorologist, who also disappeared in the snow in October. Mr. Lawton, accompanied by a Mrs. Lucille Bridgeman, still missing, set out at that time in search of one Kirby Bridgeman, the woman's son. It was believed that this young man had gone into the wastes with a party of Eskimos and Indians, though no trace of this party has since been found. The recovery of Mr. Lawton's body will have to wait until the spring thaw; Constables McCauley and Sterling report that the body is frozen in a great block of clear ice that also encloses a canvas shelter and bivouac. The detailed report mentions that the eyes of the corpse are open and staring, as though the freezing took place with great rapidity....

NELSON RECORDER
A Christmas Horror!

Carol singers in the High Hill quarter of Nelson were astounded and horrified when, at 11:00 P.M., the frozen body of a young man crashed out of the upper branches of a tree in the grounds of No. 10 Church Street where they were caroling. Such was the force of its fall that the icy, naked figure brought down many branches with it. At least two of the witnesses state that the horribly mauled and mangled youth—whose uncommonly large and strangely webbed feet may help to identify him—fell not out of the tree but through it, as from the sky! Investigations are continuing.

THE FAIRGROUND HORROR

This one was written in the first half of 1972. Kirby McCauley sold it on my behalf to editor Edward F. Berglund for an anthology that would be called "The Disciples of Cthulhu." And indeed The Fairground Horror was so published—by DAW Books in 1976, in an attractive and now much sought after paperback edition—since when it has been reprinted variously, most recently in my TOR Books collection, "Beneath the Moors and Darker Places." My Lovecraft dependency (and its resultant purple prose) is not so much visible as unmistakable in this novella…!

The funfair was as yet an abject failure. Drizzling rain dulled the chrome of the dodgem-cars and stratojets; the neons had not even nearly achieved the garishness they display by night; the so-called "crowd"was hardly worth mentioning as such. But it was only 2:00 P. M. and things could yet improve.

Had the weather been better—even for October it was bad—and had Bathley been a town instead of a mere village, then perhaps the scene were that much brighter. Come evening, when the neons and other bright naked bulbs would glow in all the painful intensity of their own natural (unnatural?) life, when the drab gypsyish dollies behind the penny-catching stalls would undergo their subtle, nightly metamorphosis into avariciously enticing Loreleis—then it *would* be brighter, but not yet.

This was the fourth day of the five when the funfair was "in town". It was an annual—event? The nomads of Hodgson's Funfair had known better times, better conditions and worse ones, but it was all the same to them and they were resigned to it. There was, though, amid all the noisy, muddy, smelly paraphernalia of the fairground, a tone of incongruity. It had been there since Anderson Tharpe, in the curious absence of his brother, Hamilton, had taken down the old freak-house frontage to repaint the boards and canvas with the new and forbidding legend: TOMB OF THE GREAT OLD ONES.

Looking up at the painted gouts of "blood" that formed the garish legend arching over a yawning, scaly, dragon-jawed entranceway, Hiram Henley frowned behind his tiny spectacles in more than casual curiosity, in something perhaps approaching concern. His lips silently formed the ominous words of that legend as if he spoke them to himself in awe and then he thrust his black-gloved hands deeper into the pockets of his fine, expensively tailored overcoat and tucked his neck down more firmly into its collar.

Hiram Henley had recognized something in the name of the place— something which might ring subconscious warning bells in even the most mundane minds—and the recognition caused an involuntary shudder to hurry up his back. "The Great Old Ones!"he said to himself yet again, and his whisper held a note of terrible fascination.

Research into just such cycles of myth and aeon-lost legend, while ostensibly he had been studying Hittite antiquities in the Middle East and Turkey, had cost Henley his position as Professor of Archaeology and Ethnology at Meldham University. "Cthulhu, Yibb-Tstll, Yog-Sothoth, Summanus— the Great Old Ones!"Again an expression of awe flitted across his bespectacled face. To be confronted with a…a *monument* such as this, and in such a place…

And yet the ex-professor was not too surprised; he had been alerted to the contents of Anderson Tharpe's queer establishment, and therefore the fact that the owner had named it thus was hardly a matter of any lasting astonishment. Nevertheless Henley knew that there were people who would have considered the naming of the fairground erection, to say nothing of the presence of its afore-hinted *contents*, blasphemous. Fortunately such persons were few and far between—the Cult of Cthulhu was still known only to a minority of serious authorities, to a few obscure occult investigators, and a scattered handful of esoteric groups—but Hiram Henley looked back to certain days of yore when he had blatantly used the university's money to go in search of just such items of awesome antiquity as now allegedly hid behind the demon-adorned ramparts of the edifice before him.

The fact of the matter was that Henley had heard how this Tomb of the Great Old Ones held within its monster-daubed board-and-canvas walls relics of an age already many millions of years dead and gone when Babylon was but a sketch in the mind's eye of Architect Thathnis III. Figures and fragments, hieroglyphed tablets and strangely scrawled papyri, weird greenstone sculpt-ings and rotting, worm-eaten tomes: Henley had reason to believe that many of these things, if not all of them, existed behind the facade of Anderson Tharpe's horror-house.

There would also be, of course, the usual nonconformities peculiar to such establishments—the two-headed foetus in its bottle of preservative, the five-legged puppy similarly suspended, the fake mummy in its red- and green-daubed wrappings, the great fruit ("vampire") bats, hanging shutter-eyed and motionless in their warm wire cages beyond the reach of giggly, shuddering women and morbidly fascinated men and boys—but Hiram Henley was not interested in any of these. Nevertheless, he sent his gloved right hand awk-wardly groping into the corner of his overcoat pocket for the silver coin which alone might open for him the door to Tharpe's house of horror.

Hiram Henley was a slight, middle-aged man. His thin figure, draped smotheringly in the heavy overcoat, his balding head and tiny specs through which his watery eyes constantly peered, his gloved hands almost lost in huge pockets, his trousers seeming to hang from beneath the hem of his overcoat and partly, not wholly covering the black patent leather shoes upon his feet; all made of him a picture which was conspicuously odd. And yet Hiram Henley's intelligence was patent; the stamp of a "higher mind"was written in erudite lines upon his brow. His were obviously eyes which had studied strange mysteries, and his feet had gone along strange ways; so that despite any other emotion or consideration which his appearance might ill-advisedly call to mind, still his shrunken frame commanded more than a little respect among his fellow men.

Anderson Tharpe, on the other hand, crouching now upon his tiny seat in the ticket-booth, was a tall man, well over six feet in height but almost as thin and emaciated as the fallen professor. His hair was prematurely grey and purposely grown long in an old-fashioned scholarly style, so that he might simulate to the crowd's satisfaction a necessary erudition; just such an erudition as was manifest in the face above the slight figure which even now pressed upon his tiny window, sixpence clutched in gloved fingers. Tharpe's beady eyes beneath blackly hypnotic brows studied Hiram Henley briefly, speculatively, but then he smiled a very genuine welcome as he passed the small man a ticket, waving away the sixpence with an expansive hand.

"Not *you*, sir, indeed no! From a gent so obviously and sincerely inter-ested in the mysteries within—from a man of your high standing"—again the expansive gesture—"why, I couldn't accept money from you, sir. It's an honour to have you visit us!"

"Thank you," Henley dryly answered, passing myopically into the great tent beyond the ticket booth. Tharpe's smile slowly faded, was replaced by a look of cunning. Quickly the tall man pocketed his few shillings in takings, then followed the slight figure of the ex-professor into the smelly sawdust-floored "museum", beyond the canvas flap.

In all, a dozen people waited within the big tent's main division. A pitifully small "crowd". But in any case, though he kept his interest cleverly veiled, Tharpe's plans involved only the ex-professor. The tall man's flattery at the ticket booth had not all been flannel; he had spotted Henley immediately as the very species of highly educated fly for which his flypaper—in the form of the new and enigmatic legend across the visage of the one-time freak-house—had been erected above Bathley Moor.

There had been, Tharpe reflected, men of outwardly similar intelligence before at the Tomb of the Great Old Ones; and more than one of them had told him that certain of his *artifacts*—those items which he kept, as his brother had kept them before him, in a separately enclosed part of the tent— were of an unbelievable antiquity. Indeed, one man had been so affected by the very sight of such ancientness that he had run from Tharpe's collection in stark terror, and he had never returned. That had been in May, and though almost six months had passed since that time, still Tharpe had come no closer to an understanding of the mysterious objects which his brother Hamilton had brought back with him from certain dark corners of the world; objects which, early in 1961, had caused him to kill Hamilton in self-defence.

Anderson had panicked then—he realized that now—for he might easily have come out of the affair blameless had he only reported Hamilton's death to the police. For a long time the folk of Hodgson's Funfair had known that there was something drastically wrong with Hamilton Tharpe; his very sanity had been questioned, albeit guardedly. Certainly Anderson would have been declared innocent of his brother's murder—the case would have gone to court only as a matter of formality—but he had panicked. And of course there had been…complications.

With Hamilton's body secretly buried deep beneath the freak-house, the folk of the fairground had been perfectly happy to believe Anderson's tale of his brother's abrupt departure on yet another of his world-spanning expeditions, the like of which had brought about all the trouble in the first place.

Now Anderson thought back on it all…

He and his brother had grown up together in the fairground, but then it had been their father's property, and "Tharpe's Funfair"had been known throughout all England for its fair play and prices. Wherever the elder Tharpe had taken his stalls and sideshows—of which the freak-house had ever been his personal favourite—his employees had been sure of good crowds. It was only after old Tharpe died that the slump started.

It had had much to do with young Hamilton's joy in old books and fancifully dubious legends; his lust for travel, adventure, and *outré* knowledge. His first money-wasting venture had been a "treasure-hunting" trip to the islands of the Pacific, undertaken solely on the strength of a vague and obviously fake map. In his absence—he had gone off with an adventurous and plausible rogue from the shooting gallery—Anderson looked after the fair. Things went badly and all the Tharpes got out of Hamilton's venture was a number of repulsively carved stone tablets and one or two patently aboriginal sculptings, not the least of which was a hideous, curiously winged octopoid idol. Hamilton placed the latter obscenity in the back of their caravan home as being simply too fantastic for display to an increasingly mundane and sceptical public.

The idol, however, had a most unsettling effect upon the younger brother. He was wont to go in to see the thing in the dead of night, when Anderson was in bed and apparently asleep. But often Anderson was awake, and during these nocturnal visits he had heard Hamilton *talking* to the idol. More disturbingly, he had once or twice dimly imagined that he heard something talking back! Too, before he went off again on his wanderings in unspoken areas of the great deserts of Arabia, the sensitive, mystery-loving traveller had started to suffer from especially bad nightmares.

Again, in Hamilton's absence, things went badly. Soon Anderson was obliged to sell out to Bella Hodgson, retaining only the freak-house as his own and his prodigal brother's property. A year passed, and another before Hamilton once more returned to the fairground, demanding his living as before but making little or no attempt to work for his needs. There was no arguing, however, for the formerly sensitive younger brother was a changed, indeed a saturnine man now, so that soon Anderson came to be a little afraid of him.

And quite apart from the less obvious alterations in Hamilton, other changes were much more apparent; changes in habit, even in appearance. The most striking was the fact that now the younger Tharpe constantly wore a shaggy black toupee, as if to disguise his partial premature baldness, which all of the funfair's residents knew about anyway and which had never caused him the least embarrassment before. Also, he had become so reticent as to be almost reclusive; keeping to himself, only rarely and reluctantly allowing himself to be drawn into even the most trivial conversations.

More than this: there had been a time prior to his second long absence when Hamilton had seemed somewhat enamoured of the young, single, dark-eyed Romany fortune-teller, "Madame Zala"—a Gypsy girl of genuine Romany ancestry—but since his return he had been especially cool towards her, and for her own part she had been seen to cross herself with a pagan sign when he had happened to be passing by. Once he had seen her make this sign, and then he had gone white with fury, hurrying off to the freak-house and remaining there for the rest of that day. Madame Zala had packed up her things and left one night in her horse-drawn caravan without a word of explanation to anyone. It was generally believed that Hamilton had threatened her in some way, though no one ever taxed him over the affair. For his own part, he simply averred that Zala had been "a charlatan of the worst sort, without the ability to conjure a puff of wind!"

All in all the members of the funfair fraternity had been quick to find Hamilton a very changed man, and towards the end there had been the aforementioned hints of a brewing madness…

On top of all this, Hamilton had again taken up his nocturnal visits to the octopoid idol, but now such visits seemed less frequent than of old. Less frequent, perhaps, but they nevertheless heralded much darker events; for soon Hamilton had installed the idol within a curtained and spacious corner of the tent, in the freak-house itself, and he no longer paid his visits alone…

Anderson Tharpe had seen, from his darkened caravan window, a veritable procession of strangers—all of them previous visitors to the freak-house, and always the more intelligent types—accompanying his brother to the tent's nighted interior. But he had never seen a one come out! Eventually, as his younger brother became yet more saturnine, reticent, and secretive, Anderson took to spying on him in earnest—and later almost wished that he had not.

In the months between, however, Hamilton had made certain alterations to the interior of the freak-house, partitioning fully a third of its area to enclose the collection of rare and obscure curiosities garnered upon his travels. At that time Anderson had been puzzled to distraction by his brother's firm refusal to let his treasures be viewed by any but a chosen few of the freak-house's patrons: those doubtfully privileged persons who later accompanied him into the private museum never again to leave.

Of course, Anderson finally reasoned, the answer was as simple as it was fantastic: somewhere upon his travels Hamilton had learned the arts of murder and thievery, arts he was now practicing in the freak-house. The bodies? These he obviously buried, to leave behind safely lodged in the dark earth

when the fair moved on. But the money…what of the money? For money—
or rather its lack—patently formed the younger brother's motive. Could he
be storing his booty away, against the day when he would go off on yet
another of his foolish trips to foreign places? Beside himself that he had not
been "cut in"on the profits of Hamilton's dark machinations, Anderson
determined to have it out with him; to catch him, as it were, red-handed.

And yet it was not until early-in-the spring of 1961 that Anderson finally
managed to "overhear" a conversation between his brother and an obviously
well-to-do visitor to the freak-house. Hamilton had singled out this patently
intelligent gentleman for attention, inviting him back to the caravan during
a break in business. Anderson, knowing most of the modus operandi by now
and, aware of the turn events must take, positioned himself outside the caravan where he could eavesdrop.

He did not catch the complete conversation, and yet sufficient to make
him aware at last of Hamilton's expert and apparently unique knowledge in
esoteric mysteries. For the first time he heard uttered the mad words Cthulhu
and Yibb-Tstll, Tsathoggua and Yog-Sothoth, Shudde-M'ell and Nyarlathotep,
discovering that these were names of monstrous "gods" from the dawn of
time. He heard mention of Leng and Lh'yib; Mnar, Ib and Sarnath; R'lyeh
and "red-litten" Yoth, and knew now that these were cities and lands ancient
even in antiquity. He heard descriptions and names given to manuscripts,
books and tablets—and here he started in recognition, for he knew that some
of these aeon-old writings existed amid Hamilton's treasures in the freak-
house—and among others he heard the strangely chilling titles of such works
as the *Necronomicon,* the *Cthaat Aquadingen,* the *Pnakotic Manuscripts* and
the *R'lyehan Texts.* This then formed the substance of Hamilton's magnetism: his amazing erudition in matters of myth and time-lost lore.

When he perceived that the two were about to make an exit from the
caravan, Anderson quickly hid himself away behind a nearby stall to continue his observations. He saw the flushed face of Hamilton's new confidant,
his excited gestures; and, at a whispered suggestion from the pale-faced
brother, he finally saw that gentleman nodding eagerly, wide-eyed in awed
agreement. And after the visitor had gone, Anderson saw the look that flitted briefly across his brother's features: a look that hinted of awful triumph,
nameless emotion—and, yes, purest evil!

But it was something about the face of the departed visitor—that
rounded gentleman of obvious substance but doubtful future—which caused
Anderson the greatest concern. He had finally recognized that face from
elsewhere, and at his first opportunity he sneaked a glance through some of

the archaeological and anthropological journals which his brother now spent so much time reading. It was as he had thought: Hamilton's prey was none other than an eminent explorer and archaeologist; one whose name, Stainton Gamber, might be even higher in the lists of famous adventurers and discoverers but for a passion for wild-goose expeditions and safaris. Then he grew even more worried, for plainly his brother could not go on forever depleting the countryside of eminent persons without being discovered.

That afternoon passed slowly for Anderson Tharpe, and when night came he went early to his bed in the caravan. He was up again, however, as soon as he heard his brother stirring and the hushed whispers that led off in the direction of the freak-house. It was as he had known it would be, when for a moment pale moonlight showed him a glimpse of Hamilton with Stainton Gamber.

Quickly he followed the two to the looming canvas tent, and in through the dragon jawed entranceway, but he paused at the door-flap to the partitioned area to listen and observe. There came the scratch of a match and its bright, sudden flare, and then a candle flickered into life. At this point the whispering recommenced, and Anderson drew back a pace as the candle began to move about the interior of Hamilton's museum. He could hear the hushed conversation quite clearly, could feel the tremulous excitement in the voice of the florid explorer:

"But these are—*fantastic!* I've believed for years now that such relics must exist. Indeed, I've often brought my reputation close to ruin for such beliefs, and now…Young man, you'll be world famous. Do you realize what you have here? Proof positive that the Cult of Cthulhu did exist! What monstrous worship—what hideous rites! Where, *where* did you find these things? I must know! And this idol—which you say is believed to invoke the spirit of the living Cthulhu himself! Who holds such beliefs? I know of course that Wendy-Smith—"

"*Hah!*" Hamilton's rasping voice cut in. "You can keep all your Wendy-Smiths and Gordon Walmsleys. They only scraped the surface. I've gone inside—*and outside!* Explorers, dreamers, mystics—mere dabblers. Why, they'd *die*, all of them, if they saw what I've seen, if they went where I've been. And none of them have ever dreamed what I *know!*"

"But why keep it hidden? Why don't you open this place up, show the world what you've got here, what you've achieved? Publish, man, publish! Why, together—"

"Together?" Hamilton's voice was darker, trembling as he suddenly snuffed the candle. "Together? Proof that the Cult of Cthulhu did exist?

Show it to the world? Publish?" His chuckle was obscene in the dark, and Anderson heard the visitor's sharp intake of breath. "The world's not ready, Gamber, and the stars are not right! What you would like to do, like many before you, is alert the world to *Their* one-time presence, the days of *Their* sovereignty—which might in turn lead to the discovery that *They are here even now!* Indeed Wendy-Smith was right, too right, and where is Wendy-Smith now? No, no—*They* aren't interested in mere dabblers, except that such are dangerous to *Them* and must be removed! *Iä, R'lyeh!* You are no true dreamer, Gamber, no believer. You're not worthy of membership in the Great Priesthood. You're...dangerous! Proof? I'll give you proof. Listen, and watch—"

Hearing his brother's injunction, the secret listener would have paid dearly to see what next occurred. A short while earlier, just before Hamilton had snuffed out the candle, Anderson had managed to find a hole in the canvas large enough to facilitate a fair view of the partitioned area. He had seen a semicircle of carved stone tablets, with the octopoid idol presiding atop or seated upon a thronelike pedestal. Now, in the dark, his view-hole was useless.

He could still listen, however, and now Hamilton's voice came—strange and vibrant, though still controlled in volume—in a chant or invocation of terrible cadence and rhythmic disorder. These were not words the younger Tharpe uttered but unintelligible *sounds*, a morbidly insane agglutination of verbal improbabilities which ought never to have issued from a human throat at all! And as the invocation ceased, to an incredulous gasping from the doomed explorer, Anderson had to draw back from his hole lest he become visible in the glow of a green radiance springing up abruptly in the centre of Hamilton's encircling relics.

The green glow grew brighter, filling the hidden museum and spilling emerald beams from several small holes in the canvas. This was no normal light, for the beams were quite alien to anything Anderson had ever seen before; the very light seemed to writhe and contort in a slow and loathsomely languid dance. Now Anderson found himself again a witness, for the shadows of Hamilton and his intended victim were thrown blackly against the wall of canvas. There was no requirement now to "spy" properly upon the pair; his view of the eerie drama could not have been clearer. The centre of the radiance seemed to expand and shrink alternatively, pulsing like an alien heart of light. Hamilton stood to one side, his arms flung wide in terrible triumph; Stainton Gamber cowered, his hands up before his face as if to shield it from some unbearable heat—or as if to ward off the unknown and inexplicable!

Anderson's shadow-view of the terrified explorer was profile, and he was suddenly astonished to note that while the man appeared to be screaming horribly he could hear nothing of his screams! It was as if Anderson had been stricken deaf. Hamilton, too, was now plainly vociferous; his throat moved in crazed cachinnations and his thrown-back head and heaving shoulders plainly announced unholy glee—but all in stark silence! Anderson knew now that the mad green light had somehow worked against normal order, annulling all sound utterly and thereby hiding in its emerald pulsings the final act in this monstrous shadow-play. As the core pulsated even faster and brighter, Hamilton moved quickly after the silently shrieking explorer, catching him by the collar of his jacket and swinging him sprawling into the core itself!

Instantly the core shrank, sucking in upon itself and dwindling in a moment to a ball of intense brightness. But where was the explorer? Horrified, Anderson saw that now *only one shadow remained faintly outlined upon the canvas—that of his brother!*

Quickly, weirdly, paling as they went, the beams of green light withdrew. Sound instantly returned, and Anderson heard his own harsh breathing. He stilled the sound, moving back to his spy-hole to see what was happening. A faint green glow with a single bright speck of a core remained within the semicircle; and now Hamilton bowed to this dimming light and his voice came again, low and tremulous with emotion:

> "Iä, naflhgn Cthulhu R'lyeh mglw'nafh,
> Eha'ungl wglw hflghglui ngah'glw,
> Engl Eha gh'eehf gnhugl,
> Nhflgng uh'eha wgah'nagl hfglufh—
> U'ng Eha'ghglui Aeeh ehn'hflgh...
> That is not dead which can eternal lie,
> And with strange aeons even death may die."

No sooner had Hamilton ceased these utterly alien mouthings and the paradoxical couplet that completed them, and while yet the green glow continued to dim and fade, than he spoke again, this time all in recognizable English. Such was his murmured modulation and deliberate spacing of the spoken sequences that his hidden brother immediately recognized the following as a translation of what had gone before:

> "Oh, Great Cthulhu, dreaming in R'lyeh,
> Thy priest offers up this sacrifice,

That thy coming be soon
And that of thy kindred dreamers.
I am thy priest and adore thee..."

It was only then that the full horror of what he had seen—the cold-blooded, premeditated murder of a man by either some monstrous occult device or a foreign science beyond his knowledge—finally went home to Anderson Tharpe, and barely managing to stifle the hysterical babble he felt welling in his throat, he took an involuntary step backwards...to collide loudly with a cage of great bats.

Three things happened then in rapid succession before Anderson could gather his wits to flee. All trace of the green glow vanished in an instant, throwing the tent once more into complete darkness; then in contrast, confusing the elder brother, the bright interior lights blinked on; finally, as he sought to recover from his confusion, Hamilton appeared through the partition's canvas door, his eyes blazing in a face contorted in fury!

"You!" Hamilton spat, striding to Anderson's side and catching him fiercely by the collar of his dressing-gown. "How much have you seen?"

Anderson twisted free and backed away. "I...I saw it all, but I had guessed as much some time ago. Murder—and you my brother!"

"Save your sanctimony," Hamilton sneered. "If you've known so much for so long, then you're as much a murderer as I am! And anyway"—his eyes seemed visibly to glaze and take on a faraway look—"it wasn't murder, not as you understand it."

"Of course not." Now it was Anderson's turn to sneer. "It was a—a 'sacrifice'—to this so-called 'god' of yours, Great Cthulhu! And were the others all sacrifices, too?"

"All of them," Hamilton answered with a nod, automatically, as in a trance.

"Oh? And where's the money?"

"Money?" The faraway look went out of the younger Tharpe's eyes immediately. "What money?"

Anderson saw that this was no bluff; his brother's motive had not been personal gain, at least not in a monetary sense. Which in turn meant—

Had those rumours and unfriendly whispers heard about the stalls and sideshows—those hints of a looming madness in his brother—had they been more than mere guesswork, then? Surely he would have known. As if in answer to his unspoken question, Hamilton spoke again—and listening to him Anderson believed he had his answer:

"You're the same as all the others, Anderson—you can't see beyond the length of your greedy nose. Money? Pah! You think that *They* are interested in wealth? *They* are not; neither am I. *They* have a wealth of aeons behind *Them; the future is Theirs…*" Again his eyes seemed to glaze over.

"Them? Who do you mean?" Anderson asked, frowning and backing farther away.

"Cthulhu and the others. Cthulhu and the Deep Ones, and *Their* brothers and kin forever dreaming in the vast vaults beneath. *"Iä, R'lyeh, Cthulhu fhtagn!"*

"You're quite—mad!"

"You think so?"Hamilton quickly followed after him, pushing his face uncomfortably close. "I'm mad, am I? Well, perhaps, but I'll tell you something: when you and the others like you are reduced to mere cattle, before the Earth is cleared off of life as you know it, a trusted handful of priests will guard the herds for *Them*—and I shall be a priest among priests, appointed to the service of Great Cthulhu Himself!"His eyes burned feverishly.

Now Anderson was certain of his brother's madness, but even so he could see a way to profit from it. "Hamilton," he said, after a moment's thought, "worship whichever gods you like and aspire to whichever priesthood—but don't you see we have to live? There could be good money in this for both of us. If only—"

"No!" Hamilton hissed. "To worship Cthulhu is enough. Indeed, it is *all!* That, in there"—he jerked his head, indicating the enclosed area behind him—"is His temple. To offer up sacrifices while yet thinking of oneself would be blasphemous, and when He comes I shall not be found wanting!" His eyes went wide and he trembled.

"You don't know Him, Anderson. He is awful, awesome, a monster, a god! He is sunken now, drowned and dead in deep R'lyeh, but His death is a sleeping death and He will awaken. When the stars are right we chosen ones will answer the Call of Cthulhu, and R'lyeh will rise up again to astound a reeling universe. Why, even the Gorgons were His priestesses in the old world! And you talk to me of money."Again he sneered, but now his madness had a firm grip on him and the sneer soon turned to a crafty smile.

"And you're helpless to do anything, Anderson, for if you breathe a word I'll swear you were in on it—that you helped me from the start! And as for bodies, why, there are none. They are gone to dreaming Cthulhu, through the light He sends me when I cry out to Him in my darkness. So you see, nothing could ever be proved…"

"Perhaps not, but I don't think it would take much to have you, well, *put away!*" Anderson quietly answered.

The barb went straight home. A look of terror crossed Hamilton's face and, plainly aware of his own mental infirmity, he visibly paled.

"Put me away? But you wouldn't. If you did, I wouldn't be able to worship, to sacrifice, and—"

"But there's no need to worry about it,"Anderson cut him off. " I won't have you put away. Just see things my way, show me how you dissolve them in that green light of yours—I mean, in, er, dreaming Cthulhu's light—and then we'll carry on as before, except that there'll be money…"

"No, Anderson," the other refused almost gently, "it can't work like that. You could never believe—not even if I showed you proof of my priesthood, which hides beneath this false head of hair that I'm obliged to wear, the very Mark of Cthulhu—and I can't worship as you suggest. I'm sorry." There was an insane sadness in his face as he drew out a long knife from its sheath inside his jacket. "I use this when they're stronger than me," he explained, "and when they're liable to fight. Cthulhu doesn't care for it much because he likes them alive initially and whole, but—" His knife hand flashed up and down.

Only Anderson's speed saved him, for he turned quickly to one side as the blade flashed down toward his breast. Then their wrists were locked and they staggered to and fro, Hamilton frothing at the mouth and trying to bite, while Anderson grimly struggled for dear life. The madman seemed to have the strength of three normal men, and soon they fell to the ground, a thrashing heap that rolled blindly in through the flap of the canvas door to Hamilton's "temple".

There it was that finally the younger brother's toupee came away from his head in the silent struggle—and in a burst of strength engendered of sheer loathing Anderson managed to turn the knife inward and drive it to the madman's heart. He was quick then to be on his feet and away from the thing that now lay twitching out its life upon the sawdust floor—the thing that had been his brother—which now, where the top of Hamilton's head had been, *wore a cap of writhing white worms of finger thickness, like some monstrous sea-anemone sucking vampirishly at the still-living brain!*

Later, when morning came, even had there been someone in whom he might safely confide, Anderson Tharpe could never have related a detailed or coherent account of the preceding hours of darkness. He recalled only the general thread of what had passed; frantic snatches of the fearful activity that followed upon the hideous death of his brother. But first there had been that half hour or so of waiting—of knowing that at any moment, attracted perhaps by strange lights or sounds, someone just might enter the tent and find him with Hamilton's body—but he had been *obliged* to wait for he could not bring himself to touch the corpse. Not while the stubby white tentacles of its head continued to writhe! Hamilton died almost immediately, but his monstrous crown had taken much longer...

Then, when the loathsome—parasite?—had shuddered into lifeless rigidity, he had gathered together his shattered nerves to dig a deep grave in the soft earth beneath the sawdust. That had been a gruesome task with the lights turned down and Cthulhu's stone effigy casting a tentacled shadow over the fearful digger. Anderson later remembered how soft the ground had been—and wet when it ought to have been dry in the weatherproof tent—and he recalled a powerful smell of deep sea, of aeon-old ocean slime and rotting seaweeds; an odour he had known on occasion before, and always after one of Hamilton's "sacrifices." The connection had not impressed itself upon his mind as anything more than mere coincidence before, but now he knew that the smell came with the green light, as did that strange state of soundlessness.

In order to clear what remained of the fetor quickly—having tamped down the earth, generally "tidied up"and removed all traces of his digging— he opened and tied back the canvas doors of the tent to allow the night air a healthy circulation. But even then, having done everything possible to hide the night's horror, he was unable to relax properly as daylight crept up and the folk of the funfair began to wake and move about.

When finally Hodgson's Funfair had opened at noon, Anderson had something of a shaky grip on himself, but even so he had found himself drenched in cold sweat at the end of each oratorial session with the crowds at the freak-house. His only moments of relaxation came between shows. The worst time had been when a leather jacketed teenager peered through the canvas inner door to the partitioned section of the tent; and Anderson had nearly knocked the youth down in his anxiety to steer him away from the place, though no trace remained of what had transpired there.

On reflection, it amazed Anderson that his fight with his brother had not attracted someone's attention, and yet it had not. Even the fairground's usually vociferous watchdogs had remained silent. And yet those same dogs, since Hamilton's return from his travels abroad, had seemed even more nervous, more given to snapping and snarling than ever before. Anderson could only tell himself that the weird "silent state" which had accompanied the green light must have spread out over the entire fairground to dissipate slowly, thus disarming the dogs. Or perhaps they had sensed something else, remaining silent out of fear...? Indeed, it appeared his second guess was correct, for he discovered later that many of the dogs had whimpered the whole night away huddled beneath the caravans of their masters...

Two days later the funfair packed up and moved on, leaving Hamilton Tharpe's body safely buried in an otherwise empty field. At last the worst of Anderson's apprehensions left him and his nerves began to settle down. To be sure his jumpiness had been marked by the folk of the funfair, who had all correctly (though for the wrong reasons) diagnosed it as a symptom of anxiety about his crazy, bad-lot brother. So it was that as soon as Hamilton's absence was remarked upon, Anderson was able simply to shrug his shoulders and answer: "Who knows? Tibet, Egypt, Australia—he's just gone off again—said nothing to me about it—could be anywhere!" And while such inquiries were always politely compassionate, he knew that in fact the inquirers were greatly relieved that his brother had "just gone off again."

Another six weeks went by, with regular halts at various villages and small towns, and during that time Anderson managed to will himself to forget all about his brother's death and his own involvement—all, that is, except the nature of that parasitic horror which had made itself manifest upon Hamilton's head. That was something he would never forget, the way that awful anemone had wriggled and writhed long after its host was dead. Hamilton had called the thing a symbol of his priesthood—in his own words: "The Mark of Cthulhu"—but in truth it could only have been some loathsomely malignant and rare form of cancer, or perhaps a kind of worm or fluke like the tapeworm. Anderson always shuddered when he recalled it, for it had looked horribly *sentient* there atop Hamilton's head; and when one thought about the depth at which it might have been rooted…

No, the insidious gropings of that horror within Hamilton's brain simply did not bear thinking about, for that had obviously been the source of his insanity. Anderson in no way considered himself weak to shudder when thoughts as terrible as these came to threaten his now calm and controlled state of mind, and when the bad dreams started he at once lay the blame at the feet of the same horror.

At first the nightmares were vague shadowy things, with misty vistas of rolling plains and yawning, empty coastlines. There were distant islands with strange pinnacles and oddly angled towers, but so far away that the unknown creatures moving about in those island cities were mere insects to Anderson's dreaming eyes. And for this he was glad. Their shapes seemed in a constant state of flux and were not—pleasant. They were primal shapes, from which the dreamer deduced that he was in a primal land of aeons lost to mankind. He always woke from such visions uneasy in mind and deflated in spirit.

But with the passing of the months into summer the dreams changed, becoming sharper visually, clearer in their insinuations, and actually frightening as opposed to merely disturbing. Their scenes were set (Anderson somehow knew) deep in the dimly lighted bowels of one of the island cities, in a room or vault of fantastic proportions and awe-inspiring angles. Always he kneeled before a vast octopoid idol…except that on occasion it was *not* an idol but a living, hideously intelligent Being!

These dreams were ever the worst when a strange voice spoke to him in words that he was quite unable to understand. He would tremble before the towering horror on its thronelike pedestal—a thing one hundred times greater in size than the stone morbidity in the freak-house—and, aware that he only dreamed, he would know that it, too, was asleep and dreaming. But its tentacles would twine and twist and its claws would scrabble at the front of the throne, and then the voice would come…

Waking from nightmares such as these he would know that they were engendered of hellish memory—of the night of the green glow, the deep-ocean smell, and the writhing thing in his brother's head—for he would always recall in his first waking moments that the awful alien voice had used sounds similar to those Hamilton had mouthed before the green light came and after it had taken the florid explorer away. The dreams were particularly bad and growing worse as the year drew to a close, and on a number of occasions the dreamer had been sure that slumbering Cthulhu was about to stir and wake up!

And then, himself waking up, all the horror would come back to Anderson, to be viewed once more in his mind's eye in vivid clarity, and knowing as he did that his brother too had been plagued by just such dreams prior to his second long absence from the fairground, Anderson Tharpe was a troubled man indeed. Yes, they *had* been the same sort of nightmares, those dreams of Hamilton's; hadn't he admitted that "Cthulhu comes to me in dreams"? And had the dreams themselves not heralded the greater horrors?

And yet, in less gloomy mood, Anderson found himself more and more often dwelling upon Hamilton's weird murder weapon, the pulsating green light. He was by no means an ignorant man, and he had read something of the recent progress in laser technology. Soon he had convinced himself that his brother had used an unknown form of foreign science to offer up his mad "sacrifices to Cthulhu". If only he could discover how Hamilton had done it…

But surely science such as that would require complex machinery? It was while pondering this very problem that Anderson hit upon what he believed must be the answer: whatever tools or engines Hamilton had used, they must be hidden in the octopoid idol, or perhaps built into those ugly stone tablets which had formed a semicircle about the idol. And perhaps, like the electric-eye beams which operated the moving floors and blasts of cool air in the fairground's Noah's Ark, Hamilton's chanted "summons" had been nothing more than a resonant trigger to set the hidden lasers or whatever to working. The smell of deep ocean and residual dampness must be the natural aftermath of such processes, in the same way that carbon monoxide and dead oil is the waste from petrol engines and the smell of ozone is attendant to electrical discharges.

The tablets, the idol too, still stood where they had stood in the time before the horror—the only change was that now the canvas partition was down and Hamilton's ancient artifacts were on display with the other paraphernalia of the freak-house—but just suppose Anderson were to arrange them exactly as they had been before, and suppose further that he could discover how to use that chanted formula. What then? Would he be able to summon the green light? If so, would he be able to use it as he had tried to convince Hamilton it should be used? Perhaps the answer lay in his dead brother's books…

Certainly that collection of ancient tomes, now slowly disintegrating in a cupboard in the caravan, were full of hints of such things. It was out of curiosity at first that Anderson began to read those books, or at least what he *could* read of them! Many were not in English but Latin or archaic German, and at least one other was in ciphers the like of which Anderson had only ever seen on the stone tablets in the freak-house.

There were among the volumes such titles as Feery's *Notes on the Cthaat Aquadingen*, and a well-thumbed copy of the same author's *Notes on the Necronomicon* ; while yet another book, handwritten in a shaky script, purported to be the *Necronomicon* itself, or a translation thereof, but Anderson could not read it for its characters were formed of an unbelievably antiquated German. Then there was a large envelope full of yellowed loose-leaves, and Hamilton had written on the envelope that this was "Ibn Shoddathua's Translation of the Mum-Nath Papyri". Among the more complete and recognizable works were such titles as *The Golden Bough* and Miss Margaret Murray's *The Witch-Cult in Western Europe*, but by comparison these were light reading.

During December and to the end of January, all of Anderson's free time was taken up in the study of these works, until finally he became in a limited way something of an authority of the dread Cthulhu Cycle of Myth. He learned of the Elder Gods, benign forces or deities that existed "in peace and glory" near Betelgeuse in the constellation Orion; and of the powers of evil, the Great Old Ones! He read of Azathoth, bubbling and blaspheming at the center of infinity—of Yog-Sothoth, the "all-in-one and one-in-all", a god-creature coexistent in all time and conterminous with all space—of Nyarlathotep, the messenger of the Great Old Ones—of Hastur the Unspeakable, hell-thing and "Lord of the Interstellar Spaces"—of fertile Shub-Niggurath, "the black goat of the woods with a thousand young"—and, finally, of Great Cthulhu himself, an inconceivable evil that seeped down from the stars like cosmic pus when Earth was young and inchoate.

There were, too, lesser gods and beings more or less obscure or distant from the central theme of the Mythos. Among these Anderson read of Dagon and the Deep Ones; of Yibb-Tstll and the Gaunts of Night; of the Tcho-Tcho people and the Mi-Go; of Yig, Chaugnar Faugn, Nygotha, and Tsathoggua; of Atlach-Nacha, Lloigor, Zhar, and Ithaqua; of burrowing Shudde-M'ell, meteor-borne Glaaki, flaming Cthugha, and the loathsome Hounds of Tindalos.

He learned how—for practicing abhorrent rites—the Great Old Ones were banished to prisoning environs where, ever ready to take possession of the Earth again, they live on eternally…Cthulhu, of course, having featured prominently in his brother's madness—now supposedly lying locked in sunken R'lyeh beneath the waves, waiting for the stars to "come right" and for his minions, human and otherwise, to perform those rites which would once more return him as ruler of his former surface dominions—held the greatest interest for Anderson.

And the more he read, the more he became aware of the fantastic *depth* of his subject—but even so he could hardly bring himself to admit that there was anything of more than passing interest in such "mumbo-jumbo". Nevertheless, on the night of the second of February, 1962, he received what should have been a warning: a nightmare of such potency that it did in fact trouble him for weeks afterwards, and particularly when he saw the connection in the *date* of this visitation. Of course, it had been Candlemas, which would have had immediate and special meaning to anyone with even the remotest schooling in the occult. Candlemas, and Anderson Tharpe had dreamed of basaltic submarine towers of titanic proportions and nightmare angles; and within those basalt walls and sepulchres, he had known that loathly Lord Cthulhu dreamed his own dreams of damnable dominion…

This had not been all. He had drifted in his dreams *through* those walls to visit once more the inner chambers and kneel before the sleeping god. But it had been an unquiet sleep the Old One slept, in which his demon claws scrabbled fitfully and his folded wings twitched and jerked as if fighting to spread and lift him up through the pressured deeps to the unsuspecting world above! Then, as before, the voice had come to Anderson Tharpe—but this time it had spoken in English!

"Do you seek," the voice had asked in awesome tones, *"to worship Cthulhu? Do you presume to His priesthood? I can see that YOU DO NOT, and yet you meddle and seek to discover His secrets! Be warned: it is a great sin against Cthulhu to destroy one of His chosen priests, and yet I see that you have done so. It is a sin, too, to scorn Him; but you have done this also. And it is a GREAT sin in His eyes to seek to use His secrets in any way other than in His service—AND THIS, TOO, YOU WOULD DO! Be warned, and live. Live and pray to your weak god that you are destroyed in the first shock of the Great Rising. It were not well for you that you live to reap Cthulhu's wrath!"*

The voice had finally receded, but its sepulchral mind-echoes had barely faded away when it seemed to the paralyzed dreamer that the face-tentacles of slumbering Cthulhu reached out, groping malignantly in his direction where he knelt in slime at the base of the massive throne!

At that a distant howling sprang up, growing rapidly louder and closer; and as the face-tentacles of the sleeping god had been about to touch him, so Tharpe came screaming awake in his sweat-drenched bed to discover that the fairground was in an uproar. All the watchdogs, big and small, chained and roaming free alike, were howling in unison in the middle of that cold night. They seemed to howl at the blindly impassive stars, and their cries were faintly answered from a thousand similarly agitated canine throats in the nearby town!

The next morning speculation was rife among the showmen as to what had caused the trouble with the dogs, and eventually, on the evidence of certain scraps of fur, they put it down to a stray cat that must have got itself trapped under one of the caravans to be pulled to pieces by a Great Dane. Nevertheless, Anderson wondered at the keen senses and interpretation of the dogs in the local town that they had so readily taken up the unnatural baying and howling…

During the next fortnight or so Anderson's slumbers were mercifully free of nightmares, so that he was early prompted to continue his researches into the Cthulhu Cycle of Myth. This further probing was born partly of curiosity and partly (as Anderson saw it) of necessity; he yet hoped to be able to gainfully employ his brother's mysterious green light, and his determination was bolstered by the fact that takings of late had been dismal. So he closed off again the previously partitioned area of the tent and his spare-time studies now became equally divided between Hamilton's books of occult lore and a patient examination of the hideous idol and carved tablets.

He discovered no evidence of hidden mechanical devices in the queer relics, but nevertheless it was not long before he found his first real clue towards implementing his ambition.

It was as simple as this: he had earlier noted upon the carved tops of the stone tablets a series of curiously intermingled cuneiform and dot-group hieroglyphs, two distinct sets to each stone. This could not be considered odd in itself, but finally Anderson had recognized the pattern of these characters and knew that they were duplicated in the handwritten *Necronomicon;* and more, there were translations in that work into at least two other languages, one of them being the antiquated German in which the bulk of the book was written.

Anderson's knowledge of German, even in its modern form, was less than rudimentary, and thus he enlisted the aid of old Hans Möller from the hoopla stall. The old German's eyesight was no longer reliable, however, and his task was made no easier by the outmoded form in which the work was written; but at last, and not without Anderson's insistent urging, Möller was able to translate one of the sequences first into more modern German (in which it read: *Gestorben ist nicht, was für ewig ruht, und mit unbekannten Äonen mag sogar der Tod noch sterben;*), and then into the following rather poor English: "It is not dead that lies still forever; Death itself dies with the passing of strange years."

When he heard the old German speak these words in his heavy accent, Anderson had to stifle the gasp of recognition which welled within him. This was nothing less than a variation of that paradoxical couplet with which his brother had once terminated his fiendish "sacrifice to Cthulhu!"

As for the other set of symbols from the tablets, frustration was soon to follow. Certainly the figures were duplicated in the centuried book, appearing in what Anderson at first took to be a code of some sort, but they had not been reproduced in German. Möller—while having not the slightest inkling of Anderson's purpose with this smelly, evil old book—finally suggested to him that perhaps the letters were not in code at all, that they might simply be the symbols of an obscure foreign language. Anderson had to agree that Möller could well be right; in the yellowed left-hand margin of the relevant page, directly opposite the frustrating cryptogram, his brother had long ago written: "Yes, but what of the *pronunciation?*"

Hamilton had done more than this: he had obligingly dated his patently self-addressed query, and the surviving Tharpe brother saw that the jotting had been made prior to the fatal second period of travel in foreign lands. Who could say what Hamilton might or might not have discovered upon that journey? Without a doubt he had been in strange places. And he had seen and done strange things to bring back with him that hellish cancer-growth sprouting in his brain.

Finally Anderson decided that this jumbled gathering of harsh and un-pronounceable letters—be it a scientific process or, more fancifully, a magical evocation—must indeed be the formula with which a clever man might call forth the green light in his dead brother's "Temple of Cthulhu". He thanked old Hans and sent him away, then sat in his caravan poring over the ancient book, puzzling and frowning long into the evening; until, as darkness fell, his eyes lit with dawning inspiration…

And so over the period of the next few days the freakhouse suffered its transition into the Tomb of the Great Old Ones. During the same week Anderson visited a printer in the local town and had new admission tickets printed. These tickets, as well as bearing the new name of the show and revised price of admission, now carried upon the reverse the following cryptic instruction:

> Any adult person desiring to speak with the proprietor of the Tomb of the Great Old Ones on matters of genuine occult phenom-ena or similar manifestations, or on subjects relating to the Great Old Ones, R'lyeh or the Cthulhu Cycle of Myth, is welcome to request a private meeting.
>
> Anderson Tharpe: Prop.

The other members of the fairground fraternity were not aware of this offer of Anderson's—nor of his authority, real or assumed, in such subjects to be able to make such an offer—until after the funfair moved into its next location, and by that time they too had discovered his advance advertising in the local press. Of course, Bella Hodgson had always looked after advance publicity in the past, but she could hardly be offended by Anderson's per-sonal efforts toward this end. Any good publicity he devised and paid for himself could only go towards attracting better crowds to the benefit of the funfair in general.

And within a very short time Anderson's plan started to bear fruit, when at last his desire for a higher percentage of rather more erudite persons among his show's clientele began to be realized. His sole purpose, of course, had been to attract just such persons in the hope that perhaps one of them might provide the baffling pronunciation he required, an *acoustical* transla-tion of the key to call up the terrible green glow.

Such authorities must surely exist; his own brother had become one in a comparatively short time, and others had spent whole lifetimes in the concentrated study of these secrets of elder lore. Surely, sooner or later, he would find a man to provide the answer, and then the secrets of the perfect murder weapon would be his. When this happened, then Anderson would test his weapon on the poor unfortunate who handed him the key, and in this way he would be sure that the secret was his alone. From then on…oh, there were many possibilities…

Through early and mid-April Anderson received a number of inquisitive callers at his caravan: some of them cranks, but at least a handful of genuinely interested and knowledgeable types. Always he pumped them for what they knew of elder mysteries in connection with the Cthulhu Cycle, especially their knowledge in ancient tongues and obscure languages, and twice over he was frustrated just when he thought himself on the right track. On one occasion, after seeing the tablets and idol, an impressed visitor presented him with a copy of Walmsley's *Notes on Deciphering Codes, Cryptograms, and Ancient Inscriptions*; but to no avail, the work itself was too deep for him.

Then, towards the end of April, in response to Anderson's continuous probing, a visitor to his establishment grudgingly gave him the address of a so-called "occult investigator", one Titus Crow, who just might be interested in his problem. Before he left the fairground this same gentleman, the weird artist Chandler Davies, strongly advised Tharpe that the whole thing were best forgotten, that no good could ever come of dabbling in such matters—be it serious study or merely idle curiosity—and with that warning he had taken his leave…

Ignoring the artist's positive dread of his line of research, that same afternoon Anderson wrote to Titus Crow at his London address, enclosing with his letter a copy of the symbols and a request for information concerning them; possibly a translation or, even better, a workable pronunciation. Impatiently then, he watched the post for an answer, and early in May was disappointed to receive a brief note from Crow advising him, as had Davies, to give up his interest in these matters and let such dangerous subjects alone. There was no explanation, no invitation regarding further correspondence; Crow had not even bothered to return the cryptic paragraph so painstakingly copied from the *Necronomicon*.

That night, as if to substantiate the double warning, Anderson once more dreamed of sunken R'lyeh, and again he knelt before slumbering Cthulhu's throne to hear the alien voice echoing awesomely in his mind.

The horror on the throne seemed more mobile in its sleep than ever before, and the voice in the dream was more insistent, more menacing:

"You have been warned, AND YET YOU MEDDLE! While the Great Rising draws ever closer and Cthulhu's shadow looms, still you choose to search out His secrets for your own use! This night there will be a sign; ignore it at your peril, lest Cthulhu bestir Himself up to visit you personally in dreams, as He has aforetime visited others!"

The following morning Anderson rose haggard and pale to learn of yet more trouble with the fairground's dogs, duplicating in detail that Candlemas frenzy of three months earlier. The coincidence was such as to cause him more than a moment's concern, and especially after reading the morning's newspapers.

What was it that the voice in his dream had said of "a sign?"—a warning which he should only ignore at his peril? Well, there had been a sign, many of them, for the night had been filled with a veritable plethora of weird and inexplicable occurrences—strange stirrings among the more dangerous inmates of lunatic asylums all over the country, macabre suicides by previously normal people—a magma of madness climaxed, so far as Anderson Tharpe was concerned, by second-page headlines in two of the national newspapers to the effect that Chandler Davies had been "put away" in Woodholme Sanatorium. The columns went on to tell how Davies had painted a monstrous "G'harne Landscape", which his outraged and terrified mistress had at once set fire to, thus bringing about in him an insane rage from which he had not recovered. More: a few days later came the news via the same organs that Davies was dead!

If Anderson Tharpe had been in any way a sensitive person, and his evil ambition less of an obsession—had his *perceptions* not been dulled by a lifetime of living close to the anomalies of the erstwhile freak-house—then perhaps he might have recognized the presence of a horror such as few men have ever known. Unlike his brother, however, Anderson was coarse-grained and not especially imaginative. All the portents and evidences, the hints and symptoms, and accumulating warnings were cast aside within a few short days of his nightmare and its accompanying manifestations, when yet again he turned to his studies in the hope that soon the secret of the green light would be his.

From then on the months passed slowly, while the crowds at the Tomb of the Great Old Ones became smaller still despite all Anderson's efforts to the contrary. His frustration grew in direct proportion to his dwindling assets, and while his continued advance advertising and the invitation on the reverse of his admission tickets still drew the occasional crank occultist or curious devotee of the macabre to his caravan, not one of them was able to further his knowledge of the Cthulhu Cycle or satisfy his growing obsession with regard to that enigmatic and cryptical "key" from the handwritten *Necronomicon*.

Twice as the seasons waxed and waned he approached old Hans about further translations from the ancient book, even offering to pay for the old German's services in this respect, but Hans was simply not interested. He was too old to become a *Dolmetscher*, he said, and his eyes were giving him trouble; he already had enough money for his simple needs, and anyway, he did not like the look of the book. What the old man did not say was that he had seen things in those yellowed pages, on that one occasion when already he had looked into the rotting volume, which simply did not bear translation! And so again Anderson's plans met with frustration.

In mid-October the now thoroughly disgruntled and morose proprietor of the Tomb of the Great Old Ones looked to a different approach. Patently, no matter how hard he personally studied Hamilton's books, he was not himself qualified to puzzle out and piece together the required information. There were those, however, who had spent a lifetime in such studies, and if he could not attract such as these to the fairground—why, then he must simply send the problem to them. True, he had tried this before, with Titus Crow; but now, as opposed to cultists, occultists, and the like, he would approach only recognized authorities. He spent the following day or two tracking down the address of Professor Gordon Walmsey of Goole, a world-renowned expert in the science of ciphers, whose book, *Notes on Deciphering Codes, Cryptograms, and Ancient Inscriptions*, had now been in his possession for almost seven months. That book was still far too deep and complicated for Anderson's fathoming, but the author of such a work should certainly find little difficulty with the piece from the *Necronomicon*.

He quickly composed a letter to the professor, and as October grew into its third week he posted it off. He was not to know it, but at that time Walmsley was engaged in the services of the Buenos Aires Museum of Antiquities, busily translating the hieroglyphs on certain freshly discovered ruins in the mountains of the Aconcaguan Range near San Juan. Anderson's letter did eventually reach him, posted on from Walmsley's Yorkshire address, but the professor was so interested in his own work that he gave it only a cursory glance. Later he found that he had misplaced it, and thus, fortunately, the scrap of paper with its deadly invocation passed into obscurity and became lost forever.

Anderson meanwhile impatiently waited for a reply, and along with the folk of the fairground prepared for the Halloween opening at Bathley, a town on the northeast border. It was then, on the night of the twenty-seventh of the month, that he received his third and final warning. The day had been chill and damp, with a bitter wind blowing off the North Sea, bringing a dankly salt taste and smell that conjured up horrible memories for the surviving Tharpe brother.

On the morning of the twenty-eighth, rising up gratefully from a sweat-soaked bed and a nightmare the like of which he had never known before and fervently prayed never to know again, Anderson Tharpe blamed the horrors of the night on yesterday's sea wind with its salty smells of ocean; but even explained away like this the dream had been a monstrous thing.

Again he had visited sunken R'lyeh—but this time there had been a vivid *reality* to the nightmare lacking in previous dreams. He had known the terrible, bone-crushing pressures of that drowned realm, had felt the frozen chill of its black waters. He had tried to scream as the pressure forced his eyes from their sockets, and then the sea had rushed into his mouth, tearing his throat and lungs and stomach as it filled him in one smashing column as solid as steel. And though the horror had lasted only a second, still he had known that there in the ponderous depths his *disintegration* had taken place before the throne of the Lord of R'lyeh, the Great Old One who seeped down from the stars at the dawn of time. He had been a sacrifice to Cthulhu…

That had been four days ago, but still Tharpe shuddered when he thought of it. He put it out of his mind now as he ushered the crowd out of the tent and turned to face the sole remaining member of that departing audience. Tharpe's oratory had been automatic; during its delivery he had allowed his mind to run free in its exploration of all that had passed since his brother's hideous death, but now he came back to earth. Hiram Henley stared back at him in what he took to be scornful disappointment. The ex-professor spoke:

"'The Tomb of the Great Old Ones,' indeed! Sir, you're a charlatan!" he said. "I could find more fearsome things in Grimm's Fairy Tales, more items of genuine antiquarian interest in my aunt's attic. I had hoped your—*show*—might prove interesting. It seems I was mistaken." His eyes glinted sarcastically behind his tiny spectacles.

For a moment Tharpes' heart beat a little faster, then he steadied himself. Perhaps this time…? Certainly the little man was worth a try. "You do me an injustice, sir—you wound me!" He waxed theatrical, an ability with which he was fluent through his years of showmanship. "Do you really believe that I would openly *display* the archaeological treasures for which this establishment was named?—I should put them out for the common herd to ogle, when not one in ten thousand could even recognize them, let alone appreciate them? Wait!"

He ducked through the canvas door-flap into the enclosed area containing Hamilton's relics, returning a few seconds later with a bronze miniature the size of his hand and wrist. The thing looked vaguely like an elongated, eyeless squid. It also looked—despite the absence of anything even remotely mundane in its appearance—utterly evil! Anderson handed the object reverently to the ex-professor, saying: "What do you make of that?" Having chosen the thing at random from the anomalies in his dead brother's collection, he hoped it really was of "genuine antiquarian interest".

His choice had been a wise one. Henley peered at the miniature, and slowly his expression changed. He examined the thing minutely, then said: "It is the burrower beneath, Shudde-M'ell, or one of his brood. A very good likeness, and ancient beyond words. Made of bronze, yet quite obviously it predates the Bronze Age!" His voice was suddenly soft. "Where did you get it?"

"You *are* interested, then?" Tharpe smiled, incapable of either admitting or denying the statements of the other.

"Of course I'm interested." Henley eagerly nodded, a bit too eagerly, Tharpe thought. "I...I did indeed do you a great injustice. This thing is *very* interesting! Do you have...more?"

"All in good time." Tharpe held up his hands, holding himself in check, waiting until the time was ripe to frame his own all-important question. "First, who are you? You understand that my—*possessions*—are not for idle scrutiny, that—"

"Yes, yes, I understand," the little man cut him off. "My name is Hiram Henley. I am—at least I was—Professor of Archaeology and Ethnology at Meldham University. I have recently given up my position there in order to carry out private research. I came here out of curiosity, I admit; a friend gave me one of your tickets with its peculiar invitation...I wasn't really expecting much, but—"

"But now you've seen something that you would never have believed possible in a place like this. Is that it?"

"Indeed it is. And you? Who are you?"

"Tharpe is my name, Anderson Tharpe, proprietor of this"—he waved his hand deprecatingly—"establishment."

"Very well, Mr. Tharpe," Henley said. "It's my good fortune to meet a man whose intelligence in my own chosen field patently must match my own—whose possessions include items such as this." He held up the heavy bronze piece and peered at it again for a moment. "Now, will you show me—the rest?"

"A glimpse, only a glimpse," Tharpe told him, aware now that Henley was hooked. "Then perhaps we can trade?"

"I have nothing. with which to trade. In what way do you mean?"

"Nothing to trade? Perhaps not," Tharpe answered, holding the canvas door open so that his visitor might step into the enclosed space beyond, "but then again…How are you on ancient tongues and languages?"

"Languages were always my—" The ex-professor started to answer, stepping into the private place. Then he paused, his eyes widening as he gazed about at the contents of the place. "Were always my—" Again he paused, reaching out his hands before him and moving forward, touching the ugly idol unbelievingly, moving quickly to the carved tablets, staring as if hypnotized at the smaller figurines and totems. Finally he turned a flushed face to Tharpe. His look was hard to define; partly awed, partly—accusing?

"I didn't steal them, I assure you," Tharpe quickly said.

"No, of course not," Henley answered, "but…you have the treasures of the aeons here!"

Now the tall showman could hold himself no longer. "Languages," he pressed. "You say you have an understanding of tongues? Can you translate from the ancient to the modern?"

"Yes, most things, providing—"

"How would you like to *own* all you see here?" Tharpe cut him off again.

Henley reached out suddenly palsied hands to take Tharpe by the forearms. "You're…joking?"

"No." Tharpe shook his head, lying convincingly. "I'm not joking. There is something of the utmost importance to my own line of—research. I need a translation of a fragment of ancient writing. Rather, I need the *original* pronunciation. If you can solve this one problem for me, all this can be yours. You can be…part of it."

"What is this fragment?" the little man cried. "*Where* is it?"

"Come with me."

"But—" Henley turned away from Tharpe, his gloved hands again reaching for those morbid items out of the aeons.

"No, no." Tharpe took his arm. "Later—you'll have all the time you need. Now there is this problem of mine. But later, tonight, we'll come back in here, and all this can be yours…"

The ex-professor voluntarily followed Tharpe out of the tent to his caravan, and there he was shown the handwritten *Necronomicon* with its cryptic "key".

"Well," Tharpe demanded, barely concealing his agitation. "Can you read it as it was written? Can you *pronounce* it in its original form?"

"I'll need a little time," the balding man mused, "and privacy; But I think…I'll take a copy of this with me, and as soon as I have the answer—"

"When? How long?"

"Tonight?"

"Good. I'll wait for you. It should be quiet here by then. It's Halloween and the fairground is open until late, but they'll all be that much more tired…" Tharpe suddenly realized that he was thinking out loud and quickly glanced at his visitor. The little man peered at him strangely through his tiny specs; *very* strangely, Tharpe thought.

"The people here are—superstitious," he explained. "It wouldn't be wise to advertise our interest in these ancient matters. They're ignorant and I've had trouble with them before. They don't like some of the things I've got."

"I understand," Henley answered. "I'll go now and work through the evening. With luck it won't take too long. Tonight—shall we say after midnight?—I'll be back." He quickly made a copy of the characters in the old book, then stood up. Tharpe saw him out of the caravan with an assumed, gravely thoughtful air, thanking him before watching him walk off in the direction of the exit; but then he laughed out loud and slapped his thigh, quickly seeking out one of the odd job boys from the stratojet thrill ride.

An hour later—to the amazement of his fellow showmen, for the crowd was thickening rapidly as the afternoon went by—Anderson Tharpe closed the Tomb of the Great Old Ones and retired to his caravan. He wanted to practice himself in the operation of the tape recorder which he had paid the odd jobber to buy for him in Bathley.

This final phase of his plan was simple; necessarily so, for of course he in no way intended to honour his bargain with Henley. He *did* intend to have the little man read out his pronunciation of the "key", and to record that pronunciation in perfect fidelity—but from then on…

If the pronunciation were imperfect, then of course the "bargain" would be unfulfilled and the ex-professor would escape with his life and nothing more; but if the invocation worked…? Why, then the professor simply could not be allowed to walk away and talk about what he had seen. No, it would be necessary for him to disappear into the green light. Hamilton would have called it a "sacrifice to Cthulhu".

And yet there had been something about the little man that disturbed Anderson; something about his peering eyes, and his eagerness to fall in with the plans of the gaunt showman. Tharpe thought of his dream of a few days past, then of those other nightmares he had known, and shuddered; and again he pondered the possibility that there had been more than met the eye in his mad brother's assertions. But what odds? Science or sorcery, it made no difference, the end result would be the same. He rubbed his hands in anticipation. Things were at last looking up for Anderson Tharpe…

At midnight the crowd began to thin out. Watching the people move off into the chill night, Anderson was glad it had started to rain again, for their festive Halloween mood might have kept them in the fairground longer, and the bright lights would have glared and the music played late into the night. Only an hour later all was quiet, with only the sporadic patter of rain on machines and tents and painted roofs to disturb the night. The last wetly gleaming light had blinked out and the weary folk of the fairground were in their beds. That was when Anderson heard the furtive rapping at his caravan door, and he was agreeably surprised that the ever-watchful dogs had not heralded his night-visitor's arrival. Possibly it was too early for them yet to distinguish between comers and goers.

As soon as he was inside Henley saw the question written on Tharpe's face. He nodded in answer: "Yes, yes, I have it. It appears to be a summons of some sort, a cry to vast and immeasurable ancient powers. Wait, I'll read it for you—"

"No, no—not here!" Tharpe silenced him before he could commence. "I have a tape recorder in the tent."

Without a word the little man followed Tharpe through the dark and into the private enclosure containing those centuried relics which so plainly fascinated him. There Tharpe illumined the inner tent with a single dim light bulb; then, switching on his tape recorder, he told the ex-professor that he was now ready to hear the invocation. And yet now Henley paused, turning to face Tharpe and gravely peering at him from where he stood by the horrible octopoid idol.

"Are you—sure?" the little man asked. "Are you sure you want me to do this?" His voice was dry, calm.

"Eh?" Anderson questioned nervously, terrible suspicions suddenly forming in his mind. "Of course I'm sure—and what do you mean, 'do this'? Do what?"

Henley shook his head sadly. "Your brother was foolish not to see that you would cause trouble sooner or later!"

Tharpe's eyes opened wide and his jaw fell slack. "Police!" he finally croaked. "You're from the police!"

"No such thing," the little man calmly answered. "I am what I told you I was—and something more than that—and to prove it…"

The sounds Henley uttered then formed an exact and fluent duplication of those Tharpe had heard once before, and shocked as he was that this frail outsider knew far too much about his affairs, still Tharpe thrilled as the inhuman echoes died and there formed in the semicircle of grim tablets an expanding, glowing greenness that sent out writhing beams of ghostly luminescence. Quickly the tall man gathered his wits. Policeman or none, Hiram Henley had to be done away with. This had been the plan in any case, once the little man—whoever he was—had done his work and was no longer required. And he had done his work well. The invocation was recorded; Anderson could call up the destroying green light any time he so desired. Perhaps Henley had been a former colleague of Hamilton's, and somehow he had come to learn of the younger Tharpe's demise? Or was he only guessing! Still, it made no difference now.

Henley had turned his back on Anderson, lifting up his arms to the hideous idol greenly illuminated in the light of the pulsating witchfire. But as the showman slipped his brother's knife from his pocket, so the little man turned again to face him, smiling strangely and showing no discernible fear at the sight of the knife. Then his smile faded and again he sadly shook his head. His lips formed the words, "No, no, my friend," but Anderson Tharpe heard nothing; once more, as it had done before, the green light had cancelled all sound within its radius.

Suddenly Tharpe was very much afraid, but still he knew what he must do. Despite the fact that the inner tent was far more chill even than the time of the year warranted, sweat glistened greenly on Anderson's brow as he moved forward in a threatening crouch, the knife raised and reflecting emerald shafts of evilly writhing light. He lifted the knife higher still as he closed with the motionless figure of the little man—*and then Hiram Henley moved!*

Anderson saw what the ex-professor had done and his lips drew back in a silent, involuntary animal snarl of the utmost horror and fear. He almost dropped the knife, frozen now in midstroke, as Henley's black gloves fell to the floor and the thick white worms twined and twisted hypnotically where his fingers ought to have been!

Then—more out of nightmare dread and loathing than any sort of rational purpose, for Anderson knew now that the ex-professor was nothing less than a Priest of Cthulhu—he carried on with his interrupted stroke and his knife flashed down. Henley tried to deflect the blow with a monstrously altered hand, his face contorting and a shriek forming silently on his lips as one of the wormish appendages was severed and fell twitching to the sawdust. He flailed his injured hand and white ichor splashed Tharpe's face and eyes.

Blindly the frantic showman struck again and again, gibbering mindlessly and noiselessly as he clawed at his face with his free hand, trying to wipe away the filthy white juice of Henley's injured hybrid member. But the blows were wild and Hiram Henley had stepped to one side.

More frantically yet, insanely, Tharpe slashed at the greenly pulsating air all about him, stumbling closer to the core of radiance. Then his knife struck something that gave like rotting flesh beneath the blow, and finally, in a short-lived revival of confidence, he opened stinging eyes to see what he had hit.

Something coiled out of the green core, something long and tapering, grayly mottled and slimy! Something that stank of deep ocean and submarine weeds! It was a tentacle—a *face*-tentacle, Tharpe knew—twitching spasmodically, even as the hand of a disturbed dreamer might twitch.

Tharpe struck again, a reflex action, and watched his blade bite through the tentacle unhindered, as if through mud—*and then saw that trembling member solidifying again where the blade had sliced!* His knife fell from a palsied hand then, and Tharpe screamed a last, desperate, silent scream as the tentacle moved more purposefully!

The now completely sentient member wrapped its tip about Tharpe's throat, constricting and jerking him forwards effortlessly into the green core. And as he went the last things he saw were the eyes in the vast face; the hellish eyes that opened briefly, saw and recognized him for what he was— a sacrifice to Cthulhu !

Quickly then, as the green light began its withdrawal and sound slowly returned to the tent, Hiram Henley put on his gloves. Ignoring as best he could the pain his injury gave him, he spoke these words:

> "Oh, Great Cthulhu, dreaming in R'lyeh,
> Thy priest offers up this sacrifice,
> That Thy coming be soon,
> And that of Thy kindred dreamers.
> I am Thy priest and adore Thee…"

And as the core grew smaller yet, he toppled the evil idol into its green center, following this act by throwing in the tablets and all those other items of fabled antiquity until the inner tent was quite empty. He would have kept all these things if he dared, but his orders—those orders he received in dreams from R'lyeh—would not allow it. When a priest had been found to replace Hamilton Tharpe, then Great Cthulhu would find a way to return those rudimentary pillars of His temple!

Finally, Henley switched off the single dim light and watched the green core as it shrank to a tiny point of intense brightness before winking out. Only the smell of deep ocean remained, and a damp circle in the dark where the sawdust floor was queerly marked and slimy…

Some little time later the folk of the fairground were awakened by the clamour of a fire engine as it sped to the blaze on the border of the circling tents, sideshows and caravans. Both Tharpe's caravan and The Tomb of the Great Old Ones were burning fiercely.

Nothing was saved, and in their frantic toiling to help the firemen the nomads of the funfair failed to note that their dogs again crouched timid and whimpering beneath the nighted caravans. They found it strange later, though, when they heard how the police had failed to discover anything of Anderson Tharpe's remains.

The gap that the destruction of the one-time freak-house had left was soon filled, for "Madame Zala", as if summoned back by the grim work of the mysterious fire, returned with her horse and caravan within the week. She is still with Hodgson's Funfair, but she will never speak of the Tharpes. At certain times of the year well known to anyone with even the remotest schooling in the occult, she is sometimes seen crossing herself with an obscure and pagan sign…

THE TAINT

The Taint was written December 2002 to January 2003, specifically for editor Steve Jones' proposed Mythos collection, "Weird Shadows Over Innsmouth," a volume dedicated to H.P. Lovecraft's darkly mysterious seaport 'town of ill repute' inhabited by the changeling Deep Ones, those less than human, amphibious worshippers of Lord Cthulhu in his house in R'lyeh. One of only a very few recent Mythos tales by my hand, apart from its unavoidable, indeed obligatory backdrop, this story escapes almost entirely from Lovecraft's literary influence to become wholly original, and I consider it on a par with Born of the Winds written all of thirty years earlier. Fedogan & Bremer published The Taint in a limited edition of "Weird Shadows Over Innsmouth" in time to launch the book at the World Fantasy Convention, Madison WI, November 2005…

James Jamieson looked through binoculars at the lone figure on the beach—a male figure, at the rim of the sea—and said, "That's pretty much what I would have wanted to do, when I was his age. Beachcombing, or writing books; maybe poetry? Or just bumming my way around the world. But my folks had other ideas. Just as well, I suppose. 'No future in poetry, son. Or in daydreaming or beachcombing.' That was my father, a doctor in his own right. Like father like son, right?" Lowering his binoculars, he smiled at the others with him. "Still, I think I would have enjoyed it."

"Beachcombing, in the summer? Oh, I could understand that well enough!" John Tremain, the middle-aged headmaster at the technical college in St. Austell, answered him. "The smell of the sea, the curved horizon way out there, sea breezes in your hair, and the wailing of the gulls? Better than the yelping of brats any time—oh yes! The sun's sparkle on the sea and warm sand between your toes—it's very seductive. But this late in the season, *and* in my career?" He shook his head. "Thanks, but no thanks. You won't find me with my hands in my pockets, sauntering along the tide-mark and picking over the seaweed."

He paused, shrugged, and continued, "Not now, anyway. But on the other hand, when I was a young fellow teaching arts and crafts: carpentry and joinery, woodcraft in general—I mean, working *with* woods as opposed to surviving in them—now would have been the ideal time for a stroll on the beach. And I used to do quite a bit of it. Yes, indeed. For it's autumn when the best pieces get washed ashore."

"Pieces?" Jilly White came back from wherever her thoughts had momentarily wandered, blinked her pretty but clouded green eyes at Tremain, then glanced from face to face in search of a hint, a clue. "I'm sorry, John, but I wasn't quite…?"

"Driftwood," the teacher smiled. "All those twisted, sandpapered roots that get tumbled in with the tide when the wind's off the sea. Those bleached, knotted, gargoyle branches. It's a long time ago now, but—" He almost sighed, gave another shrug, and finished off, "But searching for driftwood was as close as I ever got to being a beachcomber."

And Doreen, his tall, slender, haughty but not unattractive wife, said, "You've visited with us often enough, Jilly. Surely you must have noticed John's carvings? They were all driftwood originally, washed up on the beach there."

And now they all looked at Jilly…

There were four of them, five if you included Jilly White's daughter, Anne, curled up with a book in the lee of a sand-dune some twenty-five yards down the beach and out of earshot. Above her, a crest of crabgrass like some buried sand-giant's eyebrow framed the girl where her curled body described a malformed eye in the dune's hollow. And that was where Jilly White's mind had been: on her fifteen-year-old daughter, there in the lee of the dune; and on the muffled, shuffling beachcomber on the far side of the dunes, near the water's edge where the waves frothed and the sand was dark and damp.

All of them were well wrapped against a breeze off the sea that wasn't so much harsh as constant, unremitting. Only endure it long enough, it would cool your ears and start to find a way through your clothes. It was getting like that now; not yet the end of September, but the breeze made it feel a lot later.

"John's carvings?" said Jilly, who was still a little distant despite that she was right there with the others on Doctor (or ex-Doctor) James Jamieson's verandah overlooking the beach. But now, suddenly, she snapped to. "Oh, his *carvings!* The driftwood! Why, yes, of course I've noticed them—and admired them, honestly—John's driftwood carvings. Silly of me, really. I'm sorry, John, but when you said 'pieces' I must have been thinking of something broken. Broken in pieces, you know?"

And Jamieson thought: *She looks rather fragile herself. Not yet broken but certainly brittle…as if she might snap quite easily.* And taking some of the attention, the weight off Jilly, he said, "Scrimshaw, eh? How interesting. I'd enjoy to see your work some time."

"Any time at all," Tremain answered. "But, er, while it's a bit rude of me to correct you, er, James, it isn't scrimshaw."

"Oh?" The old man looked taken aback. "It isn't?"

The headmaster opened his mouth to explain, but before he could utter another word his wife, Doreen, cut in with, "Scrimshaw is the art or handicraft of old-time sailors, Doctor." She could be a little stiff with first names. "Well, art of a sort, anyway." And tut-tutting—apparently annoyed by the breeze—she paused to brush back some ruffled, dowdy-looking strands of hair from her forehead before explaining further. "Scrimshaw is the name they've given to those odd designs that they carve on shells and old whalebones and such."

"Ah!" Jamieson exclaimed. "But of course it is!" And glancing at Jilly, now huddling to herself, shivering a little and looking pale, he smiled warmly and said, "So you see, Jilly my dear, you're not alone in mixing things up this afternoon. What with driftwood and scrimshaw and the wind—which is picking up I think, and blowing our brains about—why, it's easy to lose track of things and fall out with the facts. Maybe we should go inside, eh? A glass of cognac will do us the world of good, and I'll treat you to something I've newly discovered: a nice slice of homemade game pie from that bakery in the village. Then I'll be satisfied that I've at least fed and watered you, and warmed your bones, before I let you go off home."

But as his visitors trooped indoors, the ex-Doctor quickly took up his binoculars to scan the beach again. In this off-the-beaten-track sort of place, one wouldn't really expect to see a great many people on the shore; none, at this time of year. The beachcomber was still there, however; hunched over and with his head down, he shambled slowly along. And it appeared that Anne, Jilly's bookish, reserved if not exactly retiring daughter, had finally noticed him. What's more, she had stood up and was making her way down the beach toward him.

Jamieson gave a start as Jilly touched his arm. And: "It's all right," she said quietly, (perhaps even confidentially, the doctor thought). "It's nothing you should feel concerned about. Young Geoff and Anne, they're just friends. They went to school together…well, for a while anyway. The infants, you know?"

"Oh dear!" Jamieson blinked his slightly rheumy old eyes at her. "I do hope you don't think I was spying on them—I mean, on your daughter. And as for this, er, Geoff?"

"It's all right," she said again, tugging him inside. "It's quite all right. You've probably bumped into him in the village and he may well have sparked some professional interest in you. That's only natural, after all. But he's really quite harmless, I assure you…"

Eating slowly, perhaps to avoid conversation, Jilly wasn't done with her food when the Tremains were ready to go. "Anyway," she said, "I'll have to wait for Anne. She won't be long…knows better than to be out when the light starts failing."

"You don't mind her walking with the village idiot?" John's words sounded much too harsh; he was probably biting his lip as he turned his face away and Doreen helped him on with his coat.

"Ignore my husband," Doreen twisted her face into something that didn't quite equal a smile. "According to him all children are idiots. It seems that's what being a teacher does to you."

Jilly said, "Personally, I prefer to think of the boy as an unfortunate. And of course in a small seaside village he stands out like a sore thumb. I'm glad he has a…a friend in Anne."

And John half relented. "You're right, of course. And maybe I'm in the wrong profession. But it's much like Doreen says. If you work all day with kids, especially bolshy teenagers, and in this day and age when you daren't even frown at the little sods let alone slap their backsides—"

At the door, Doreen lifted her chin. "I don't recall saying anything like that. Nothing as rude as that, anyway."

"Oh, you know what I mean!" John said testily, trailing her outside, and colliding with her where she'd paused on the front doorstep. Then—in unison but almost as an afterthought—they stuck their heads back inside to thank Jamieson for his hospitality.

"Not at all," their host answered. "And I'll be dropping in on you soon, to have a look at those carvings."

"Please do," John told him.

And Doreen added, "Evenings or weekends, you'll be welcome. We're so glad that you've settled in here, Doctor."

"Oh, call me James, for goodness sake!" Jamieson waved them goodbye, closed the door, turned to Jilly and raised an enquiring, bushy grey eyebrow.

She shrugged. "A bit pompous maybe, but they're neighbours. And it does get lonely out here."

They went to the bay window in the end wall and watched the Tremains drive off down the road to their home less than a mile away. Jilly lived half a mile beyond that, and the tiny village—a huddle of old fishermen's houses, really—stood some four or five hundred yards farther yet, just out of sight behind the rising, rocky promontory called South Point. On the far side of the village, a twin promontory, North Point, formed a bay, with the harbour lying sheltered in the bight.

For a moment more Jamieson watched the Tremains's car speed into the distance, then turned a glance of covert admiration on Jilly. She noticed it, however, cocked her head on one side and said, "Oh? Is there something…?"

Caught out and feeling just a little uncomfortable now, the old man said, "My dear, I hope you won't mind me saying so, but you're a very attractive woman. And even though I'm a comparative stranger here, a newcomer, I can't say I've come across too many eligible bachelors in the village."

Now Jilly frowned. Her lips began to frame a question—or perhaps a sharp retort, an angry outburst—but he beat her to it.

"I'm sorry, I'm so sorry!" He held up his hands. "It's none of my business, I know. And I keep forgetting that your husband…that he—"

"—Died less than eighteen months ago, yes," Jilly said.

The old man sighed. "My bedside manner hasn't improved any with age," he said. "I retired here for what I thought would be solitude—an absence of everything that's gone before—only to find that I can't seem to leave my practice behind me! To my patients I was a healer, a father confessor, a friend, a champion. I didn't realize it would be so hard not to continue being those things."

She shook her pretty head, smiled wanly and said, "James, I don't mind your compliments, your concern, or your curiosity. I find it refreshing that there are still people who…who care about anyone. Or anything for that matter!"

"But you frowned."

"Not at what you said," she answered, "but the way you said it. Your accent, really."

"My accent?"

"Very similar to my husband's. He was an American, too, you know."

"No, I didn't know that. And he had a similar accent? A New England accent, you say?" Suddenly there was a new, a different note of concern in Jamieson's voice, unlike the fatherly interest he'd taken in Jilly earlier. "And may I ask where he hailed from, your husband? His home town?"

"George was from Massachusetts, a town on or near the coast—pretty much like this place, I suppose—called, er, Ipswich? Or maybe Arkham or Innsmouth. He would talk about all three, so I can't be certain. And I admit to being a dunce where American geography is concerned. But I'm sure I have his birth certificate somewhere in the house, if you're that interested?"

Sitting down, the old man bade Jilly do the same. "Interested?" he said. "Well, perhaps not. Let sleeping dogs lie, eh?"

"Sleeping dogs?" Now she was frowning again.

And he sighed before answering. "Well, I did practice for a few months— *just* a few months—in Innsmouth. A very strange place, Jilly, even for this day and age. But no, you don't want to know about that."

"But now you've got *me* interested," she said. "I mean, what was so strange about the place?"

"Well, if you must know, it was mainly the people—degenerate, inbred, often retarded—in fact much like young Geoff. I have bumped into him, yes, and there's that about the boy…there's a certain look to him…" But there the old man paused, probably because he'd seen how Jilly's hands fluttered, trembling on the arms of her chair. Seeing where he was looking, she put her hands in her lap, clasping them until her fingers went white. It was obvious that something he had said had disturbed her considerably. And so:

"Let's change the subject," he said, sitting up straighter. "And let me apologise again for being so personal. But a woman like you—still young and attractive, in a place like this—surely you should be looking to the future now, realizing that it's time to go, time to get out of here. Because while you're here there are always going to be memories. But there's an old saying that goes 'out of sight—'"

"'—Out of mind?'" She finished it for him.

"Something like that." He nodded. "A chance to start again, in a place, some town or city, that *does* have its fair share of eligible bachelors…" And then he smiled, however wryly. "But there I go, being personal again!"

Jilly didn't return his smile but told him, "I do intend to get away, I have intended it, but there are several things that stop me. For one, it's such a short time since George…well, since he…"

"I understand." Jamieson nodded. "You haven't yet found the time or the energy to get around to it."

"And two, it's not going to be easy to sell up—not for a decent price, anyway. I mean, look how cheaply you were able to secure this place."

Again the old man nodded. "When people die or move away, no one moves in, right? Well, except for old cheapskates like me."

"And all perfectly understandable," said Jilly. "There's no school in the village, and no work; the fishing has been unproductive for years now, though of late it has seemed to pick up just a little. As for amenities: the nearest supermarket is in St. Austell! And when the weather gets bad the old road out of the village is like a death trap; it's always getting potholed or washed out. So there's no real reason why anyone would want to come here. A few holidaymakers, maybe, in the summer season, and the very rare occasion when someone like you might want to retire here. But apart from that…"

"Yes?" He prompted her, slyly. "But apart from that? Jilly, almost everything you've said seems to me contradictory. You've given some very excellent reasons why you *shouldn't* stay, and a few pretty bad ones why you *should*. Or haven't I heard them all yet?"

She shrank down into herself a little, and Jamieson saw her hands go back to the arms of her chair, fluttering there like a pair of nervous birds…

"It's my daughter," she said after a while. "It's Anne. I think we'll have to stay here a little longer, if only for her sake."

"Oh?"

"Yes. She's…she's doing piano with Miss Harding in the village, and twice a week she studies languages at night school in St. Austell. She loves it; she's quite a little interpreter, you know, and I feel I have to let her continue."

"Languages, you say?" The old man's eyebrows went up. "Well, she'll find plenty of work as an interpreter—or as a teacher, for that matter."

"Yes, I think so, too!" said Jilly, more energetically now. "It's her future, and she has a very real talent. Why, she even reads sign!"

"I'm sorry?"

"Sign language, as used by the deaf and dumb."

"Oh, yes, of course. But no, er, higher education?"

"She had the grades," said Jilly, protectively. "She would have no trouble getting into university. But what some desire, others put aside. And to be totally honest…well, she's not the communal type. She wouldn't be happy away from home."

Again Jamieson's nod of understanding. "A bit of a loner," he said.

"She's a young girl," Jilly quickly replied, "and so was I, once upon a time. And I know that we all go through our phases. She's unsettled enough—I mean, what with her father's death and all—so any move will just have to wait. And that's that."

Now, having firmly indicated that she no longer desired to talk about her daughter, it was Jilly's turn to change the subject. And in doing so she returned to a previous topic.

"You know," she said, after a moment, "despite that you'll probably think it's a morbid sort of fascination, I can't help being interested in what you were saying about Innsmouth—the way its denizens were, well, strange."

Denizens, Jamieson repeated her, but silently, to himself. *Yes, I suppose you could describe them that way.*

He might have answered her. But a moment earlier, as Jilly had spoken the last few words, so the verandah door had glided open to admit Anne. There she stood framed against the evening, her hair blowing in the unrelenting sea breeze, her huge green eyes gazing enquiringly into the room. But her face was oh-so-pale, and her gaze cold and unsmiling. Maybe she'd been out in the wind too long and the chill had finally got to her.

Sliding the door shut behind her, and going to the fire to warm herself she said, "What was that you were saying, Mother? Something about strange denizens?"

But Jilly shrugged it off. "Mr Jamieson and I were engaged in a private conversation, dear, and you shouldn't be so nosy."

That was that; Anne's return had called a halt to any more talk. But when Jamieson drew the verandah curtains he couldn't help noticing that hulking, shambling, head-down figure silhouetted against the sand dunes; the shape of Geoff, casting long ugly shadows as he headed back toward the village.

Following which it was time to drive Anne and Jilly home…

There was a week of bad weather. James Jamieson would sit in a chair by his sliding patio window and gaze out across the decking of the verandah, across the dunes and beach, at the roaring, rearing ocean. But no matter the driving rain and pounding surf, the roiling sky split by flashes of lightning and shuddering to drum rolls of thunder, sooner or later there would be a hulking figure on the sands: "Young Geoff," as Jilly White had seen fit to call him, the "unfortunate" youth from the village.

Sometimes the boy—or young man, whatever—would be seen shambling along the tidemark; at others he'd walk too close to the turbulent water, and end up sloshing through the foam when waves cast their spume across his route. Jamieson made a point of watching him through his expensive high-resolution binoculars, and now and then he would bring Geoff's face into sharper focus.

The sloping forehead and almost bald head; the wide, fleshy mouth, bulging eyes and scaly bump of a chin, with the bristles of a stubby beard poking through; the youth's skin—its roughness in general, with those odd folds or wattles—especially the loose flaps between his ears and his collar…

One afternoon toward the end of the week, when the weather was calmer, Jamieson also spied John Tremain on the beach. The link road must have washed out again, relieving the headmaster of his duties for a day or so and allowing him time to indulge his hobby. And sure enough as he walked the tidemark, he would stoop now and then to examine this or that piece of old driftwood. But at the same time "the village idiot" was also on the beach, and their paths crossed. Jamieson watched it all unfold in the cross hairs of his binoculars:

Tremain, crouching over a dark patch of seaweed, and Geoff coming over the dunes on a collision course. Then the meeting; the headmaster seeing the youth and jerking upright, lurching backward from the advancing figure and apparently threatening him with the knobby end of a stripped branch! The other coming to an awkward halt, and standing there with his arms and hands flapping uselessly, his flabby mouth opening and closing as if in silent protest.

But was it revulsion, hatred, or stark terror on Tremain's part? Or simply shock? Jamieson couldn't make up his mind. But whichever, it appeared that Tremain's dislike of "bolshy" teenagers went twice for those who weren't so much bolshy as, well, unfortunate.

That, however, was all there was to it; hardly a confrontation as such, and over and done with as quickly as that. Then Tremain scuttling for home, and Geoff standing there, watching him go. The end. But at least it had served to remind Jamieson of his promise to go and see John's driftwood carvings—which was one reason at least why he should pay a return visit…

At the weekend Jamieson called the Tremains on the telephone to check that the invitation was still open, and on Sunday evening he drove the solitary mile to his neighbour's place, parking by the side of the road. Since he, the Whites and the Tremains had the only properties on this stretch of pot-holed road, it wasn't likely that he'd be causing any traffic problems.

"Saw you on the beach the other day," he told John when he was seated and had a drink in his hand. "Beachcombing, hey?"

The other nodded. "It seems our talking about it must have sparked me off again. I found one or two rather nice pieces."

"You certainly have an eye for it," the old man commented, his flattery very deliberate. "Why, I can see you have several 'nice pieces'—expertly finished pieces, that is—right here. But if you'll forgive my saying so, it seems to me these aren't so much carvings as wind-, sea-, and sand-sculptures really, which you have somehow managed to revitalize with sandpaper and varnish, imagination and infinite skill. So much so that you've returned them to a new, dramatic life of their own!"

"Really?" Tremain was taken aback; he didn't see Jamieson's flattery for what it really was, as a means to an end, a way to ingratiate himself into the Tremains's confidence. For Jamieson found himself in such a close-knit microcosm of isolated community society that he felt sure the headmaster and his wife would have knowledge of almost everything that had gone on here; they would have the answers to questions he couldn't possibly put to Jilly, not in her condition.

For the old man suspected—indeed, he more than suspected—that Jilly White's circumstances had brought her to the verge of nervous exhaustion. But what exactly were her circumstances? As yet there were loose ends here, which Jamieson must at least attempt to tie up before making any firm decision or taking any definite course of action.

Which was why the ex-Doctor was here at the Tremains's this evening. They were after all his and Jilly's closest neighbours and closest in status, too. Whereas the people of the village—while they might well be the salt of the earth—were of a very different order indeed. And close-mouthed? Oh, he'd get nothing out of them.

And so back to the driftwood:

"Yes, really," the old man finally answered John Tremain's pleased if surprised inquiry. "I mean, this table we're sitting at, drinking from: a table of driftwood—but see how the grain stands out, the fine polish!" In fact the table was quite ugly. Jamieson pointed across the room. "And who could fail to admire your plant stand there, so black it looks lacquered."

"Yacht varnish," Tremain was all puffed up now. "As for why it's so black, it's ebony."

"*Diospyros,*" said Doreen Tremain, entering from the kitchen with a tray of food. "A very heavy wood, and tropical. Goodness only knows how long it was in the sea, to finally get washed up here."

"Amazing!" Jamieson declared. "And not just the stand. Your knowledge of woods—and indeed of most things, as I've noted—does both of you great credit."

And now she preened and fussed no less than her husband. "I do so hope you like turbot, er, James?"

"*Psetta maxima*," said Jamieson, not to be outdone. "If it's fish, dear lady, then you need have no fear. I'm not the one to turn my nose up at a good piece of fish."

"I got it from Tom Foster in the village," she answered. "I like his fish, if not his company." And she wrinkled her nose.

"Tom Foster?" Jamieson repeated her, shaking his head. "No, I don't think I know him."

"And you don't want to," said John, helping the old man up, and showing him to the dining table. "Tom might be a good fisherman, but that's all he's good for. Him and his Gypsy wife."

Sitting down, Jamieson blinked his rheumy eyes at the other and enquired, "His Gypsy wife?"

"She's not a Gypsy," Doreen shook her head. "No, not Romany at all, despite her looks. It seems her great-grandmother was a Polynesian woman. Oh, there are plenty such throwbacks in Devon and Cornwall, descendants of women brought back from the Indies and South Pacific when the old sailing ships plied their trade. Anyway, the Fosters are the ones who have charge of that young Geoff person. But there again, I suppose we should be thankful that someone is taking care of him."

"*Huh!*" John Tremain grunted. "Surely his mother is the one who should be taking care of him. Or better far his father, except we all know that's no longer possible."

"And never would have been," Doreen added. "Well, not without all sorts of complications, accusations, and difficulties in general."

Watching the fish being served, Jamieson said, "I'm afraid you've quite lost me. Do you think you could…I mean, would you mind explaining?"

The Tremains looked at each other, then at the old man.

"Oh?" he said. "Do I sense some dark secret here, one from which I'm excluded? But that's okay—if I don't need to know, then I don't need to know. After all, I am new around here."

"No," said Doreen, "it's not that. It's just that—"

"It's sort of delicate," her husband said. "Or not exactly delicate, not any longer, but not the kind of thing people like to talk about. Especially when it's your neighbour, or your ex-neighbour, who is concerned."

"My *ex*-neighbour?" Jamieson frowned. "George White? He was *your* neighbour, yes, but never mine. So, what's the mystery?"

"You've not sensed anything?" This was Doreen again. "With poor Jilly? You've not wondered why she and Anne always seem to be sticking up for—"

"For that damned idiot in the village?" John saw his opportunity to jump in and finish it for her.

And the old man slowly nodded. "I think I begin to see," he said. "There's some connection between George White, Jilly and Anne, and—"

"And Geoff, yes," said Doreen. "But do you think we should finish eating first? I see no reason why we can't tell you all about it. You are or were a doctor, after all—and we're sure you've heard of similar or worse cases—but I'd hate the food to spoil."

And so they ate in relative silence. Doreen Tremain's cooking couldn't be faulted, and her choice of white wine was of a similar high quality…

"It was fifteen, sixteen years ago," John Tremain began, "and we were relative newcomers here, just as you are now. In those days this was a prosperous little place; the fish were plentiful and the village booming; in the summer there were people on the beaches and in the shops. Nowadays—there's only the post office, the pub, and the bakery. The post office doubles as a general store and does most of the business, and you can still buy a few fresh fish on the quayside before what's left gets shipped inland. And that's about it right now. But back then:

"They were even building a few new homes here, extending the village, as it were. This house and yours, they were the result. That's why they're newish places. But the road got no further than your place and hasn't been repaired to any great extent since. Jilly and George's place was maybe twenty years older; standing closer to the village, it wasn't as isolated. As for the other houses they'd planned to build on this road, they just didn't happen. Prices of raw materials were rocketing, the summers weren't much good any more, and fish stocks had begun a rapid decline.

"The Whites had been here for a year or two. They had met and married in Newquay, and moved here for the same reason we did: the housing was cheaper than in the towns. George didn't seem to have a job. He'd inherited some fabulous art items in gold and was gradually selling them off to a dealer in Truro. And Jilly was doing some freelance editing for local publishers."

Now Doreen took over. "As for George's gold: it was jewellery, and quite remarkable. I had a brooch off him that I wear now and then. It's unique,

I think. Beautiful but very strange. Perhaps you'd like to see it?"

"Certainly," said the old man. "Indeed I would." While she went to fetch it, John continued the story.

"Anyway, Jilly was heavy with Anne at the time, but George wasn't a home body. They had a car—the same wreck she's got now, more off the road than on it—which he used to get into St. Austell, Truro, Newquay, and goodness knows where else. He would be away for two or three days at a time, often for whole weekends. Which wasn't fair on Jilly who was very close to her time. But look, let me cut a long story short.

"Apparently George had been a bit of a louse for quite some time. In fact as soon as Jilly had declared her pregnancy, that was when he'd commenced his…well, his—

"—Womanizing?" The old man sat up straighter in his chair. "Are you saying he was something of a rake?"

By now Doreen had returned with a small jewellery box. "Oh, George White was much more than *something* of a rake," she said. "He was a great deal of a rake, in fact a roue! And all through poor Jilly's pregnancy he'd been, you know, doing it in most of the towns around."

"Really?" said Jamieson. "But you can't know that for sure, now can you?"

"Ah, but we can," said John, "for he was seen! Some of the locals had seen him going into…well, 'houses of ill repute,' shall we put it that way? And a handful of the village's single men, whose morals also weren't all they might be, learned about George's reputation in those same, er, houses. But you'll know, James—and I'm sure that in your capacity as a doctor you *will* know—it's a sad but true fact that you do actually reap what you sow. And in George White's case, that was true in more ways than one."

"Which is where this becomes even more indelicate," Doreen got to her feet. "And I have things to do in the kitchen. So if you'll excuse me…" And leaving her jewellery box on the table she left the room and closed the door behind her. Then:

"George caught something," said John, quietly.

"He what?"

"Well, that's the only way I can explain it. He caught this bloody awful disease, presumably from some woman with whom he'd, er, associated. But that wasn't all."

"There's more?" Jamieson shook his head. "Poor Jilly."

"Poor Jilly, indeed! For little Anne was only a few months old when this slut from Newquay arrived in the village with her loathsome child—a baby she blamed on George White."

"Ah!" Jamieson nodded knowingly. "And the child was Geoff, right?"

"Of course. That same cretin, adopted by the Fosters, who shambles around the village even now. A retarded youth of some fifteen years—but who looks like and has the strength of an eighteen-year-old—who in fact is George White's illegitimate son and young Anne's half-brother. And because I'm quite fond of Jilly, I find that...that *creature* perfectly unbearable!"

"Not to mention dangerous," said Jamieson.

"Eh? What's that?" The other looked startled.

"I was out on my verandah," said the old man. "It was just the other day, and I saw you with...with that young man. You seemed to be engaged in some sort of confrontation."

"But that's it exactly!" said Tremain. "He's suddenly there—he comes upon you, out of nowhere—and God only knows what goes on in that misshapen head of his. Enough to scare the life out of a man, coming over the dunes like that, and blowing like a stranded fish! A damn great fish, yes, that's what he reminds me of. *Ugh!* And it's how Tom Foster uses him, too!"

"What? Foster uses him?" Jamieson seemed totally engrossed. "In what way? Are we talking about physical abuse?"

"No, no, nothing that bad!" Tremain held up his hands. "No, but have you seen that retard swim? My God, if he had more than half a brain he'd be training for the olympics! What? Why, he's like a porpoise in the water! *That's* how Foster uses him."

"I'm afraid I'm still not with you," Jamieson admitted, his expression one of complete bafflement. "You're saying that this Foster somehow uses the boy to catch fish?"

"Yes." The other nodded. "And if the weather hadn't been so bad recently you wouldn't have seen nearly so much of the idiot on the beach. No, for he'd have been out with Tom Foster in his boat. The lad swims—in all weathers, apparently—to bring in the fish for that degenerate who looks after him."

Jamieson laughed out loud, then stopped abruptly and asked, "But...do you actually believe that? That a man can herd fish? I mean, that's quite incredible!"

"Oh?" Tremain answered. "You think so? Then don't just take my word for it but the next time you're in town go have a drink in the Sailor's Rest. Get talking with any of the local fishermen and ask them how come Foster always gets the best catches."

"But herding fish—" the old man began to protest.

And Tremain cut him off: "Now, I didn't say that. I said he brings them in—somehow attracts them." Then he offered a weak grin. "Yes, I'm well aware that sounds almost as silly. But—" He pursed his lips, shrugged and fell silent.

"So," said Jamieson. "Some truths, some rumours. But as far as I'm concerned, I still don't know it all. For instance, what was this awful disease you say George White contracted? What do you mean by 'awful'? All venereal diseases are pretty awful."

"Well, I suppose they are," Tremain answered. "But not like this one. There's awful and awful, but this was hideous. And he passed it down to his idiot child, too."

"He did what?"

"The way 'young Geoff' looks now, that was how George White looked in the months before he—"

"Died?"

"No." The other shook his head, grimly. "It's not as simple as that. George didn't just die, he took his own life." And:

"Ah!" said the old man. "So it was suicide."

Tremain nodded. "And I know this is a dreadful thing to say, but with a man like that—with his sexual appetites—surely it's just as well. A disease like that…why, he was a walking time bomb!"

"My goodness!" Jamieson exclaimed. "Was it never diagnosed? Can we put a name to it? Who was his doctor?"

"He wouldn't see a doctor. The more Jilly pressed him to do so, the more he retreated into himself. And only she could tell you what life must have been like with him, during his last few weeks. But since she'd already stuck it out for fifteen or more years, watching it gradually come out in him during all of that time…God, how strong she must have been!"

"Terrible, terrible!" said Jamieson—and then he frowned. "Yet Jilly and *her* child, I mean Anne—apparently they didn't come down with anything."

"No, and we can thank God for that!" said Tremain. "I think we'll have to assume that as soon as Jilly knew how sick George was, she—or they—stopped…well, you know what I mean."

"Yes." Jamieson nodded. "I do know: they were man and wife in name only. But if both Anne and Geoff were born within a few months of each other—and if young Geoff was, well, *defective* from birth—then Anne is a very fortunate young woman indeed."

"Exactly," said Tremain. "And is it any wonder her mother's nerves are so bad? My wife and I, we've known the White's a lot longer than you, James, and I can assure you that there's never been a woman more watchful of her child than Jilly is of Anne."

"Watchful?"

Doreen had come back in, and she said, "Oh, yes. That girl, she can't cough or catch a cold, or even develop a pimple without having her mother fussing all over her. Why, Anne's skin is flawless, but if you should see them on the beach together next summer—and if Anne's skin gets a little red or rough from the sun and the sand—you watch Jilly's reaction."

And Tremain concurred. "It's a wonder Jilly so much as lets that kid out of the house…"

The subject changed; the conversation moved on; half an hour or so later Jamieson looked at his watch. "Almost time I was on my way," he said. "There are some programmes I want to watch on TV tonight." He turned to Doreen. "Before I go, however, you might like to show me that brooch of yours. You were, er, busy in the kitchen for a while when we were talking and I didn't much like to open the box in your absence."

"Yes," she said. "It was very thoughtful of you to wait for me." She opened the small velvet-lined box and passed it across to him. The brooch was pinned to a pad in the bottom of the box and the old man let it lie there, simply turning the box in his hand and looking at the brooch from all angles.

"You're absolutely right." He nodded after a moment or two. "Without a doubt it has a certain beauty, but it's also a very odd piece. And it's not the first time I've seen gold worked in this style. But you know…" Here he paused and frowned, apparently uncertain how best to continue.

"Oh?" she said. "Is something wrong?"

"Well—" he began to answer, then paused again and bit his lip. "Well, it's just that…I don't know. Perhaps I shouldn't mention it."

Doreen took back the box and brooch, and said, "But now you really *must* mention it! You have to! Do you think there's something wrong with the brooch? But then, what could be wrong with it? Some kind of fake, maybe? Poor quality gold? Or not gold at all!" Her voice was more strident, more high-pitched, moment by moment. "Is that it, James? Have I been cheated?"

"At the price, whatever it was you paid? Probably not. It's the meaning of the thing. It's what it stands for. Doreen, this isn't a lucky item."

"It's unlucky? In what way?"

"Well, anthropology was a hobby of mine no less than driftwood art is your husband's. And as for the odd style and native workmanship we see here…I believe you'll find this brooch is from the South Seas, where it was probably crafted by a tribal witchdoctor."

"What? A witchdoctor?" Doreen's hand went to her throat.

"Oh, yes." Jamieson nodded. "And having fashioned it from an alloy of local gold and some other lustrous metal, the idea would have been to lay a curse upon it, then to ensure it fell into the hands of an enemy. A kind of sympathetic magic—or in the poor victim's case, quite unsympathetic."

Now Doreen took the box back, and staring hard at its contents said, "To be honest, I've never much liked this thing. I only bought it out of some misguided sense of loyalty to Jilly, so that I could tell myself that at least some money was finding its way into that household. What with George's philandering and all, they couldn't have been very well off."

Her husband took the box off her, peered at the brooch for a few moments, and said, "I think you must be right, James. It isn't a very pleasant sort of thing at all. It's quite unearthly, really. These weird arabesques, not of any terrestrial foliage but more of…what? Interwoven seaweeds, kelp, suckered tentacles? And these scalloped edges you see in certain shells. I mean, it's undeniably striking in its looks—well, until you look closer. And then, why, you're absolutely right! It's somehow crude, as if crafted by some primitive islander."

He handed the box back to his wife who said, "I'll sell it at once! I believe I know the jewellers where George White got rid of those other pieces." And glancing at the old man: "It's not that I'm superstitious, you understand, but better not to risk it. You never know where this thing's been."

"Dear lady, you're so right," Jamieson said. "But myself, having an interest in this sort of thing—and being a doctor of an entirely different stamp—I find the piece fascinating So if you do decide to sell it, don't take it to a dealer but offer it to me first. And whatever you paid for it, I think we can safely say you won't be the worse off."

"Why, that's so very kind of you!" she said, seeing him to the door. "But are you sure?"

"Absolutely," the old man answered. "Give me a ring in the morning when you've had time to think it over, and let me know what I owe you."

With which the Tremains walked him to his car…

The winter came in quickly and savagely, keeping almost everyone in the village to their houses. With the fishermen's boats sheltering within the harbour wall, only the old Sailor's Rest was doing anything like good business.

Driving his car to work at the college in St. Austell over frequently washed-out and ever potholed roads, headmaster John Tremain cursed the day he'd bought his place (a) for its cheapness and (b) for its "seclusion and wild dramatic beauty." The seclusion was fine and dandy but he could do without the wildness of winters like this one, and of drama he'd had more than enough. Come spring and the first half-decent offer he got, he and Doreen would be out of here for a more convenient place in St. Austell. It would be more expensive, but what the hell…he'd sell the car, cycle to work, and save money on petrol and repairs.

As for the Whites: Jilly and Anne were more or less housebound, but they did have a regular visitor in the old American gentleman. James Jamieson had seemed to take to them almost as family, and never turned up on their doorstep without bringing some gift or other with him. Often as not it was food: a fresh pie from the bakery, a loaf of bread and slab of cheese, maybe a bottle of good wine. All to the good, for Jilly's old car was well past reliable, and Anne had to attend her piano and language lessons. Jamieson would drive the girl to and fro without complaint, and wouldn't accept a penny for all his kindness.

Also, when Anne went down with a sore throat, which served to drive her mother frantic with worry, Jamieson gave the girl a thorough examination and diagnosed a mild case of laryngitis. His remedy—one aspirin three times daily, and between times a good gargle with a spoonful of salt in water—worked wonders, for mother and daughter both! But his ministrations didn't stop there. For having now seen Jilly on several occasions when her nervous condition was at its worst, the old man had in fact prescribed for her, too; though not without protesting that in fact he shouldn't for he'd retired from all that. Nevertheless, the pills he made up for her did the trick, calming her nerves like nothing she'd tried before. They couldn't entirely relieve her obsession or anxieties with regard to Anne, however, though now when she felt compelled to fuss and fret her hands wouldn't shake so badly, and her at best fluffy mind would stay focussed for longer. Moreover, now that certain repetitive nightmares of long-standing no longer visited her quite so frequently, Jilly was pleased to declare that she was sleeping better…

Occasionally, when the weather was a little kinder, Anne would walk to her piano lesson at Miss Harding's thatched cottage on the far side of the village. Jilly would usually accompany her daughter part way, and use the occasion to visit the bakery or collect groceries at the post office. The winter being a hard one, such times were rare; more often than not, James Jamieson would arrive in his car in time to give Anne a lift. It got so that Jilly even expected him, and Anne—normally so retiring—had come to regard him as some kind of father or grandfather figure.

One day in mid-January, when the wind drove the waves high up the beach, and stinging hail came sleeting almost horizontally off the sea, the old man and his young passenger arrived at Miss Harding's place to find an agitated Tom Foster waiting for them—in fact waiting for Jamieson.

The old man had bumped into Foster once or twice before in the Sailor's Rest, and had found him a surly, bearded, weatherbeaten brute with a gravelly voice and a habit of slamming his empty mug on the bar by way of catching the barman's attention and ordering another drink. He had few friends among the other fishermen and was as much a loner as any man Jamieson had ever known. Yet now, today, he was in need of a friend—or rather, in need of a doctor.

The village spinster, Miss Julia Harding, had kept Foster waiting in the small conservatory that fronted her cottage; he wasn't the sort of person she would allow in the house proper. But Foster, still shaking rain from his lank hair, and pacing to and fro—a few paces each way, which was all the conservatory allowed—pounced on Jamieson as soon as the old man was ushered into view by Miss Harding.

"It's the boy," he rasped, grabbing Jamieson's arm. "Can't get no sleep, the way um itches. I know'd you'd be comin' with the lass fer the teachin', and so I waited. But I do wish you'd come see the boy. I'd consider it a real favour, and Tom Foster dun't forget um that does um a favour. But it's more fer young Geoff'n fer me. Um's skin be raw from scratchin', so it be. And I got no car fer gettin' um inter the city...beside which, um dun't want no big city doctor. But um won't fuss any with you, if you'll come see um."

"I don't any longer practice..." The old man appeared at a loss what to do or say.

But Anne took his other arm. "Please go," she said. "Oh do *please* go and see Geoff! And I'll go with you."

Miss Harding wagged her finger at Anne, and said, "Oh? And what of your lesson, young lady?" But then, looking for support from Tom Foster and Jamieson, and seeing none, she immediately shook her head in self denial. "No, no—whatever was I thinking? If something ails that poor lad, it's surely more important than a piano lesson. It must be, for Mr. Foster here, well, he's hardly one to get himself all stirred up on a mere whim—nor for anything much else, except maybe his fishing—and not even that on a bad day!"

"That I'm not," growled Foster, either ignoring or failing to recognize the spinster's jibe for what it really was. And to Jamieson: "Will you come?"

"Well," the old man sighed, "I don't suppose it can do any harm to see the boy, and I always carry my old medicine bag in the back of the car…not that there's a lot of medicine in it these days. But—" He threw up his hands, took Anne and Foster back out to his car, and drove them to the latter's house where it stood facing the sea across the harbour wall in Fore Street.

Tom Foster's wife, a small, black-haired, dark-complexioned woman, but not nearly as gnarled or surly as her husband, wiped her hands on her apron to clasp Jamieson's hand as she let them into the house. She said nothing but simply indicated a bedroom door where it stood ajar.

Geoff was inside, a bulky shape under a coarse blanket, and the room bore the unmistakable odour of fish—but then, so did the entire house. Wrinkling his nose, Jamieson glanced at Anne, but she didn't seem to have noticed the fish stink; all she was interested in was Geoff's welfare. As she approached the bed so its occupant seemed to sense her presence; the youth's bulbous, ugly head came out from under the blanket, and he stared at her with luminous green eyes. But:

"No, no, lass!" Tom Foster grunted. "I knows you be friends but you can't be in 'ere. Um's naked under that blanket, and um ain't nice ter look at what wi' um's scratchin' and all. So out you goes and Ma Foster'll see ter you in the front." And coarse brute of a man that he was, he gentled her out of the room.

As Foster closed the door behind her, so Jamieson drew up a chair close to the bed, and said, "Now then, young man, try not to be alarmed. I'm here to see what the trouble is." With which he began to turn back the blanket. A squat hand, short-fingered and thickly webbed, at once grasped the top edge of the blanket and held it fast. The old man saw blood under the sharp fingernails, the trembling of the unfortunate's entire body under the blanket, and the terror in his huge, moist, oh-so-deep eyes.

Foster immediately stepped forward. "Now, dun't you take on so, lad," he said. "This un's a doctor, um be. A friend ter the lass and 'er Ma. If you let um, um'll see ter your scratchin'."

The thing called Geoff (for close up he was scarcely human) opened his mouth and Jamieson saw his teeth, small but as sharp as needles. There was no threat in it, however—just a popping of those pouty lips, a soundless pleading almost—as the hand slowly relaxed its grip, allowing the old man to turn back the cover without further hindrance.

Despite that Foster was hovering over the old man, watching him closely, he saw no evidence of shock at what was uncovered: that scaly body—which even five years ago a specialist in St. Austell had called the worst case of ichthyosis he'd ever seen, now twice as bad at least—that body under a heavily wattled neck and sloping but powerful shoulders, and the raw, red areas on the forearms and under the ribcage where the rough grey skin had been torn. And as the old man opened his bag and called for hot water and a clean towel, Foster nodded his satisfaction. He had done the right thing sure enough, and Jamieson was a doctor good and true who would care for a life even if it were such as this one under the blanket.

But as Foster turned away to answer Jamieson's request, the old man took his arm and said, "Tom, do you care for him?"

"Eh?" Foster grunted. "Why, me and my old girl, we've cared fer um fer fifteen years! And in fifteen years you can get used ter things, even them things that never gets no better but only worse. And as fer folks—even poorly made 'uns such as the boy—why, in time you can even get fond of 'em, so you can!"

Jamieson nodded and said, "Then look after him better." And he let Foster go…

Anne saw the wet, pink-splotched towels when Mrs Foster brought them out of Geoff's room. And then Tom Foster allowed her in.

The old man was putting his things back into his bag as she hurried to the bedside. There was a clean white sheet under the blanket now, and it was tucked up under Geoff's blob of a chin. The youth's neck was bandaged to hold a dressing under his left ear; his right arm lay on top of the blanket, the forearm bandaged where a red stain was evidence of some small seepage.

"What was it?" Anne snatched a breath, touching her hand to her lips and staring at Jamieson wide-eyed, her face drawn and pale, even paler than usual. "Oh, what was it?"

"A skin disorder," he told her. "Something parasitic—like lice or scabies—but I think I got all of it. No need to worry about it, however. It must have been uncomfortable for him, but it certainly wasn't deadly. Geoff will recover, I assure you."

And Tom Foster said, "Anythin' I can do fer you, Mr. Jamieson, sir, jus' you ask. I dun't forget um who's done me or mine a favour—no, not never."

"Well, Tom," Jamieson answered, "I might come to you for a nice piece of fish some time, and that would be payment enough for what little I've done here. Right now, though, we've other things to talk about." He turned to the girl. "Anne, if you'll wait in the car?"

Anne had sat down in the chair by the bed. She was holding Geoff's hand and they were looking at each other, and Jamieson couldn't help noticing a striking similarity in the deep green colour of their eyes…but *only* in their colour. It was true that Anne's eyes were slightly, almost unnoticeably protuberant, but as for the other's…

…In his current physical condition, and despite that his eyes were huge and bulging, even more so than was usual, still the old man had to grant them the dubious distinction of being Geoff's most human feature!

And now the youth had taken his hand from the girl's, and his stubby fingers were moving rapidly, urgently, making signs which she appeared to understand and began answering in a like fashion. This "conversation" lasted only a moment or so longer, until Geoff turned his watery gaze on Jamieson and twisted his face into what had to be his version of a smile. At which Anne said:

"He says I'm to thank you for him. So thank you." Then she stood up and left the room and the house…

Inside the front door, Jamieson spoke to Tom Foster in lowered tones. "Do you know what I dug out and scraped off him?"

"How'd I know that?" the other protested. "You be the doctor."

"Oh?" said the old man. "And you be the fisherman, but you tell me you've never seen such as that before? Very well, then I'll tell you: they were fish-lice, Tom. Copepods, small crustaceans that live on fish as parasites. Now then, Mr. Fisherman—tell me you've never seen fish-lice before."

The other looked away, then slowly nodded. "I've seen 'em, sure enough. Usually on plaice or flounder, flatties or bottomfeeders. But on a man? In the flesh of a man?" And now he shook his head. "I jus' dint want ter believe it, that's all."

"Well, now you can believe it," said Jamieson. "And the only way he could have got them was by frequent periods of immersion in the sea. They got under his skin where it's especially scaly and fed there like ticks on a dog. They were dug in quite deep, so I know he's had them for a long time."

"Oh? And are you sayin' I ain't looked after um, then?" Tom was angry now. "Well, I'm tellin' you as how I din't see 'em on um afore! And anyways, you answer me this—if um's had 'em so long, why'd they wait ter flare up now, eh?"

The old man nodded. "Oh, I think I can tell you that, Tom. It's because his skin was all dried out. And because they need it damp, they started digging in for the moisture in his blood. So all of a sudden the boy was itching and hurting. And when he scratched, the hurt only got worse. That's what happened here. So now then, you can tell me something: when were you last out at sea, Tom? *Not recently*, I'll wager!"

"Ah-*hah!*" The other narrowed his eyes, thrust his chin out. "So then, Mr. Jamieson. You've been alistenin' ter rumours, eh? And what did them waggin' village tongues tell you…that Tom Foster makes um's poor dumb freak swim fer um? And that um gets um ter chase up the fish fer um? *Hah!*" He shook his head. "Well it ain't so! That 'un swims 'cos um *likes* ter swim, and 'cos um *wants* ter swim—and in all weathers if I dun't be watchin' um! That's all there be ter such tall stories. But if you be askin' does um know where the best fish can be found? Then you're damn right um do, and that's why I gets the best catch—always! So then, what else can I tell you?"

"Nothing, Tom," said Jamieson. "But there is something you can do for that youth. If he wants to swim, let him—you don't need to let the village see it. And if he gets…well, infested again, you saw me working and know what to do. But whatever you do, you mustn't let him dry out like that again. No, for it seems to me his skin needs that salt water…"

It had stopped hailing, and protected by the building Anne was waiting just outside the door. Since the door had been standing ajar, she must have heard the old man's and Foster's conversation. But she said nothing until they were in the car. Then:

"He had fish-lice?" It wasn't a shocked exclamation, just a simple enquiry.

And starting up the car Jamieson answered, "Oh, people are prone to all kinds of strange infections and infestations. I've heard it said that AIDS—a disease caused by immune deficiency—came from monkeys; and there's that terrible CJD that you can get from eating contaminated or incorrectly processed beef. And how about psittacosis? From parrots, of all things! As for that poor boy: well, what can I say? He likes to swim."

"It's very strange," she said, as Jamieson drove out of the village, "but my father…he didn't like the sea. Not at all. He had those books about it—about the sea and other things—and yet was afraid of it. He used to say it lured him. They say he killed himself, suicide, and perhaps he did; but at least he did it his way. I remember he once said to me, 'If a time comes when I must go, it won't take me alive.' Toward the end he used to say all sorts of things that didn't make a lot of sense, but I think he was talking about the sea."

"And what makes you think that?" Jamieson asked her, glancing at her out of the corner of his eye, and aware that she was watching him, probably to gauge his reaction.

"Well, because of the way he did it…jumped off the cliff at South Point, down onto the rocks. He washed up on the beach, all broken up."

"How awful!" The old man swung the car onto the lonely road to Jilly White's house. "And yet you and your mother, you continue to live right here, almost on the beach itself."

"I think that's because she needs to be sure about certain things," the girl answered. "Needs to be sure of me, perhaps?"

Jamieson saw Jilly standing on the doorstep and stopped the car outside the house. He would have liked to carry on talking, to have the girl clarify her last cryptic remark, or learn more about the books she'd mentioned—her father's books, about the sea. But Jilly was already coming forward. And now Anne touched the old man's arm and said, "It's best she doesn't know we were at the Fosters'. If she knew about Geoff's fish-lice, it might only set her off again."

Then, lifting her voice a little as she got out of the car, she said, "Thank's again for the ride." And in a whisper added, "And for what you did for Geoff…"

The winter dragged on. Jamieson spent some of the time driving, visiting the local towns, even going as far afield as Falmouth and Penzance. And to break the boredom a little, usually there would be a weekly "social evening" alternating between Jilly's, the Tremains's, and Jamieson's place. The old man even managed to inveigle Jilly into joining him and the Tremains in a visit to the dilapidated Sailor's Rest one night.

On that occasion Anne went with them. She was under age for drinking—even for being in the pub—but the proprietor knew her, of course, and served her orange juice; and in any case it wasn't as if the place was about to be raided.

Their table was close to a great open fireplace where logs popped and hissed, and the pub being mainly empty, the service couldn't be faulted. In an atmosphere that was quietly mellow, the country food bought fresh from the village bakery was very good. Even Jilly appeared clear-headed and in good spirits for once, and as for the Tremains: putting their customary, frequently unwarranted snobbery aside, they were on their very best behaviour.

That was the up-side, but the down-side was on its way. It came as the evening drew to a close in the forms of the fisherman Tom Foster, and that of his ward the shambling Geoff, when the pair came in from the cold and took gloomy corner seats at a small table. It was doubtful that they had noticed the party seated near the fire on the far side of the room, but Foster's narrowed eyes had certainly scanned the bar area before he ushered his ward and companion to their more discreet seats.

And as suddenly as that the evening turned sour. "Checking that his enemies aren't in," said Tremain under his breath. "I can understand that. He's probably afraid they'll report him."

"His enemies?" said Jamieson. "The other village fishermen, you mean? Report him for what?"

"See for yourself," said the other, indicating the barman, who was on his way to Foster's corner with a tray. "A pint for Tom, and a half for that...for young Geoff. He lets that boy drink here—alcohol, mind—and him no older than Anne here. I mean, it's one thing to have that...well, that poor unfortunate in the village, but quite another to deliberately addle what few brains he's got with strong drink!"

Anne, visibly stiffening in her chair, at once spoke up in the youth's defence. "Geoff isn't stupid," she said. "He can't speak very well, and he's different, but he isn't stupid." And staring pointedly at Tremain, "He isn't ignorant, either."

The headmaster's mouth fell open. "Well, I...!" But before he could say more:

"John, you asked for that," Doreen told him. "You're aware that Anne is that youth's friend. Why, she's probably the only friend he's got! You should mind what you say."

"But I..." Tremain began to protest, only to have Jamieson step in with:

"Oh, come, come! Let's not ruin the pleasant evening we're having. Surely our opinions can differ without that we have to fight over them? If Tom Foster does wrong, then he does wrong. But I say let that youth have whatever pleasures he can find."

"And I agree," said Doreen, glowering at her husband. "God only knows he'll find few enough!"

With which they fell silent, and that was that. Things had been said that couldn't be retracted, and as for the evening's cosy atmosphere and light-hearted conversation: suddenly everything had fallen flat. They tried to hang on to it but were too late. John Tremain took on a haughty, defensive attitude, while his wife turned cold and distant. Jilly retreated quietly into herself again, and young Anne's presence continued to register only by virtue of her physically being there—but as for her thoughts, they could be anywhere...

❖ ❖ ❖

After that, such get-togethers were few and far between. Their friendship—the fact that the Tremains, Whites, and Jamieson stuck together at all—continued on a far less intimate level, surviving mainly out of necessity; being of the village's self-appointed upper crust, they couldn't bring themselves to mingle too freely with those on the lower rungs of the social ladder.

The old man was the odd-man-out—or rather the pig-in-the-middle; while he maintained contact with the Tremains, Jamieson never failed to assist Jilly and Anne White whenever the opportunity presented itself. Moreover, he visited the Sailor's Rest from time to time, building at least tentative friendships with several of the normally taciturn locals. The Tremains reckoned him either a fool or a saint, while the Whites—both of them—saw him as a godsend.

One evening in early March Jilly called the old man, ostensibly to tell him she was running low on medication, the pills which he'd prescribed and made up for her. But Jamieson sensed there was more than that to her call. The woman's voice hinted of loneliness, and the old man's intuition was that she wanted someone to talk to…or someone to talk to her.

He at once drove to her house.

Waiting for his knock, Jilly made him welcome with a glass of sherry. And after he had handed over a month's supply of her pills, and she had offered him a chair, she said, "I feel such an idiot calling you so late when I've had all day to remember my medication was getting low. I hope you don't mind?"

"Not at all, my dear," the old man answered. "If anything, I'm just a little concerned that you may be taking too many of those things. I mean, by my calculations you should still have a fortnight's supply at least. Of course, I could be wrong. My memory's not as keen as it used to be. But…?"

"Oh!" she said. And then, quickly recovering: "Ah! No—not at all—your memory's fine. I'm the one at fault. For like a fool I…well, I *spilled* some pills the other day, and didn't like to use them after they'd been on the floor."

"Very sensible, too!" he answered. "And anyway, I've let it go too long without asking you how you've been feeling. But you see, Jilly, I'm not getting any younger, and what used to be my bedside manner is all shot to pieces. I certainly wouldn't like to think those pills of mine were doing you any harm."

"Doing me harm? On the contrary," she replied. "I think I'm feeling better. I'm calmer—perhaps a little easier in my mind—but….Well, just a moment ago, James, you were complaining about your memory. *Huh!* I should be so lucky! No, I don't think it's your pills—though it could be a side effect—but I do seem to stumble a lot. And I don't just mean in my speech or my memory, but also physically. My balance is off, and I sometimes feel quite weak. You may have noticed?"

"Side effects, yes." He nodded. "You could be right. But in a remote place like this it's easy to get all vague and forgetful. I mean, who do you talk to? You see me occasionally—and of course there's Anne—but that's about it." He looked around the room, frowning. "Talking about Anne, where is she?"

"Sleeping." Jilly held a finger to her lips. "What with the weather improving and all, she's been doing a lot of walking on the beach. Walking and reading, and so intelligent! Haven't you ever wondered why she isn't at school? They had nothing more to teach her, that's why. She left school early, shortly after her father…after George…after he…" She paused, touched her hand to her brow, looked suddenly vague.

"Yes, I understand," said the old man, and waited.

In another moment Jilly blinked; and shaking her head as if to clear it, she said, "I'm sorry, what were you saying?"

"I was just wondering if there was anything else I could do for you," Jamieson answered. "Apart from delivering your pills, that is. Did you want to talk, perhaps? For after all, we could all of us use a little company, some friendly conversation from time to time."

"Talk?" she said—and then the cloud lifted from her brow. "Ah, *talk!* Now I remember! It was something you were telling me one time, but we were somehow interrupted. I think it was Anne. Yes, she came on the scene just as you were going to talk about…about…wasn't it that coastal town in America, the place that George came from, that you were telling me about?"

"Innsmouth?" said the old man. "Yes, I believe I recall the occasion. But I also recall how nervous you were. And Jilly, in my opinion—from what I've observed of you, er, in my capacity as a doctor or ex-doctor—it seems to me that odd or peculiar subjects have a very unsettling effect on you. Are you sure you want to hear about Innsmouth?"

"While it's true that certain subjects have a bad affect on me," she began slowly, "at the same time I'm fascinated by anything concerning my husband's history or his people. Especially the latter, his genealogy." She speeded up a little. "After all what do we really know of genetics—those traits we carry down the generations with us—traits passed on by our forebears? And I think to myself, perhaps I've been avoiding George's past for far too long. Things have happened here, James…" She clutched his arm. "Weird alterations, alienations, and I need to be sure they can't ever happen again, not to me or mine!" She was going full tilt now. "Or if they do happen, that I'll know what to do—what to do about—do about…"

But there Jilly stopped dead, with her mouth still open, as if she suddenly realized that she'd said too much, too quickly, and even too desperately.

And after a long moment's silence the old man quietly said, "Maybe I'd better ask you again, my dear: are you sure you want me to tell you about Innsmouth?"

She took a deep breath, deliberately stilled the twitching of her slender hands on the arms of her chair, and said "Yes, I really would like to know all about that place and its people."

"And after I've gone, leaving you on your own here tonight? What of your dreams, Jilly? For I feel I must warn you: you may well be courting nightmares."

"I want to know," she answered at once. "As for nightmares: you're right, I can do without them. But still I *have* to know."

"Anne has told me there are some books that belonged to her father." Jamieson tried to reason with her. "Perhaps the answer you're seeking can be found in their pages?"

"George's books?" She shuddered. "Those ugly books! He used to bury himself in them. But when they were heaping the seaweed and burning it last summer, I asked Anne to throw them into the flames!" She offered a nervous, perhaps apologetic shrug. "What odds? I couldn't have read them anyway, for they weren't in English; they weren't in any easily recognizable language. But the worst thing was the way they felt. Why, just touching them made me feel queasy!"

The old man narrowed his eyes, nodded and said, "And do you really expect me to talk about Innsmouth, when the very thought of a few mouldy old books makes you look ill? And you asked the girl to burn them, without even knowing their value or what was in them? You know, it's probably a very good thing I came along when I did, Jilly. For it's fairly obvious that you're obsessed about something, and obsessions can all too easily turn to psychoses. Wherefore—"

"—You're done with me," she finished it for him, and fell back in her chair. "I'm ill with worry—or with my own, well, 'obsession' if you like—and you're not going to help me with it."

The old man took her hand, squeezed it, and shook his head. "Oh, Jilly!" he said. "You've got me all wrong. Psychology may be one of our more recently accepted medical sciences, but I'm not so ancient that I predate it in its entirety! Yes, I know a thing or two about the human psyche; more than enough to assure you that there's not much wrong with yours."

She looked bewildered, and so Jamieson continued, "You see, my dear, you're finally opening up, deliberately exposing yourself to whatever your problem is, taking your first major step toward getting rid of it. So of course I'm going to help you."

She sighed her relief, then checked herself and said, "But, if that involves telling me about Innsmouth—?"

"Then so be it," said the old man. "But I would ask you not to interrupt me once I start, for I'm very easily sidetracked." And after Jilly nodded her eager assent, he began…

"During my time at my practice in Innsmouth, I saw some strange sad cases. Many locals are inbred, to such an extent that their blood is tainted. I would very much like to be able to put that some other way, but no other way says it so succinctly. And the 'Innsmouth look'—a name given to the very weird, almost alien appearance of some of the town's inhabitants—is the principal symptom of that taint.

"However, among the many myths and legends I've heard about that place and those with 'the look,' some of the more fanciful have it the other way round; they insist that it wasn't so much inbreeding that caused the taint as miscegenation…the *mixed* breeding between the town's old-time sea captains and the women of certain South Sea island tribes with which they often traded during their voyages. And what's more, the same legends have it that it wasn't only the native *women* with whom these degenerate old sea dogs associated, but…but I think it's best to leave that be for now, for tittle-tattle of that nature can so easily descend into sheer fantasy.

"Very well, but whatever the origin or source of the town's problems— the *real* source, that is—it's still possible that it may at least have some *connection* with those old sea-traders and the things they brought back with them from their ventures. Certainly some of them married and brought home native women—which in this day and age mightn't cause much of a stir, but in the mid-19th century was very much frowned upon—and in their turn these women must surely have brought some of their personal belongings and customs with them: a few native gewgaws, some items of clothing, their 'cuisine,' of course…possibly even something of their, er, religions? Or perhaps 'religion' is too strong a word for what we should more properly accept as primitive native beliefs.

"In any case, that's as far back as I was able to trace the blood taint—if such it is,—but as for the 'Innsmouth look' itself, and the horrible way it manifested itself in the town's inhabitants…well, I think the best way to describe that is as a disease; yes, and perhaps more than one disease at that.

"As to the form or forms this affliction takes," (now Jamieson began to lie, or at least to step aside from the truth,) "well, if I didn't know any better, I might say that there's a fairly representative example or specimen, as it were, right here in our own backyard: that poor unfortunate youth who lives with the Fosters, Anne's friend, young Geoff. Of course, I don't know of any connection—and can't see how there could possibly be one—but that youth would seem to have something much akin to the Innsmouth stigma, if not the selfsame affliction. Just take a look at his condition:

"The unwholesome scaliness of the skin, far worse than any mere ichthyosis; the strange, shambling gait; the eyes, larger than normal and increasingly difficult to close; the speech—where such exists at all—or the guttural gruntings that pass for speech; and those gross anomalies or distortions of facial arrangement giving rise to fishy or froggy looks…and all of these features present in young Geoff. Why, John Tremain tells me that the youth reminds him of nothing so much as a stranded fish! And if somehow there is something of the Innsmouth taint in him…well then, is it any wonder that such dreadful fantasies came into being in the first place? I think not…"

Pausing, the old man stared hard at Jilly. During his discourse she had turned very pale, sunk down into her chair, and gripped its arms with white-knuckled hands. And for the first time he noticed grey in her hair, at the temples. She had not, however, given way to those twitches and jerks normally associated with her nervous condition, and all of her attention was still rapt upon him.

Now Jamieson waited for Jilly's reaction to what he'd told her so far, and in a little while she found her voice and said, "You mentioned certain gewgaws that the native women might have brought with them from those South Sea islands. Did you perhaps mean jewellery, and if so have you ever seen any of it? I mean, what *kind* of gewgaws, exactly? Can you describe them for me?"

For a moment the old man frowned, then said, "Ah!" and nodded his understanding. "But I think we may be talking at cross purposes, Jilly. For where those native women are concerned—in connection with their belongings— I actually *meant* gewgaws: bangles and necklaces made from seashells, and ornaments carved out of coconut shells…that sort of thing. But it's entirely possible I know what *you* mean by gewgaws…for of course I've seen that brooch that Mrs. Tremain purchased from your husband. Oh yes; and since I have a special interest in such items, I bought it back from her! But in fact the only genuine 'gewgaws' in the tales I've heard were the cheap trinkets which those old sea captains offered the islanders in so-called 'trade.' Trade?

Daylight robbery, more like! While the gewgaws that *you* seem to be interested in have to be what those poor savages parted with in exchange for those worthless beads and all that useless frippery—by which I mean the quaintly-worked jewellery, but *real jewellery*, in precious golden alloy, that Innsmouth's seafarers as good as stole from the natives! And you ask have I actually seen such? Indeed I have, and not just the piece I bought from Doreen Tremain…"

The old man had seemed to be growing more and more excited, carried away by his subject, apparently. But now, calming down, he paused to collect his thoughts and settled himself deeper in his chair before continuing. And:

"There now," he finally said. "Didn't I warn you that I was easily sidetracked? And wouldn't you know it, but now I've completely lost the thread!"

"I had asked you about that native jewellery," she reminded him. "I thought maybe you could describe it for me, or at least tell me where you saw it. And there was something else you said—something about the old sea captains and…and *things* they associated with other than the natives?—that I somehow found, well, interesting."

"Ah!" the old man answered. "But I can assure you, my dear, that last was sheer fantasy. And as for the jewellery…where did I see it? Why, in Innsmouth itself, where else? In a museum there—well, a sort of museum—but more properly a shrine, or a site of remembrance, really. I suppose I could tell you about it if you still wish it? And if you're sure none of this is too troubling for you?" The way he looked at her, his gaze was very penetrating. But having come this far, Jilly wasn't about to be put off.

"I do wish it," she nodded. "And I promise you I'll try not…not to be troubled. So do please go on."

The old man nodded and stroked his chin, and after a while carried on with his story.

"Anthropology, the study of man's origins and ways of life, was always something of a hobby of mine," he began. "And crumbling old Innsmouth, despite its many drawbacks, was not without its sources—its own often fascinating history and background—which as yet I've so poorly delineated.

"Some of the women—I can't really call them ladies—who attended my practice were of the blood. Not necessarily tainted blood but native blood, certainly. Despite the many generations separating them from their dusky forebears, still there was that of the South Sea islands in them. And it was a handful of these patients of mine, my clients, so to speak, that led to my enquiries after the jewellery they wore…the odd clasp or brooch, a wrist bangle or necklace. I saw quite a few, all displaying a uniform, somehow rude style of workmanship, and all very similarly adorned or embellished.

"But as for a detailed description, that's rather difficult. Floral? No, not really. Arabesque? That would more properly fit the picture; weird foliage and other plant forms, curiously and intricately intertwined…but not foliage of the land. It was oceanic: seaweeds and sea grasses, with rare conches and fishes hidden in the design—particularly fishes—forming what may only be described as an unearthly piscine or perhaps batrachian depiction. And occasionally, as a backdrop to the seaweeds and grasses, there were hinted buildings: strange, squat pyramids, and oddly-angled towers. It was as if the unknown craftsman—who or whatever—had attempted to convey the lost Atlantis or some other watery civilization…"

The old man paused again, then said, "There. As a description, however inadequate, that will have to suffice. Of course, I was never so close to the Innsmouth women that I was able to study their clasps and brooches in any great detail, but I did enquire of them as to their origin. Ah, but they were a closemouthed lot and would say very little…well, except for one, who was younger and less typical of her kind; and she directed me to the museum.

"In its heyday it had been a church—that was before the tainted blood had moved in and the more orthodox religions out,—a squat-towered stone church, yes, but long since desanctified. It stood close to another once-grand building: a pillared hall of considerable size, still bearing upon its pediment the faded legend, 'Esoteric Order of Dagon.'

"Dagon, eh? But here a point of great interest:

"Many years ago, this great hall, too, had been a place of worship…or obeisance of some sort, certainly. And how was this for an anthropological puzzle? For of course the fish-god Dagon—half man, half fish—had been a deity of the Philistines, later to be adopted by the Phoenicians who called him Oannes. And yet these Polynesian islanders, thousands of miles away around the world, had offered up their sacrifices—or at least their prayers— to the selfsame god. And in the Innsmouth of the 1820s their descendants were carrying on that same tradition! But you know, my dear, and silly as it may seem, I can't help wondering if perhaps they're doing it still…I mean today, even now.

"But there you go, I've sidetracked myself again! So where was I? Ah, yes! The old church, or rather the museum.

"The place was gothic in its looks, with shuttered windows and a disproportionately high basement. And it was there in the half-sunken basement—

the museum proper—that the 'exhibits' were housed. There under dusty glass in unlocked boxwood cases, I saw such a fabulous collection of golden jewellery and ornaments…why, it amazed me that there were no labels to describe the treasure, and more so that there was no curator to guard it against thieves or to enlighten casual visitors with its story! Not that there were many visitors. Indeed, on such occasions as I was there I saw no one—not even a church mouse.

"But that jewellery, made of those strange golden alloys…oh, it was truly fascinating! As was a small, apparently specialized library of some hundreds of books; all of them antiques, and all quietly rotting away on damp, easily accessible shelves. Apart from one or two titles of particularly unpleasant connotation, I recognized nothing that I saw; and, since most of those titles were in any case beyond me, I never so much as paused to turn a page. But as with the exotic, alien jewellery—and *if* I had been a thief, of course—I'm sure I might have walked out of there with a fortune in rare and forbidden volumes under my coat, and no one to stop, accuse or search me. In fact, searching my memory, I believe I've heard mention that certain books and a quantity of jewellery were indeed stolen from the museum some twenty-odd years ago. Not that gold was ever of any great rarity in Innsmouth, for those old sea captains had brought it home in such large amounts that back in the 1800's one of them had even opened up a refinery in order to purify his holdings! I tried to visit the refinery, too, only to find it in a state of total dereliction…as was much of the old town itself in the wake of a…well, of a rumoured epidemic, and subsequent government raids in 1927-28. But there, that's another story."

And fidgeting a very little—seeming suddenly reticent—Jamieson brought his narrative to an abrupt halt, saying, "And there you have it, my dear. With regard to your question about the strange jewellery…well, I've tried to answer it as best possible. So, er, what else can I tell you? Nothing, I fear…"

But now it was Jilly White's eyes searching the old man's face, and not the other way about. For she had noticed several vague allusions and some major omissions in his narrative, for which she required explanations.

"About the jewellery…yes, I believe I understand," she said. "But you've said some other things that aren't nearly so clear. In fact you seemed to be avoiding certain subjects. And I w-w-want…I *wan-w-w…!*" She slammed her arms down on the arms of her chair, trying to control her stammering. "I *want* to know! About—how did you put it?—the *associations* of those old sea captains with something other than the island women, which you said was sheer fantasy. But fantasy or not, I want to know. And about…about their beliefs…their religion and d-d-*dedication* to Dagon. Also, w-w-with regard to that foreign jewellery, you said something about its craftsman, *'who or whatever!'* Now what did you mean by that? And that epidemic you mentioned: what was all that about? What, an epidemic that warranted government raids? James—if you're my friend at all—surely you m-m-*must* see that I have to know!"

"I can see that I've upset you," he answered, reaching out and touching her hand. "And I believe I know what it is that's so unsettling for you. You're trying to connect all of this to George, aren't you? You think that his blood, too, was tainted. Jilly, it may be so, but it's not your fault. And if the taint is in fact a disease, it probably wasn't his fault either. You can't blame yourself that your husband may have been some kind of…of carrier. And even if he was, surely his influence is at an end now? You mustn't go on believing that it…that it isn't over yet."

"Then convince me otherwise," she answered, a little calmer now that she could speak openly of what was on her mind. "Tell me about these things, so that I'll better understand them and be able to make up my own mind."

Jamieson nodded. "Oh, I can tell you," he said, "if only by repeating old wives tales—myths and rumours—and fishermen's stories of mermaids and the like. But the state of your nerves, I'd really rather not."

"My nerves, yes," she said. "Wait." And she fetched a glass of water and took two of her pills. "There, and now you can see that I'm following doctor's orders. Now *you* must follow my orders and tell me." And leaning forward in her chair, she gripped his forearms. "Please. If not for my sake…for Anne's?"

And knowing her meaning, how could he refuse her?

"Very well," the old man answered. "But my dear, this thing you're worrying about, it is—it *has* to be—a horrible disease, and nothing more. So don't go mixing fantasy and reality, for that way lies madness."

And after a moment's thought he told her the rest of it…

"The stories I've heard…well, they were incredible. Legends born of primitive innocence and native ignorance both. You see, with regard to Dagon, those islanders had their own myths which had been handed down from generation to generation. Their blood and looks being so debased, and the taint having such a hold on them—probably since time immemorial— they reasoned that they had been created in the image of their maker, the fish-god himself, Dagon.

"Indeed they told those old sea captains just such stories, and also that in return for worshipping Dagon they'd been given all the wealth of the oceans in the abundance of fish they were able to catch, and in the strange golden alloy, which was probably washed out of their mountains in rainy-season streams. It would be the native priests, of course—their witch doctors, priests of Dagon or his 'esoteric order'—who secretly worked the gold into the jewellery whose remnants we occasionally see today.

"But the modern legend—the one you'll hear in Innsmouth and its environs—is that in return for the good fishing and the gold, the natives gave of their children to the sea, or to manlike beings who lived in the sea: the so-called 'Deep Ones,' servitors of Dagon and other alleged, er, 'deities' of the deep, such as Great Cthulhu and Mother Hydra. And the same legend has it that Innsmouth's sea captains, in their lust for alien gold, the favours of mainly forgotten gods out of doubtful myths, and the promise of life everlasting, followed suit in the sacrifice of *their* young to Dagon and the Deep Ones. Except they were not sacrifices as such but matings! Thus in *both* legends, it became possible to blame the 'Innsmouth look' or taint on this miscegenation: the mingling of Deep One and clean human blood. But of course no such matings took place because there's no such thing as a merman! Nor was there ever, but that didn't stop a handful of the more degenerate Innsmouth people from adopting the cult, as witness that weathered, white-pillared hall dedicated to the Esoteric Order of Dagon.

"Which leaves only the so-called 'epidemic' of 1927-28…

"Well, seventy years ago our society was far less tolerant. And sad to say that when stories leaked out of Innsmouth of the sheer scale of the taint—the numbers of inbred, diseased and malformed people living there—the federal government's reaction was excessive in the extreme. But there's little doubt that it would have been the same if AIDS had been found there in the same period: panic, and a knee-jerk reaction, yes. And so there followed a vast series of raids and many arrests, and a burning and dynamiting of large numbers of rotting old houses along the waterfront. But no criminal charges were brought and no one was committed for trial; just vague statements about malignant diseases, and the covert dispersal of a great many detainees into various naval and military prisons.

"Thus old Innsmouth was depopulated, and these seventy-odd years later its recovery is still only very sluggish. There is, however, a modern laboratory there now, where pathologists and other scientists—some of them Innsmouth people themselves—continue to study the taint and to offer what help they may to the descendants of survivors of those frenzied federal raids. I worked there myself, however briefly, but it was disheartening work to say the least. I saw sufferers in every stage of degeneration, and could only offer the most basic assistance to any of them. For among the doctors and other specialists there…well, the general concensus is that there's no hope for a cure as yet for those with the Innsmouth blood. And until or unless the taint is allowed to die out by gradual dispersion or depletion of that diseased foreign gene pool, there shall always be those with the Innsmouth look…"

Jilly was as calm as Jamieson had ever seen her now—too calm, he thought—like the calm before a storm. Her eyes were unblinking and had a distant quality, but her look was reflective rather than vague or vacant. And finally, after a few long moments of silence, the old man prompted her, "What now, Jilly? Is something still bothering you?"

Her gaze focussed on him and she said, "Yes. I think there is one more thing. You said something about everlasting life—that the Innsmouth seafarers had been promised everlasting life if they embraced the worship of Dagon and these other cult figures. But…what if they reneged on the cult, turned back from such worship? You see, toward the end George frequently rambled in his sleep, and I'd often hear him say that he didn't *want* to live forever, not like that. He meant his condition, of course. But I can't believe— no, no, I *can*! I *do*!—that *he* believed in s-s-such things. So, do you think—I mean, is it p-p-possible—that my husband was once a m-member of that old Innsmouth c-c-cult? And could there be anything of t-truth in it? I mean, anything at all?"

Jamieson shook his head. "Anything to it? Only in his mind, my dear. For you see, as George's condition worsened, it would have been more than a merely physical thing. He would have been doing what you are doing: looking for an explanation where none exists. And having had to do with those cultists—and knowing the legends—he might have come to believe that certain things were true. But as for you, you mustn't. You simply mustn't!"

"B-b-but that tainted blood," she said, her voice a whisper now, as if from far away. "His blood, and Geoff's blood, and…and w-w-what of Anne's?"

"Jilly, now I want you to listen." The old man took hold of her arms, grasping her very firmly. And of all the lies or half truths he had told her in the past half hour, the next would be his biggest deceit of all. "Jilly, I have known you and Anne—especially Anne—for quite a while now, and from my knowledge of the Innsmouth taint, and also from what I know and have seen of your daughter, I would be glad to stake my reputation on the fact that she is as normal as you or I."

At which she sighed, relaxing a little in her chair…

And taking that as his signal to depart, Jamieson stood up. "I must be off," he said. "It's late and I've some things to do before bed." Then, as he made his way to the door, he said: "Do give my regards to Anne, won't you? It's a shame I missed her—or perhaps not, since we needed to have our talk."

Jilly had followed him—rather stumblingly, he thought—and at the door said, "I really d-d-don't know how to thank you. My mind feels so much more at ease now. But then it always does after I-I-I've spoken with you." She waited until he'd got into his car, and waved him a shaky goodbye before closing the door.

Pulling away from the house, the old man noticed an almost furtive flicker of movement in the drapes of an upstairs window. It was Anne's bedroom; and very briefly he saw her face—those huge eyes of hers—in the gap of partly drawn-aside curtains. At which he wondered how long she had been awake; even wondered if she had been asleep! And if not, how much she'd overheard.

Or had she perhaps already known it all...?

The long winter with its various ailments—Anne White's laryngitis, and Doreen Tremain's 'flu—merged slowly into spring; green shoots became flowers in village gardens or window boxes; lowering skies brightened, becoming bluer day to day.

But among these changes were others, not nearly so natural and far less benign, and old Jamieson was witness to them all.

He would see the beachcomber—"young Geoff," indeed, as if he were just another village youth—shambling along the tidemark. But he wasn't like other youths, and he was ailing.

Jamieson watched him in his binoculars, that tired shambler on the shore: his slow lurching, feet flip-flopping, shoulders sloping, head down and collar up. And despite that the weather was much improved, he no longer went out to sea. Oh, he *looked* at the sea—constantly pausing to lift his ugly head and gaze out across that wide wet horizon—gaze longingly, the old man thought, as he attempted to read something of emotion into the near-distant visage— but the youth's great former ability in the water, and his untried but suspected strength on dry land, these seemed absent now. Plainly put, he was in decline.

The old man had heard rumours in the village pub. The fishing was much improved but Tom Foster wasn't doing as well as in previous years; he'd lost his good luck charm, the backward boy who guided his boat to the best fishing grounds. At least, that was how they saw it, the other fishermen, but it was Tom Foster himself who had told the old man the truth of it one evening in the Sailor's Rest.

"It's the boy," he said, concernedly. "Um's not umself. Um says the sea lures um, and um's afeared of it. Oh, um walks the shore and watches all the whitecaps, the seahorses come rollin' in, but um ain't about ter go aridin' on 'em. I dun't know what um means, but um keeps complainin' as how um 'ain't ready,' and doubts um ever will be, but if um 'goes now' it'll be the end of um. Lord only knows where um's thinkin' of goin'! And truth is, um sickens. So while I knows um'd come out with me if I was ter ask um, I won't fer um's sake. The only good thing: um lies in the bath a lot, keeps umself well soaked in fresh water so um's skin dun't suffer much and there be no more of them fish-lice."

And the leathery old seaman had shrugged—though in no way negligently—as he finished his pint, and then his ruminations with the words, "No more sea swimmin', no more fish-lice—it's as simple as that. But as fer the rest of it...I worries about um, that I do."

"Answer me one question," the old man had begged of Foster then. "Tell me, why did you take him in? You had no obligation in that respect. I mean, it wasn't as if the youth—the child—was of your blood. He was a foundling, and there were, well, complications right from the start."

Foster had nodded. "It were my woman, the missus, who took ter um. Her great-granny had told of just such young 'uns when um were a little 'un out in the islands. And Ma Foster felt fer um, um did. Me too, 'ventually, seein' as how we've had um all this time. But we always knew who um's dad were. No big secret that, fer um were here plain ter see. Gone now, though, but um did used ter pay um's share."

"George White gave you money?"

"Fer Geoff's upkeep, yes." Foster had readily admitted it. "That's a fact. The poor bugger were sellin' off bits of precious stuff—jewell'ry and such—in all the towns around. Fer the lad, true enough, but also fer um's own pleasure...or so I've heard it said. But that's none of my business..."

Then there was poor Jilly White. She, too—her health—was very obviously in decline. Her nightmares were of constant concern, having grown repetitive and increasingly weird to the point of grotesque. Also, her speech and mobility were suffering badly; she stuttered, often repeated herself, occasionally fell while negotiating the most simple routines both in and out of doors. Indeed, she had become something of a prisoner in her own home; she only rarely ventured down onto the beach, to sit with her daughter in the weak but welcome spring sunshine.

As to her dreams:

It had been a long-drawn-out process, but Jamieson had been patient; he had managed to extract something of the nightmarish contents of Jilly's dreams from the lady herself, the rest from Anne during the return journey from a language lesson trip into St. Austell. Unsurprisingly, all of the worst dreams were centered upon George White, Jilly's ex-husband; not on his suicide, as might at least in some part be expected, but on his disease: its progression and acceleration toward the end.

In particular she dreamed of frogs or the batrachia in general, and of fish…but *not* as creatures of Nature. The horror of these visitations was that they were completely alien, gross mutations or hybrids of man and monster. And the man was George White, his human face and something of his form transposed upon those of the amphibia and fishes alike—and all too often upon beings who had the physical components of both genera *and more!* In short, Jilly dreamed of Deep Ones, where George was a member of that aquatic society!

And Anne White told of how her mother mumbled and gibbered, gasping her horror of "great wet eyes that wouldn't or couldn't close;" or "scales as sharp and rough as a file;" or "the flaps in George's neck, going right through to the inside and pulsing like…like *gills* when he snorted or choked in his sleep!" But these things with regard to her mother's nightmares weren't all that Anne had spoken of on the occasion of that revealing drive home from her language lesson. For she had also been perfectly open in telling Jamieson:

"I know you saw me at my window that time when you brought her pills and spoke to my mother at length, the night you told her about Innsmouth. I heard you start to talk, got out of bed, and sat listening at the head of the stairs. I was as quiet as could be and must have heard almost everything you said."

And Jamieson had nodded. "Things she probably wouldn't have spoken of if she'd known you were awake? Did it…bother you, our conversation?"

"Perhaps a little…but no, not really," she had answered. "I know more than my mother gives me credit for. But about what you told her, in connection with my father and what she dreamed about him, well, there is something I'd like to know—without that you need to repeat it to her."

"Oh?"

"Yes. You said that you'd seen those sick Innsmouth people, 'in every stage of degeneration.' And I wondered…"

"…You wondered just what those stages were?" The old man had prompted her, and then gone on: "Well, there are stages and there are states. It usually depends on how they start out. The taint might occur from birth, or it might come much later. Some scarcely develop the Innsmouth look at all…while others are born with it."

"Like Geoff?"

"Like him, yes." Again Jamieson nodded. "It rather depends on the strength of the Innsmouth blood in the parents…or in at least one of them, obviously. Or in the ancestral blood line in general."

And then, out of the blue and without any hesitation, she'd said, "I know that Geoff is my half-brother. It's why my mother let's us be friends. She feels guilty for my father's sake—in his place, I mean. And so she thinks of Geoff as 'family.' Well, of a sort."

"And you? How do you think of him?"

"As my brother, do you mean?" She had offered an indecisive shake of her head. "I'm not really sure. In a way, I suppose. I don't find him horrible, if that's what you mean."

"No, of course not, and neither do I!" The old man had been quick to answer. "As a doctor, I've grown used to accepting too many abnormalities in people to be repulsed by any of them."

"Abnormalities?" Anne had cocked her head a little, favouring Jamieson with a curious, perhaps challenging look. And:

"Differences, then," he had told her.

And after a moment's silence she'd said, "Go on, then. Tell me about them: these states or stages."

"There are those born with the look, as I've mentioned," he had answered, "and those who gradually develop it, some of whom stay mostly, well, *normal*-looking. There are plenty of those in Innsmouth right now. Also, there is always a handful who retain their, er, agreeable—their acceptably, well, *human*—features for a great many years, changing only towards the end, when the metamorphosis occurs very rapidly indeed. At the hospital where I worked, some of the geneticists—Innsmouth people themselves—were trying to alter certain genes in their patients; if not to kill off the process entirely, at least to prolong the human looks of those who were likely to suffer the change."

"'Human-looking', and 'metamorphosis', and 'geneticists', Anne had nodded, thoughtfully. "But with those words—and the way you explained it—it doesn't sound so much a disease as a, well, a 'metamorphosis,' yes; and that *is* your own word! Like a pupa into a butterfly, or rather a tadpole into a frog. Except, instead of a tadpole…"

But there she'd frowned, broken off and sat back musing in her seat. "It's all very puzzling, but I think the answers are coming and that I'm beginning to understand." Then, sitting up straight again until she strained against her safety belt, she had said. "But look—we're almost home!" And urgently turning to stare at Jamieson's profile: "We're through the village and there are still some things I wanted to ask—just one or two more, that's all."

At which the old man had slowed down, allowing her time to speak, and prompting her, "Go on then, ask away."

"This cult of Dagon," she had said then. "This religion or 'Esoteric Order' in Innsmouth—does it still exist? I mean, do they still worship? And if so, what if someone with the look or the blood—what if he doesn't want to be one of them—what if he reneges and…and runs away? My mother asked you much the same question, I know. But you didn't quite answer her."

"I think," Jamieson had said then, bringing his vehicle to a halt outside the Whites' house, "I think that would be quite bad for this hypothetical person. What would he do, if or when the change came upon him? With no one to help him; none of his own kind, that is."

Anne's mother had come to the door of the house, and stood there all pale and uncertain. But Anne, getting out of the car, had looked at the old man with her penetrating gaze, and he had seen that it was all coming together for her—and that indeed she knew more than her mother had given her credit for…

In the second week of May things came to a head.

The first handful of tourists and early holidaymakers were in the village, staying at two or three cheap bed-and-breakfast places; and these city folk were making their way down onto the beaches each day, albeit muffled against the still occasionally brisk weather.

And in the lenses of Jamieson's binoculars, the gnarled Tom Foster and his malformed ward had also been seen—as often as not arguing, apparently—the younger one pulling himself away, and the elder dragging after him, shaking his head and pointing back imploringly the way they'd come. And despite that the ill-favoured youth was failing, he yet retained enough strength to power him stumblingly, stubbornly on, leaving his foster-father panting and cursing in his wake. But when the youth was alone—fluttering there like a stumpy scarecrow on the sands, with his few wisps of coarse hair blowing back from his head in the wind off the ocean—then as always he would be seen gazing out over the troubled waters, as if transfixed by their vast expanse…

It happened on a reasonably warm Sunday afternoon that the Tremains,

Jamieson, and Anne White were on the beach together, or rather at the same time. And so was young Geoff.

For ease of walking the old man held to firmer ground set back from the dunes, on a heading that would take him past the Tremains's house as he visited Jilly White's place. Doreen and John Tremain were taking the air maybe two hundred yards ahead of Jamieson; with their backs to him, they hadn't as yet observed him. And Anne was a small dot in the distance, huddled with a book in the lee of a grass-crested dune, a favourite location of hers, just one hundred or so yards this side of her mother's house. Today she stayed close to home out of necessity, for the simple reason that Jilly had taken to her bed four days ago as the result of some sort of physical or mental collapse, if not a complete nervous breakdown.

There were a very few holidaymakers on the beach...fewer still in bathing costumes, daring the water for the first time. But closer to the sea than the rest—coming from the direction of the village and avoiding the small family groups—there was young Geoff. Jamieson had his binoculars with him; he paused to focus on the youth, finding himself mildly concerned on noting his poor condition.

He was stumbling very badly now; his flabby mouth had fallen fully open, and his bulbous chin wobbled on his chest. Even at this distance, the youth's eyes seemed filmed over, and the scaly skin of his face was grey. He seemed to be gasping at the air, and his broad, rounded shoulders went up and down with the heaving of his chest.

As the old man watched, so that strange figure tore off its shapeless jacket and threw it aside, then angled its route even closer to the band of damp sand at the sea's rim. Some children paddling and splashing there, laughing as they jumped the small waves in six inches of water, noticed Geoff's approach. They at once quit their play and fell silent, backed away from him, and finally turned to run up the beach.

And sensing that something was about to happen here, Jamieson put on a little more speed. Likewise the Tremains; they too were walking faster, cresting the dunes, heading for the softer sands of the beach proper. Being that much closer to the youth, they had obviously witnessed his antics and noted his poor condition, and like the old man they'd sensed something strange in the air.

Anne, on the other hand, remained seated, reading in the scoop of her dune, as yet unaware of the drama taking shape close by.

Jamieson, no longer showing any sign of his age or possible infirmity, put on yet more speed; he was anxious to be as close as possible to whatever was happening here. He only paused when he heard a weird cry—a strange, ululant howling—following which he hurried on and crested the dunes in the prints left by the Tremains. Then, from that slightly higher elevation, and at a distance of less than one hundred and fifty yards, he scanned the scene ahead.

Having heard the weird howling, Anne was on her feet now at the crest of her dune, looking down across the beach. And there was her half-brother, up to his knees in the water, tearing off his shirt and dropping his ragged trousers, making these nerve-jangling noises as he howled, hissed, and shrieked at the sea!

Anne ran down across the beach; the Tremains hurried after, and Jamieson raced to catch up. He was vaguely aware that Jilly White had appeared on the decking at the back of her house, and was standing or staggering there in her dressing-gown. White as a ghost, clutching at the handrail with one shaking hand, Jilly held the other to her mouth.

Anne was into the water now, wading out toward the demented—or tormented—youth. John Tremain had kicked off his shoes; he tested the water, hoisted the cuffs of his trousers uselessly, and went splashing toward the pair. And meanwhile Jamieson, puffing and panting with the effort, had closed in on the scene as a whole.

Geoff had stopped hissing and howling; he grasped at Anne's hand, held it tight, pointed urgently out to sea. Then, releasing her, he made signs: *Come with me, sister, for I have to go! I am not ready, but still I must go! It calls to me…the sea is calling and I can no longer resist…I must go!*

Then he saw her uncertainty, her denial, stopped making his signs, and began dragging her deeper into the water. But it was now clear that he was deranged, unhinged, and his teeth gleamed the yellowy-white of fish-bone as he recommenced his gibbering, his howling, his awful cries of supplication…his liturgy to the unknown lords of the sea.

Jamieson was much closer now, and Tremain closer still. The headmaster grabbed at Anne, tried to fight the youth off. Geoff released Anne's hand and turned on Tremain, fastening his sharp teeth on the other's shoulder and biting through his thin shirt. Tremain gave a cry of pain! Lurching backwards, he stumbled and fell into the water, which momentarily covered his head.

But the youth saw what he had done—knew he'd done wrong and with Tremain's blood staining his face, and streaming from his gaping circle of a mouth, he appeared to regain his senses…at least partly. And shaking his head, Geoff signalled his farewell to Anne, waddled a foot deeper into the water's surge, let himself fall forward and began to swim.

He swam, and it was at once apparent that this was his natural element. And seeing him go, Jamieson thought, *Alas that he isn't equipped for it…*

Tremain had dragged himself to the beach; Anne had returned to where the water reached her knees, and watched Geoff's progress as his form diminished with distance. Jamieson helped John Tremain up out of the shallows, dampened a handkerchief in salt water, applied it to the raw, bleeding area between the other's neck and shoulder. Doreen Tremain hurried forward, wringing her hands and asking what she should do.

"Take him home," said the old man. "Keep my handkerchief on the wound to staunch the bleeding. Treat it with an antiseptic, then pad and bandage it. When John recovers from the shock take him into St. Austell for shots: anti-tetanus, and whatever else is prescribed. But don't delay. Do you understand?" She nodded, helped her husband up the beach and away.

Anne was at the water's rim. Soaked from the waist down and shocked to her core—panting and gasping—she stared at the old man with her mouth wide open. And turning her head, looking out to sea, she said, "Geoff…Geoff!"

"Let's get you home," said Jamieson, taking her hand.

"But Geoff…what of Geoff?"

"We'll call the coastguard." The old man nodded reassuringly, and threw his jacket round her shoulders.

"He said…said he wasn't ready." She allowed him to lead her from the water.

"None of us were," Jamieson muttered under his breath. "Not for this."

Half-way up the beach toward the house, they heard a gurgling cry. It was Jilly White, staggering on the decking of her ocean-facing patio, one hand on the rail, the other pointing at the sky, the horizon, the sea, the beach…and finally at her daughter and Jamieson. Her drawn face went through a variety of changes; vacant one moment, it showed total horror in the next, and finally nothing as her eyes rolled up like white marbles.

Then, as her knees gave way beneath her, Jilly crumpled to the decking and lay there jerking, drooling, and mouthing incoherently…

The coastguard found no sign of Geoff, despite that their boat could be seen slicing through the off-shore water all that day, and then on Monday from dawn till dark. A doctor—a specialist from St. Austell—gave Jilly White a thorough examination, and during a quiet, private discussion with Jamieson out of earshot of Anne, readily agreed with the old man's diagnosis. Of course

Anne asked about it after the specialist had left, but Jamieson told her it could wait until all had settled down somewhat; and in any case things being as they were, for the moment incapable of improvement, Jilly's best interests lay in resting. He, Jamieson himself, would remain in attendance, and with Anne's help he would care for her mother until other decisions were made if such should become necessary.

In the event, however, the old man didn't expect or receive too much help from Anne; no, for she was out on the beach, walking its length mile upon mile, watching the sea and only coming home to eat and sleep when she was exhausted. This remained her routine for four days, until Geoff's bloated body was washed up on a shingle beach some miles down the coast.

Then Anne slept, and slept, a day and a night.

And the next morning—after visiting her mother's bedside and finding her sleeping, however fitfully—Anne went to the old man in the hollow of her dune, and sat down with him in the sand on the first truly warm day of the year.

He was in shirt-sleeves, grey slacks, canvas shoes; dressed for the fine weather. And he had her book in his lap, unopened. Handing it over, he said, "I found it right here where you left it the other day. I was going to return it to you. You're lucky no one else stumbled on it, and that it hasn't rained."

She took the heavy old book and put it down away from him, asking, "Did you look at it?"

He shook his head. "It's your property. For all I know you might have written in it. I believe in privacy, both for myself and for others."

She took his hand and leaned against him, letting him know that come what may they were friends. "Thank you for everything that you've done, especially for my mother," she said. "I mean, I'm so glad you came here, to the village. Even knowing you *had* to come—" (a sly sideways glance at him,) "—still I'm glad. You've been here just a few months, yet I feel like I've known you, oh, for a very long time."

"I'll take that as a compliment," Jamieson answered her.

"I feel I can talk to you," she quickly went on. "I've felt that way since the first time I saw you. And after you treated Geoff when he was sick…well, then I knew it was so."

"And indeed we do talk," said the old man. "Nothing really deep, or not *too* deep, not yet—or until now?—but we talk. Perhaps it's a question of trust, of a sort of kinship?"

"Yes." She nodded. "I know I can tell you things, secrets. I've needed to tell someone things. I'd like to have been able to tell my mother, but she wouldn't have listened. Her nerves. She used to get worried, shake her head, walk away. Or rather, she would stumble away. Which has been getting worse every day. But you…you're very different."

He smiled. "Ah, well, but that's always been my lot. As I believe I once told Jilly, sometimes I'm seen as a father confessor. Sort of odd, really, because I'm not a catholic."

"Then what are you?" Anne tilted her head on one side. "I mean, what's your religion? Are you an atheist?"

"Something like that." Jamieson shrugged. "Actually, I do have certain beliefs. But I'm not one to believe in a conventional god, if that's what you're asking. And you? What do you believe in?"

"I believe in the things my father told me," she answered dreamily. "Some beautiful things, some ugly, and some strange as the strangest myths and fables in the strangest books. But of course *you* know what I mean, even if I'm not sure myself." As she spoke, she took up her book and hugged it to her chest. Bound in antique leather, dark as old oak and glossy with age, the book's title, glimpsed between Anne's spread fingers, consisted of just three ornately tooled letters: E.O.D.

"Well," said Jamieson, "and here you are with just such a book. One of your strange books, perhaps? Certainly its title is very odd. Your mother once told me she gave you such books to burn…"

She looked at the book in her hands and said, "My father's books? There were some she wanted rid of, yes. But I couldn't just burn them. This is one of them. I've read them a lot and tried to make sense of them. Sometimes I thought I understood them; at others I was at a loss. But I knew they were important and now I know why." And then, suddenly galvanized, gripping his arm below the elbow. "Can we please stop pretending? I know almost everything now…so won't you please tell me the rest? And I swear to you—whatever you tell me—it will be safe with me. I think you must know that by now."

The old man nodded and gently disengaged himself. "I think I can do that, yes. That is, as long as you're not going to be frightened by it, and provided you won't run away…like your father."

"He was very afraid, wasn't he?" she said. "But I'll never understand why he stole the books and the Innsmouth jewellery. If he hadn't taken them, maybe they'd have just let him go."

"I think that perhaps he planned to sell those books," the old man answered. "In order to support himself, naturally. For of course he would have known that they were very rare and valuable. But after he fled Innsmouth, changed his name, got back a little self-confidence and started to think clearly, he must also have realized that wherever the books surfaced they would be a sure link—a clue, a pointer—to his whereabouts. And so he kept them."

"And yet he sold the jewellery." She frowned.

"Because gold is different than books." Jamieson smiled. "It becomes very personal; the people who buy jewellery wear it, of course, but they also guard it very closely and they don't keep it on library shelves or places where others might wonder about it. Also, your father was careful not to spread it too thickly. Some here, some there; never too much in any one place. Perhaps at one time he'd reasoned that just like the books he shouldn't sell the jewellery—but then came the time when he had to."

"Yet the people of the Esoteric Order weren't any too careful with it," she said, questioningly.

"Because they consider Innsmouth their town and safe," Jamieson answered. "And also because their members rarely betray a trust. Which in turn is because there are penalties for any who do."

"Penalties?"

"There are laws, Anne. Doesn't every society have laws?"

Her huge eyes studied his, and Jamieson felt the trust they conveyed...a mutual trust, passing in both directions. And he said, "So is there anything else I should tell you right now?"

"A great many things," Anne answered, musingly. "It's just that I'm not quite sure how to ask about them. I have to think things through." But in the next moment she was alert again:

"You say my father changed his name?"

"Oh yes, as part of the merry chase he's led us—led me—all these years. But the jewellery did in the end let him down. All winter long, when I've been out and about, I've been buying it back in the towns around. I have most of it now. As for your father's name: actually, he wasn't a White but a Waite, from a long line—a very, *very* long line—of Innsmouth Waites. One of his ancestors, and mine, sailed with Obed Marsh on the Polynesian trade routes. But as for myself...well, chronologically I'm a lot closer to those old seafarers than poor George was."

She blinked, shook her head in bewilderment; the first time the old man had seen her caught unawares, which made him smile. And: "You're a Waite, too?" she said. "But...Jamieson?"

"Well, actually it's Jamie's son." He corrected her. "Jamie Waite's son, out of old Innsmouth. Have I shocked you? Is it so awful to discover that the kinship you've felt is real?"

And after the briefest pause, while once again she studied his face: "No," she answered, and shook her head. "I think I've probably guessed it—some of it—all along. And Geoff, poor Geoff…Why, it would also make you kin to him, and I think he knew it, too! It was in his eyes when he looked at you."

"Geoff?" The old man's face fell and he gave a sad shake of his head. "What a pity. But he was a hopeless case who couldn't ever have developed fully. His gills were rudimentary, useless, unformed, atrophied. Atavisms, throwbacks in bloodlines that we hoped had been successfully conditioned out, still occur occasionally. That poor boy was in one such 'state,' trapped between his ancestral heritage and his—or his father's—scientifically engineered or altered genes. And instead of cojoining, the two facets fought."

"A throwback," she said, softly. "What a horrible description!"

And the old man shrugged, sighed, and said, "Yes. Yet what else can we call him, the way Geoff was, and the way he looked? But one day, my dear, our ambassadors—our agents—will walk among people and look no different from them, and be completely accepted by them. Until eventually we Deep Ones will be the one race, the true amphibious race which nature always intended. We were the first…why, we *came* from the sea, the cradle of life itself! Given time, and the land and sea both shall be ours."

"Ambassadors…" Anne repeated him, letting it all sink in. "But in actual fact agents. Spies and fifth columnists."

"Our advance guard." He nodded. "And who knows—you may be one of them? Indeed, that's my intention."

She stroked her throat, looked suddenly alarmed. "But Geoff and me, we were of an age, of a blood. And if his—his gills? —those flaps were gills? But…" Again she stroked her throat, searchingly now. Until he caught at her hand.

"Yours are on the inside, like mine. A genetic modification which reproduced itself perfectly in you, just as in me. That's why your father's desertion was so disappointing to us, and one of the reasons why I had to track him down: to see how he would spawn, and if he'd spawn true. In your case he did. In Geoff's, he didn't."

"My gills?" Yet again she stroked her throat, and then remembered something. "Ah! My *laryngitis!* When my throat hurt last December, and you examined me! Two or three aspirins a day was your advice to my mother, and I should gargle four or five times daily with a spoonful of salt dissolved in warm water."

"You wouldn't let anyone else see you." The old man reminded her. "And why was that, I wonder? Why me?"

"Because I didn't *want* any other doctor looking at me," she replied. "I didn't want anyone else examining me. Just you."

"Kinship," he said. "And you made the right choice. But you needn't worry. Your gills—at present the merest of pink slits at the base of your windpipe—are as perfect as in any foetal or infant land-born Deep One. And they'll stay that way for…oh, a long time—as long or even longer than mine have stayed that way, and will until I'm ready—when they'll wear through. For a month or so then they'll feel tender as their development progresses, with fleshy canals like empty veins that will carry air to your land lungs. At which time you'll be as much at home in the sea as you are now on dry land. And that will be *wonderful*, my dear!"

"You want me to…to come with you? To be a…a…?"

"But you already are! There's a certain faint but distinct odour about you, Anne. Yes, and I have it, too, and so did your half-brother. But you can dilute it with pills we've developed, and then dispel it utterly with a dab of special cologne."

A much longer silence, and again she took his bare forearms in her hands, stroking down from the elbow. His skin felt quite smooth in that direction. But when she stroked upwards from the wrist…

"Yes," she said, "I suppose I am. My skin is like yours…the scales don't show. They're fine and pink and golden. But if I'm to come with you, what of my mother? You still haven't told me what's wrong with her."

And now, finally, after all these truths, the old man must tell a lie. He must, because the truth was one she'd never accept—or rather she would—and all faith gone. But there had been no other way. And so:

"Your mother," the old man hung his head, averted his gaze, started again. "Your mother, your own dear Jilly…I'm afraid she won't last much longer." That much at least was the truth.

But Anne's hand had flown to her mouth, and so he hurriedly continued. "She has CJD, Anne—Creutzfeldt-Jacob disease—the so-called mad cow disease, at a very advanced stage." (That was another truth, but not the whole truth.)

Anne's mouth had fallen open. "Does she know?"

"But how can I tell her? And how can you? She may never be herself again. And if or when she were herself, she would only worry about what will become of you. And there's no way we can tell her about…well, you know what I mean. But Anne, don't look at me like that, for there's nothing that can be done for her. There's no known cure, no hospital can help her. I wanted her to have her time here, with you. And of course I'm here to help in the final stages. That specialist from St. Austell, he agrees with me."

Finally the girl found her voice. "Then your pills were of no use to her."

"A placebo." *Now* Jamieson lied. "They were sugar pills, to give her some relief by making her *think* I was helping her."

No, not so…and no help for Jilly, who would never have let her daughter go; whose daughter never *would* have gone while her mother lived. And those pills filled with synthetic prions—rogue proteins indistinguishable from the human form of the insidious bovine disease, developed in a laboratory in shadowy old Innsmouth—eating away at Jilly's brain even now, faster and faster.

Anne's hand fell from her face. "How long?"

He shook his head. "Not long. After witnessing what happened the other day, not long at all. Days, maybe? No more than a month at best. But we shall be here, you and I. And Anne, we can make up for what she'll miss. Your years, like mine…oh, you shall have years without number!"

"It's true, then?" Anne looked at him, and Jamieson looked back but saw no sign of tears in her eyes, which was perfectly normal. "It's true that we go on—that our lives go on—for a long time? But not everlasting, surely?"

He shook his head. "Not everlasting, no—though it sometimes feels that way! I often lose count of my years. But I am your ancestor, yes."

Anne sighed and stood up. And brushing sand from her dress, she took his hand, helping him to his feet. "Shall we go and be with my mother…grandfather?"

Now his smile was broad indeed—a smile he showed only to close intimates—which displayed his small, sharp, fish-like teeth. And:

"Grandfather?" he said. "Ah, no. In fact I'm your *father's* great-great-grandfather! And as for yourself, Anne…well you must add another great."

And hand in hand they walked up the beach to the house. The young girl and the old—the *very* old—man…?

RISING WITH SURTSEY

Another jump back in time—way back, some thirty-eight years in fact, as I make this record—to my very first year of writing. For I produced Rising With Surtsey—a title that Derleth found very much to his taste—in December 1967, during the so-called Cold War, when my Military Police duties included patrolling the all-but ensieged city of Berlin. As previously stated, I was completely absorbed in Lovecraftian prose in that period, and so it shouldn't come as a surprise if the writing is flawed both by purple prose (my fault) and adjectivitis (Lovecraft's). The horror too is highly Lovecraftian, but its introduction is not nearly as subtle as it could be. If he had still been alive and working at the time, I think that HPL might have been able to do a decent revision job on this one. Also, I like to think that the storyline might have appealed to him as it did to Derleth, who published it in an anthology called "Dark Things" in 1971...

It appears that with the discovery of a live coelacanth—a fish thought to have been extinct for over seventy millions of years—we may have to revise our established ideas of the geological life spans of certain aquatic animals...
—Linkages Wonders of the Deep

Surname	—Haughtree
Christian Names	—Phillip
Date of Birth	—2 Dec 1927
Age (years)	—35

Place of Birth	—Old Beldry, Yorks.
Address	—Not applicable
Occupation	—Author

WHO STATES: (Let here follow the body of the statement)

I have asked to be cautioned in the usual manner but have been told that in view of my alleged *condition* it is not necessary…The implication is obvious, and because of it I find myself obliged to begin my story in the following way: I must clearly impart to the reader—before advising any unacquainted perusal of this statement—that I was never a fanatical believer in the supernatural. Nor was I ever given to hallucinations or visions, and I have never suffered from my nerves or been persecuted by any of the mental illnesses. There is no record to support any evidence of madness in any of my ancestors—and Dr. Stewart was quite wrong to declare me insane.

It is necessary that I make these points before permitting the reading of this, for a merely casual perusal would soon bring any conventionally minded reader to the incorrect conclusion that I am either an abominable liar or completely out of my mind, and I have little wish to reinforce Dr. Stewart's opinions…

Yet I admit that shortly after midnight on the 15th November 1963 the body of my brother did die by my hand; but at the same time I must clearly state that I am not a murderer. It is my intention in the body of this statement—which will of necessity be long, for I insist I must tell the whole story—to prove conclusively my innocence. For, indeed, I am guilty of no heinous crime, and that act of mine which terminated life in the body of my brother was nothing but the reflex action of a man who had recognized a hideous threat to the sanity of the whole world. Wherefore, and in the light of the allegation of madness levelled against me, I must now attempt to tell this tale in the most detailed fashion; I must avoid any sort of garbled sequence and form my sentences and paragraphs with meticulous care, refraining from even *thinking* on the end of it until that horror is reached…

Where best to start?

If I may quote Sir Amery Wendy-Smith:

There are fabulous legends of Star-Born creatures who inhabited this Earth many millions of years before Man appeared and who were still here, in certain black places, when he eventually evolved. They are, I am sure, to an extent here even now.

It may be remembered that those words were spoken by the eminent antiquary and archeologist before he set out upon his last, ill-fated trip into the interior of Africa. Sir Amery was hinting, I know, at the same breed of hell-spawned horror which first began to make itself apparent to me at that ghastly time eighteen months ago; and I take this into account when I remember the way in which he returned, alone and raving, from that dark continent to civilization.

At that time my brother Julian was just the opposite of myself, insofar as he was a firm believer in dark mysteries. He read omnivorously of fearsome books uncaring whether they were factual—as Frazer's *Golden Bough* and Miss Murray's *Witch-Cult*—or fanciful—like his collection of old, nigh-priceless volumes of *Weird Tales* and similar popular magazines. Many friends, I imagine, will conclude that his original derangement was due to this unhealthy appetite for the monstrous and the abnormal. I am not of such an opinion, of course, though I admit that at one time I was.

Of Julian: he had always been a strong person physically, but had never shown much strength of character. As a boy he had had the size to easily take on any bully—but never the determination. This was also where he failed as a writer, for while his plots were good he was unable to make his characters live. Being without personality himself, it was as though he was only able to reflect his own weaknesses into his work. I worked in partnership with him, filling-in plots and building life around his more or less clay figures. Up until the time of which I write, we had made a good living and had saved a reasonable sum. This was just as well, for during the period of Julian's illness, when I hardly wrote a word, I might well have found myself hard put to support both my brother and myself. Fortunately, though sadly, he was later taken completely off my hands; but that was after the onset of his trouble…

It was in May 1962 that Julian suffered his actual breakdown, but the start of it all can be traced back to the 2nd of February of that year—Candlemas—a date which I know will have special meaning to anyone with even the slightest schooling in the occult. It was on that night that he dreamed his dream of titanic basalt towers—dripping with slime and ocean ooze and fringed with great sea-mats—their weirdly proportioned bases buried in grey-green muck and their non-Euclidean-angled parapets fading into the watery distances of that unquiet submarine realm.

At the time we were engaged upon a novel of eighteenth-century romance, and I remember we had retired late. Still later I was awakened by

Julian's screams, and he roused me fully to listen to an hysterical tale of nightmare. He babbled of what he had seen lurking behind those monolithic, slimy ramparts, and I remember remarking—after he had calmed himself somewhat—what a strange fellow he was, to be a writer of romances and at the same time a reader and dreamer of horrors. But Julian was not so easily chided, and such was his fear and loathing of the dream that he refused to lie down again that night but spent the remaining hours of darkness sitting at his typewriter in the study with every light in the house ablaze.

One would think that a nightmare of such horrible intensity might have persuaded Julian to stop gorging himself with his nightly feasts of at least two hours of gruesome reading. Yet, if anything, it had the opposite effect—but now his studies were all channelled in one certain direction. He began to take a morbid interest in anything to do with oceanic horror, collecting and avidly reading such works as the German *Unter-Zee Kulten*, Gaston le Fe's *Dwellers in the Depths*, Gantley's *Hydrophinnae*, and the evil *Cthaat Aquadingen* by an unknown author. But it was his collection of fictional books which in the main claimed his interest. From these he culled most of his knowledge of the Cthulhu Mythos—which he fervently declared was not myth at all— and often expressed a desire to see an original copy of the *Necronomicon* of the mad Arab Abdul Alhazred, as his own copy of Feery's *Notes* was practically useless, merely hinting at what Julian alleged Alhazred had explained in detail.

In the following three months our work went badly. We failed to make a deadline on a certain story and, but for the fact that our publisher was a personal friend, might have suffered a considerable loss financially. It was all due to the fact that Julian no longer had the urge to write. He was too taken up with his reading to work and could no longer even be approached to talk over story plots. Not only this, but that fiendish dream of his kept returning with ever increasing frequency and vividness. Every night he suffered those same silt-submerged visions of obscene terrors the like of which could only be glimpsed in such dark tomes as were his chosen reading. But did he really suffer? I found myself unable to make up my mind. For as the weeks passed, my brother seemed to become all the more uneasy and restless by day, whilst eagerly embracing the darkening skies of evening and the bed in which he sweated out the horrors of hideous dream and nightmare…

We were leasing, for a reasonable monthly sum, a moderate house in Glasgow where we had separate bedrooms and a single study which we shared. Although he now looked forward to them, Julian's dreams had grown even worse and they had been particularly bad for two or three nights when,

in the middle of May, it happened. He had been showing an increasing interest in certain passages in the *Cthaat Aquadingen* and had heavily underscored a section in that book which ran thus:

> *Rise!*
> *O Nameless Ones:*
> *That in Thy Season*
> *Thine Own of Thy choosing.*
> *Through Thy Spells and Thy Magic,*
> *Through Dreams and Enchantry,*
> *May know of Thy Coming;*
> *And rush to Thy Pleasure,*
> *For the Love of Our Master,*
> *Knight of Cthulhu,*
> *Deep Slumberer in Green,*
> *Othuum...*

This and other bits and pieces culled from various sources, particularly
certain partly suppressed writings by a handful of authors, all allegedly "missing persons" or persons who had died in strange circumstances—namely: Andrew Phelan, Abel Keane, Claiborne Boyd, Nayland Colum, and Horvath
Blayne—had had a most unsettling effect upon my brother, so that he was
close to exhaustion when he eventually retired late on the night that the
horror really started. His condition was due to the fact that he had been
studying his morbid books almost continually for a period of three days, and
during that time had taken only brief snatches of sleep—and then only during the daylight hours, never at night. He would answer, if ever I attempted
to remonstrate with him, that he did not *want* to sleep at night "when the
time is so near" and that "there was so much that would be strange to him
in the Deeps." Whatever *that* was supposed to mean...

After he had retired that night I worked on for an hour or so before
going to bed myself. But before leaving our study I glanced at that with
which Julian had last been so taken up, and I saw—as well as the above non-
sense, as I then considered it—some jottings copied from the *Life of St. Brendan* by the sixth-century Abbot of Clonfert in Galway:

> All that day the brethren, even when they were no longer in
> view of the island, heard a loud wailing from the inhabitants thereof,
> and a noisome stench was perceptible at a great distance. Then

St. Brendan sought to animate the courage of the brethren, saying: "Soldiers of Christ, be strong in faith unfeigned and in the armour of the spirit, for we are now on the confines of hell!"

I have since studied the *Life of St. Brendan*, and have found that which made me shudder in awful recognition—though at the reading I could not correlate the written word and my hideous disquiet; there was just something in the book which was horribly disturbing—and, moreover, I have found other references to historic oceanic eruptions; namely, those which sank Atlantis and Mu, those recorded in the *Liber Miraculorem* of the monk and chaplain Herbert of Clairvaux in France in the years 1178-80, and that which was closer to the present and which is known only through the medium of the suppressed *Johansen Narrative*. But at the time of which I write, such things only puzzled me and I could never, not even in my wildest dreams, have guessed what was to come.

I am not sure how long I slept that night before I was eventually roused by Julian and half awoke to find him crouching by my bed, whispering in the darkness. I could feel his hand gripping my shoulder, and though I was only half-awake I recall the pressure of that strong hand and something of what he said. His voice had the trance-like quality of someone under deep hypnosis, and his hand jerked each time he put emphasis on a word.

"They are *preparing*…They will *rise*…They have not mustered *The Greater Power*, nor have they the blessing of *Cthulhu*, and the rising will not be *permanent* nor go recorded…But the effort will suffice for the *Mind-Transfer*…For the *Glory* of Othuum…

"Using those *Others* in Africa, those who took Sir Amery Wendy-Smith, *Shudde-M'ell* and his hordes, to relay their messages and dream-pictures, they have finally defeated the magic *spell* of deep water and can now *control* dreams as of old—despite the oceans which cover them! Once more they have mastery of dreams, but to perform the Transfer they need not even break the surface of the water—a lessening of the pressure will suffice.

"Ce'haie, ce'haie!!!

"*They rise even now*; and He knows me, searching me out…And my mind, which they have prepared in dreams, will be here to meet Him, for I am *ready* and they need wait no longer. My ignorance is nothing—I do not *need* to know or understand! They will *show* me; as, in dreams, they have showed me the *Deep Places*. But they are unable to draw from my weak mind, or from *any* mortal brain, *knowledge of the surface*…The mental images of men are not *strongly* enough transmitted…And the deep water—even though, through the work of Shudde-M'ell, they have mostly conquered its ill effects—*still* interferes with those blurred images which they *have* managed to obtain...

"*I am the chosen one*...Through *His* eyes in my *body* will they again acquaint themselves *entirely* with the surface; that in time, when the stars are *right*, they may perform the *Great Rising*...Ah! The Great Rising! *The damnation of Hastur!* The dream of *Cthulhu* for countless ages...When *all* the deep dwellers, the dark denizens, the *sleepers* in silted cities, will *again* confound the world with their powers...

"For that is not dead which can lie *forever*, and when mysterious times have passed, *it shall be again as it once was*...Soon, when the Transfer is done, He shall walk the Earth *in my guise*, and I the great deeps *in His*! So that where they ruled *before* they may one day rule *again*—aye—even the brethren of *Yibb-Tstll* and the sons of dreaming *Cthulhu* and their servants— *for the Glory of R'lyeh...*"

That is as much of it as I can remember, and even then not at all clearly, and as I have said, it was nothing to me at that time but gibberish. It is only since then that I have acquainted myself with certain old legends and writings; and in particular, in connection with the latter part of my brother's fevered mouthings, the inexplicable couplet of the mad Arab Abdul Alhazred:

"That is not dead which can eternal lie,
And with strange aeons even death may die."

But I digress.

It took me some time, after the drone of Julian's outré monologue had died away, to realize that he was no longer in the room with me and that there was a chill morning breeze blowing through the house. In his own room his clothes still hung neatly where he had left them the night before— but Julian had gone, leaving the door to the house swinging open.

I dressed quickly and went out to search the immediate neighbourhood— with negative results. Then, as dawn was breaking, I went into a police-station to discover—to my horror—that my brother was in "protective custody." He had been found wandering aimlessly through the northern streets of the city mumbling about "giant Gods" waiting for something in the ocean deeps. He did not seem to realize that his sole attire was his dressing-gown, nor did he appear to recognize me when I was called to identify him. Indeed, he seemed to be suffering from the aftereffects of some terrible shock which had left him in a trauma-like state, totally incapable of rational thought. He would only mumble unguessable things and stare blankly towards the northern wall of his cell; an awful, mad light glowing in the back of his eyes...

My tasks were sufficient that morning to keep me amply occupied, and horribly so; for Julian's condition was such that on the orders of a police psychiatrist he was transferred from his police-station cell to Oakdeene Sanatorium for "observation." Nor was it easy to get him attended to at the sanatorium. Apparently the supervisors of that institute had had their own share of trouble the previous night. When I did eventually get home, around noon, my first thought was to check the daily newspapers for any reference to my brother's behaviour. I was glad, or as glad as I could be in the circumstances, to find that Julian's activities had been swamped from a more prominent place of curious interest—which they might well have otherwise claimed—by a host of far more serious events.

Strangely, those other events were similar to my brother's trouble in that they all seemed concerned with mental aberrations in previously normal people or, as at Oakdeene, increases in the activities of the more dangerous inmates of lunatic asylums all over the country. In London a businessman of some standing had hurled himself bodily from a high roof declaring that he must "fly to Yuggoth on the rim." Chandler Davies, who later died raving mad at Woodholme, painted "in a trance of sheer inspiration" an evil black and grey *G'harne Landscape* which his outraged and frightened mistress set on fire upon its completion. Stranger still, a Cotswold rector had knifed to death two members of his congregation who, he later protested to the police, "had no right to exist," and from the coast, near Harden in Durham, strange midnight swimmers had been seen to make off with a fisherman who screamed of "giant frogs" before disappearing beneath the still sea...It was as if, on that queer night, some madness had descended—or, as I now believe, had risen—to blanket the more susceptible minds of certain people with utter horror.

But all these things, awful as they were, were not that which I found most disturbing. Looking back on what Julian had murmured in my bedroom while I lay in half-slumber, I felt a weird and inexplicable chill sweep over me as I read, in those same newspapers, of an amateur seismologist who believed he had traced *a submarine disturbance in the ocean between Greenland and the northern tip of Scotland...*

What was it Julian had whispered about a rising which would not go recorded? Certainly something had been recorded happening in the depths of the sea!…But, of course, that was ridiculous, and I shook off the feeling of dread which had gripped me on reading the item. Whatever that deep oceanic disturbance had been, its cause could only be coincidental to my brother's behaviour.

So it was that rather than ponder the reason for so many outré happenings that ill-omened night I thanked our lucky stars that Julian had got away with so light a mention in the press; for what had occurred could have been damaging to both of us had it been given greater publicity.

Not that any of this bothered Julian! Nothing bothered him, for he stayed in that semi-conscious state in which the police had found him for well over a year. During that year his weird delusions were of such a fantastic nature that he became, as it were, the psychological pet and project of a well-known Harley Street alienist. Indeed, after the first month or so, so strong did the good doctor's interest in my brother's case become, he would accept no fee for Julian's keep or treatment; and, though I visited Julian frequently, whenever I was in London, Dr. Stewart would never listen to my protests or hear of me paying for his services. Such was his patient's weird case that the doctor declared himself extremely fortunate to be in a position where he had the opportunity to study such a fantastic mind. It amazes me now that the same man who proved so understanding in his dealings with my brother should be so totally devoid of understanding with me; yet that is the pass to which the turn of events has brought me. Still, it was plain my brother was in good hands, and in any case I could hardly afford to press the matter of payment; Dr. Stewart's fees were usually astronomical.

It was shortly after Dr. Stewart "took Julian in" that I began to study my brother's star-charts, both astronomical and astrological, and delved deep into his books on the supernatural arts and sciences. I read many peculiar volumes during that period and became reasonably familiar with the works of Fermold, Lévi, Prinn, and Gezrael, and—in certain darker reaches of the British Museum—I shuddered to the literacy lunacy of Magnus, Glynnd, and Alhazred. I read the *R'lyeh Text* and the *Johansen Narrative* and studied the fables of lost Atlantis and Mu. I crouched over flaking tomes in private collections and tracked down all sources of oceanic legend and myth with which I came into contact. I read the manuscript of Andrew Phelan, the deposition of Abel Keane, the testament of Claiborne Boyd, the statement of Nayland Colum, and the narrative of Horvath Blayne. The papers of Jefferson Bates fell to my unbelieving scrutiny, and I lay awake at nights thinking of the hinted fate of Enoch Conger.

And I need never have bothered.

All the above delvings took the better part of a year to complete, by which time I was no nearer a solution to my brother's madness than when I began. No, perhaps that is not quite true. On reflection I think it quite possible that a man might go mad after exploring such dark avenues as these I have mentioned—and especially a man such as Julian, who was more than normally sensitive to begin with. But I was by no means satisfied that this was the whole answer. After all, his interest in such things had been lifelong; I could still see no reason why such an interest should suddenly accumulate so terribly. No, I was sure that the start of it all had been that Candlemas dream.

But at any rate, the year had not been totally lost. I still did not believe in such things—dark survivals of elder times; great ancient gods waiting in the ocean depths; impending doom for the human race in the form of nightmare ocean-dwellers from the beginning of time—how could I and retain my own sanity? But I had become fairly erudite as regards these darker mysteries of elder Earth. And certain facets of my strange research had been of particular interest to me. I refer to what I had read of the oddly similar cases of Joe Slater, the Catskill Mountains vagabond in 1900-01, Nathaniel Wingate Peaslee of Miskatonic University in 1908-13, and Randolph Carter of Boston, whose disappearance in 1928 was so closely linked with the inexplicable case of the Swami Chandraputra in 1930. True, I had looked into other cases of alleged demonic possession—all equally well authenticated— but those I have mentioned seemed to have a special significance, as they paralleled more than roughly that case which I was researching and which involved so terribly my brother.

But time had passed quickly and it was a totally unexpected shock to me, though one of immeasurable relief and pleasure, to find in my letter-box one July morning in 1963 a letter from Dr. Stewart which told of Julian's rapid improvement. My joy and amazement can be well imagined when, on journeying down to London the very next day, to the practice of Dr. Stewart, I found my brother returned—so far as could be ascertained in such a short time—to literally complete mental recovery. Indeed, it was the doctor himself who, on my arrival, informed me that Julian's recovery was now complete, that my brother had *fully* recovered almost overnight: but I was not so sure—there appeared to be one or two anomalies.

These apart, though, the degree of recovery which had been accomplished was tremendous. When I had last seen my brother, only a month earlier, I had felt physically sickened by the unplumbed depths of his delusions. I had, on that occasion, gone to stand beside him at the barred window from which I was told he always stared blindly northwards, and in answer to my careful greeting he had said: "Cthulhu, Othuum, Dagon: the Deep Ones in Darkness; all deeply dreaming, awaiting awakening…" Nor had I been able to extract anything from him at all except such senseless mythological jargon.

What a transformation! Now he greeted me warmly—though I imagined his recognition of me to be a trifle slow—and after I had delightedly talked with him for a while I came to the conclusion that so far as I could discern, and apart from one new idiosyncrasy, he seemed to be the same man I had known before the onset of the trouble. This oddity I have mentioned was simply that he seemed to have developed a weird photophobia and now wore large, shielded, dark-lensed spectacles which denied one the slightest glimpse of his eyes even from the sides. But, as I later found out, there was an explanation even for these enigmatic-looking spectacles.

While Julian prepared himself for the journey back to Glasgow, Dr. Stewart took me to his study where I could sign the necessary release documents and where he could tell me of my brother's fantastic recovery. It appeared that one morning only a week earlier, on going to his exceptional patient's room, the doctor had found Julian huddled beneath his blankets. Nor would my brother come out or allow himself to be brought out until the doctor had agreed to bring him that pair of very dark-lensed spectacles. Peculiar though this muffled request had been, it had delighted the astonished alienist, constituting as it did the first conscious recognition of existence that Julian had shown since the commencement of his treatment.

And the spectacles had proved to be worth their weight in gold, for since their advent Julian had rapidly progressed to his present state of normalcy. The only point over which the doctor seemed unhappy was that to date my brother had point-blank refused to relinquish the things; he declared simply that the light *hurt his eyes!* To some degree, however, the good doctor informed me, this was only to be expected. During his long illness Julian had departed so far from the normal world as it were, that his senses, unused, had partly atrophied—literally ceasing to function. His recovery had left him in the position of a man who, trapped in a dark cave for a long period of time, is suddenly released to face the bright outside world: which also explained in part the clumsiness which had attended Julian's every physical action during the first days of his recovery. One of the doctor's assistants has found occasion to remark upon the most odd way in which my brother had tended to wrap his arms around things which he wanted to lift or examine—even small things—as though he had forgotten what his fingers were for! Also, at first, the patient had tended to waddle rather than walk, almost in the manner of a penguin, and his recently reacquired powers of intelligent expression had lapsed at times in the queerest manner—when his speech had degenerated to nothing more than a guttural, hissing parody of the English language. But all these abnormalities had vanished in the first few days, leaving Julian's recovery as totally unexplained as had been his decline.

In the first-class compartment on the London-Glasgow train, on our way north, having exhausted the more obvious questions I had wanted to put to my restored brother—questions to which, incidentally, his answers had seemed guardedly noncommittal—I had taken out a pocketbook and started to read. After a few minutes, startled by a passing train, I had happened to glance up...and was immediately glad that Julian and I were alone in the compartment. For my brother had obviously found something of interest in an old newspaper, and I do not know what others might have thought of the look upon his face...As he read his face bore an unpleasant and, yes, almost evil expression. It was made to look worse by those strange spectacles; a mixture of cruel sarcasm, black triumph, and tremendous contempt. I was taken aback, but said nothing, and later—when Julian went into the corridor for a breath of fresh air—I picked up the newspaper and turned to the section he had been reading, which perhaps had caused the weird distortion of his features. I saw at once what had affected him, and a shadow of the old fear flickered briefly across my mind as I read the article. It was not strange that what I read was new to me—I had hardly seen a newspaper since the horror began a year previously—but it was as though this was the same report I had read at that time. It was all there, almost a duplicate of the occurrences of that night of evil omen: the increased activities of lunatics all over the country, the sudden mad and monstrous actions of previously normal people, the cult activity and devil-worship in the Midlands, the sea-things sighted off Harden on the coast, and more inexplicable occurrences in the Cotswolds.

A chill as of strange ocean-floors touched my heart, and I quickly thumbed through the remaining pages of the paper—and almost dropped the thing when I came across that which I had more than half expected. For submarine disturbances had been recorded in the ocean between Greenland and the northern tip of Scotland. And more—I instinctively glanced at the date at the top-centre of the page, *and saw that the newspaper was exactly one week old*...It had first appeared on the stands on the very morning when Dr. Stewart had found my brother huddled beneath the blankets in the room with the barred windows.

✤ ✤ ✤

Yet apparently my fears were groundless. On our return to the house in Glasgow the first thing my brother did, to my great delight and satisfaction, was destroy all his old books of ancient lore and sorcery; but he made no attempt to return to his writing. Rather he mooned about the house like some lost soul, in what I imagined to be a mood of frustration over those mazed months of which he said he could remember nothing. And not once, until the night of his death, did I see him without those spectacles. I believe he even wore the things to bed—but the significance of this, and something he had mumbled that night in my room, did not dawn on me until much later.

But of those spectacles: I had been assured that this photophobia would wear off, yet as the days went by it became increasingly apparent that Dr. Stewart's assurances had gone for nothing. And what was I to make of that other change I had noticed? Whereas before Julian had been almost shy and retiring, with a weak chin and a personality to match, he now seemed to be totally out of character, in that he asserted himself over the most trivial things whenever the opportunity arose, and his face—his lips and chin in particular—had taken on a firmness completely alien to his previous physiognomy.

It was all most puzzling, and as the weeks passed I became ever more aware that far from all being well with that altered brother of mine something was seriously wrong. Apart from his brooding, a darker horror festered within him. Why would he not admit the monstrous dreams which constantly invaded his sleep? Heaven knows he slept little enough as it was; and when he did he often roused me from my own slumbers by mumbling in the night of those same horrors which had featured so strongly in his long illness.

But then, in the middle of October, Julian underwent what I took to be a real change for the better. He became a little more cheerful and even dabbled with some old manuscripts long since left abandoned—though I do not think he did any actual work on them—and towards the end of the month he sprang a surprise. For quite some time, he told me, he had had a wonderful story in mind, but for the life of him he could not settle to it. It was a tale he would have to work on himself; and it would be necessary for him to do much research, as his material would have to be very carefully prepared. He asked that I bear with him during the period of his task and allow him as much privacy as our modest house could afford. I agreed to everything he suggested, though I could not see why he found it so necessary to have a lock put on his door; or, for that matter, why he cleared out the spacious cellar beneath the house "for future use." Not that I questioned his actions. He had asked for privacy, and as far as I could assist him he would have it. But I admit to having been more than somewhat curious.

From then on I saw my brother only when we ate—which for him was not any too often—and when he left his room to go to the library for books, a thing he did with clockwork regularity every day. With the first few of these excursions I made a point of being near the door of the house when he returned, for I was puzzled as to what form his work was going to take and I thought I might perhaps gain some insight if I could see his books of reference.

If anything, the materials Julian borrowed from the library only served to add to my puzzlement. What on Earth could he want with Lauder's *Nuclear Weapons and Engines*, Schall's *X-Rays*, Couderc's *The Wider Universe*, Ubbelohde's *Man and Energy*, Keane's *Modern Marvels of Science*, Stafford Clarke's *Psychiatry Today*, Schubert's *Einstein*, Geber's *The Electrical World*, and all the many volumes of *The New Scientist* and *The Progress of Science* with which he returned each day heavily burdened? Still, nothing he was doing gave me any cause to worry as I had in the old days, when his reading had been anything but scientific and had involved those dreadful works which he had now destroyed. But my partial peace of mind was not destined to last for very long.

One day in mid-November—elated by a special success which I had achieved in the writing of a difficult chapter it my own slowly shaping book—I went to Julian's room to inform him of my triumph. I had not seen him at all that morning, but the fact that he was out did not become apparent until, after knocking and receiving no reply, I entered his room. It had been Julian's habit of late to lock his door when he went out, and I was surprised that on this occasion he had not done so. I saw then that he had left the door open purposely so that I might see the note he had left for me on his bedside table. It was scribbled on a large sheet of white typing paper in awkward, tottering letters, and the message was blunt and to the point:

Phillip,
    Gone to London for four or five days. Research. Brit. Museum…
                                   Julian

Somewhat disgruntled, I turned to leave the room and as I did so noticed my brother's diary lying open at the foot of his bed where he had thrown it. The book itself did not surprise me—before his trouble he had always, kept such notes—and not being a snoop I would have left the room there and then had I not glimpsed a word—*or name*—which I recognized on the open, hand-written pages: *"Cthulhu."*

Simply that…yet it set my mind awhirl with renewed doubts. Was Julian's trouble reasserting itself? Did he yet require psychiatric treatment and were his original delusions returning? Remembering that Dr. Stewart had warned me of the possibility of a relapse, I considered it my duty to read all that my brother had written—which was where I met with a seemingly insurmountable problem. The difficulty was simply this: I was *unable* to read the diary, for it was written in a completely alien, cryptically cuneiform script the like of which I had ever seen only in those books which Julian had burned. There was a distinct resemblance in those weird characters to the minuscules and dot-groups of the *G'harne Fragments*—I remembered being struck by an article on them in one of Julian's books, an archeological magazine—but only a resemblance; the diary contained nothing I could understand except that one word, *Cthulhu,* and even that had been scored through by Julian, as if on reflection, and a weird squiggle of ink had been crammed in above it as a replacement.

I was not slow to come to a decision as to what my proper course of action should be. That same day, taking the diary with me, I went down to Wharby on the noon train. That article on the *G'harne Fragments* which I had remembered reading had been the work of the curator of the Wharby Museum, Professor Gordon Walmsley of Goole; who, incidentally, had claimed the first translation of the fragments over the claim of the eccentric and long-vanished antiquarian and archeologist Sir Amery Wendy-Smith. The professor was an authority on the Phitmar Stone—that contemporary of the famous Rosetta Stone with its key inscriptions in two forms of Egyptian hieroglyphs—and the Geph Columns Characters, and had several other translations or feats of antiquarian deciphering to his credit. Indeed, I was extremely fortunate to find him in at the museum, for he planned to fly within the week to Peru where yet another task awaited his abecedarian talents. None the less, busy with arrangements as he was, he was profoundly interested in the diary; enquiring where the hieroglyphics within had been copied, and by whom and to what purpose? I lied, telling him my brother had copied the inscriptions from a black stone monolith somewhere in the mountains of Hungary; for I knew that just such a stone exists, having once seen mention of it in one of my brother's books. The professor squinted his eyes suspiciously at my lie but was so interested in the diary's strange characters that he quickly forgot whatever it was that had prompted his suspicion. From then until I was about to leave his study, located in one of the museum's rooms, we did not speak. So absorbed did he become with the diary's contents that I think he completely forgot my presence in the room. Before I left, however, I managed to extract a promise from him that the diary would be returned to my Glasgow address within three days and that a copy of his translation, if any, would accompany it. I was glad that he did not ask me why I required such a translation.

My faith in the professor's abilities was eventually borne out—but not until far too late. For Julian returned to Glasgow on the morning of the third day—earlier by twenty-four hours than I had been led to believe, and his diary still had not been returned—nor was he slow to discover its loss.

I was working half-heartedly at my book when my brother made his appearance. He must have been to his own room first. Suddenly I felt a presence in my room with me. I was so lost in my half-formed imaginings and ideas that I had not heard my door open; nevertheless I knew something was in there with me. I say *something*; and that is the way it was! I was being observed—but not, I felt, by a human being! Carefully, with the short hair of my neck prickling with an uncanny life of its own, I turned about. Standing in the open doorway with a look on his face which I can only describe as being utterly hateful was Julian. But even as I saw him, his horribly writhing features composed themselves behind those enigmatic dark glasses and he forced an unnatural smile.

"I seem to have mislaid my diary, Phillip," he said slowly. "I'm just in from London and I can't seem to find the thing anywhere. I don't suppose you've seen it, have you?" There was the suggestion of a sneer in his voice, an unspoken accusation. "I don't need the diary really, but there are one or two things in it which I wrote in code—ideas I want to use in my story. I'll let you in on a secret! It's a *fantasy* I'm writing! I mean—horror, science fiction, and fantasy—they're all the rage these days; it's about time we broke into the field. You shall see the rough work as soon as it's ready. But now, seeing as you obviously haven't seen my diary, if you'll excuse me, I want to get some of my notes together."

He left the room quickly, before I could answer, and I would be lying if I said I was not glad to see him go. And I could not help but notice that with his departure the feeling of an alien presence also departed. My legs felt suddenly weak beneath me as a dreadful aura of foreboding settled like a dark cloud over my room. Nor did that feeling disperse—rather it tightened as night drew on.

Lying in my bed that night I found myself going again and again over Julian's strangeness, trying to make some sense of it all. A fantasy? Could it be?

It was so unlike Julian; and why, if it was only a story, had his look been so terrible when he was unable to find his diary? And why write a story in a diary at all? Oh! He had liked reading weird stuff—altogether too much, as I have explained—but he had never before shown any urge to *write* it! And what of the books he had borrowed from the library? They had not seemed to be works he could possibly use in connection with the construction of a fantasy! And there was something else, something which kept making brief appearances in my mind's eye but which I could not quite bring into focus. Then I had it—the thing which had been bothering me ever since I first saw that diary: *where in the name of all that's holy had Julian learned to write in hieroglyphics?*

That cinched it!

No, I did not believe that Julian was writing a story at all. That was only an excuse he had created to put me off the track. But what track? What did he think he was doing? Oh! It was obvious; he was on the verge of another breakdown, and the sooner I got in touch with Dr. Stewart the better. All these tumultuous thoughts kept me awake until a late hour, and if my brother was noisy again that night I did not hear him. I was so mentally fatigued that when I eventually nodded off I slept the sleep of the dead.

Is it not strange how the light of day has the power to drive away the worst terrors of night? With the morning my fears were much abated and I decided to wait a few more days before contacting Dr. Stewart. Julian spent all morning and afternoon locked in the cellar, and finally—again becoming alarmed as night drew near—I determined to reason with him, if possible, over supper. During the meal I spoke to him, pointing out how strangely he seemed to be acting and lightly mentioning my fears of a relapse. I was somewhat taken aback by his answers. He argued it was my own fault he had had to resort to the cellar in which to work, stating that the cellar appeared to be the only place where he could be sure of any privacy. He laughed at my mention of a relapse, saying he had never felt better in his life! When he again mentioned "privacy" I knew he must be referring to the unfortunate incident of the missing diary and was shamed into silence. I mentally cursed Professor Walmsley and his whole museum.

Yet, in direct opposition to all my brother's glib explanations, that night was the worst; for Julian gibbered and moaned in his sleep, making it impossible for me to get any rest at all; so that when I arose, haggard and withdrawn, late on the morning of the 13th, I knew I would soon have to take some definite action.

I saw Julian only fleetingly that morning, on his way from his room to the cellar, and his face seemed pale and cadaverous. I guessed that his dreams were having as bad an effect upon him as they were on me; yet rather than appearing tired or hag-ridden he seemed to be in the grip of some feverish excitement.

Now I became more worried than ever and even scribbled two letters to Dr. Stewart, only later to ball them up and throw them away. If Julian was genuine in whatever he was doing, I did not want to spoil his faith in me—what little of it was left—and if he was not genuine? I was becoming morbidly curious to learn the outcome of his weird activities. None the less, twice that day, at noon and later in the evening, when as usual my fears got the better of me, I hammered at the cellar door demanding to know what was going on in there. My brother completely ignored these efforts of mine at communication, but I was determined to speak to him. When he finally came out of the cellar, much later that night, I was waiting for him at the door. He turned the key in the lock behind him, carefully shielding the cellar's contents from my view, and regarded me curiously from behind those horrid dark glasses before offering me the merest parody of a smile.

"Phillip, you've been very patient with me," he said, taking my elbow and leading me up the cellar steps, "and I know I must have seemed to be acting quite strangely and inexplicably. It's all very simple really, but for the moment I can't explain just what I'm about. You'll just have to keep faith with me and wait. If you're worried that I'm heading for another bout of, well, *trouble*—you can forget it. I'm perfectly all right. I just need a little more time to finish off what I'm doing—and then, the day after tomorrow, I'll take you in there"—he nodded over his shoulder—"into the cellar, and show you what I've got. All I ask is that you're patient for just one more day. Believe me, Phillip, you've got a revelation coming which will shake you to your very roots; and afterwards—you'll understand everything. Don't ask me to explain it all now—you wouldn't believe it! But seeing is believing, and when I take you in there you'll be able to see for yourself."

He seemed so reasonable, so sensible—if a trifle feverish—and so excited, almost like a child about to show off some new toy. Wanting to believe him, I allowed myself to be easily talked around and we went off together to eat a late meal.

❖ ❖ ❖

Julian spent the morning of the 14th transferring all his notes—great sheaves of them which I had never suspected existed—together with odds and ends in small cardboard boxes, from his room to the cellar. After a meagre lunch he was off to the library to "do some final checking" and to return a number of books lately borrowed. While he was out I went down to the cellar—only to discover that he had locked the door and taken the key with him. He returned and spent the entire afternoon locked in down there, to emerge later at night looking strangely elated. Still later, after I had retired to my room, he came and knocked on my door.

"The night is exceptionally clear, Phillip, and I thought I'd have a look at the sky…the stars have always fascinated me, you know? But the window in my room doesn't really show them off too well; I'd appreciate it if you'd allow me to sit in here and look out for a while?"

"By all means do, old fellow, come on in," I answered, agreeably surprised. I left my easy chair and went to stand beside him after he crossed the room to lean on the windowsill. He peered through those strange, dark lenses up and out into the night. He was, I could see, intently studying the constellations, and as I glanced from the sky to his face I mused aloud: "Looking up there, one is almost given to believe that the stars have some purpose other than merely making the night look pretty."

Abruptly my brother's manner changed. "What d'you mean by that?" He snapped, staring at me in an obviously suspicious fashion. I was taken aback. My remark had been completely innocuous.

"I mean that perhaps those old astrologers had something after all," I answered.

"Astrology is an ancient and exact science, Phillip—you shouldn't talk of it so lightly." He spoke slowly, as though restraining himself from some outburst. Something warned me to keep quiet, so I said no more. Five minutes later he left. Pondering my brother's odd manner, I sat there a while longer; and, as I looked up at the stars winking through the window across the room, I could not help but recall a few of those words he had mumbled in the darkness of my bedroom so long ago at the onset of his breakdown. He had said:

"That in time, *when the stars are right*, they may perform the Great Rising…"

There was no sleep at all for me that night; the noises and mutterings, the mouthings and gibberings which came, loud and clear, from Julian's room would not permit it. In his sleep he talked of such eldritch and inexplicable things as the Deep Green Waste, the Scarlet Feaster, the Chained Shoggoth, the Lurker at the Threshold, Yibb-Tstll, Tsathoggua, the Cosmic Screams, the Lips of Bugg-Shash, and the Inhabitants of the Frozen Chasm. Towards morning, out of sheer exhaustion, I eventually nodded off into evil dreams which claimed my troubled subconscious until I awoke shortly before noon on the 15th.

Julian was already in the cellar, and as soon as I had washed and dressed, remembering his promise to "show me" what he had got, I started off down there. But at the top of the cellar steps my feet were suddenly arrested by the metallic *clack* of the letter-box flap in the front door of the house.

The diary!

Unreasonably fearing that Julian might also have heard the noise, I raced back along the passage to the door, snatched up the small stamped and addressed brown-paper parcel which lay on the inside door-mat, and fled with the thing to my room. I locked myself in and ripped open the parcel. I had tried Julian's door earlier and knew it to be unlocked. Now I planned to go in and drop the diary down behind the headboard of his bed while he was still in the cellar. In this way he might be led to believe he had merely misplaced the book. But, after laying aside the diary to pick up and read the stapled sheets which had fallen loose and fluttered to the floor, I forgot all about my planned deception in the dawning knowledge of my brother's obvious impending insanity. Walmsley had done as he had promised. I cast his brief, eagerly enquiring letter aside and quickly, in growing horror, read his translation of Julian's cryptical notes. It was all there, all the proof I needed, in neat partially annotated paragraphs; but I did not need to read it all. Certain words and phrases, lines and sentences, seemed to leap upon the paper, attracting my frantically searching eyes:

"This shape/form? sickens me. Thanks be there is not long to wait. There is difficulty in the fact that this form/body/shape? would not obey me at first, and I fear it may have alerted—(?—?) to some degree. Also, I have to hide/protect/conceal ? that of me which also came through with the transfer/journey/passage?

"I know the mind of (?—?) fares badly in the Deeps…and of course his eyes were ruined/destroyed? completely…

"Curse the water that quiets/subdues? Great (?)'s power. In these few times/periods? I have looked upon/seen/ observed? much and studied what I have seen and read—but I have had to gain such knowledge secretly. The mind-sendings/mental messages (telepathy?) from my kin/brothers? at (?—?) near that place which men call Devil—(?) were of little use to me, for the progress these beings/creatures? have made is fantastic in the deep times/moments/ periods? since their (?) attack on those at Devil—(?).

"I have seen much and I know the time is not yet ripe for the great rising/coming? They have developed weapons of (?) power. We would risk/chance? defeat—and that must never be.

"But if (??????? they ???) turn their devices against themselves (??? bring ?) nation against nation (?? then ??) destructive/cataclysmic? war rivalling (name—possibly *Azathoth*, as in *Pnakotic Mss)*.

"The mind of (?—?) has broken under the strain of the deeps…It will now be necessary to contact my rightful shape in order to rebecome one/re-enter? it.

"*Cthulhu?* (?) triumph (???) I am eager to return to my own shape/form/body? I do not like the way this brother—(the word brother implying falseness?) has looked at me…but he suspects nothing…"

There was more, much more, but I skipped over the vast majority of the translation's remaining contents and finished by reading the last paragraph which, presumably, had been written in the diary shortly before Julian took himself off to London:

"(Date?)…six more (short periods of time?) to wait…Then the stars should be right/in order/positioned? and if all goes well the transfer can be performed/accomplished?"

That was all; but it was more than enough. That reference about my not "suspecting" anything, in connection with those same horrors which had been responsible for his first breakdown, was sufficient finally to convince me that my brother was seriously ill!

Taking the diary with me, I ran out of my room with one thought in my mind. Whatever Julian thought he was doing I had to stop him. Already his delvings constituted a terrible threat to his health, and who could say but that the next time a cure might not be possible? If he suffered a second attack, there was the monstrous possibility that he would remain permanently insane.

Immediately I started my frantic hammering, he opened the cellar door and I literally fell inside. I say I fell; indeed, I did—I fell from a sane world into a lunatic, alien, nightmare dimension totally outside any previous experience. As long as I live I shall never forget what I saw. The floor in the centre of the cellar had been cleared, and upon it, chalked in bold red strokes, was a huge and unmistakable evil symbol. I had seen it before in those books which were now destroyed…and now I recoiled at what I had later read of it! Beyond the sign, in one corner, a pile of ashes was all that remained of Julian's many notes. An old iron grating had been fixed horizontally over bricks, and the makings of a fire were already upon it. A cryptographic script, which I recognized as being the blasphemous *Nyhargo Code*, was scrawled in green and blue chalk across the walls, and the smell of incense hung heavily in the air. The whole scene was ghastly, unreal, a living picture from Eliphas Lévi—nothing less than the lair of a sorcerer! Horrified, I turned to Julian—in time to see him lift a heavy iron poker and start the stunning swing downwards towards my head. Nor did I lift a finger to stop him. I could not—*for he had taken off those spectacles, and the sight of his terrible face had frozen me rigid as polar ice...*

Regaining consciousness was like swimming up out of a dead, dark sea. I surfaced through shoals of night-black swimmers to an outer world where the ripples of the ocean were dimly lit by the glow from a dying orange sun. As the throbbing in my head subsided, those ripples resolved themselves into the pattern of my pin-stripe jacket—but the orange glow remained! My immediate hopes that it had all been a nightmare were shattered at once; for as I carefully raised my head from its position on my chest the whole room slowly came under my unbelieving scrutiny. Thank God Julian had his back to me and I could not see his face. Had I but *glimpsed* again, in those first moments of recovery, those hellish eyes I am certain the sight would have returned me to instant oblivion.

I could see now that the orange glow was reflected from the now blazing fire on the horizontal grill, and I saw that the poker which had been used to strike me down was buried in the heart of the flames with red-heat creeping visibly up the metal towards the wooden handle. Glancing at my watch, I saw that I had been unconscious for many hours—it was fast approaching the midnight hour. That one glance was also sufficient to tell me that I was tied to the old wicker-chair in which I had been seated, for I saw the ropes. I flexed my muscles against my bonds and noticed, not without a measure of satisfaction, that there was a certain degree of slackness in them. I had managed to keep my mind from dwelling on Julian's facial differences; but, as he turned towards me, I steeled myself to the coming shock.

His face was an impassive white mask in which shone, cold and malevolent and indescribably alien, those eyes! As I live and breathe, I swear they were twice the size they ought to have been—and they bulged, uniformly scarlet, outwards from their sockets in chill, yet aloof hostility.

"Ah ! You've returned to us, dear brother. But why d'you stare so? Is it that you find this face so awful? Let me assure you, you don't find it half so hideous as I!"

Monstrous truth, or what I thought was the truth, began to dawn in my mazed and bewildered brain. "The dark spectacles!" I gasped. "No wonder you had to wear them, even at night. You couldn't bear the thought of people seeing those diseased eyes!"

"Diseased? No, your reasoning is only partly correct. I had to wear the glasses, yes; it was that or give myself away—which wouldn't have pleased those who sent me in the slightest, believe me. For Cthulhu, beneath the waves on the far side of the world, has already made it known to Othuum, my master, of his displeasure. They have spoken in dreams, and Cthulhu is *angry!*" He shrugged, "Also, I needed the spectacles; these eyes of mine are accustomed to piercing the deepest depths of the ocean! Your surface world was an agony to me at first—but now I am used to it. In any case, I don't plan to stay here long, and when I go I will take this body with me," he plucked at himself in contempt, "for my pleasure."

I knew that what he was saying was not, could not, be possible, and I cried out to him, begging him to recognize his own madness. I babbled that modern medical science could probably correct whatever was wrong with his eyes. My words were drowned out by his cold laughter. "Julian!" I cried.

"Julian?" he answered. "Julian Haughtree?" He lowered his awful face until it was only inches from mine. "Are you blind, man? *I am Pesh-Tlen, Wizard of deep Gell-Ho to the North!*" He turned away from me, leaving my tottering mind to total up a nerve-blasting sum of horrific integers. The Cthulhu Mythos—those passages from the *Cthaat Aquadingen* and the *Life of St. Brendan*—Julian's dreams; "They can now control dreams as of old." The Mind Transfer—"They will rise"—"through his eyes in my body"— giant gods waiting in the ocean deeps—" He shall walk the Earth in my guise"—a submarine disturbance off the coast of Greenland! *Deep Gell-Ho to the North…*

God in heaven! Could such things be? Was this all, in the end, not just some fantastic delusion of Julian's but an incredible fact? This thing before me! Did he—*it*—really see through the eyes of a monster from the bottom of the sea? And if so—*was it governed by that monster's mind?*

After that, it was not madness that gripped me—not then—rather was it the refusal of my whole being to accept that which was unacceptable. I do not know how long I remained in that state, but the spell was abruptly broken by the first, distant chime of the midnight hour.

At that distant clamour my mind became crystal clear and the eyes of the being called Pesh-Tlen blazed even more unnaturally as he smiled—if that word describes what he *did* with his face—in final triumph. Seeing that smile, I knew that something hideous was soon to come and I struggled against my bonds. I was gratified to feel them slacken a little more about my body. The—creature—had meanwhile turned away from me and had taken the poker from the fire. As the chimes of the hour continued to ring out faintly from afar it raised its arms, weaving strange designs in the air with the tip of the redly glowing poker, and commenced a chant or invocation of such a loathsome association of discordant tones and pipings that my soul seemed to shrink inside me at the hearing. It was fantastic that what was grunted, snarled, whistled, and hissed with such incredible fluency could ever have issued from the throat of something I had called brother, regardless what force motivated his vocal cords; but, fantastic or not, I heard it. Heard it? Indeed, as that mad cacophony died away, tapering off to a high-pitched, screeching end—*I saw its result!*

Writhing tendrils of green smoke began to whirl together in one corner of the cellar. I did not see the smoke arrive, nor could I say whence it came—it was just suddenly there! The tendrils quickly became a column, rapidly thickening, spinning faster and faster, forming—*a shape!*

Outside in the night freak lightning flashed and thunder rumbled over the city in what I have since been told was the worst storm in years—but I barely heard the thunder or the heavy downpour of rain. All my senses were concentrated on the silently spinning, rapidly coalescing thing in the corner. The cellar had a high ceiling, almost eleven feet, but what was forming seemed to fill that space easily.

I screamed then, and mercifully fainted. For once again my mind had been busy totalling the facts as I knew them, and I had mentally questioned Pesh-Tlen's reason for calling up this horror from the depths—or from wherever else it came. Upstairs in my room, unless Julian had been up there and removed it, the answer lay where I had thrown it—Walmsley's translation! Had not Julian, or Pesh-Tlen, or whatever the thing was, written in that diary: *"It will now be necessary to contact my natural form in order to re-enter it"*?

My black-out could only have been momentary, for as I regained consciousness for the second time I saw that the thing in the corner had still not completely formed. It had stopped spinning and was now centrally opaque, but its outline was infirm and wavering, like a scene viewed through smoke. The creature that had been Julian was standing to one side of the cellar, arms raised towards the semi-coherent object in the corner, features strained and twitching with hideous expectancy.

"Look," it spoke coldly, half turning towards me. "See what I and the Deep Ones have done! Behold, mortal, your brother—*Julian Haughtree!*"

For the rest of my days, which I believe will not number many, I will never be able to rid my memory of that sight! While others lie drowning in sleep I will claw desperately at the barrier of consciousness, not daring to close my eyes for fear of that which lingers yet beyond my eyelids. As Pesh-Tlen spoke those words—the thing in the corner finally materialized!

Imagine a black, glistening, ten-foot heap of twisting, ropey tentacles and gaping mouths...Imagine the outlines of a slimy, alien face in which, sunk deep in gaping sockets, are the remains of ruptured *human* eyes...Imagine shrieking in absolute clutching, leaping fear and horror—and imagine the thing which I have here described answering your screams in a madly familiar voice; *a voice which you instantly recognize!*

"Phillip! Phillip, where are you? What's happened? I can't see...We came up out of the sea, and then I was whirled away somewhere and I heard your voice." The horror rocked back and forth. "Don't let them take me back, Phillip!"

The voice was that of my brother, all right—but not the old sane Julian I had known! That was when I, too, went mad; but it was a madness with a purpose, if nothing else. When I had previously fainted, the sudden loosening of my body must have completed the work which I had started on the ropes. As I lurched to my feet they fell from me to the floor. The huge, blind monstrosity in the corner had started to lumber in my direction, vaguely twisting its tentacles before it as it came. At the same time the red-eyed demon in Julian's form was edging carefully towards it, arms eagerly outstretched.

"Julian," I screamed, "look out—only by contact can he re-enter—and then he intends to kill you, to take you back with him to the deeps."

"Back to the deeps? No! No, he can't! I won't go!" The lumbering horror with my brother's mad voice spun blindly around, its flailing tentacles knocking the hybrid sorcerer flying across the floor. I snatched the poker from the fire where it had been replaced and turned threateningly upon the sprawling half-human.

"Stand still, Julian!" I gibbered over my shoulder at the horror from the sea as the wizard before me leapt to his feet. The lumberer behind me halted. "You, Pesh-Tlen, get back." There was no plan in my bubbling mind; I only knew I had to keep the two—*things*—apart. I danced like a boxer, using the glowing poker to ward off the suddenly frantic Pesh-Tlen.

"But it's time—it's time! The contact must be now!" The red-eyed thing screeched. "Get out of my way…" Its tones were barely human now. "You can't stop me…I must…must…must make strong…strong contact! I must…*bhfg—ngyy fhtlhlh hegm—yeh'hhg narcchhh'yy!* You won't cheat me!"

A pool of slime, like the trail of a great snail, had quickly spread from the giant shape behind me; and, even as he screamed, Pesh-Tlen suddenly leapt forward straight onto it, his feet skidding on the evil-smelling mess. He completely lost his balance. Arms flailing he fell, face down, sickeningly, onto the rigid red-hot poker in my hand. Four inches of the glowing metal slid, like a warm knife through butter, into one of those awful eyes. There was a hissing sound, almost drowned out by the creature's single shrill scream of agony, and a small cloud of steam rose mephitically from the thing's face as it pitched to the floor.

Instantly the glistening black giant behind me let out a shriek of terror. I spun round, letting the steaming poker fall, to witness that monstrosity from the ocean floor rocking to and fro, tentacles wrapped protectively round its head. After a few seconds it became still, and the rubbery arms fell listlessly away to reveal the multi-mouthed face with its ruined, rotting eyes.

"You've killed him, I know it," Julian's voice said, calmer now. "He is finished and I am finished—already I can feel them recalling me." Then, voice rising hysterically *"They won't take me alive!"*

The monstrous form trembled and its outline began to blur. My legs crumpled beneath me in sudden reaction, and I pitched to the floor. Perhaps I passed out again—I don't know for sure—but when I next looked in its direction the horror had gone. All that remained was the slime and the grotesque corpse.

I do not know where my muscles found the strength to carry my tottering and mazed body out of that house. Sanity did not drive me, I admit that, for I was quite insane. I wanted to stand beneath the stabbing lightning and scream at those awful, rain-blurred stars. I wanted to bound, to float in my madness through eldritch depths of unhallowed black blood. I wanted to cling to the writhing breasts of Yibb-Tstll. Insane—insane, I tell you, I gibbered and moaned, staggering through the thunder-crazed streets until, with a roar and a crash, sanity-invoking lightning smashed me down…

You know the rest. I awoke to this world of white sheets; to you, the police psychiatrist, with your soft voice…Why must you insist that I keep telling my story? Do you honestly think to make me change it? It's *true*, I tell you! I admit to killing my brother's body—but it wasn't *his mind* that I burned out! You stand there babbling of awful eye diseases. *Julian had no eye disease!* D'you really imagine that the other eye, the unburnt one which you found in that body—in my brother's face—was his? And what of the pool of slime in the cellar and the stink? Are you stupid or something? You've asked for a statement, and here it is! Watch, damn you, watch while I scribble it down...you damn great crimson eye...always watching me...who would have thought that the lips of Bugg-Shash could *suck* like that? Watch, you redness you...and look out for the Scarlet Feaster! *No, don't take the paper away...*

NOTE:
Sir,

Dr. Stewart was contacted as you suggested, and after seeing Haughtree he gave his expert opinion that the man was madder than his brother ever had been. He also pointed out the possibility that the disease of Julian Haughtree's eyes had started soon after his partial mental recovery—probably brought on by constantly wearing dark spectacles. After Dr. Stewart left the police ward, Haughtree became very indignant and wrote the above statement.

Davies, our specialist, examined the body in the cellar himself and is convinced that the younger brother must, indeed, have been suffering from a particularly horrible and unknown ocular disease.

It is appreciated that there are one or two remarkable coincidences in the wild fancies of both brothers in relation to certain recent factual events— but these are, surely, only coincidences. One such event is the rise of the volcanic island of Surtsey. Haughtree must somehow have heard of Surtsey after being taken under observation. He asked to be allowed to read the following newspaper account, afterwards yelling very loudly and repeatedly: "By God! They've named it after the wrong mythos!" Thereafter he was put into a straitjacket of the arm-restricting type:

—BIRTH OF AN ISLAND—

Yesterday morning, the 16th November, the sun rose on a long, narrow island of tephra, lying in the sea to the north of Scotland. at latitude 63° 18' North and longitude 20° 36½?' West. Surtsey, which was born on the 15th November, was then 130 feet high and growing all the time. The fantastic "birth" of the island was witnessed by the crew of the fishing vessel *Isleifer II*, which was lying west of Geirfuglasker, southernmost of the Vestmann

Islands. Considerable disturbance of the sea—which hindered clear observation—was noticed, and the phenomena, the result of submarine volcanic activity, involved such awe-inspiring sights as columns of smoke reaching to two and a half miles high, fantastic lightning storms, and the hurling of lava-bombs over a wide area of the ocean. Surtsey has been named after the giant Surter, who—in Norse Mythology—"Came from the South with Fire to fight the God Freyr at Ragnarok," which battle preceded the end of the world and the Twilight of the Gods. More details and pictures inside…

Still in the "jacket," Haughtree finally calmed himself and begged that further interesting items in the paper be read to him. Dr. Davies did the reading, and when he reached the following report Haughtree grew very excited:

—BEACHES FOULED—

Garvin Bay, on the extreme North coast, was found this morning to be horribly fouled. For a quarter of a mile deposits of some slimy, black grease were left by the tide along the sands. The stench was so great from these unrecognizable deposits that fishermen were unable to put to sea. Scientific analysis has already shown the stuff to be of an organic base, and it is thought to be some type of oil. Local shipping experts are bewildered, as no known tankers have been in the area for over three months. The tremendous variety of dead and rotting fish also washed up has caused the people of nearby Belloch to take strong sanitary precautions. It is hoped that tonight's tide will clear the affected area…

At the end of the reading Haughtree said: "Julian said they wouldn't take him alive." Then, still encased in the jacket, he somehow got off the bed and flung himself through the third-story window of his room in the police ward. His rush at the window was of such tremendous ferocity and strength that he took the bars and frame with him. It all happened so quickly there was nothing anyone could do to stop him.

Submitted as an appendix to my original report.

Sgt. J.T. Muir

23 November 1963.

Glasgow City Police

LORD OF THE WORMS

Lord of the Worms *is another one of those stories that escapes Lovecraft's influence, with the usual caveat in respect of its backdrop, of course. For how may one write a Mythos story without its customary theme? Well, whether or not, I did my best to do just that. In 1982, a year after leaving the Army following twenty-two years of service, and after Kirby McCauley had found himself more or less obliged to concentrate his agenting skills rather more exclusively on behalf of his most successful client (someone called Stephen King?), I sent Paul Ganley of Weirdbook Press—a semi-professional small press: basically a one-man-show—a copy of this novella. Paul's reaction was immediate; he loved the story and bought it word for word after one reading. Later it dawned on me that I might have tried it first on "F&SF", the magazine that had published* Born of the Winds *some six years earlier; it was that sort of story. "F&SF" would have paid somewhat better and I certainly needed the money, but Paul and his "Weirdbook Magazine" had been accepting and publishing my stories for quite some time and we had become firm friends. Another one of my personal favourites, LOTW features the occult investigator Titus Crow as a young man shortly after World War Two, long before he became involved with the Burrowers Beneath or suffered his Transition. The story made its debut in "Weirdbook 17," 1983, and has seen its most recent reprint in my TOR collection, "Harry Keogh: Necroscope & Other Weird Heroes."*

Twenty-two is the Number of the Master! A 22 may only be described in glowing terms, for he is the Great Man. Respected, admired by all who know him, he has the Intellect and the Power and he has the Magic! Aye, he is the Master Magician. But a word of

warning: just as there are Day and Night, so are there two sorts of Magic—
White, and Black!

—*Grossmann's* Numerology
VIENNA, 1776

I

The war was well over. Christmas 1945 had gone by and the New Year
festivities were still simmering, and Titus Crow was out of a job. A young
man whose bent for the dark and mysterious side of life had early steeped
him in obscure occult and esoteric matters, his work for the War Department had moved in two seemingly unconnected, highly secretive directions.
On the one hand he had advised the ministry in respect of certain of *Der
Führer's* supernatural interests, and on the other he had used the skills of the
numerologist and cryptographer to crack the codes of his goose-stepping war
machine. In both endeavors there had been a deal of success, but now the
thing was finished and Titus Crow's talents were superfluous. Now he was
at a loss how best to employ himself. Not yet known as one of the world's
foremost occultists, nor even suspecting the brilliance he was yet to achieve
in many diverse fields of study and learning—and yet fully conscious of the
fact that there was much to be done and a course to be run—for the moment
he felt without a purpose, a feeling not much to his liking. And this after living and working in bomb-ravaged London through the war years, with the
fever and stress of that conflict still bottled inside him.

For these reasons he was delighted when Julian Carstairs—the so-called
Modern Magus, or Lord of the Worms, an eccentric cult or coven leader—
accepted his agreeable response to an advertisement for a young man to un-
dertake a course of secretarial duties at Carstairs' country home, the tenure
of the position not to exceed three months. The money seemed good
(though that was not of prime importance), and part of the work would
consist of cataloging Carstairs' enviable occult library. Other than this the
advertisement had not been very specific; but Titus Crow had little doubt
but that he would find much of interest in the work and eagerly awaited the
day of his first meeting with Carstairs, a man he assumed to be more eccentric than necromantic.

Wednesday, 9 January 1946, was that day, and Crow found the address,
The Barrows—a name which immediately conjured mental pictures of tu-
muli and cromlechs—at the end of a wooded, winding private road not far

from the quaint and picturesque town of Haslemere in Surrey. A large, two-story house surrounded by a high stone wall and expansive gardens of dark shrubbery, overgrown paths and gaunt-limbed oaks weighed down with festoons of unchecked ivy, the place stood quite apart from any comparable habitation.

That the house had at one time been a residence of great beauty seemed indisputable; but equally obvious was the fact that recently, possibly due to the hostilities, it had been greatly neglected. And quite apart from this air of neglect and the generally drear appearance of any country property in England during the first few weeks of the year, there was also a gloominess about The Barrows. Something inherent in its grimy upper windows, in the oak-shaded brickwork and shrouding shrubbery, so that Crow's pace grew measured and just a trifle hesitant as he entered the grounds through a creaking iron gate and followed first the drive, then a briar-tangled path to the front door.

And then, seeming to come too close on the heels of Crow's ringing of the bell, there was the sudden opening of the great door and the almost spectral face and figure of Julian Carstairs himself, whose appearance the young applicant saw from the start was not in accordance with his preconceptions. Indeed, such were Carstairs' looks that what little remained of Crow's restrained but ever-present exuberance was immediately extinguished. The man's aspect was positively dismal.

Without introduction, without even offering his hand, Carstairs led him through the gloomy interior to the living room, a room somber with shadows which seemed almost painted into the dark oak paneling. There, switching on lighting so subdued that it did absolutely nothing to dispel the drabness of the place or its fungal taint of dry rot, finally Carstairs introduced himself and bade his visitor be seated. But still he did not offer his hand.

Now, despite the poor light, Crow was able to take in something of the aspect of this man who was to be, however temporarily, his employer; and what he saw was not especially reassuring. Extremely tall and thin almost to the point of emaciation, with a broad forehead, thick dark hair and bushy eyebrows, Carstairs' pallor was one with the house. With sunken cheeks and slightly stooped shoulders, he could have been any age between seventy and eighty-five, perhaps even older. Indeed, there was that aura about him, hinting of a delayed or altered process of aging, which one usually associates with mummies in their museum alcoves.

Looking yet more closely at his face (but guardedly and as unobtrusively as possible), Crow discovered the pocks, cracks and wrinkles of years without number; as if Carstairs had either lived well beyond his time, or had packed far too much into a single lifespan. And again the younger man found himself comparing his host to a sere and dusty mummy.

And yet there was also a wisdom in those dark eyes, which at least redeemed for the moment an otherwise chill and almost alien visage. While Crow could in no wise appreciate the outer shell of the man, he believed that he might yet find virtue in his knowledge, the occult erudition with which it was alleged Carstairs had become endowed through a life of remote travels and obscure delvings. And certainly there was that of the scholar about him, or at least of the passionate devotee.

There was a hidden strength there, too, which seemed to belie the supposed age lines graven in his face and bony hands; and as soon as he commenced to speak, in a voice at once liquid and sonorous, Crow was aware that he was up against a man of great power. After a brief period of apparently haphazard questioning and trivial discourse, Carstairs abruptly asked him the date of his birth. Having spoken he grew silent, his eyes sharp as he watched Crow's reaction and waited for his answer.

Caught off guard for a moment, Crow felt a chill strike him from nowhere, as if a door had suddenly opened on a cold and hostile place; and some sixth sense warned him against all logic that Carstairs' question was fraught with danger, like the muzzle of a loaded pistol placed to his temple. And again illogically, almost without thinking, he supplied a fictitious answer which added four whole years to his actual age:

"Why, second December 1912," he answered with a half-nervous smile. "Why do you ask?"

For a moment Carstairs' eyes were hooded, but then they opened in a beaming if cadaverous smile. He issued a sigh, almost of relief, saying: "I was merely confirming my suspicion, astrologically speaking, that perhaps you were a Saggitarian—which of course you are. You see, the sidereal science is a consuming hobby of mine, as are a great many of the so-called 'abstruse arts.' I take it you are aware of my reputation? That my name is linked with all manner .of unspeakable rites and dark practices? That according to at least one daily newspaper I am, or believe myself to be, the very Antichrist?" And he nodded and mockingly smiled. "Of course you are. Well, the truth is far less damning, I assure you. I dabble a little, certainly—mainly to entertain my friends with certain trivial talents, one of which happens to be astrology—but as for necromancy and the like…I ask you, Mr. Crow—in this day and age?" And again he offered his skull-like smile.

Before the younger man could make any sort of comment to fill the silence that had fallen over the room, his host spoke again, asking, "And what are your interests, Mr. Crow?"

"My interests? Why, I—" But at the last moment, even as Crow teetered on the point of revealing that he, too, was a student of the esoteric and oc-cult—though a white as opposed to a black magician—so he once more felt that chill as of outer immensities and, shaking himself from a curious lethargy, noticed how large and bright the other's eyes had grown. And at that moment Crow knew how close he had come to falling under Carstairs' spell, which must be a sort of hypnosis. He quickly gathered his wits and feigned a yawn.

"You really must excuse me, sir," he said then, "for my unpardonable boorishness. I don't know what's come over me that I should feel so tired. I fear I was almost asleep just then."

Then, fearing that Carstairs' smile had grown more than a little forced— thwarted, almost—and that his nod was just a fraction too curt, he quickly continued: "My interests are common enough. A little archaeology, paleon-tology…"

"Common, indeed!" answered Carstairs with a snort. "Not so, for such in-terests show an inquiring nature, albeit for things long passed away. No, no, those, are admirable pastimes for such a young man." And he pursed his thin lips and fingered his chin a little before asking:

"But surely, what with the war and all, archaeological work has suffered greatly. Not much of recent interest there?"

"On the contrary," Crow answered at once, "1939 was an exceptional year. The rock art of Hoggar and the excavations at Brek in Syria; the Niger-ian Ife bronzes; Bleger's discoveries at Pylos and Wace's at Mycenae; Sir Leonard Woolley and the Hittites…myself, I was greatly interested in the Oriental Institute's work at Megiddo in Palestine. That was in '37. Only a bout of ill health held me back from accompanying my father out to the site."

"Ah! Your interest is inherited, then? Well, do not concern yourself that you missed the trip. Megiddo was not especially productive. Our inscrutable Oriental friends might have found more success to the northeast, a mere twenty-five or thirty miles."

"On the shores of Galilee?" Crow was mildly amused at the other's as-sumed knowledge of one of his pet subjects.

"Indeed," answered Carstairs, his tone bone dry. "The sands of time have buried many interesting towns and cities on the shores of Galilee. But tell me: what are your thoughts on the Lascaux cave paintings, discovered in, er, '38?"

"No, in 1940." Crow's smile disappeared as he suddenly realized he was being tested, that Carstairs' knowledge of archaeology—certainly recent digs and discoveries—was at least the equal of his own. "September 1940. They are without question the work of Cro-Magnon man, some twenty to twenty-five thousand years old."

"Good!" Carstairs beamed again, and Crow suspected that he had passed the test.

Now his gaunt host stood up to tower abnormally tall even over his tall visitor. "Very well, I think you will do nicely, Mr. Crow. Come then, and I'll show you my library. It's there you will spend most of your time, after all, and you'll doubtless be pleased to note that the room has a deal more natural light than the rest of the house. Plenty of windows. Barred windows, for of course many of my books are quite priceless."

Leading the way through gloomy and mazy corridors, he mused: "Of course, the absence of light suits me admirably. I am hemeralopic. You may have noticed how large and dark my eyes are in the gloom? Yes, and that is why there are so few strong electric lights in the house. I hope that does not bother you?"

"Not at all," Crow answered, while in reality he felt utterly hemmed in, taken prisoner by the mustiness of dry rot and endless, stifling corridors.

"And you're a rock hound, too, are you?" Carstairs continued. "That is interesting. Did you know that fossil lampshells, of the sort common here in the South, were once believed to be the devil's cast-off toenails?" He laughed a mirthless, baying laugh. "Ah, what it is to live in an age enlightened by science, eh?"

II

Using a key to unlock the library door, he ushered Crow into a large room, then stooped slightly to enter beneath a lintel uncomfortably shallow for a man of his height. "And here we are," he unnecessarily stated, staggering slightly and holding up a hand to ward off the weak light from barred windows. "My eyes," he offered by way of an explanation. "I'm sure you will understand…"

Quickly crossing the carpeted floor, he drew shades until the room stood in somber shadows. "The lights are here," he said, pointing to switches on the wall. "You are welcome to use them when I am not present. Very well, Mr. Crow, this is where you are to work. Oh, and by the way: I agree to your request as stated in your letter of introduction, that you be allowed your freedom at weekends. That suits me perfectly well, since weekends are really the only suitable time for our get-togethers—that is to say, when I entertain a few friends.

"During the week, however, you would oblige me by staying here. Behind the curtains in the far wall is a lighted alcove, which I have made comfortable with a bed, a small table and a chair. I assure you that you will not be disturbed. I will respect your privacy—on the understanding, of course, that you will respect mine; with regard to which there are certain house rules, as it were. You are not to have guests or visitors up to the house under any circumstances—The Barrows is forbidden to all outsiders. And the cellar is quite out of bounds. As for the rest of the house: with the sole exception of my study, it is yours to wander or explore as you will—though I suspect you'll have little enough time for that. In any case, the place is quite empty. And that is how I like it.

"You do understand that I can only employ you for three months? Good. You shall be paid monthly, in advance, and to ensure fair play and goodwill on both sides I shall require you to sign a legally binding contract. I do not want you walking out on me with the job only half completed.

"As for the work: that should be simple enough for anyone with the patience of the archaeologist, and I will leave the system entirely up to you. Basically, I require that all my books should be put in order, first by category, then by author, and alphabetically in the various categories. Again, the breakdown will be entirely your concern. All of the work must, however, be cross-referenced; and finally I shall require a complete listing of books by title, and once again alphabetically. Now, are you up to it?"

Crow glanced around the room; at its high shelves and dusty, book-littered tables. Books seemed to be piled everywhere. There must be close to seven or eight thousand volumes here! Three months no longer seemed such a great length of time. On the other hand, from what little he had seen of the titles of some of these tomes…

"I am sure," he finally answered, "that my work will be to your complete satisfaction."

"Good!" Carstairs nodded. "Then today being three-quarters done, I suggest we now retire to the dining room for our evening meal, following which you may return here if you so desire and begin to acquaint yourself with my books. Tomorrow, Thursday, you begin your work proper, and I shall only disturb you on those rare occasions when I myself visit the library, or perhaps periodically to see how well or ill you are progressing. Agreed?"

"Agreed," answered Crow, and he once more followed his host and employer out into the house's airless passages.

On their way Carstairs handed him the key to the library door, saying: "You shall need this, I think." And seeing Crow's frown he explained, "The house has attracted several burglars in recent years, hence the bars at most of the windows. If such a thief did get in, you would be perfectly safe locked in the library."

"I can well look after myself, Mr. Carstairs," said Crow.

"I do not doubt it," answered the other, "but my concern is not entirely altruistic. If you remain safe, Mr. Crow, then so do my books." And once again his face cracked open in that hideous smile…

They ate at opposite ends of a long table in a dimly lighted dining room whose gloom was one with the rest of the house. Titus Crow's meal consisted of cold cuts of meat and red wine, and it was very much to his liking; but he did note that Carstairs' plate held different fare, reddish and of a less solid consistency, though the distance between forbade any closer inspection. They ate in silence and when finished Carstairs led the way to the kitchen, a well-equipped if dingy room with a large, well-stocked larder.

"From now on," Carstairs explained in his sepulchral voice, "you are to prepare your own meals. Eat what you will, everything here is for you. My own needs are slight and I usually eat alone; and of course there are no servants here. I did note, however, that you enjoy wine. Good, so do I. Drink what you will, for there is more than sufficient and my cellar is amply stocked."

"Thank you," Crow answered. "And now, if I may, there are one or two points…"

"By all means."

"I came by car, and—"

"Ah! Your motorcar, yes. Turn left on the drive as you enter through the gate. There you will find a small garage. Its door is open. Better that you leave your car there during the week, or else as winter lengthens the battery is sure to suffer. Now then, is there anything else?"

"Will I need a key?" Crow asked after a moment's thought. "A key to the house, I mean, for use when I go away at weekends?"

"No requirement," Carstairs shook his head. "I shall be here to see you off on Fridays, and to welcome you when you return on Monday mornings."

"Then all would appear to be very satisfactory. I do like fresh air, however, and would appreciate the occasional opportunity to walk in your gardens."

"In my wilderness, do you mean?" and Carstairs gave a throaty chuckle. "The place is so overgrown I should fear to lose you. But have no fear—the door of the house will not be locked during the day. All I would ask is that when I am not here you are careful not to lock yourself out."

"Then that appears to be that," said Crow. "It only remains for me to thank you for the meal—and of course to offer to wash the dishes."

"Not necessary." Again Carstairs shook his head. "On this occasion I shall do it; in future we shall do our own. Now I suggest you garage your car."

He led Crow from the kitchen through gloomy passages to the outer door, and as they went the younger man remembered a sign he had seen affixed to the ivy-grown garden wall. When he mentioned it, Carstairs once more gave his throaty chuckle. "Ah, yes—Beware of the Dog! There is no dog, Mr. Crow. The sign is merely to ensure that my privacy is not disturbed. In fact I hate dogs, and dogs hate me!"

On that note Crow left the house, parked his car in the garage provided, and finally returned to Carstairs' library. By this time his host had gone back to the study or elsewhere and Crow was left quite alone. Entering the library he could not help but lick his lips in anticipation. If only one or two of the titles he had seen were the actual books they purported to be…then Carstairs' library was a veritable gold mine of occult lore! He went directly to the nearest bookshelves and almost immediately spotted half a dozen titles so rare as to make them half-fabulous. Here was an amazingly pristine copy of du Nord's *Liber Ivonie*, and another of Prinn's *De Vermis Mysteriis*. And these marvelous finds were simply inserted willy-nilly in the shelves, between such mundane or common treatises as Miss Margaret Murray's *Witch-Cult* and the much more doubtful works of such as Mme. Blavatsky and Scott-Elliot.

A second shelf supported d'Erlette's *Cultes des Goules*, Gauthier de Metz's *Image du Mond*, and Artephous' *The Key of Wisdom*. A third was filled with an incredible set of volumes concerning the theme of oceanic mysteries and horrors, with such sinister-sounding titles as Gantley's *Hydrophinnae*, the *Cthaat Aquadingen*, the German *Unter Zee Kulten*, le Fe's *Dwellers in the Depths*, and Konrad von Gerner's *Fischbuch*, circa 1598.

Moving along the shelved wall, Crow felt his body break out in a sort of cold sweat at the mere thought of the *value* of these books, let alone their contents, and such was the list of recognizably "priceless" volumes that he soon began to lose all track of the titles. Here were the *Pnakotic Manuscripts*, and here *The Seven Cryptical Books of Hsan*; until finally, on coming across the *R'lyeh Text* and, at the very last, an ancient, ebony-bound, gold-and-silver-arabesqued tome which purported to be none other than the *Al Azif* itself!…He was obliged to sit down at one of the dusty tables and take stock of his senses.

It was only then, as he unsteadily seated himself and put a hand up to his fevered brow, that he realized all was not well with him. He felt clammy from the sweat which had broken out on him while looking at the titles of the books, and his mouth and throat had been strangely dry ever since he sampled (too liberally, perhaps?) Carstairs' wine. But this dizziness clinched it. He did not think that he had taken overmuch wine, but then again he had not recognized the stuff and so had not realized its potency. Very well, in future he would take only a single glass. He did not give thought, not at this point, to the possibility that the wine might have been drugged.

Without more ado, still very unsteady on his feet, he got up, put on the light in the alcove where his bed lay freshly made, turned off the library lights proper, and stumblingly retired. Almost before his head hit the pillow he was fast asleep.

He dreamed.

The alcove was in darkness but dim moonlight entered the library through the barred windows in beams which moved with the stirring of trees in the garden. The curtains were open and four dark-robed, hooded strangers stood about his bed, their half-luminous eyes fixed upon him. Then one of them bent forward and Crow sensed that it was Carstairs.

"Is he sleeping, Master?" an unknown voice asked in a reedy whisper.

"Yes, like a baby," Carstairs answered. "The open, staring eyes are a sure sign of the drug's efficacy. What do you think of him?"

A third voice, deep and gruff, chuckled obscenely. "Oh, he'll do well enough, Master. Another forty or fifty years for you here."

"Be quiet!" Carstairs immediately snarled, his dark eyes bulging in anger. "You are never to mention that again, neither here nor anywhere else!"

"Master," the man's voice was now a gasp. "I'm sorry! I didn't realize—"

Carstairs snorted his contempt. "None of you ever realizes," he said.

"What of his sign, Master?" asked the fourth and final figure, in a voice as thickly glutinous as mud. "Is it auspicious?"

"Indeed it is. He is a Saggitarian, as am I. And his numbers are…most propitious." Carstairs' voice was now a purr. "Not only does his name have nine letters, but in the orthodox system his birth number is twenty-seven—a triple nine. Totaled individually, however, his date gives an even better result, for the sum is eighteen!"

"The triple six!" The other's gasp was involuntary.

"Indeed," said Carstairs.

"Well, he seems tall and strong enough, Master," said the voice of the one already chastised. "A fitting receptacle, it would seem."

"Damn you!" Carstairs rounded on him at once. "Fool! How many times must I repeat—" and for a moment, consumed with rage, his hissing voice broke. Then, "Out! Out! There's work for you fools, and for the others. But hear me now: He is The One, I assure you—and he came of his own free will, which is as it must always be."

Three of the figures melted away into darkness but Carstairs stayed. He looked down at Crow one last time, and in a low, even whisper said, "It was a dream. Anything you may remember of this was only a dream. It is not worth remembering, Mr. Crow. Not worth it at all. Only a dream…a dream…a dream…" Then he stepped back and closed the curtains, shutting out the moonbeams and leaving the alcove in darkness. But for a long time it seemed to the sleeping man in the bed that Carstairs' eyes hung over him in the night like the smile of the Cheshire Cat in Alice.

Except that they were malign beyond mortal measure….

III

In the morning, with weak, grime-filtered January sunlight giving the library a dull, time-worn appearance more in keeping with late afternoon than morning, Crow awakened, stretched and yawned. He had not slept well and had a splitting headache, which itself caused him to remember his vow of the previous night: to treat his employer's wine with more respect in future. He remembered, too, something of his dream—something vaguely frightening—but it had been only a dream and not worth remembering. Not worth it at all…

Nevertheless, still lying abed, he struggled for a little while to force memories to the surface of his mind. They were there, he was sure, deep down in his subconscious. But they would not come. That the dream had concerned Carstairs and a number of other, unknown men, he was sure, but its details…(he shrugged the thing from his mind) were not worth remembering.

Yet still he could not rid himself of the feeling that he should remember, if only for his own peace of mind. There was that frustrating feeling of having a word on the tip of one's tongue, only to find it slipping away before it can be voiced. After the dream there had been something else—a continuation, perhaps—but this was far less vague and shadowy. It had seemed to Crow that he had heard droning chants or liturgies of some sort or other echoing up from the very bowels of the house. From the cellars? Well, possibly that had been a mental hangover from Carstairs' statement that the cellars were out of bounds. Perhaps, subconsciously, he had read something overly sinister into the man's warning in that respect.

But talking—or rather thinking—of hangovers, the one he had was developing into something of a beauty! Carstairs' wine? Potent?…Indeed!

He got up, put on his dressing gown, went in search of the bathroom and from there, ten minutes later and greatly refreshed, to the dining room. There he found a brief note, signed by Carstairs, telling him that his employer would be away all day and urging an early start on his work. Crow shrugged, breakfasted, cleared up after himself and prepared to return to the library. But as he was putting away his dishes he came upon a packet of Aspros, placed conspicuously to hand. And now he had to smile at Carstairs' perception. Why, the man had known he would suffer from last night's overindulgence, and these pills were to ensure Crow's clearheadedness as he commenced his work!

His amusement quickly evaporated, however, as he moved from kitchen to library and paused to ponder the best way to set about the job. For the more he looked at and handled these old books, the more the feeling grew within him that Carstairs' passion lay not in the ownership of such volumes but in their use. And if that were the case, then yesterday's caution—however instinctive, involuntary—might yet prove to have stood him in good stead. He thought back to Carstairs' question about his date of birth, and of the man's alleged interest—his "consuming" interest—in astrology. Strange, then, that there was hardly a single volume on that subject to be found among all of these books.

Not so strange, though, that in answer to Carstairs' question he had lied. For as a numerologist Crow had learned something of the importance of names, numbers, and dates—especially to an occultist! No magician in all the long, macabre history of mankind would ever have let the date of his birth be known to an enemy, nor even his name, if that were at all avoidable. For who could tell what use the other might make of such knowledge, these principal factors affecting a man's destiny?

In just such recesses of the strange and mystical mind were born such phrases of common, everyday modern usage as: "That bullet had his number on it," and "His number is up!" And where names were concerned, from Man's primal beginnings the name was the identity, the very spirit, and any wizard who knew a man's name might use it against him. The Holy Bible was full of references to the secrecy and sanctity of names, such as the third and "secret" name of the rider of the Horse of Revelations, or that of the angel visiting Samson's father, who asked: "Why asketh thou then after my name, seeing it is secret?" And the Bible was modern fare compared with certain Egyptian legends concerning the use of names in inimical magic. Well, too late to worry about that now; but in any case, while Carstairs had Crow's name, at least he did not have his number.

And what had been that feeling, Crow wondered, come over him when the occultist had asked about his interests, his hobbies? At that moment he would have been willing to swear that the man had almost succeeded in hypnotizing him. And again, for some reason he had been prompted to lie; or if not to lie, to tell only half the truth. Had that, too, been some mainly subconscious desire to protect his identity? If so, why? What possible harm could Carstairs wish to work upon him? The idea was quite preposterous.

As for archaeology and paleontology: Crow's interest was quite genuine and his knowledge extensive, but so too (apparently) was Carstairs'. What had the man meant by suggesting that the Oriental Institute's expedition might have had more success digging in Galilee?

On impulse Crow took down a huge, dusty atlas of the world—by no means a recent edition—and turned its thick, well-thumbed pages to the Middle East, Palestine and the Sea of Galilee. Here, in the margin, someone had long ago written in reddish, faded ink the date 1602; and on the map itself, in the same sepia, three tiny crosses had been marked along the north shore of Galilee. Beside the center cross was the word *Chorazin*.

Now, this was a name Crow recognized at once. He went back to the shelves and after some searching found a good copy of John Kitto's *Illustrated Family Bible* in two volumes, carrying the bulky second volume back to his table. In Matthew and in Luke he quickly located the verses he sought, going from them to the notes at the end of Chapter 10 of Luke. There, in respect of Verse 13, he found the following note:

> Chorazin—This place is nowhere mentioned but in this and the parallel texts, and in these only by way of reference. It would seem to have been a town of some note, on the shores of the Lake of Galilee, and near Capernaum, along with which and Bethsaide its name occurs. The answer of the natives to Dr. Richardson, when he inquired concerning Capernaum (see the note on iv, 31) connected Chorazin in the same manner with that city….

Crow checked the specified note and found a further reference to Chorazin, called by present-day natives Chorasi and lying in extensive and ancient ruins. Pursing his lips, Crow now returned to the atlas and frowned again at the map of Galilee with its three crosses. If the central one was Chorazin, or the place now occupied by its ruins, then the other two probably identified Bethsaide and Capernaum, all cursed and their destruction foretold by Jesus. As Carstairs had observed: the sands of time had indeed buried many interesting towns and cities on the shores of Galilee.

And so much for John Kitto, D.D., F. S.A. A massive and scholarly work to be sure, his great Bible—but he might have looked a little deeper into the question of Chorazin. For to Crow's knowledge this was one of the birthplaces of "the Antichrist"—whose birth, in its most recent manifestation, had supposedly taken place about the year 1602…

Titus Crow would have dearly loved to research Carstairs' background, discover his origins and fathom the man's nature and occult directions; so much so that he had to forcefully remind himself that he was not here as a spy but an employee, and that as such he had work to do. Nor was he loath to employ himself on Carstairs' books, for the occultist's collection was in a word, marvelous.

With all of his own esoteric interest, Crow had never come across so fantastic an assemblage of books in his life, not even in the less public archives of such authoritative establishments as the British Museum and the Bibliothèque Nationale. In fact, had anyone previously suggested that such a private collection existed, Crow might well have laughed. Quite apart from the expense necessarily incurred in building such a collection, where could a man possibly find the time required and the dedication in a single lifetime? But it was another, and to Crow far more astonishing, aspect of the library which gave him his greatest cause to ponder: namely the incredible carelessness or sheer ignorance of anyone who could allow such a collection to fall into such disorder, disuse, and decay.

For certainly decay was beginning to show; there were signs of it all about, some of them of the worst sort. Even as midday arrived and he put aside his first rough notes and left the library for the kitchen, just such a sign made itself apparent. It was a worm—a bookworm, Crow supposed, though he had no previous experience of them—which he spotted crawling on the carpeted floor just within the library door. Picking the thing up, he discovered it to be fat, pinkish, vaguely morbid in its smell and cold to the touch. He would have expected a bookworm to be smaller, drier, more insectlike. This thing was more like a maggot! Quickly he turned back into the room, crossed the floor, opened a small window through the vertical bars and dropped the offensive creature into the dark shrubbery. And before making himself a light lunch he very scrupulously washed and dried his hands.

The rest of the day passed quickly and without incident, and Crow forswore dinner until around 9:00 P.M. when he began to feel hungry and not a little weary. In the interim he had made his preliminary notes, decided upon categories, and toward the last he had begun to move books around and clear a shelf upon which to commence the massive job of work before him.

For a meal this time he heated the contents of a small flat tin of excellent sliced beef, boiled a few potatoes and brewed up a jug of coffee; and last but not least, he placed upon the great and otherwise empty table a single glass and one of Carstairs' obscure but potent bottles. On this occasion, however, he drank only one glass, and then not filled to the brim. And later, retiring to his alcove with a book—E.L. de Marigny's entertaining *The Tarot: A Treatise*—he congratulated himself upon his restraint. He felt warm and pleasantly drowsy, but in no way as intoxicated as he had felt on the previous night. About 10:30, when he caught himself nodding, he went to bed and slept soundly and dreamlessly all through the night.

Friday went by very quietly, without Crow once meeting, seeing or hearing Carstairs, so that he could not even be sure that the man was at home. This suited him perfectly well, for he still entertained certain misgivings with regard to the occultist's motives. As Carstairs had promised, however, he was there to see Crow off that evening, standing thin and gaunt on the drive, with a wraith of ground mist about his ankles as the younger man drove away.

At his flat in London Crow quickly became bored. He did not sleep well that Friday night, nor on Saturday night, and Sunday was one long misery of boredom and depression, sensations he was seldom if ever given to experience. On two occasions he found himself feeling unaccountably dry and licking his lips, and more than once he wished he had brought a bottle of Carstairs' wine home with him. Almost without conscious volition, about 7:30 on Sunday evening, he began to pack a few things ready for the return journey. It had completely escaped his usually pinpoint but now strangely confused memory that he was not supposed to return until Monday morning.

About 10:00 P.M. he parked his car in the small garage in the grounds of The Barrows, and walked with his suitcase past three other cars parked on the drive. Now, approaching the house, he began to feel a little foolish; for Carstairs was obviously entertaining friends, and of course he would not be expecting him. If the door should prove to be unlocked, however, he might just be able to enter without being heard and without disturbing his employer.

The door was unlocked; Crow entered and went quietly to the library, and there, on a table beside his open notebook, he discovered a bottle of wine and this note:

> Dear Mr. Crow,
> I have perused your notes and they seem very thorough. I am well pleased with your work so far. I shall be away most of Monday, but expect to see you before I depart. In the event that you should return early, I leave you a small welcome.
> Sleep well.
>
> > J. C.

All of which was very curious. The note almost made it seem that Carstairs had known he would return early! But at any rate, the man seemed in a good humor; and it would be boorish of Crow not to thank him for the gift of the bottle. He could at least try, and then perhaps he would not feel so bad about sneaking into the house like a common criminal. The hour was not, after all, unreasonable.

So thinking, Crow took a small glass of wine to fortify himself, then went quietly into the gloomy passages and corridors and made his unlighted way to Carstairs' study. Seeing a crack of feeble electric light from beneath the occultist's door and hearing voices, he paused, reconsidered his action and was on the point of retracing his steps when he heard his name mentioned. Now he froze and all his attention concentrated itself upon the conversation being carried on in Carstairs' study. He could not catch every word, but—

"The date ordained...Candlemas Eve," Carstairs was saying. "Meanwhile, I...my will on him. He *works* for me—do you understand?—and so was partly...power from the start. My will, aided...wine, will do the rest. Now, I...decided upon it, and will...no argument. I have said it before and now...again: he *is* the one. Garbett, what has he in the way of vices?"

A thick, guttural voice answered—a voice which Crow was almost certain he knew from somewhere—saying: "None at all, that I...discover.

Neither women—not as a vice—nor drugs, though…very occasionally likes a cigarette. He…not gamble…no spendthrift, he—"

"Is pure!" Carstairs' voice again. "But you…worked for the War Department? In…capacity?"

"That is a stone wall, Master…as well try…into…Bank of England! And it…dangerous to press too far."

"Agreed," answered Carstairs. "I want as little as possible to link him with us and this place. Afterward, he will seem to return…old haunts, friends, interests. Then the gradual breaking away—and nothing…connect him and me. Except…shall be one!"

"And yet, Master," said another voice, which again Crow thought he knew, a voice like a windblown reed, "you seem less…completely satisfied…"

After a pause Carstairs' voice came yet again. "He is not, as yet, a subject…hypnotism. On our first…resisted strongly. But that is not necessarily a bad sign. There is one…need to check. I shall attend to that tomorrow, by letter. It is possible, just possible…lied…birthdate. In which case…time to find another."

"But…*little* time!" a fourth voice said. "They mass within you, Master, ravenous and eager to migrate—and Candlemas…so close." This voice was thickly glutinous, as Crow had somehow suspected it would be; but Carstairs' voice when it came again had risen a note or two. While it still had that sonorous quality, it also seemed to ring—as in a sort of triumph?

"Aye, they mass, the Charnel Horde—for they know it nears their time! Then—that which remains shall be theirs, and they shall have a new host!" His voice came down a fraction, but still rang clear. "If Crow has lied, I shall deal with him. Then—" and his tone took on a sudden, demonic bite, a sort of crazed amusement, "perhaps you would volunteer, Durrell, for the feasting of the worm? Here, *see how taken they are with you!*"

At that there came a scuffle of feet and the scraping sound of table and chairs sharply moved. A gurgling, glutinous cry rang out, and Crow had barely sufficient time to draw back into a shallow, arched alcove before the study door flew open and a frantic figure staggered out into the corridor, almost toppling a small occasional table which stood there. White-faced, with bulging eyes, a man of medium build hurried past Crow and toward the main door of the house. He stumbled as he went and uttered a low moan, then threw something down which plopped on the fretted carpet.

When the house door slammed after him, Crow made his way breathlessly and on tiptoe back to the library. He noted, in passing, that something small and leprous-white crawled on the floor where Durrell had thrown it. And all the while the house rang with Carstairs' baying laughter…

IV

It might now reasonably be assumed that Titus Crow, without more ado, would swiftly take his leave of The Barrows and Carstairs forever; that he would go home to London or even farther afield, return the month's wages that Carstairs had paid him in advance, revoke the contract he had signed and so put an end to the…whatever it was that his employer planned for him. And perhaps he would have done just that; but already the wine was working in him, that terribly potent and rapidly addictive wine which, along with Carstairs' sorcerous will, was binding him to this house of nameless evil.

And even sensing his growing dependence on the stuff, having heard it with his own ears from Carstairs' own lips, still he found himself reaching with trembling hand for that terrible bottle, and pouring another glass for himself in the suddenly morbid and prisonlike library. All sorts of nightmare visions now raced through Crow's mind as he sat there atremble— chaotic visions of immemorial madness, damnable conclusions totalled from a mass of vague and fragmentary evidences and suspicions—but even as his thoughts whirled, so he sipped, until his senses became totally confounded and he slipped into sleep slumped at the table, his head cushioned upon his arm.

And once more he seemed to dream….

This time there were only three of them. They had come silently, creeping in the night, and as they entered so one of them, probably Carstairs, had switched off the library lights. Now, in wan moonlight, they stood about him and the hour was midnight.

"See," said Carstairs, "my will and the wine combined have sufficed to call him back, as I said they would. He is now bound to The Barrows as by chains. In a way I am disappointed. His will is not what I thought it. Or perhaps I have made the wine too potent."

"Master," said the one called Garbett, his voice thickly glutinous as ever, "it may be my eyes in this poor light, but—"

"Yes?"

"I think he is trembling! And why is he not in his bed?"

Crow felt Garbett's hand, cold and clammy, upon his fevered brow. "See, he trembles!" said the man. "As if in fear of something…"

"Ah!" came the occultist's voice. "Yes, your powers of observation do you credit, friend Garbett, and you are a worthy member of the coven. Yes, even though the wine holds him fast in its grip, still he trembles. Perhaps he has heard something of which it were better he remained in ignorance. Well, that can be arranged. Now help me with him. To leave him here like this would not be a kindness, and prone upon his bed he will offer less resistance."

Crow felt himself lifted up by three pairs of hands, steadied and guided across the floor, undressed, put to bed. He could see dimly, could feel faintly, could hear quite sharply. The last thing he heard was Carstairs' hypnotic voice, telling him to forget…forget. Forget anything he might have overheard this night. For it was all a dream and unimportant, utterly unimportant…

On Monday morning Crow was awakened by Carstairs' voice. The weak January sun was up and the hands on his wristwatch stood at 9:00 A.M. "You have slept late, Mr. Crow. Still, no matter…Doubtless you need the rest after a hectic weekend, eh? I am going out and shall not be back before nightfall. Is there anything you wish me to bring back for you? Something to assist you in your work, perhaps?"

"No," Crow answered, "nothing that I can think of. But thanks anyway." He blinked sleep from his eyes and felt the first throb of a dull ache developing in the front of his skull. "This is unpardonable—my sleeping to this hour. Not that I slept very well…"

"Ah?" Carstairs tut-tutted. "Well, do not concern yourself—nothing is amiss. I am sure that after breakfast you will feel much better. Now you must excuse me. Until tonight, then." And he turned and strode from the room.

Crow watched him go and lay for a moment thinking, trying to ignore the fuzziness inside his head. There had been another dream, he was sure, but very little of it was clear, and fine details utterly escaped him. He remembered coming back to The Barrows early…after that nothing. Finally he got up, and as soon as he saw the half-empty bottle on the table he understood—or believed he understood—what had happened. That damned wine!

Angry with himself, at his own stupidity, he went through the morning's routine and returned to his work on Carstairs' books. But now, despite the fact that the sun was up and shining with a wintry brightness, it seemed to Crow that the shadows were that much darker in the house and the gloom that much deeper.

❖ ❖ ❖

The following day, with Carstairs again absent, he explored The Barrows from attic to cellar, but not the cellar itself. He did try the door beneath the stairs, however, but found it locked. Upstairs the house had many rooms, all thick with dust and sparsely furnished; with spots of mold on some of the walls and woodworm in much of the furniture. The place seemed as disused and decayed above as it was below, and Crow's inspection was mainly perfunctory. Outside Carstairs' study he paused, however, as a strange and shuddery feeling took momentary possession of him.

Suddenly he found himself trembling and breaking out in a cold sweat; and it seemed to him that half-remembered voices echoed sepulchrally and ominously in his mind. The feeling lasted for a moment only, but it left Crow weak and full of a vague nausea. Again angry with himself and not a little worried, he tried the study door and found it to be open. Inside the place was different from the rest of the house.

Here there was no dust or disorder but a comparatively well-kept room of fair size, where table and chairs stood upon an Eastern-style carpet, with a great desk square and squat beneath a wall hung with six oil paintings in matching gilt frames. These paintings attracted Crow's eyes and he moved forward the better to see them. Proceeding from right to left, the pictures bore small metallic plaques which gave dates but no names.

The first was of a dark, hawk-faced, turbaned man in desert garb, an Arab by his looks. The dates were 1602-68. The second was also of a Middle Eastern type, this time in the rich dress of a sheik or prince, and his dates were 1668-1734. The third was dated 1734-90 and was the picture of a statuesque, high-browed Negro of forceful features and probably Ethiopian descent; while the fourth was of a stern-faced young man in periwig and smallclothes, dated 1790-1839. The fifth was of a bearded, dark-eyed man in a waistcoat and wearing a monocle—a man of unnatural pallor—dated 1839-88; and the sixth—

The sixth was a picture of Carstairs himself, looking almost exactly as he looked now, dated 1888-1946!

Crow stared at the dates again, wondering what they meant and why they were so perfectly consecutive. Could these men have been the previous leaders of Carstairs' esoteric cult, each with dates which corresponded to the length of his reign? But 1888…yes, it made sense; for that could certainly not be Carstairs' birth date. Why, he would be only fifty-seven years of age! He looked at least fifteen or twenty years older than that; certainly he gave the impression of advanced age, despite his peculiar vitality. And what of that final date, 1946? Was the man projecting his own death?—or was this to be the year of the next investiture?

Then, sweeping his eyes back across the wall to the first picture, that of the hawk-faced Arab, something suddenly clicked into place in Crow's mind. It had to do with the date 1602…and in another moment he remembered that this was the date scrawled in reddish ink in the margin of the old atlas. The date of birth of the supposed Antichrist, 1602, in a place once known as Chorazin the Damned!

Still, it made very little sense—or did it? There was a vague fuzziness in Crow's mind, a void desperately trying to fill itself, like a mental jigsaw puzzle with so many missing pieces that the picture could not come together. Crow knew that somewhere deep inside he had the answers—and yet they refused to surface.

As he left Carstairs' study he cast one more half-fearful glance at the man's sardonic picture. A white crawling thing, previously unnoticed, dropped from the ledge of the frame and fell with a plop to the Boukhara rug…

Left almost entirely on his own now, Crow worked steadily through the rest of Tuesday, through Wednesday and Thursday morning; but after a light lunch on Thursday he decided he needed some fresh air. This coincided with his discovering another worm or maggot in the library, and he made a mental note that sooner or later he must speak to Carstairs about the possibility of a health hazard.

Since the day outside was bright, he let himself out of the house and into the gardens, choosing one of the many overgrown paths rather than the wide, gravelly drive. In a very little while all dullness of the mind was dissipated and he found himself drinking gladly and deeply of the cold air. This was something he must do more often, for all work and no play was beginning to make Titus Crow a very dull boy indeed.

He was not sure whether his employer was at home or away; but upon reaching the main gate by a circuitous route he decided that the latter case must apply. Either that or the man had not yet been down to collect the mail. There were several letters in the box, two of which were holding the metal flap partly open. Beginning to feel the chill, Crow carried the letters with him on a winding route back to the house. Out of sheer, curiosity he scanned them as he went, noting that the address on one of them was all wrong. It was addressed to a Mr. Castaigne, Solicitor, at The Burrows. Alongside the postage stamps the envelope had been faintly franked with the name and crest of Somerset House in London.

Somerset House, the central registry for births and deaths? Now, what business could Carstairs have with—

And again there swept over Titus Crow that feeling of nausea and faintness. All the cheeriness went out of him in a moment and his hand trembled where it held the suspect envelope. Suddenly his mind was in motion, desperately fighting to remember something, battling with itself against an invisible inner voice which insisted that it did not matter. But he now knew that it did.

Hidden by a clump of bushes which stood between himself and the house, Crow removed the crested envelope from the bundle of letters and slipped it into his inside jacket pocket. Then, sweating profusely if coldly, he delivered the bulk of the letters to the occasional table outside the door of Carstairs' study. On his way back to the library he saw that the cellar door stood open under the stairs, and he heard someone moving about down below. Pausing, he called down:

"Mr. Carstairs, there's mail for you. I've left the letters outside your study."

The sounds of activity ceased and finally Carstairs' voice replied: "Thank you, Mr. Crow. I shall be up immediately."

Not waiting, Crow hurried to the library and sat for a while at the table where he worked, wondering what to do and half-astonished at the impulse which had prompted him to steal the other's mail; or rather, to take this one letter. He had previously installed an electric kettle in the library with which to make himself coffee, and as his eyes alighted upon the kettle, an idea dawned. For it was far too late now for anything else but to let his suspicions carry him all the way. He must now follow his instincts.

Against the possibility of Carstairs' sudden, unannounced entry, he prepared the makings of a jug of instant coffee, an invention of the war years which found a certain favor with him; but having filled the jug to its brim with boiling water, he used the kettle's surplus steam to saturate the envelope's gummed flap until it came cleanly open. With trembling fingers, he extracted the letter and placed the envelope carefully back in his pocket. Now he opened the letter in the pages of his notebook, so that to all intents and purposes he would seem to be working as he read it.

The device was unnecessary, since he was not disturbed; but this, written in a neat hand upon the headed stationery of Somerset House, was what he read:

Dear Mr. Castaigne,

In respect of your inquiry on behalf of your client, we never answer such by telephone. Nor do we normally divulge information of this nature except to proven relatives or, occasionally, the police. We expect that now that hostilities are at an end, these restrictions may soon be lifted. However, since you have stressed that this is a matter of some urgency, and since, as you say, the person you seek could prove to be beneficiary of a large sum of money, we have made the necessary inquiries.

There were several Thomas Crows born in London in 1912 and one Trevor Crow; but there was no Titus. A Timeus Crow was born in Edinburgh, and a Titus Crew in Devon.

The name Titus Crow is, in fact, quite rare, and the closest we can come to your specifications is the date 1916, when a Titus Crow was indeed born in the city on the 2nd December. We are sorry if this seems inconclusive.

If you wish any further investigations made, however, we will require some form of evidence, such as testimonials, of the validity of your credentials and motive.

Until then, we remain,

etc...

Feeling a sort of numbness spreading through all his limbs, his entire body and mind, Crow read the letter again and yet again. Evidence of Carstairs' credentials and motive, indeed!

Very well, whatever it was that was going on, Titus Crow had now received all the warnings he needed. Forewarned is forearmed, they say, and Crow must now properly arm himself—or at least protect himself—as best he could. One thing he would not do was run, not from an as-yet-undefined fear, an unidentified threat. His interest in the esoteric, the occult, had brought him to The Barrows, and those same interests must now sustain him.

And so, in his way, he declared war. But what were the enemy's weapons, and what was his objective? For the rest of the afternoon Crow did very little of work but sat in thoughtful silence and made his plans...

V

At 4:45 P.M. he went and knocked on Carstairs' door. Carstairs answered but did not invite him in. Instead he came out into the corridor. There, towering cadaverously over Crow and blocking out even more of the gloomy light of the place, he said, "Yes, Mr. Crow? What can I do for you?"

"Sir," Crow answered, "I'm well up to schedule on my work and see little problem finishing it in the time allowed. Which prompts me to ask a favor of you. Certain friends of mine are in London tonight, and so—"

"You would like a long weekend, is that it? Well, I see no real problem, Mr. Crow..." But while Carstairs' attitude seemed genuine enough, Crow suspected that he had in fact presented the man with a problem. His request had caught the occultist off guard—surprised and puzzled him—as if Carstairs had never for a moment considered the possibility of Crow's wishing to take extra time off. He tried his best not to show it, however, as he said: "By all means, yes, do go off and see your friends. And perhaps you would do me the honor of accepting a little gift to take with you? A bottle of my wine, perhaps? Good! When will you be going?"

"As soon as possible," Crow answered at once. "If I leave now I'll have all of tomorrow and Saturday to spend with my friends. I may even be able to return early on Sunday, and so make up for lost time."

"No, I wouldn't hear of it." Carstairs held up long, tapering hands. "Besides, I have friends of my own coming to stay this weekend—and this time I really do not wish to be disturbed." And he looked at Crow pointedly. "Very well, I shall expect to see you Monday morning. Do enjoy your weekend and I do urge you to take a bottle of my wine with you." He smiled his ghastly smile.

Crow said, "Thank you," and automatically stuck out his hand—which Carstairs ignored or pretended not to see as he turned and passed back into his study....

At 5:20 P.M. Crow pulled up at a large hotel on the approaches to Guildford and found a telephone booth. On his first day at The Barrows Carstairs had given him his ex-directory number, in case he should ever need to contact him at short notice. Now he took out the letter from Somerset House, draped his handkerchief over the mouthpiece of the telephone and called Carstairs' number.

The unmistakable voice of his employer answered almost at once. "Carstairs here. Who is speaking?"

"Ah, Mr. Castaigne," Crow intoned. "Er—you did say Castaigne, didn't you?"

There was a moment's silence, then: "Yes, Mr. Castaigne, that's correct. Is that Somerset House?"

"Indeed, sir, I am calling in respect of your inquiry about a Mr. Crow?"

"Of course, yes. Titus Crow," Carstairs answered. "I was expecting a communication of one sort or another."

"Quite," said Crow. "Well, the name Titus Crow is in fact quite rare, and so was not difficult to trace. We do indeed have one such birth on record, dated second December 1912."

"Excellent!" said Carstairs, his delight clearly in evidence.

"However," Crow hastened on, "I must point out that we do not normally react to unsolicited inquiries of this nature and advise you that in future—"

"I quite understand," Carstairs cut him off. "Do not concern yourself, sir, for I doubt that I shall ever trouble you again." And he replaced his telephone, breaking the connection.

And that, thought Crow as he breathed a sigh of relief and put down his own handset, is that. His credentials were now authenticated, his first line of defense properly deployed.

Now there were other things to do…

Back in London, Crow's first thought was to visit a chemist friend he had known and studied with in Edinburgh. Taylor Ainsworth was the man, whose interests in the more obscure aspects of chemistry had alienated him from both tutors and students alike. Even now, famous and a power in his field, still there were those who considered him more alchemist than chemist proper. Recently returned to London, Ainsworth was delighted to renew an old acquaintance and accepted Crow's invitation to drinks at his flat that night, with one reservation: he must be away early on a matter of business.

Next Crow telephoned Harry Townley, his family doctor. Townley was older than Crow by at least twenty years and was on the point of giving up his practice to take the cloth, but he had always been a friend and confidant; and he, too, in his way was considered unorthodox in his chosen field. Often referred to as a charlatan, Townley held steadfastly to his belief in hypnotism, homeopathy, herbalism and such as tremendous aids to more orthodox treatments. Later it would be seen that there was merit in much of this, but for now he was considered a crank.

The talents of these two men, as opposed to those of more mundane practitioners, were precisely what Crow needed. They arrived at his flat within minutes of each other, were introduced and then invited to sample—in very small doses—Carstairs' wine. Crow, too, partook, but only the same minute amount as his friends, sufficient to wet the palate but no more. Oh, he felt the need to fill his glass, certainly, but he now had more than enough of incentives to make him refrain.

"Excellent!" was Harry Townley's view.

"Fine stuff," commented Taylor Ainsworth. "Where on earth did you find it, Titus?" He picked up the bottle and peered closely at the label. "Arabic, isn't it?"

"The label is, yes," Crow answered. "It says simply, 'table wine,' that much at least I know. So you both believe it to be of good quality, eh?"

They nodded in unison and Townley admitted, "I wouldn't mind a bottle or two in my cellar, young Crow. Can you get any more?"

Crow shook his head. "I really don't think I want to," he said. "It seems I'm already partly addicted to the stuff—and it leaves me with a filthy headache! Oh, and you certainly shouldn't take it if you're driving. No, Harry, I've other stuff here you can drink while we talk. Less potent by far. This bottle is for Taylor."

"For me?" Ainsworth seemed pleasantly surprised. "A gift, do you mean? That's very decent of you…" Then he saw Crow's cocked eyebrow. "Or is there a catch in it?"

Crow grinned. "There's a catch in it, yes. I want an analysis. I want to know if there's anything in it. Any drugs or such like."

"I should be able to arrange that okay," said the other. "But I'll need a sample."

"Take the bottle," said Crow at once, "and do what you like with it afterward—only get me that analysis. I'll be in touch next weekend, if that's all right with you?"

Now Crow pulled the cork from a commoner brand and topped up their glasses. To Townley he said, "Harry, I think I'm in need of a checkup. That's why I asked you to bring your tools."

"What, you?" The doctor looked surprised. "Why, you're fit as a fiddle—you always have been."

"Yes," said Crow. "Well, to my knowledge the best fiddles are two hundred years old and stringy! And that's just how I feel," and he went on to describe in full his symptoms of sudden nausea, headaches, bouts of dizziness and apparent loss of memory. "Oh, yes," he finished, "and it might just have something to do with that wine which both of you find so excellent!"

While Townley prepared to examine him, Ainsworth excused himself and went off to keep his business appointment. Crow let him go but made him promise not to breathe a word of the wine or his request for an analysis to another soul. When he left, Carstairs' bottle was safely hidden from view in a large inside pocket of his overcoat.

Townley now sounded Crow's chest and checked his heart, then examined his eyes—the latter at some length—following which he frowned and put down his instruments. Then he seated himself facing Crow and tapped with his fingers on the arms of his chair. The frown stayed on his face as he sipped his wine.

"Well?" Crow finally asked.

"You may well say 'well,' young Crow," Townley answered. "Come on, now, what have you been up to?"

Crow arched his eyebrows. "Up to? Is something wrong with me, then?"

Townley sighed and looked a little annoyed. "Have it your own way, then," he said. "Yes, there is something wrong with you. Not a great deal, but enough to cause me some concern. One: there is some sort of drug in your system. Your pulse is far too slow, your blood pressure too high—oh, and there are other symptoms I recognize, including those you told me about. Two: your eyes. Now, eyes are rather a specialty of mine, and yours tell me a great deal. At a guess—I would say you've been playing around with hypnosis."

"I most certainly have not!" Crow denied, but his voice faltered on the last word. Suddenly he remembered thinking that Carstairs had a hypnotic personality.

"Then perhaps you've been hypnotized," Townley suggested, "without your knowing it?"

"Is that possible?"

"Certainly." Again the doctor frowned. "What sort of company have you been keeping just lately, Titus?"

"Fishy company indeed, Harry," the other answered. "But you've interested me. Hypnosis and loss of memory, eh? Well now," and he rubbed his chin thoughtfully. "Listen, could you possibly dehypnotize me? Trace the trouble back to its source, as it were?"

"I can try. If you've been under once—well, it's usually far easier the second time. Are you game?"

"Just try me," Crow grimly answered. "There's something I have to get to the bottom of, and if hypnosis is the way—why, I'll try anything once!"

An hour later, having had Crow in and out of trance half a dozen times, the good doctor finally shook his head and admitted defeat. "You have been hypnotized, I'm sure of it," he said. "But by someone who knows his business far better than I. Do you remember any of the questions I asked you when you were under?"

Crow shook his head.

"That's normal enough," the other told him. "What's extraordinary is the fact that I can get nothing out of you concerning the events of the last couple of weeks!"

"Oh?" Crow was surprised. "But I'll gladly tell you all about the last few weeks if you like—without hypnosis."

"*All* about them?"

"Of course."

"I doubt it." Townley smiled. "For that's the seat of the trouble. You don't *know* all about them. What you remember isn't the whole story."

"I see," Crow slowly answered, and his thoughts went back again to those dim, shadowy dreams of his and to his strange pseudomemories of vague snatches of echoing conversation. "Well, thank you, Harry," he finally said. "You're a good friend and I appreciate your help greatly."

"Now, listen, Titus." The other's concern was unfeigned. "If there's anything else I can do—anything at all—just let me know, and—"

"No, no, there's nothing." Crow forced himself to smile into the doctor's anxious face. "It's just that I'm into something beyond the normal scope of things, something I have to see through to the end."

"Oh? Well, it must be a damned funny business that you can't tell me about. Anyway, I'm not the prying type—but I do urge you to be careful."

"It *is* a funny business, Harry," Crow nodded, "and I'm only just beginning to see a glimmer of light at the end of the tunnel. As for my being careful—you may rely upon that!"

Seeing Townley to the door, he had second thoughts. "Harry, do I remember your having a gun, a six-shooter?"

"A forty-five revolver, yes. It was my father's. I have ammunition, too."

"Would you mind if I borrowed it for a few weeks?"

Townley looked at him very hard, but finally gave a broad grin. "Of course you can," he said. "I'll drop it round tomorrow. But there is such a thing as being *too* careful, you know!"

VI

Following a very poor night's sleep, the morning of Friday, 18 January, found Titus Crow coming awake with a start, his throat dry and rough and his eyes gritty and bloodshot. His first thought as he got out of bed was of Carstairs' wine—and his second was to remember that he had given it to

Taylor Ainsworth for analysis. Stumbling into his bathroom and taking a shower, he cursed himself roundly. He should have let the man take only a sample. But then, as sleep receded and reason took over, he finished showering in a more thoughtful if still sullen mood.

No amount of coffee seemed able to improve the inflamed condition of Crow's throat, and though it was ridiculously early he got out the remainder of last night's bottle of his own wine. A glass or two eased the problem a little, but within the hour it was back, raw and painful as ever. That was when Harry Townley turned up with his revolver, and seeing Crow's distress he examined him and immediately declared the trouble to be psychosomatic.

"What?" said Crow hoarsely. "You mean I'm imagining it? Well, that would take a pretty vivid imagination!"

"No," said Townley, "I didn't say you were imagining it. I said it isn't a physical thing. And therefore there's no physical cure."

"Oh, I think there is," Crow answered. "But last night I gave the bottle away!"

"Indeed?" And Townley's eyebrows went up. "Withdrawal symptoms, eh?"

"Not of the usual sort, no," answered Crow. "Harry, have you the time to put me into trance just once more? There's a certain precaution I'd like to take before I resume the funny business we were talking about last night."

"Not a bad idea," said the doctor, "at least where this supposed sore throat of yours is concerned. If it is psychosomatic, I might be able to do something about it. I've had a measure of success with cigarette smokers."

"Fine," said Crow, "but I want you to do more than just that. If I give you a man's name, can you order me never to allow myself to fall under his influence—never to be hypnotized by him—again?"

"Well, it's a tall order," the good doctor admitted, "but I can try."

Half an hour later when Townley snapped his fingers and Crow came out of trance, his throat was already feeling much better, and by the time he and Townley left his flat the trouble had disappeared altogether. Nor was he ever bothered with it again. He dined with the doctor in the city, then caught a taxi and went on alone to the British Museum.

Through his many previous visits to that august building and establishment he was well-acquainted with the curator of the Rare Books Department, a lean, learned gentleman thirty-five years his senior, sharp-eyed and with a dry and wicked wit. Sedgewick was the man's name, but Crow invariably called him sir.

"What, you again?" Sedgewick greeted him when Crow sought him out. "Did no one tell you the war was over? And what code-cracking business are you on this time, eh?"

Crow was surprised. "I hadn't suspected you knew about that," he said.

"Ah, but I did! Your superiors saw to it that I received orders to assist you in every possible way. You didn't suppose I just went running all over the place for any old body, did you?"

"This time," Crow admitted, "I'm here on my own behalf. Does that change things, sir?"

The other smiled. "Not a bit, old chap. Just tell me what you're after and I'll see what I can do for you. Are we back to cyphers, codes, and cryptograms again?"

"Nothing so common, I'm afraid," Crow answered. "Look, this might seem a bit queer, but I'm looking for something on worm worship."

The other frowned. "Worm worship? Man or beast?"

"I'm sorry?" Crow looked puzzled.

"Worship of the annelid—family, *Lumbricidae*—or of the man, Worm?"

"The man-worm?"

"Worm with a capital W." Sedgewick grinned. "He was a Danish physician, an anatomist. Olaus Worm. Around the turn of the sixteenth century, I believe. Had a number of followers. Hence the word *Wormian*, relating to his discoveries."

"You get more like a dictionary every day!" Crow jokingly complained. But his smile quickly turned to a frown. "Olaus Worm, eh? Could a Latinized version of that be Olaus Wormius, I wonder?"

"What, old Wormius who translated the Greek *Necronomicon?* No, not possible, for he was thirteenth century."

Crow sighed and rubbed his brow. "Sir," he said, "you've thrown me right off the rails. No, I meant worship of the beast—the annelid, if you like— worship of the maggot."

Now it was Sedgewick's turn to frown. "The maggot!" he repeated. "Ah, but now you're talking about a different kettle of worms entirely. A maggot is a grave -worm. Now, if that's the sort of worm you mean…have you tried *The Mysteries of the Worm?*"

Crow gasped. *The Mysteries of the Worm!* He had seen a copy in Carstairs' library, had even handled it. Old Ludwig Prinn's *De Vermis Mysteriis!*

Seeing his look, Sedgewick said: "Oh? Have I said something right?"

"Prinn." Crow's agitation was obvious. "He was Flemish, wasn't he?"

"Correct! A sorcerer, alchemist and necromancer. He was burned in Brussels. He wrote his book in prison shortly before his execution, and the manuscript found its way to Cologne where it was posthumously published."

"Do you have a copy in English?"

Sedgewick smiled and shook his head. "I believe there is such a copy—circa 1820, the work of one Charles Leggett, who translated it from the German black-letter—but we don't have it. I can let you see a black-letter, if you like."

Crow shook his head. "No, it gives me a headache just thinking of it. My knowledge of antique German simply wouldn't run to it. What about the Latin?"

"We have half of it. Very fragile. You can see but you can't touch."

"Can't touch? Sir—I want to borrow it!"

"Out of the question, old chap. Worth my job."

"The black-letter, then." Crow was desperate. "Can I have a good long look at it? Here? Privately?"

The other, pursed his lips and thought it over for a moment or two, and finally smiled. "Oh, I daresay so. And I suppose you'd like some paper and a pen, too, eh? Come on, then."

A few minutes later, seated at a table in a tiny private room, Crow opened the black-letter—and from the start he knew he was in for a bad time, that the task was near hopeless. Nonetheless he struggled on, and two hours later Sedgewick looked in to find him deep in concentration, poring over the decorative but difficult pages. Hearing the master librarian enter, Crow looked up.

"This could be exactly what I'm looking for," he said. "I think it's here—in the chapter called 'Saracenic Rituals.'"

"Ah, the Dark Rites of the Saracens, eh?" said Sedgewick. "Well, why didn't you say so? We have the 'Rituals' in a translation!"

"In English?" Crow jumped to his feet.

Sedgewick nodded. "The work is anonymous, I'm afraid—by Clergyman X, or some such, and of course I can't guarantee its reliability—but if you want it—"

"I do!" said Crow.

Sedgewick's face grew serious. "Listen, we're closing up shop soon. If I get it for you—that is if I let you take it with you—I must have your word that you'll take infinite care of it. I mean, my heart will quite literally be in my mouth until it's returned."

"You know you have my word," Crow answered at once.

Ten minutes later Sedgewick saw him out of the building. Along the way Crow asked him, "Now how do you suppose Prinn, a native of Brussels, knew so much about the practice of black magic among the Syria-Arabian nomads?"

Sedgewick opened his encyclopedic mind. "I've read something about that somewhere," he said. "He was a much-traveled man, Prinn, and lived for many years among an order of Syrian wizards in the Jebel el Ansariye. That's where he would have learned his stuff. Disguised as beggars or holy men, he and others of the order would make pilgrimages to the world's most evil places, which were said to be conducive to the study of demonology. I remember one such focal point of evil struck me as singularly unusual, being as it was situated on the shore of Galilee! Old Prinn lived in the ruins there for some time. Indeed, he names it somewhere in his book." Sedgewick frowned. "Now, what was the place called…?"

"Chorazin!" said Crow flatly, cold fingers clutching at his heart.

"Yes, that's right," answered the other, favoring Crow with an appraising glance. "You know, sometimes I think you're after my job! Now, do look after that pamphlet, won't you?"

That night, through Saturday and all of Sunday, Crow spent his time engrossed in the "Saracenic Rituals" reduced to the early nineteenth-century English of Clergyman X, and though he studied the pamphlet minutely still it remained a disappointment. Indeed, it seemed that he might learn more from the lengthy preface than from the text itself. Clergyman X (whoever he had been) had obviously spent a good deal of time researching Ludwig Prinn, but not so very much on the actual translation.

In the preface the author went into various dissertations on Prinn's origins, his lifestyle, travels, sources and sorceries—referring often and tantalizingly to other chapters in *De Vermis Mysteriis*, such as those on familiars, on the demons of the Cthulhu Myth Cycle, on divination, necromancy, elementals and vampires—but when it came to actually getting a few of Prinn's blasphemies down on paper, here he seemed at a loss. Or perhaps his religious background had deterred him.

Again and again Crow would find himself led on by the writer, on the verge of some horrific revelation, only to be let down by the reluctance of X to divulge Prinn's actual words. As an example, there was the following passage with its interesting extract from Alhazred's *Al Azif*, which in turn gave credit to an even older work by Ibn Schacabao:

And great Wisdom was in Alhazred, who had seen the Work of the Worm and knew it well. His Words were ever cryptic, but never less than here, where he discusses the Crypts of the Worm-Wizards of olden Irem, and something of their Sorceries:

"The nethermost Caverns," (said he) "are not for the fathoming of Eyes that see; for their Marvels are strange and terrific. Cursed the

Ground where dead Thoughts live new and oddly bodied, and evil the Mind that is held by no Head. Wisely did Ibn Schacabao say, that happy is the Town whose Wizards are all Ashes. For it is of old Rumor, that the Soul of the Devil-bought hastes not from his charnel Clay, but fats and instructs *the very Worm that gnaws*, till out of corruption horrid Life springs, and the dull Scavengers of Earth wax crafty to vex it and swell monstrous to plague it. Great Holes secretly are digged where Earth's Pores ought to suffice, and Things have learned to walk that ought to crawl..."

In Syria, with my own Eyes, I Ludwig Prinn saw one Wizard of Years without Number transfer himself to the Person of a younger man, whose Number he had divined; when at the appointed Hour he spoke the Words of the Worm. And this is what I saw..." [Editor's note: Prinn's description of the dissolution of the wizard and the investment of himself into his host is considered too horrific and monstrous to permit of any merely casual or unacquainted perusal—X]

Crow's frustration upon reading such as this was enormous; but in the end it was this very passage which lent him his first real clue to the mystery, and to Carstairs' motive; though at the time, even had he guessed the whole truth, still he could not have believed it. The clue lay in the references to the wizard knowing the younger man's number—and on rereading that particular line Crow's mind went back to his first meeting with Carstairs, when the man had so abruptly inquired about his date of birth. Crow had lied, adding four whole years to his span and setting the date at 2 December 1912. Now, for the first time, he considered that date from the numerologists' point of view, in which he was expert.

According to the orthodox system, the date 2 December 1912 would add up thus:

$$2$$
$$12$$
$$1$$
$$9$$
$$1$$
$$\underline{2}$$

$= 27$ and $2 + 7 = 9$

Or: $27 =$ Triple 9

Nine could be considered as being either the Death Number or the number of great spiritual and mental achievement. And of course the finding would be reinforced by the fact that there were nine letters in Crow's name—*if* that were the true date of his birth, which it was not.

To use a different system, the fictional date's numbers would add up thus:

$$
\begin{array}{r}
2 \\
1 \\
2 \\
1 \\
9 \\
1 \\
\underline{2} \\
=18 \\
\end{array}
$$

and $1 + 8 = 9$

Or: $18 =$ Triple 6

Triple six! The number of the Beast in Revelations! Crow's head suddenly reeled. Dimly, out of some forgotten corner of his mind, he heard an echoing voice say, *"His numbers are most propitious…propitious…propitious…"* And when he tried to tie that voice down it wriggled free, saying, *"Not worth it…just a dream…unimportant…utterly unimportant…"*

He shook himself, threw down his pen—then snatched it back up. Now Crow glared at the familiar room about him as a man suddenly roused from nightmare. "It *is* important!" he cried. "Damned important!"

But of course there was no one to hear him.

Later, fortified with coffee and determined to carry on, he used the Hebrew system to discover his number, in which the letters of the alphabet stand for numbers and a name's total equals the total of the man. Since this system made no use of the 9, he might reasonably expect a different sort of answer. But this was his result:

1	2	3	4	5	6	7	8
A	B	C	D	E	U	O	F
I	K	G	M	H	V	Z	P
Q	R	L	T	N	W		
J		S			X		
Y							

Titus Crow equals T,4 I,1 T,4 U,6 S,3 C,3 R,2 O,7 W,6. Which is 4 + 1 + 4 + 6 + 3 + 3 + 2 + 7 + 6 = 36. And 3 + 6 = 9. Or 36, a double 18. The Beast redoubled!

Propitious? In what way? For whom? Certainly not for himself!

For Carstairs?

Slowly, carefully, Titus Crow put down his pen…

VII

To Carstairs, waiting in the shadow of his doorway, it seemed that Crow took an inordinately long time to park his car in the garage, and when he came into view there were several things about him which in other circumstances might cause concern. A semidisheveled look to his clothes; a general tiredness in his bearing; an unaccustomed hang to his leonine head and a gritty redness of eye. Carstairs, however, was not at all concerned; on the contrary, he had expected no less.

As for Crow: despite his outward appearance, he was all awareness! The inflammation of his eyes had been induced by a hard rubbing with a mildly irritating but harmless ointment; the disheveled condition of his dress and apparent lack of will were deliberately affected. In short, he was acting, and he was a good actor.

"Mr. Crow," said Carstairs as Crow entered the house. "Delighted to have you back." And the other sensed a genuine relief in the occultist's greeting. Yes, he *was* glad to have him back. "Have you breakfasted?"

"Thank you, yes—on my way here." Crow's voice was strained, hoarse, but this too was affected.

Carstairs smiled, leading the way to the library. At the door he said, "Ah, these long weekends! How they take it out of one, eh? Well, no doubt you enjoyed the break."

As Crow passed into the library, Carstairs remained in the corridor. "I shall look in later," he said, "when perhaps you'll tell me something of the system you've devised for your work—and something of the progress you are making. Until then…" And he quietly closed the door on Crow.

Now the younger man straightened up. He went directly to his worktable and smiled sardonically at the bottle of wine, its cork half-pulled, which stood there waiting for him. He pulled the cork, poured a glass, took the bottle to the barred windows and opened one a crack, then stuck the neck of the bottle through the bars and poured the filthy stuff away into the garden. The empty bottle he placed in his alcove bedroom, out of sight.

Then, seating himself and beginning to work, he forced himself to concentrate on the task in hand—the cataloging of Carstairs' books, as if that were the real reason he was here—and so without a break worked steadily through the morning. About midday, when he was sure that he had done enough to satisfy his employer's supposed curiosity, should that really be necessary, he made himself coffee. Later he would eat, but not for an hour or so yet.

The morning had not been easy. His eyes had kept straying to the library shelf where he knew an edition of Prinn's book stood waiting for his eager attention. But he dared not open the thing while there was a chance that Carstairs might find him with it. He must be careful not to arouse the occultist's suspicions. Also, there was the glass of red wine close to hand, and Crow had found himself tempted. But in removing the symptoms of his supposed addiction, Harry Townley had also gone a good deal of the way toward curbing the need itself; so that Crow half suspected it was his own perverse nature that tempted him once more to taste the stuff, as if in contempt of Carstairs' attempted seduction of his senses.

And the glass was still there, untouched, when half an hour later Carstairs quietly knocked and strode into the room. His first act on entering was to go directly to the windows and draw the shades, before moving to the table and picking up Crow's notes. Saying nothing, he studied them for a moment, and Crow could see that he was mildly surprised. He had not expected Crow to get on quite so well, that much was obvious. Very well, in future he would do less. It made little difference, really, for by now he was certain that the "work" was very much secondary to Carstairs' real purpose in having him here. If only he could discover what that purpose really was…

"I am very pleased, Mr. Crow," said Carstairs presently. "Extremely so. Even in adverse conditions you appear to function remarkably well."

"Adverse conditions?"

"Come, now! It is dim here—drab, lonely and less than comfortable. Surely these are adverse conditions?"

"I work better when left alone," Crow answered. "And my eyes seem to have grown accustomed to meager light."

Carstairs had meanwhile spotted the glass of wine, and turning his head to scan the room he casually searched for the bottle. He did not seem displeased by Crow's apparent capacity for the stuff.

"Ah…" Crow mumbled. "Your wine. I'm afraid I—"

"Now, no apologies, young man," Carstairs held up a hand. "I have more than plenty of wine. Indeed, it gives me pleasure that you seem to enjoy it so. And perhaps it makes up for the otherwise inhospitable conditions, which I am sure are not in accordance with your usual mode of existence. Very well, I leave you to it. I shall be here for the rest of today—I have work in my study—but tomorrow I expect to be away. I shall perhaps see you on Wednesday morning?" And with that he left the library.

Satisfied that he was not going to be disturbed any further, without bothering to open the window shades, Crow took down *De Vermis Mysteriis* from its shelf and was at once dismayed to discover the dark, cracked leather bindings of the German black-letter, almost the duplicate of the book he had looked into in the British Museum. His dismay turned to delight, however, on turning back the heavy cover and finding, pasted into the old outer shell a comparatively recent work whose title page declared it to be:

THE MYSTERIES OF THE WORM
being
THE COMPLETE BOOK
in sixteen chapters
With many dozens wood engravings;
representing
THE ORIGINAL WORK
of
LUDWIG PRINN,
after translation
By Charles Leggett,
and including his notes;
this being Number Seven
of a very Limited Edition,
LONDON
1821

Crow immediately took the book through into his alcove room and placed it under his pillow. It would keep until tonight. Then he unpacked a few things, hiding Townley's gun under his mattress near the foot of the bed. Finally, surprised to find he had developed something of an appetite, he decided upon lunch.

But then, as he drew the curtains on the alcove and crossed the room toward the library door, something caught his eye. It was an obscene, white wriggling shape on the faded carpet where Carstairs had stood. He took it to the window but there, even as he made to toss it into the garden, discovered a second worm crawling on the wainscotting. Now he was filled with revulsion. These were two worms too many!

He disposed of the things, poured the still-untouched glass of wine after them and went straight to Carstairs' study. Knocking, he heard dull movements within, and finally the occultist's voice:

"Come in, Mr. Crow."

This surprised him, for until now the room had supposedly been forbidden to him. Nevertheless he opened the door and went in. The gloom inside made shadows of everything, particularly the dark figure seated at the great desk. A thick curtain had been drawn across the single window and only the dim light of a desk lamp, making a pool of feeble yellow atop the desk, gave any illumination at all. And now, here in these close quarters, the musty smell of the old house had taken to itself an almost charnel taint which was so heavy as to be overpowering.

"I was resting my eyes, Mr. Crow," came Carstairs' sepulchral rumble. "Resting this weary old body of mine. Ah, what it must be to be young! Is there something?"

"Yes," said Crow firmly. "A peculiar and very morbid thing. I just thought I should report it."

"A peculiar thing? Morbid? To what do you refer?" Carstairs sat up straighter behind his desk.

Crow could not see the man's face, which was in shadow, but he saw him start as he answered, "Worms! A good many of them. I've been finding them all over the house."

The figure in the chair trembled, half stood, sat down again. "Worms?" There was a badly feigned tone of surprise in his voice, followed by a short silence in which Crow guessed the other sought for an answer to this riddle. He decided to prompt him.

"I really think you should have it seen to. They must be eating out the very heart of the house."

Now Carstairs sat back and appeared to relax. His chuckle was throaty when he answered. "Ah, no, Mr. Crow—for they are not of the house-eating species. I rather fancy they prefer richer fare. Yes, I too have seen them. They are maggots!"

"Maggots?" Crow could not keep the disgusted note out of his voice, even though he had half suspected it. "But…is there something dead here?"

"There was," Carstairs answered. "Shortly after you arrived here I found a decomposing rabbit in the cellar. The poor creature had been injured on the road or in a trap and had found a way into my cellar to die. Its remains were full of maggots. I got rid of the carcass and put down chemicals to destroy the maggots. That is why you were forbidden to go into the cellar; the fumes are harmful."

"I see…"

"As for those few maggots you have seen, doubtless some escaped and have found their way through the cracks and crevices of this old house. There is nothing for them here, however, and so they will soon cease to be a problem."

Crow nodded.

"So do not concern yourself."

"No, indeed." And that was that.

Crow did not eat after all. Instead, feeling queasy, he went out into the garden for fresh air. But even out there the atmosphere now seemed tainted. It was as if a pall of gloom hovered over the house and grounds, and that with every passing minute the shadows deepened and the air grew heavy with sinister presences.

Some sixth, psychic sense informed Crow that he walked the strands of an incredibly evil web, and that a great bloated spider waited, half hidden from view, until the time was just right—or until he took just one wrong step. Now a longing sprang up in him to be out of here and gone from the place, but there was that obstinate streak in his nature which would not permit flight. It was a strange hand that Fate had dealt, where at the moment Carstairs seemed to hold more than his fair share of the aces and Titus Crow held only one trump card.

Even now he did not realize how much depended upon that card, but he felt sure that he would very soon find out.

VIII

Crow did little or no work that afternoon but, affected by a growing feeling of menace—of hidden eyes watching him—searched the library wall to wall and over every square inch of carpeting, wainscotting, curtains and alcove, particularly his bed, for maggots. He did not for one moment believe Carstairs' explanation for the presence of the things, even though logic told him it might just be plausible. But for all that his search was very thorough and time-consuming he found nothing.

That night, seated uneasily in the alcove behind drawn curtains, he took out *De Vermis Mysteriis* and opened it to the "Saracenic Rituals," only to discover that the greater part of that chapter was missing, the pages cleanly removed with a razor-sharp knife. The opening to the chapter was there, however, and something of its middle. Reading what little remained, Crow picked out three items which he found particularly interesting. One of these fragments concerned that numerology in which he was expert, and it was an item of occult knowledge written down in terms no one could fail to understand:

> The Names of a Man, along with his Number, are all-important. Knowing the First, a Magician knows something of the Man; knowing the Second, he knows his Past, Present, and Future; and he may control the Latter by means of his Sorceries, even unto the Grave and beyond!

Another offered a warning against wizardly generosity:

> Never accept a Gift from a Necromancer, or any Wizard or Familiar. Steal which may be stolen, buy which may be bought, earn it if that be at all possible and if it must be had—but do *not* accept it, neither as a Gift nor as a Legacy…

Both of these seemed to Crow to have a bearing on his relationship with Carstairs; but the last of the three interested and troubled him the most, for he could read in it an even stronger and far more sinister parallel:

> A Wizard will not offer the Hand of Friendship to one he would seduce. When a Worm-Wizard refuses his Hand, that is an especially bad Omen. And having once refused his Hand, if he then offers it, that is even worse!

Finally, weary and worried. but determined in the end to get to the root of the thing, Crow went to bed. He lay in darkness and tossed and turned for a long time before sleep finally found him; and this was the first time, before sleeping, that he had ever felt the need to turn his key in the lock of the library door.

On Tuesday morning Crow was awakened by the sound of a motorcar's engine. Peeping through half-closed window shades he saw Carstairs leave the house and get into a car which waited on the winding drive. As soon as the car turned about and bore the occultist away, Crow quickly dressed and went to the cellar door under the stairs in the gloomy hall. The door was locked, as he had expected.

Very well, perhaps there was another way in. Carstairs had said that a rabbit had found its way in; and even if that were untrue, still it suggested that there might be such an entry from the grounds of the house. Going into the garden, Crow first of all ensured that he was quite alone, then followed the wall of the house until, at the back, he found overgrown steps leading down to a basement landing. At the bottom a door had been heavily boarded over, and Crow could see at a glance that it would take a great deal of work to get into the cellar by that route. Nor would it be possible to disguise such a forced entry. To one side of the door, completely opaque with grime, a casement window next offered itself for inspection. This had not been boarded up, but many successive layers of old paint had firmly welded frame and sashes into one. Using a penknife, Crow worked for a little while to gouge the paint free from the joint; but then, thinking he heard an unaccustomed sound, he stopped and hastily returned to the garden. No one was there, but his nerves had suffered and he did not return to his task. That would have to wait upon another day.

Instead he went back indoors, washed, shaved and breakfasted (though really he did not have much of an appetite) and finally climbed the stairs to scan the countryside all around through bleary windows. Seeing nothing out of the ordinary, he returned to the ground floor and once more ventured along the corridor to Carstairs' study. That door, too, was locked; and now Crow's frustration and jumpiness began to tell on him. Also he suspected that he was missing the bolstering—or deadening—effect of the occultist's wine. And Carstairs had not been remiss in leaving him a fresh bottle of the stuff upon the breakfast table.

Now, fearing that he might weaken, he rushed back to the kitchen and picked up the bottle on the way. Only when he had poured it down the sink, every last drop, did he begin to relax; and only then did he realize how tired he was. He had not slept well; his nerves seemed frayed; at this rate he would never have the strength to solve the mystery, let alone see it through to the end.

At noon, on the point of preparing himself a light meal, he found yet another maggot—this time in the kitchen itself. That was enough. He could not eat here. Not now.

He left the house, drove into Haslemere and dined at a hotel, consumed far too many brandies and returned to The Barrows cheerfully drunk. All the rest of the day he spent sleeping it off—for which sheer waste of time he later cursed himself—and awakened late in the evening with a nagging hangover.

Determined now to get as much rest as possible, he made himself a jug of coffee and finally retired for the night. The coffee did not keep him awake; and once again he locked the library door.

Wednesday passed quickly and Crow saw Carstairs only twice. He did a minimum of "work" but searched the library shelves for other titles which might hint at his awful employer's purpose. He found nothing, but such was his fascination with these old books—the pleasure of reading and handling them—that his spirits soon rose to something approaching their previous vitality. And throughout the day he kept up the pretense of increasing dependence on Carstairs' wine, and he continued to effect a hoarse voice and to redden his eyes by use of the irritating ointment.

On Thursday Carstairs once again left the house, but this time he forgot to lock his study door. By now Crow felt almost entirely returned to his old self, and his nerves were steady as he entered that normally forbidden room. And seeing Carstairs' almost antique telephone standing on an occasional table close to the desk, he decided upon a little contact with the outside world.

He quickly rang Taylor Ainsworth's number in London. Ainsworth answered, and Crow said: "Taylor, Titus here. Any luck yet with that wine?"

"Ah!" said the other, his voice scratchy with distance. "So you couldn't wait until the weekend, eh? Well, funny stuff, that wine, with a couple of really weird ingredients. I don't know what they are or how they work, but they do. They work on human beings like aniseed works on dogs! Damned addictive!"

"Poisonous?"

"Eh? Dear me, no! I shouldn't think so, not in small amounts. You wouldn't be talking to me now if they were! Listen, Titus, I'd be willing to pay a decent price if you could—"

"Forget it!" Crow snapped. Then he softened. "Listen, Taylor, you're damned *lucky* there's no more of that stuff, believe me. I think it's a recipe that goes back to the very blackest days of Man's history—and I'm pretty sure that if you knew those secret ingredients you'd find them pretty ghastly! Thanks anyway, for what you've done." And despite the other's distant protests he put down the telephone.

Now, gazing once more about that dim and malodorous room, Crow's eyes fell upon a desk calendar. Each day, including today, had been scored through with a thick black line. The 1st February, however, Candlemas Eve, had been ringed with a double circle.

Candlemas Eve, still eight days away…

Crow frowned. There was something he should remember about that date, something quite apart from its religious connections. Dim memories stirred sluggishly. *Candlemas Eve, the date ordained.*

Crow started violently. The date ordained? Ordained for what? Where had that idea come from? But the thought had fled, had sunk itself down again into his subconscious mind.

Now he tried the desk drawers. All were locked and there was no sign of a key. Suddenly, coming from nowhere, Crow had the feeling that there were eyes upon him! He whirled, heart beating faster—and came face-to-face with Carstairs' picture where it hung with the others on the wall. In the dimness of that oppressive room, the eyes in the picture seemed to glare at him piercingly…

After that the day passed uneventfully and fairly quickly. Crow visited the sunken casement window again at the rear of the house and did a little more work on it, scraping away at the old, thick layers of paint, seeming to make very little impression. As for the rest of the time: he rested a good deal and spent an hour or so on Carstairs' books, busying himself with the "task" he had been set, but no more than that.

About 4:30 P.M. Crow heard a car pull up outside and going to the half-shaded windows he saw Carstairs walking up the drive as the car pulled away. Then, giving his eyes a quick rub and settling himself at his worktable, he assumed a harassed pose. Carstairs came immediately to the library, knocked and walked in.

"Ah, Mr. Crow. Hard at it as usual, I see?"

"Not really," Crow hoarsely answered, glancing up from his notebook. "I can't seem to find the energy for it. Or maybe I've gone a bit stale. It will pass."

Carstairs seemed jovial. "Oh, I'm sure it will. Come, Mr. Crow, let's eat. I have an appetite. Will you join me?" Seeing no way to excuse himself, Crow followed Carstairs to the dining room. Once there, however, he remembered the maggot he had found in the kitchen and could no longer contemplate food under any circumstances.

"I'm really not very hungry," he mumbled.

"Oh?" Carstairs raised an eyebrow. "Then I shall eat later. But I'm sure you wouldn't refuse a glass or two of wine, eh?"

Crow was on the point of doing just that—until he remembered that he could not refuse. He was not supposed to be able to refuse! Carstairs fetched a bottle from the larder, pulled its cork and poured two liberal glasses. "Here's to you, Mr. Crow," he said. "No—to us!"

And seeing no way out, Crow was obliged to lift his glass and drink…

IX

Nor had Carstairs been satisfied to leave it at that. After the first glass there had been a second, and a third, until Titus Crow's head was very quickly spinning. Only then was he able to excuse himself, and then not before Carstairs had pressed the remainder of the bottle into his hand, softly telling him to take it with him, to enjoy it before he retired for the night.

He did no such thing but poured it into the garden; and then, reeling as he went, made his way to the bathroom where he drank water in such amounts and so quickly as to make himself violently ill. Then, keeping everything as quiet as possible, he staggered back to the library and locked himself in.

He did not think that a great deal of wine remained in his stomach—precious little of anything else, either—but his personal remedy for any sort of excess had always been coffee. He made and drank an entire jug of it, black, then returned to the bathroom and bathed, afterward thoroughly dousing himself with cold water. Only then did he feel satisfied that he had done all he could to counteract the effects of Carstairs' wine.

All of this had taken it out of him, however, so that by 8:00 P.M. he was once again listless and tired. He decided to make an early night of it, retiring to his alcove with *De Vermis Mysteriis*. Within twenty minutes he was nodding over the book and feeling numb and confused in his mind. The unvomited wine was working on him, however gradually, and his only hope now was that he might sleep it out of his system.

Dazedly returning the heavy book to its shelf, he stumbled back to his bed and collapsed onto it. In that same position, spread-eagled and facedown, he fell asleep; and that was how he stayed for the next four hours.

Crow came awake slowly, gradually growing aware that he was being addressed, aware too of an unaccustomed feeling of cold. Then he remembered what had gone before and his mind began to work a little faster. In the darkness of the alcove he opened his eyes a fraction, peered into the gloom and made out two dim figures standing to one side of his bed. Some instinct told him that there would be more of them on the other side, and only by the greatest effort of will was he able to restrain himself from leaping to his feet.

Now the voice came again, Carstairs' voice, not talking to him this time but to those who stood around his bed. "I was afraid that the wine's effect was weakening, but apparently I was wrong. Well, my friends, you are here tonight to witness an example of my will over the mind and body of Titus Crow. He cannot be allowed to go away this weekend, of course, for the time is too near. I would hate anything to happen to him."

"So would we all, Master," came a voice Crow recognized. "For—"

"For then I would need to make a second choice, eh, Durrell? Indeed, I know why you wish nothing to go amiss. But you *presume*, Durrell! You are no fit habitation."

"Master, I merely—" the other began to protest.

"Be quiet!" Carstairs snarled. "And watch." Now his words were once more directed at Crow, and his voice grew deep and sonorous.

"Titus Crow, you are dreaming, only dreaming. There is nothing to fear, nothing at all. It is only a dream. Turn over onto your back, Titus Crow."

Crow, wide awake now—his mind suddenly clear and realizing that Harry Townley's counterhypnotic device was working perfectly—forced himself to slow, languid movement. With eyes half-shuttered, he turned over, relaxed and rested his head on his pillow.

"Good!" Carstairs said. "That was good. Now sleep, Titus Crow, sleep and dream."

Now Garbett's voice said: "Apparently all is well, Master."

"Yes, all is well. His Number is confirmed, and he comes more fully under my spell as the time approaches. Now we shall see if we can do a little more than merely command dumb movement. Let us see if we can make him talk. Mr. Crow, can you hear me?"

Crow, mind racing, opened parched lips and gurgled, "Yes, I hear you."

"Good! Now, I want you to remember something. Tomorrow you will come to me and tell me that you have decided to stay here at The Barrows over the weekend. Is that clear?"

Crow nodded.

"You do want to stay, don't you?"

Again he nodded.

"Tell me you wish it."

"I want to stay here," Crow mumbled, "over the weekend."

"Excellent!" said Carstairs. "There'll be plenty of wine for you here, Titus Crow, to ease your throat and draw the sting from your eyes."

Crow lay still, forcing himself to breathe deeply.

"Now I want you to get up, turn back your covers and get into bed," said Carstairs. "The night air is cold and we do not wish you to catch a chill, do we?"

Crow shook his head, shakily stood up, turned back his blankets and sheets and lay down again, covering himself.

"Completely under your control!" Garbett chuckled, rubbing his hands together. "Master, you are amazing!"

"I have been amazing, as you say, for almost three and a half centuries," Carstairs replied with some pride. "Study my works well, friend Garbett, and one day you too may aspire to the Priesthood of the Worm!"

On hearing these words so abruptly spoken, Crow could not help but give a start—but so too did the man Durrell, a fraction of a second earlier, so that Crow's movement went unnoticed. And even as the man on the bed sensed Durrell's frantic leaping, so he heard him cry out: "*Ugh!* On the floor! I trod on one! The maggots!"

"Fool!" Carstairs snarled. "Idiot!" And to the others, "Get him out of here. Then come back and help me collect them up."

After that there was a lot of hurried movement and some scrambling about on the floor, but finally Crow was left alone with Carstairs; and then the man administered that curious droning caution which Crow was certain he had heard before.

"It was all a dream, Mr. Crow. Only a dream. There is nothing really you should remember about it, nothing of any importance whatsoever. But you will come to me tomorrow, won't you, and tell me that you plan to spend the weekend here? Of course you will!"

And with that Carstairs left, silently striding from the alcove like some animated corpse into the dark old house. But this time he left Crow wide awake, drenched in a cold sweat of terror and with little doubt in his mind but that this had been another attempt of Carstairs' to subvert him to his will—at which he had obviously had no little success in the recent past!

Eyes staring in the darkness, Crow waited until he heard engines start up and motorcars draw away from the house—waited again until the old place settled down—and when far away a church clock struck one, only then did he get out of bed, putting on lights and slippers, trembling in a chill which had nothing at all to do with that of the house. Then he set about to check the floor of the alcove, the library, to strip and check and reassemble his bed blanket by blanket and sheet by sheet; until at last he was perfectly satisfied that there was no crawling thing in this area he had falsely come to think of as his own place, safe and secure. For the library door was still locked, which meant either that Carstairs had a second key, or—

Now, with Harry Townley's .45 tucked in his dressing-gown pocket, he examined the library again, and this time noticed that which very nearly stood his hair on end. It had to do with a central section of heavy shelving set against an internal wall. For in merely looking at this mighty bookcase, no one would ever suspect that it had a hidden pivot—and yet such must be the case. Certain lesser books where he had left them stacked on the carpet along the frontage of the bookshelves had been moved, swept aside in an arc; and now indeed he could see that a small gap existed between the bottom of this central part and the carpeted floor proper.

Not without a good deal of effort, Crow finally found the trick of it and caused the bookcase to move, revealing a blackness and descending steps which spiraled steeply down into the bowels of the house. At last he had discovered a way into the cellar; but for now he was satisfied simply to close that secret door and make for himself a large jug of coffee, which he drank to its last drop before making another.

And so he sat through the remaining hours of the night, sipping coffee, occasionally trembling in a preternatural chill, and promising himself that above all else, come what may, he would somehow sabotage whatever black plans Carstairs had drawn up for his future…

The weekend was nightmarish.

Crow reported to Carstairs Saturday morning and begged to be allowed to stay at The Barrows over the weekend (which, it later occurred to him in the fullness of his senses, whether *he himself* willed it or not, was exactly what he had been instructed to do) to which suggestion, of course, the master of the house readily agreed. And after that things rapidly degenerated.

Carstairs was there for every meal, and whether Crow ate or not his host invariably plied him with wine; and invariably, following a routine which now became a hideous and debilitating ritual, he would hurry from dining room to bathroom there to empty his stomach disgustingly of its stultifying contents. And all of this time he must keep up the pretense of falling more and more willingly under Carstairs' spell, though in all truth this was the least of it. For by Sunday night his eyes were inflamed through no device of his own, his throat sore with the wine and bathroom ritual, and his voice correspondingly hoarse.

He did none of Carstairs' "work" during those hellish days, but at every opportunity pored over the man's books in the frustrated hope that he might yet find something to throw more light on the occultist's current activities. And all through the nights he lay abed, desperately fighting the drugs which dulled his mind and movements, listening to cellar-spawned chantings and howlings until with everything else he could very easily imagine himself the inhabitant of bedlam.

Monday, Tuesday, and Wednesday passed in like fashion—though he did manage to get some food into his system, and to avoid excessive contact with Carstairs' wine—until, on Wednesday evening over dinner, the occultist offered him the break he so desperately longed for. Mercifully, on this occasion, the customary bottle of wine had been more than half-empty at the beginning of the meal; and Crow, seizing the opportunity to pour, had given Carstairs the lion's share, leaving very little for himself; and this without attracting the attention of the gaunt master of the house, whose thoughts seemed elsewhere. Crow felt relieved in the knowledge that he would not have to concern himself yet again with the morbid bathroom ritual.

At length, gathering his thoughts, Carstairs said: "Mr. Crow, I shall be away tomorrow morning, probably before you are up and about. I will return about midafternoon. I hesitate to leave you alone here, however, for to be perfectly frank you do not seem at all well."

"Oh?" Crow hoarsely mumbled. "I feel well enough."

"You do not look it. Perhaps you are tasking yourself too hard." His eyes bored into Crow's along the length of the great table, and his voice assumed its resonant, hypnotic timber. "I think you should rest tomorrow, Mr. Crow. Rest and recuperate. Lie late abed. Sleep and grow strong."

At this Crow deliberately affected a fluttering of his eyelids, nodding and starting where he sat, like an old man who has difficulty staying awake. Carstairs laughed.

"Why!" he exclaimed, his voice assuming a more casual tone. "Do you see how right I am? You were almost asleep at the table! Yes, that's what you require, young man: a little holiday from work tomorrow. And Friday should see you back to normal, eh?"

Crow dully nodded, affecting disinterest—but his mind raced. Whatever was coming was close now. He could feel it like a hot wind blowing from hell, could almost smell the sulfur from the fires that burned behind Carstairs' eyes...

Amazingly, Crow slept well and was awake early. He remained in bed until he heard a car pull up to the house, but even then some instinct kept him under his covers. Seconds later Carstairs parted the alcove's curtains and silently entered; and at the last moment hearing his tread, with no second to spare, Crow fell back upon his pillow and feigned sleep.

"That's right, Titus Crow, sleep," Carstairs softly intoned. "Sleep deep and dreamlessly—for soon your head shall know no dreams, no thoughts but mine! Sleep, Titus Crow, sleep..." A moment later the rustling of the curtains signaled his leaving; but still Crow waited until he heard the receding crunch of the car's tires on the gravel of the drive.

After that he was up in a moment and quickly dressed. Then: out of the house and around the grounds, and upstairs to spy out the land all around. Finally, satisfied that he was truly alone, he returned to the library, opened the secret bookcase door and descended to the Stygian cellar. The narrow stone steps turned one full circle to leave him on a landing set into an arched alcove in the cellar wall, from which two more paces sufficed to carry him into the cellar proper. Finding a switch, he put on subdued lighting—and at last saw what sort of wizard's lair the place really was!

Now something of Crow's own extensive occult knowledge came to the fore as he moved carefully about the cellar and examined its contents; something of that, and of his more recent readings in Carstairs' library. There were devices here from the very blackest days of Man's mystical origins, and Titus Crow shuddered as he read meaning into many of the things he saw.

The floor of the cellar had been cleared toward its center, and there he found the double interlocking circles of the Persian Mages, freshly daubed in red paint. In one circle he saw a white-painted ascending node, while in the other a black node descended. A cryptographic script, immediately known to him as the blasphemous Nyhargo Code, patterned the brick wall in green and blue chalks, its huge Arabic symbols seeming to leer where they writhed in obscene dedication. The three remaining walls were draped with tapestries so worn as to be threadbare—due to their being centuries-old—depicting the rites of immemorial necromancers and wizards long passed into the dark pages of history; wizards robed, Crow noted, in the forbidden pagan cassocks of ancient *deserta Arabia*, lending them an almost holy aspect.

In a cobwebbed corner he found scrawled pentacles and zodiacal signs; and hanging upon hooks robes similar to those in the tapestries, embroidered with symbols from the *Lemegeton*, such as the Double Seal of Solomon. Small jars contained hemlock, henbane, mandrake, Indian hemp and a substance Crow took to be opium—and again he was given to shudder and to wonder at the constituents of Carstairs' wine…

Finally, having seen enough, he retraced his steps to the library and from there went straight to Carstairs' study. Twice before he had found this door unlocked, and now for the third time he discovered his luck to be holding. This was hardly unexpected, however: knowing Crow would sleep the morning through, the magician had simply omitted to take his customary precautions. And inside the room…another piece of luck! The keys to the desk dangled from a drawer keyhole.

With trembling hands Crow opened the drawers, hardly daring to disturb their contents; but in the desk's bottom left-hand drawer at last he was rewarded to find that which he most desired to see. There could be no mistaking it: the cleanly sliced margins, the woodcut illustrations, the precise early nineteenth-century prose of one Charles Leggett, translator of Ludwig Prinn. This was the missing section from Leggett's book: these were the "Saracenic Rituals," the Mysteries of the Worm!

Closing the single window's shades, Crow switched on the desk lamp and proceeded to read, and as he read so time seemed to suspend itself in the terrible lore which was now revealed. Disbelievingly, with eyes that opened wider and wider, Crow read on; and as he turned the pages, so the words seemed to leap from them to his astonished eyes. An hour sped by, two, and Crow would periodically come out of his trance long enough to glance at his watch, or perhaps pass tongue over parched lips, before continuing. For it was all here, all of it—and finally everything began to click into place.

Then…it was as if a floodgate had opened, releasing pent-up, forbidden memories to swirl in the maelstrom of Crow's mind. He suddenly *remembered* those hypnotically erased night visits of Carstairs', the conversations he had been willed to forget; and rapidly these pieces of the puzzle slotted themselves together, forming a picture of centuries-old nightmare and horror out of time. He *understood* the mystery of the paintings with their consecutive dates, and he *knew* Carstairs' meaning when the man had spoken of a longevity dating back almost three and a half centuries. And at last, in blinding clarity, he could see the part that the wizard had planned for him in his lust for sorcerous survival.

For Crow was to be the receptacle, the host body, youthful haven of flesh for an ancient black phoenix risen again from necromantic ashes! As for Crow himself, the *Identity*, Titus Crow: that was to be cast out—exorcised and sent to hell—*replaced by the mind and will of Carstairs, a monster born of the blackest magicks in midnight ruins by the shore of Galilee in the year 1602!…*

Moreover, he knew when the deed was to be done. It was there, staring at him, ringed in ink on Carstairs' desk calendar: the first day of February, 1946.

Candlemas Eve, "the day ordained."

Tomorrow night!

X

That night, though he had never been much of a believer, Titus Crow said his prayers. He did manage to sleep—however fitfully and with countless startings awake, at every tiniest groan and creak of the old place—and in the morning looked just as haggard as this last week had determined he should look. Which was just as well, for as the time approached Carstairs would hardly let him out of his sight.

On four separate occasions that morning, the man came to visit him in the library, eyeing him avidly, like a great and grotesque praying mantis. And even knowing Carstairs' purpose with him—*because* he knew that purpose—Crow must keep up his pretense of going. to the slaughter like a lamb, and not the young lion his looks normally suggested.

Lunch came and went, and Crow—mainly by deft sleight of hand—once more cut his wine intake to a minimum; and at 6:00 P.M. he negotiated the evening repast with similar skill and success. And through all of this it was plain to him that a morbid excitement was building in Carstairs, an agitation of spirit the man could barely contain.

At 7:30 P.M.—not long after Crow had finished off an entire jug of coffee and as he sat in silence by the light of one dim lamp, memorizing tonight's monstrous rite from what he had read of it in the "Saracenic Rituals"—Carstairs came and knocked upon the library door, walking in as usual before Crow could issue the customary invitation. No need now for Crow to feign haggardness or the weary slump of his shoulders, for the agonizingly slow buildup to the night's play had itself taken care of these particulars.

"Mr. Crow," said Carstairs in unusually unctuous tones, "I may require a little assistance tonight..."

"Assistance?" Crow peered at the other through red-rimmed eyes. "My assistance?"

"If you have no objection. I have some work to do in the cellar, which may well keep me until the middle of the night. I do not like to keep you from your bed, of course, but in the event I should call for you"—his voice stepped slyly down the register—"you will answer, won't you?"

"Of course," Crow hoarsely answered, his eyes now fixed on the burning orbs of the occultist.

"You will come when I call?" Carstairs now droned, driving the message home. "No matter how late the hour? You will awaken and follow me? You will come to me in the night, when I call?"

"Yes," Crow mumbled.

"Say it, Titus Crow. Tell me what you will do, when I call."

"I shall come to you," Crow obediently answered. "I will come to you when you call me."

"Good!" said Carstairs, his face ghastly as a skull. "Now rest, Titus Crow. Sit here and rest—and wait for my call. Wait for my call..." Silently he turned and strode from the room, quietly closing the door behind him.

Crow got up, waited a moment, switched off the one bulb he had allowed to burn. In his alcove bedroom he drew the curtains and put on the light, then quickly changed into his dressing gown. He took Harry Townley's .45 revolver out from under his mattress, loaded it and tucked it out of sight in the large pocket of his robe. Now he opened the curtains some twelve inches and brushed through them into the library proper, pacing the floor along the pale path of light from the alcove.

To and fro he paced, tension mounting, and more than once he considered flight; even now, close as he was to those dark mysteries which at once attracted and repelled him. The very grit of his makeup would not permit it, however, for his emotions now were running more to anger than the terror he had expected. He was to be, to *have been*, this monster Carstairs' victim! How now, knowing what the outcome would be—praying that it *would be* as he foresaw it—could he possibly turn away? No, flight was out of the question; Carstairs would find a substitute: the terror would continue. Even if Crow were to go, who could say what revenge might or might not fly hot on his heels?

At 9:30 P.M. cars pulled up at the house, quiet as hearses and more of them than at any other time, and through a crack in his shades Crow watched shadowy figures enter the house. For a little while then there were faint, subdued murmurings and creakings; all of which Crow heard with ears which strained in the library's darkness, fine-tuned to catch the merest whisper. A little later, when it seemed to him that the noises had descended beneath the house, he put out the alcove light and sat in unmitigated darkness in the chair where Carstairs had left him. And all about him the night grew heavy, until it weighed like lead upon his head and shoulders.

As the minutes passed he found his hand returning again and again to the pocket where Townley's revolver lay comfortably heavy upon his thigh, and every so often he would be obliged to still the nervous trembling of his limbs. Somewhere in the distance a great clock chimed the hour of eleven, and as at a signal Crow heard the first susurrations of a low chanting from beneath his feet. A cold sweat immediately stood out upon his brow, which he dabbed away with a trembling handkerchief.

The Ritual of the Worm had commenced!

Angrily Crow fought for control of himself…for he knew what was coming. He cursed himself for a fool—for several fools—as the minutes ticked by and the unholy chanting took on rhythm and volume. He stood up, sat down, dabbed at his chill brow, fingered his revolver…and started at the sudden chiming of the half hour.

Now, in an instant, the house seemed full of icy air, the temperature fell to zero! Crow breathed the black, frigid atmosphere of the place and felt the tiny hairs crackling in his nostrils. He smelled sharp fumes—the unmistakable reek of burning henbane and opium—and sat rigid in his chair as the chanting from the cellar rose yet again, in a sort of frenzy now, throbbing and echoing as with the acoustics of some great cathedral.

The time must surely approach midnight, but Crow no longer dared glance at his watch.

Whatever it had been, in another moment his terror passed; he was his own man once more. He sighed raggedly and forced himself to relax, knowing that if he did not, that the emotional exhaustion must soon sap his strength. Surely the time—

—Had come!

The chanting told him: the way it swelled, receded and took on a new meter. For now it was his own name he heard called in the night, just as he had been told he would hear it.

Seated bolt upright in his chair, Crow saw the bookshelf door swing open, saw Carstairs framed in the faintly luminous portal, a loose-fitting cassock belted about his narrow middle. Tall and gaunt, more cadaverous than ever, the occultist beckoned.

"Come, Titus Crow, for the hour is at hand. Rise up and come with me, and learn the great and terrible mysteries of the worm!"

Crow rose and followed him, down the winding steps, through reek of henbane and opium and into the now luridly illumined cellar. Braziers stood at the four corners, glowing red where heated metal trays sent aloft spirals of burned incense, herbs, and opiates; and round the central space a dozen robed and hooded acolytes stood, their heads bowed and facing inward, toward the painted, interlocking circles. Twelve of them, thirteen including Carstairs, a full coven.

Carstairs led Crow through the coven's ring and pointed to the circle with the white-painted ascending node. "Stand there, Titus Crow," he commanded. "And have no fear."

Doing as he was instructed, Crow was glad for the cellar's flickering lighting and its fume-heavy atmosphere, which made faces ruddy and mobile and his trembling barely noticeable. And now he stood there, his feet in the mouth of the ascending node, as Carstairs took up his own position in the adjoining circle. Between them, in the "eye" where the circles interlocked, a large hourglass trickled black sand from one almost empty globe into another which was very nearly full.

Watching the hourglass and seeing that the sands had nearly run out, now Carstairs threw back his cowl and commanded: "Look at me, Titus Crow, and heed the Wisdom of the Worm!" Crow stared at the man's eyes, at his face and cassocked body.

The chanting of the acolytes grew loud once more, but their massed voice no longer formed Crow's name. Now they called on the Eater of Men himself, the loathsome master of this loathsome ritual:

"Wamas, Wormius, Vermi, WORM!"

"Wamas, Wormius, Vermi, WORM!"

"Wamas, Wormius, Vermi—"

And the sand in the hourglass ran out!

"Worm!" Carstairs cried as the others fell silent. *"Worm, I command thee—come out!"*

Unable, not daring to turn his eyes away from the man, Crow's lips drew back in a snarl of sheer horror at the transition which now began to take place. For as Carstairs convulsed in a dreadful agony, and while his eyes stood out in his head as if he were splashed with molten metal, still the man's mouth fell open to issue a great baying laugh.

And out of that mouth—out from his ears, his nostrils, even the hair of his head—there now appeared a writhing white flood of maggots, grave worms erupting from his every orifice as he writhed and jerked in his hellish ecstasy!

"Now, Titus Crow, now!" cried Carstairs, his voice a glutinous gabble as he continued to spew maggots. "Take my hand!" And he held out a trembling, quaking mass of crawling horror.

"No!" said Titus Crow. "No, I will not!"

Carstairs gurgled, gasped, cried, *"What?"* His cassock billowed with hideous movement. "Give me your hand—*I command it!*"

"Do your worst, wizard," Crow yelled. back through gritted teeth.

"But…I have your Number! You *must* obey!"

"Not my Number, wizard," said Crow, shaking his head, and at once the acolyte circle began to cower back, their sudden gasps of terror filling the cellar.

"You lied!" Carstairs gurgled, seeming to shrink into himself. "You…*cheated!* No matter—a small thing." In the air he shaped a figure with a forefinger. "Worm, he is yours. I command you—*take him!*"

Now he pointed at Crow, and now the tomb horde at his feet rolled like a flood across the floor—and drew back from Crow's circle as from a ring of fire. "Go on!" Carstairs shrieked, crumbling into himself, his head wobbling madly, his cheeks in tatters from internal fretting. "Who is *he?* What does he know? I command you!"

"I know many things," said Crow. "They do not want me—they dare not touch me. And I will tell you why: I was born not in 1912 but in 1916—on second December of that year. Your ritual was based on the wrong date, Mr. Carstairs!"

The 2nd December 1916! A concerted gasp went up from the wavering acolytes. *"A Master!"* Crow heard the whisper. *"A twenty-two!"*

"No!" Carstairs fell to his knees. *"No!"*

He crumpled, crawled to the rim of his circle, beckoned with a half-skeletal hand. "Durrell, to me!" His voice was the rasp and rustle of blown leaves.

"Not me!" shrieked Durrell, flinging off his cassock and rushing for the cellar steps. "Not me!" Wildly he clambered from sight—and eleven like him hot on his heels.

"No!" Carstairs gurgled once more.

Crow stared at him, still unable to avert his eyes. He saw his features melt and flow, changing through a series of identities and firming in the final—the first!—dark, Arab visage of his origin. Then he fell on his side, turned that ravaged, sorcerer's face up to Crow. His eyes fell in and maggots seethed in the red orbits. The horde turned back, washed over him. In a moment nothing remained but bone and shreds of gristle, tossed and eddied on a ravenous tide.

Crow reeled from the cellar, his flesh crawling, his mind tottering on the brink. Only his Number saved him, the 22 of the Master Magician. And as he fumbled up the stone steps and through that empty, gibbering house, so he whispered words half forgotten, which seemed to come to him from nowhere:

"For it is of old renown that the soul of the devil-bought hastes not from his charnel clay, but fats and instructs *the very worm that gnaws;* till out of corruption horrid life springs…"

Later, in his right mind but changed forever, Titus Crow drove away from The Barrows into the frosty night. No longer purposeless, he knew the course his life must now take. Along the gravel drive to the gates, a pinkish horde lay rimed in white death, frozen where they crawled. Crow barely noticed them.

The tires of his car paid them no heed whatever.

THE HOUSE OF THE TEMPLE

Let's step back a year or two from Lord of the Worms. In April 1980, while serving out my last year at the Training Centre of the Royal Military Police, I mistakenly sent out two copies of The House of the Temple...a genuine error on my part—in no way my usual practice—as double submissions of that sort are much frowned upon. However, one copy went to editor Lin Carter who was editing a line of newly revived, mass market paperback issues of "Weird Tales" under the Zebra imprint, and the other to my then good friend Francesco Cova in Genoa, Italy. Cova was looking for quality stories for his exceptional Italian/English-language semi-pro "Kadath" magazine, and I had promised to do my very best for him. This novella is one of my best, I fancy, not least because both Carter and Cova bought it and brought it out uncomfortably close together in respectively, "Weird Tales" vol. 48, No. 3, and "Kadath" vol. 1, No. 3—the latter being in fact the true first in November 1980. This last quarter century has seen the story reprinted more than once, most notably in my Fedogan & Bremer collection "A Coven of Vampires."

(Incidentally, when that last-mentioned collection went out of print very quickly after publication, it became Fedogan & Bremer's fastest selling book. While there's no direct association, F&B picked up the Best Small press award at the very next World Fantasy Convention.)

I. The Summons

I suppose under the circumstances it is only natural that the police should require this belated written statement from me; and I further suppose it to be in recognition of my present highly nervous condition and my totally unwarranted confinement in this place that they are allowing me to draw the thing up without supervision. But while every kindness has been shown me, still I most strongly protest my continued detainment here. Knowing what I now know, I would voice the same protest in respect of detention in any prison or institute anywhere in Scotland…anywhere in the entire British Isles.

Before I begin, let me clearly make the point that, since no charges have been levelled against me, I make this statement of my own free will, fully knowing that in so doing I may well extend my stay in this detestable place. I can only hope that upon its reading, it will be seen that I had no alternative but to follow the action I describe.

You the reader must therefore judge. My actual sanity—if indeed I am still sane—my very *being*, may well depend upon your findings…

I was in New York when the letter from my uncle's solicitors reached me. Sent from an address in the Royal Mile, that great road which reaches steep and cobbled to the esplanade of Edinburgh Castle itself, the large, sealed manila envelope had all the hallmarks of officialdom, so that even before I opened it I feared the worst.

Not that I had been close to my uncle in recent years (my mother had brought me out of Scotland as a small child, on the death of my father, and I had never been back) but certainly I remembered Uncle Gavin. If anything I remembered him better than I did my father; for where Andrew McGilchrist had always been dry and introverted, Uncle Gavin had been just the opposite. Warm, outgoing and generous to a fault, he had spoilt me mercilessly.

Now, according to the letter, he was dead and I was named his sole heir and beneficiary; and the envelope contained a voucher which guaranteed me a flight to Edinburgh from anywhere in the world. And then of course there was the letter itself, the contents of which further guaranteed my use of that voucher; for only a fool could possibly refuse my uncle's bequest, or fail to be interested in its attendant though at present unspecified conditions.

Quite simply, by presenting myself at the offices of Macdonald, Asquith and Lee in Edinburgh, I would already have fulfilled the first condition toward inheriting my uncle's considerable fortune, his estate of over three hundred acres and his great house where it stood in wild and splendid solitude at the foot of the Pentlands in Lothian. All of which seemed a very far cry from New York…

As to what I was doing in New York in the first place:

Three months earlier, in mid-March of 1976—when I was living alone in Philadelphia in the home where my mother had raised me—my fiancée of two years had given me back my ring, run off and married a banker from Baltimore. The novel I was writing had immediately metamorphosed from a light-hearted love story into a doom-laden tragedy, became meaningless somewhere in the transformation, and ended up in my waste-paper basket. That was that. I sold up and moved to New York, where an artist friend had been willing to share his apartment until I could find a decent place of my own.

I had left no forwarding address, however, which explained the delayed delivery of the letter from my uncle's solicitors; the letter itself was post-marked March 26th, and from the various marks, labels and redirections on the envelope, the US Mail had obviously gone to considerable trouble to find me. And they found me at a time when the lives of both myself and my artist friend, Carl Earlman, were at a very low ebb. I was not writing and Carl was not drawing, and despite the arrival of summer our spirits were on a rapid decline.

Which is probably why I jumped at the opportunity the letter presented, though, as I have said, certainly I would have been a fool to ignore or refuse the thing...Or so I thought at the time.

I invited Carl along if he so desired, and he too grasped at the chance with both hands. His funds were low and getting lower; he would soon be obliged to quit his apartment for something less ostentatious; and since he, too, had decided that he needed a change of locale—to put some life back into his artwork—the matter was soon decided and we packed our bags and headed for Edinburgh.

It was not until our journey was over, however—when we were settled in our hotel room in Princes Street—that I remembered my mother's warning, delivered to me deliriously but persistently from her deathbed, that I should never return to Scotland, certainly not to the old house. And as I vainly attempted to adjust to the jet-lag and the fact that it was late evening while all my instincts told me it should now be day, so my mind went back over what little 1 knew of my family roots, of the McGilchrist line itself, of that old and rambling house in the Pentlands where I had been born, and especially of the peculiar reticence of Messrs Macdonald, Asquith and Lee, the Scottish solicitors.

Reticence, yes, because I could almost feel the hesitancy in their letter. It seemed to me that they would have preferred *not* to find me; and yet, if I were asked what it was that gave me this impression, then I would be at a loss for an answer. Something in the way it was phrased, perhaps—in the dry, professional idiom of solicitors—which too often seems to me to put aside all matters of emotion or sensibility; so that I felt like a small boy offered a candy…and warned simultaneously that it would ruin my teeth. Yes, it seemed to me that Messrs Macdonald, Asquith and Lee might actually be *apprehensive* about my acceptance of their conditions—or rather, of my uncle's conditions—as if they were offering a cigar to an addict suffering from cancer of the lungs.

I fastened on that line of reasoning, seeing the conditions of the will as the root of the vague uneasiness which niggled at the back of my mind. The worst of it was that these conditions were not specified; other than to say that if I could not or would not meet them, still I would receive fifteen thousand pounds and my return ticket home, and that the residue of my uncle's fortune would then be used to carry out his will in respect of "the property known as Temple House."

Temple House, that rambling old seat of the McGilchrists where it stood locked in a steep re-entry; and the Pentland Hills a grey and green backdrop to its frowning, steep-gabled aspect; with something of the Gothic in its structure, something more of Renaissance Scotland, and an aura of antiquity all its own which, as a child, I could still remember loving dearly. But that had been almost twenty years ago and the place had been my home. A happy home, I had thought; at least until the death of my father, of which I could remember nothing at all.

But I did remember the pool—the deep, grey pool where it lapped at the raised, reinforced, east-facing garden wall—the pool and its ring of broken quartz pillars, the remains of the temple for which the house was named. Thinking back over the years to my infancy, I wondered if perhaps the pool had been the reason my mother had always hated the place. None of the McGilchrists had ever been swimmers, and yet water had always seemed to fascinate them. I would not have been the first of the line to be found floating face-down in that strange, pillar-encircled pool of deep and weedy water; and I had used to spend hours just sitting on the wall and staring across the breeze-rippled surface…

So my thoughts went as, tossing in my hotel bed late into the night, I turned matters over in my mind…And having retired late, so we rose late, Carl and I; and it was not until 2 P.M. that I presented myself at the office of Macdonald, Asquith and Lee on the Royal Mile.

II. The Will

Since Carl had climbed up to the esplanade to take in the view, I was alone when I reached my destination and entered MA and L's offices through a door of yellow-tinted bull's-eye panes, passing into the cool welcome of a dim and very *Olde Worlde* anteroom; and for all that this was the source of my enigmatic summons, still I found a reassuring air of charm and quiet sincerity about the place. A clerk led me into an inner chamber as much removed from my idea of a solicitor's office as is Edinburgh from New York, and having been introduced to the firm's Mr. Asquith I was offered a seat.

Asquith was tall, slender, high-browed and balding, with a mass of freckles which seemed oddly in contrast with his late middle years, and his handshake was firm and dry. While he busied himself getting various documents, I was given a minute or two to look about this large and bewilderingly cluttered room of shelves, filing cabinets, cupboards and three small desks. But for all that the place seemed grossly disordered, still Mr. Asquith quickly found what he was looking for and seated himself opposite me behind his desk. He was the only partner present and I the only client.

"Now, Mr. McGilchrist," he began. "And so we managed to find you, did we? And doubtless you're wondering what it's all about, and you probably think there's something of a mystery here? Well, so there is, and for me and my partners no less than for yourself."

"I don't quite follow," I answered, searching his face for a clue.

"No, no of course you don't. Well now, perhaps this will explain it better. It's a copy of your uncle's will. As you'll see, he was rather short on words; hence the mystery. A more succinct document—which nevertheless hints at so much more—I've yet to see!"

"I Gavin McGilchrist," (the will began) "of Temple House in Lothian, hereby revoke all Wills, Codicils or Testamentary Dispositions heretofore made by me, and I appoint my Nephew, John Hamish McGilchrist of Philadelphia in the United States of America, to be the Executor of this my Last Will and direct that all my Debts, Testamentary and Funeral Expenses shall be paid as soon as conveniently may be after my death.

"I give and bequeath unto the aforementioned John Hamish McGilchrist everything I possess, my Land and the Property standing thereon, with the following Condition: namely that he alone shall open and read the Deposition which shall accompany this Will into the hands of the Solicitors; and that furthermore he, being the Owner, shall destroy Temple House to its last stone within a Threemonth of accepting this Condition. In the event that he shall refuse this undertaking, then shall my Solicitors, Macdonald, Asquith and Lee of Edinburgh, become sole Executors of my Estate, who shall follow to the letter the Instructions simultaneously deposited with them."

The will was dated and signed in my uncle's scratchy scrawl.

I read it through a second time and looked up to find Mr. Asquith's gaze fixed intently upon me. "Well," he said, "and didn't I say it was a mystery? Almost as strange as his death…" He saw the immediate change in my expression, the frown and the question my lips were beginning to frame, and held up his hands in apology. "I'm sorry," he said, "so very sorry—for of course you know nothing of the circumstances of his death, do you? I had better explain:

"A year ago," Asquith continued, "your uncle was one of the most hale and hearty men you could wish to meet. He was a man of independent means, as you know, and for a good many years he had been collecting data for a book. Ah! I see you're surprised. Well, you shouldn't be. Your great-grandfather wrote *Notes on Nessie: the Secrets of Loch Ness;* and your grandmother, under a pseudonym, was a fairly successful romanticist around the turn of the century. You, too, I believe, have published several romances? Indeed," and he smiled and nodded, "it appears to be in the blood, you see?

"Like your great-grandfather, however, your Uncle Gavin McGilchrist had no romantic aspirations. He was a researcher, you see, and couldn't abide a mystery to remain unsolved. And there he was at Temple House, a bachelor and time on his hands, and a marvellous family tree to explore and a great mystery to unravel."

"Family tree?" I said. "He was researching the biography of a family? But which fam—" And I paused.

Asquith smiled. "You've guessed it, of course," he said. "Yes, he was planning a book on the McGilchrists, with special reference to the curse…" And his smile quickly vanished.

It was as if a cold draught, coming from nowhere, fanned my cheek. "The curse? My family had…a curse?"

He nodded. "Oh, yes. Not the classical sort of curse, by any means, but a curse nevertheless—or at least your uncle thought so. Perhaps he wasn't really serious about it at first, but towards the end—"

"I think I know what you mean," I said. "I remember now: the deaths by stroke, by drowning, by thrombosis. My mother mentioned them on her own deathbed. A curse on the McGilchrists, she said, on the old house."

Again Asquith nodded, and finally he continued. "Well, your uncle had been collecting material for many years, I suspect since the death of your father; from local archives, historical annals, various chronicles, church records, military museums, and so on. He had even enlisted our aid, on occasion, in finding this or that old document. Our firm was founded one hundred and sixty years ago, you see, and we've had many McGilchrists as clients.

"As I've said, up to a time roughly a year ago, he was as hale and hearty a man as you could wish to meet. Then he travelled abroad; Hungary, Romania, all the old countries of antique myth and legend. He brought back many books with him, and on his return he was a changed man. He had become, in a matter of weeks, the merest shadow of his former self. Finally, nine weeks ago on March 22nd, he left his will in our hands, an additional set of instructions for us to follow in the event you couldn't be found, and the sealed envelope which he mentions in his will. I shall give that to you in a moment. Two days later, when his gillie returned to Temple House from a short holiday—"

"He found my uncle dead," I finished it for him. "I see...And the strange circumstances?"

"For a man of his years to die of a heart attack..." Asquith shook his head. "He wasn't old. What?—an outdoors man, like him? And what of the shotgun, with both barrels discharged, and the spent cartridges lying at his feet just outside the porch? What had he fired at, eh, in the dead of night? And the look on his face—monstrous !"

"You saw him?"

"Oh, yes. That was part of our instructions; I was to see him. And not just myself but Mr. Lee also. And the doctor, of course, who declared it could only have been a heart attack. But then there was the post-mortem. That was also part of your uncle's instructions..."

"And its findings?" I quietly asked.

"Why, that was the reason he wanted the autopsy, do you see? So that we should know he was in good health."

"No heart attack?"

"No," he shook his head, "not him. But dead, certainly. And that look on his face, Mr. McGilchrist—that terrible, pleading look in his wide, wide eyes..."

3. The House

Half an hour later I left Mr. Asquith in his office and saw myself out through the anteroom and into the hot, cobbled road that climbed to the great grey castle. In the interim I had opened the envelope left for me by my uncle and had given its contents a cursory scrutiny, but I intended to study them minutely at my earliest convenience.

I had also offered to let Asquith see the contents, only to have him wave my offer aside. It was a private thing, he said, for my eyes only. Then he had asked me what I intended to do now, and I had answered that I would go to Temple House and take up temporary residence there. He then produced the keys, assured me of the firm's interest in my business—its complete confidentiality and its readiness to provide assistance should I need it—and bade me good day.

I found Carl Earlman leaning on the esplanade wall and gazing out over the city. Directly below his position the castle rock fell away for hundreds of feet to a busy road that wound round and down and into the maze of streets and junctions forming the city centre. He started when I took hold of his arm.

"What—? Oh, it's you, John! I was lost in thought. This fantastic view; I've already stored away a dozen sketches in my head. Great!" Then he saw my face and frowned. "Is anything wrong? You don't quite look yourself."

As we made our way down from that high place I told him of my meeting with Asquith and all that had passed between us, so that by the time we found a cab (a "taxi") and had ourselves driven to an automobile rental depot, I had managed to bring him fully up to date. Then it was simply a matter of hiring a car and driving out to Temple House…

We headed south-west out of Edinburgh with Carl driving our Range Rover at a leisurely pace, and within three-quarters of an hour turned right off the main road onto a narrow strip whose half-metalled surface climbed straight as an arrow toward the looming Pentlands. Bald and majestic, those grey domes rose from a scree of gorse-grown shale to cast their sooty, mid-afternoon shadows over lesser mounds, fields and streamlets alike. Over our vehicle, too, as it grew tiny in the frowning presence of the hills.

I was following a small-scale map of the area purchased from a filling station (a "garage"), for of course the district was completely strange to me. A lad of five on leaving Scotland—and protected by my mother's exaggerated fears at that, which hardly ever let me out of her sight—I had never been allowed to stray very far from Temple House.

Temple House…and again the name conjured strange phantoms, stirred vague memories I had thought long dead.

Now the road narrowed more yet, swinging sharply to the right before passing round a rocky spur. The ground rose up beyond the spur and formed a shallow ridge, and my map told me that the gully or re-entry which guarded Temple House lay on the far side of this final rise. I knew that when we reached the crest the house would come into view, and I found myself holding my breath as the Range Rover's wheels bit into the cinder surface of the track.

"There she is!" cried Carl as first the eaves of the place became visible, then its oak-beamed gables and greystone walls, and finally the entire frontage where it projected from behind the sheer rise of the gully's wall. And now, as we accelerated down the slight decline and turned right to follow a course running parallel to the stream, the whole house came into view where it stood half in shadow. That strange old house in the silent gully, where no birds ever flew and not even a rabbit had been seen to sport in the long wild grass.

"Hey!" Carl cried, his voice full of enthusiasm. "And your uncle wanted this place pulled down? What in hell for? It's beautiful—and it must be worth a fortune!"

"I shouldn't think so," I answered. "It might look all right from here, but wait till you get inside. Its foundations were waterlogged twenty years ago. There were always six inches of water in the cellar, and the panels of the lower rooms were mouldy even then. God only knows what it must be like now!"

"Does it look the way you remember it?" he asked.

"Not quite," I frowned. "Seen through the eyes of an adult, there are differences."

For one thing, the pool was different. The level of the water was lower, so that the wide, grass-grown wall of the dam seemed somehow taller. In fact, I had completely forgotten about the dam, without which the pool could not exist, or at best would be the merest pebble-bottomed pool and not the small lake which it now was. For the first time it dawned on me that the pool was artificial, not natural as I had always thought of it, and that Temple House had been built on top of the dam's curving mound where it extended to the steep shale cliff of the defile itself.

With a skidding of loose chippings, Carl took the Range Rover up the ramp that formed the drive to the house, and a moment later we drew to a halt before the high-arched porch. We dismounted and entered, and now Carl went clattering away—almost irreverently, I thought—into cool rooms, dark stairwells and huge cupboards, his voice echoing back to me where I stood with mixed emotions, savouring the atmosphere of the old place, just inside the doorway to the house proper.

"But this is *it!*" he cried from somewhere. "This is for me! My studio, and no question. Come and look, John—look at the windows letting in all this good light. You're right about the damp, I can feel it—but that aside, it's perfect!"

I found him in what had once been the main living-room, standing in golden clouds of dust he had stirred up, motes illumined by the sun's rays where they struck into the room through huge, leaded windows. "You"ll need to give the place a good dusting and sweeping out," I told him.

"Oh, sure," he answered, "but there's a lot wants doing before that. Do you know where the master switch is?"

"Umm? Switch ?"

"For the electric light," he frowned impatiently at me. "And surely there's an icebox in the kitchen."

"A refrigerator?" I answered. "Oh, yes, I'm sure there is…Look, you run around and explore the place and do whatever makes you happy. Me, I'm just going to potter about and try to waken a few old dreams."

During the next hour or two—while I quite literally "pottered about" and familiarized myself once again with this old house so full of memories—Carl fixed himself up with a bed in his "studio," found the main switch and got the electricity flowing, examined the refrigerator and satisfied himself that it was in working order, then searched me out where I sat in the mahogany-panelled study upstairs to tell me that he was driving into Penicuik to stock up with food.

From my window I watched him go, until the cloud of dust thrown up by his wheels disappeared over the rise to the south, then stirred myself into positive action. There were things to be done—things I must do for myself, others for my uncle—and the sooner I started the better. Not that there was any lack of time; I had three whole months to carry out Gavin McGilchrist's instructions, or to fail to carry them out. And yet somehow…yes, there was this feeling of urgency in me.

And so I switched on the light against gathering shadows, took out the envelope left for me by my uncle—that envelope whose contents, a letter and a notebook, were for my eyes only—sat down at the great desk used by so many generations of McGilchrists, and began to read…

4. The Curse

"My dear, dear nephew," the letter in my uncle's uneven script began, "— so much I would like to say to you, and so little time in which to say it. And all these years grown in between since last I saw you.

"When first you left Scotland with your mother I would have written to you through her, but she forbade it. In early 1970 I learned of her death, so that even my condolences would have been six months too late; well, you have them now. She was a wonderful woman, and of course she was quite right to take you away out of it all. If I'm right in what I now suspect, her woman's intuition will yet prove to have been nearer the mark than anyone ever could have guessed, and—

"But there I go, miles off the point and rambling as usual; and such a lot to say. Except—I'm damned if I know where to begin! I suppose the plain fact of the matter is quite simply stated—namely, that for you to be reading this is for me to be gone forever from the world of men. But gone...*where?* And how to explain?

"The fact is, I cannot tell it all, not and make it believable. Not the way I have come to believe it. Instead you will have to be satisfied with the barest essentials. The rest you can discover for yourself. There are books in the old library that tell it all—if a man has the patience to look. And if he's capable of putting aside all matters of common knowledge, all laws of science and logic; capable of unlearning all that life has ever taught him of truth and beauty.

"Four hundred years ago we weren't such a race of damned sceptics. They were burning witches in these parts then, and if they had suspected of anyone what I have come to suspect of Temple House and its grounds...

"Your mother may not have mentioned the curse—the curse of the McGilchrists. Oh, she believed in it, certainly, but it's possible she thought that to tell of it might be to invoke the thing. That is to say, by telling you she might bring the curse down on your head. Perhaps she was right, for unless my death is seen to be *entirely natural*, then certainly I shall have brought it down upon myself.

"And what of you, Nephew?

"You have three months. Longer than that I do not deem safe, and nothing is guaranteed. Even three months might be dangerously overlong, but I pray not. Of course you are at liberty, if you so desire, simply to get the thing over and done with. In my study, in the bottom right-hand drawer of my desk, you will find sufficient fuses and explosive materials to bring down the wall of the defile onto the house, and the house itself into the pool, which should satisfactorily put an end to the thing.

"But...you had an enquiring mind as a child. If you look where I have looked and read what I have read, then you shall learn what I've learned and know that it is neither advanced senility nor madness but my own intelligence which leads me to the one, inescapable conclusion—that this House of the Temple, this Temple House of the McGilchrists, is accursed. Most terribly…

"I could flee this place, of course, but I doubt if that would save me. And if it did save me, still it would leave the final questions unanswered and the riddle unsolved. Also, I loved my brother, your father, and I saw his face when he was dead. If for nothing else, that look on your father's dead face has been sufficient reason for me to pursue the thing thus far. I thought to seek it out, to know it, destroy it—but now…

"I have never been much of a religious man, Nephew, and so it comes doubly hard for me to say what I now say: that while your father is dead these twenty years and more, I now find myself wondering if he is truly at rest! And what will be the look on *my* face when the thing is over, one way or the other? Ask about that, Nephew, ask how I looked when they found me.

"Finally, as to your course of action from this point onward: do what you will, but in the last event be sure you bring about the utter dissolution of the seat of ancient evil known as Temple House. There are things hidden in the great deserts and mountains of the world, and others sunken under the deepest oceans, which never were meant to exist in any sane or ordered universe. Yes, and certain revenants of immemorial horror have even come among men. One such has anchored itself here in the Pentlands, and in a little while I may meet it face to face. If all goes well…But then you should not be reading this.

"And so the rest is up to you, John Hamish; and if indeed man has an immortal soul, I now place mine in your hands. Do what must be done and if you are a believer, then say a prayer for me…

Yr. Loving Uncle—
Gavin McGilchrist."

I read the letter through a second time, then a third, and the shadows lengthened beyond the reach of the study's electric lights. Finally, I turned to the notebook—a slim, ruled, board-covered book whose like might be purchased at any stationery store—and opened it to page upon page of scrawled and at first glance seemingly unconnected jottings, references, abbreviated notes and memoranda concerning…Concerning what? Black magic? Witchcraft? The "supernatural"? But what else would you call a curse if not supernatural?

Well, my uncle had mentioned a puzzle, a mystery, the McGilchrist curse, the thing he had tracked down almost to the finish. And here were all the pointers, the clues, the keys to his years of research. I stared at the great bookcases lining the walls, the leather spines of their contents dully agleam in the glow of the lights. Asquith had told me that my uncle brought many old books back with him from his wanderings abroad.

I stood up and felt momentarily dizzy, and was obliged to lean on the desk until the feeling passed. The mustiness of the deserted house, I supposed, the closeness of the room and the odour of old books. Books... yes, and I moved shakily across to the nearest bookcase and ran my fingers over titles rubbed and faded with age and wear. There were works here which seemed to stir faint memories—perhaps I had been allowed to play with those books as a child?—but others were almost tangibly strange to the place, whose titles alone would make aliens of them without ever a page being turned. These must be those volumes my uncle had discovered abroad. I frowned as I tried to make something of their less than commonplace names.

Here were such works as the German *Unter-Zee Kulten* and Feery's *Notes on the Necronomicon* in a French edition; and here Gaston le Fe's *Dwellers in the Depths* and a black-bound, iron-hasped copy of the *Cthäat Aquadingen*, its harsh title suggestive of both German and Latin roots. Here was Gantley's *Hydrophinnae*, and here the *Liber Miraculorem* of the Monk and Chaplain Herbert of Clairvaux. Gothic letters proclaimed of one volume that it was Prinn's *De Vermis Mysteriis*, while another purported to be the suppressed and hideously disquieting *Unaussprechlichen Kulten* of Von Junzt—titles which seemed to leap at me as my eyes moved from shelf to shelf in a sort of disbelieving stupefaction.

What possible connection could there be between these ancient, foreign volumes of elder madness and delirium and the solid, down-to-earth McGilchrist line of gentlemen, officers and scholars? There seemed only one way to find out. Choosing a book at random. I found it to be the *Cthäat Aquadingen* and returned with it to the desk. The light outside was failing now and the shadows of the hills were long and sooty. In less than an hour it would be dusk, and half an hour after that dark.

Then there would only be Carl and I and the night. And the old house. As if in answer to unspoken thoughts, settling timbers groaned somewhere overhead. Through the window, down below in the sharp shadows of the house, the dull green glint of water caught my eye.

Carl and I, the night and the old house—

And the deep, dark pool.

5. The Music

It was almost completely dark by the time Carl returned, but in between I had at least been able to discover my uncle's system of reference. It was quite elementary, really. In his notebook, references such as "CA 121/7" simply indicated an item of interest in the *Cthäat Aquadingen*, page 121, the seventh paragraph. And in the work itself he had carefully underscored all such paragraphs or items of interest. At least a dozen such references concerning the *Cthäat Aquadingen* occurred in his notebook, and as night had drawn on I had examined each in turn.

Most of them were meaningless to me and several were in a tongue or glyph completely beyond my comprehension, but others were in a form of old English which I could transcribe with comparative ease. One such, which seemed a chant of sorts, had a brief annotation scrawled in the margin in my uncle's hand. The passage I refer to, as nearly as I can remember, went like this:

"Rise, O Nameless Ones;
It is Thy Season
When Thine Own of Thy Choosing,
Through Thy Spells & Thy Magic,
Through Dreams & Enchantry,
May know Thou art come.
They rush to Thy Pleasure,
For the Love of Thy Masters—
—the Spawn of Cthulhu."

And the accompanying annotation queried: "Would they have used such as this to call the Thing forth, I wonder, or was it simply a blood lure? What causes it to come forth now? When will it next come?"

It was while I was comparing references and text in this fashion that I began to get a glimmer as to just what the book was, and on further considering its title I saw that I had probably guessed correctly: "Cthäat" frankly baffled me, unless it had some connection with the language or being of the pre-Nacaal Kthatans; but "Aquadingen" was far less alien in its sound and formation. It meant (I believed), "water-things", or "things of the waters"; and the—*Cthäat Aquadingen* was quite simply a compendium of myths and legends concerning water sprites, nymphs, demons, naiads and other supernatural creatures of lakes and oceans, and the spells or conjurations by which they might be evoked or called out of their watery haunts.

I had just arrived at this conclusion when Carl returned, the lights of his vehicle cutting a bright swath over the dark surface of the pool as he parked in front of the porch. Laden down, he entered the house and I went down to the spacious if somewhat old fashioned kitchen to find him filling shelves and cupboards and stocking the refrigerator with perishables. This done, bright and breezy in his enthusiasm, he enquired about the radio.

"Radio?" I answered. "I thought your prime concern was for peace and quiet? Why, you've made enough noise for ten since we got here !"

"No, no," he said. "It's not *my* noise I'm concerned about but yours. Or rather, the radio's. I mean, you've obviously found one for I heard the music."

Carl was big, blond and blue-eyed; a Viking if ever I saw one, and quite capable of displaying a Viking's temper. He had been laughing when he asked me where the radio was, but now he was frowning. "Are you playing games with me, John?"

"No, of course I'm not," I answered him. "Now what's all this about? What music have you been hearing?"

His face suddenly brightened and he snapped his fingers. "There's a radio in the Range Rover," he said. "There has to be. It must have gotten switched on, very low, and I've been getting Bucharest or something." He made as if to go back outside.

"Bucharest?" I repeated him.

"Hmm?" he paused in the kitchen doorway. "Oh, yes—gypsyish stuff. Tambourines and chanting—and fiddles. Dancing around campfires. Look, I'd better switch it off or the battery will run down."

"I didn't see a radio," I told him, following him out through the porch and onto the drive.

He leaned inside the front of the vehicle, switched on the interior light and searched methodically. Finally he put the light out with an emphatic click. He turned to me and his jaw had a stubborn set to it. I looked back at him and raised my eyebrows. "No radio?"

He shook his head. "But I heard the music."

"Lovers," I said.

"Eh?"

"Lovers, out walking. A transistor radio. Perhaps they were sitting in the grass. After all, it is a beautiful summer night."

Again he shook his head. "No, it was right there in the air. Sweet and clear. I heard it as I approached the house. It came from the house, I thought. And you heard nothing?"

"Nothing," I answered, shaking my head.

"Well then—damn it to hell!" he suddenly grinned. "I've started hearing things, that's all! Skip it…Come on, let's have supper…"

Carl stuck to his "studio" bedroom but I slept upstairs in a room adjacent to the study. Even with the windows thrown wide open, the night was very warm and the atmosphere sticky, so that sleep did not come easily. Carl must have found a similar problem for on two or three occasions I awakened from a restless half-sleep to sounds of his moving about downstairs. In the morning over breakfast both of us were a little bleary-eyed, but then he led me through into his room to display the reason for his nocturnal activity.

There on the makeshift easel, on one of a dozen old canvasses he had brought with him, Carl had started work on a picture…of sorts.

For the present he had done little more than lightly brush in the background, which was clearly the valley of the house, but the house itself was missing from the picture and I could see that the artist did not intend to include it. The pool was there, however, with its encircling ring of quartz columns complete and finished with lintels of a like material. The columns and lintels glowed luminously.

In between and around the columns vague figures writhed, at present insubstantial as smoke, and in the foreground the flames of a small fire were driven on a wind that blew from across the pool. Taken as a whole and for all its sketchiness, the scene gave a vivid impression of savagery and pagan excitement—strange indeed considering that as yet there seemed to be so little in it to excite any sort of emotion whatever.

"Well," said Carl, his voice a trifle edgy, "what do you think?"

"I'm no artist, Carl," I answered, which I suppose in the circumstances was saying too much.

"You don't like it?" he sounded disappointed.

"I didn't say that," I countered. "Will it be a night scene?"

He nodded.

"And the dancers there, those wraiths…I suppose they *are* dancers?"

"Yes," he answered, "and musicians. Tambourines, fiddles…"

"Ah!" I nodded. "Last night's music."

He looked at me curiously. "Probably…Anyway, I'm happy with it. At least I've started to work. What about you?"

"You do your thing," I told him, "and I"ll do mine."

"But what are you going to do?"

I shrugged. "Before I do anything I'm going to soak up a lot of atmosphere.

But I don't intend staying here very long. A month or so, and then—"

"And then you'll burn this beautiful old place to the ground." He had difficulty keeping the sour note out of his voice.

"It's what my uncle wanted," I said. "I'm not here to write a story. A story may come of it eventually, even a book, but that can wait. Anyway, I won't burn the house." I made a mushroom cloud with my hands. "She goes—up!"

Carl snorted. "You McGilchrists," he said. "You're all nuts!" But there was no malice in his statement.

There was a little in mine, however, when I answered "Maybe—but I don't hear music when there isn't any!"

But that was before I knew everything...

6. The Familiar

During the course of the next week Scotland began to feel the first effects of what is now being termed "a scourge on the British Isles," the beginning of an intense, ferocious and prolonged period of drought. Sheltered by the Pentlands, a veritable suntrap for a full eight to ten hours a day, Temple House was no exception. Carl and I took to lounging around in shorts and T-shirts, and with his blond hair and fair skin he was particularly vulnerable. If we had been swimmers, then certainly we should have used the pool; as it was we had to content ourselves by sitting at its edge with our feet in the cool mountain water.

By the end of that first week, however, the drought's effect upon the small stream which fed the pool could clearly be seen. Where before the water had rushed down from the heights of the defile, now it seeped, and the natural overflow from the sides of the dam was so reduced that the old course of the stream was now completely dry. As for our own needs: the large water tanks in the attic of the house were full and their source of supply seemed independent, possibly some reservoir higher in the hills.

In the cool of the late afternoon, when the house stood in its own and the Pentlands' shade, then we worked; Carl at his drawing or painting, I with my uncle's notebook and veritable library of esoteric books. We also did a little walking in the hills, but in the heat of this incredible summer that was far too exhausting and only served to accentuate a peculiar mood of depression which had taken both of us in its grip. We blamed the weather, of course, when at any other time we would have considered so much sunshine and fresh air a positive blessing.

By the middle of the second week I was beginning to make real sense of my uncle's fragmentary record of his research. That is to say, his trail was becoming easier to follow as I grew used to his system and started to detect a pattern.

There were in fact two trails, both historic, one dealing with the McGilchrist line itself, the other more concerned with the family seat, with the House of the Temple. Because I seemed close to a definite discovery, I worked harder and became more absorbed with the work. And as if my own industry was contagious, Carl too began to put in longer hours at his easel or drawing board.

It was a Wednesday evening, I remember, the shadows lengthening and the atmosphere heavy when I began to see just how my uncle's mind had been working. He had apparently decided that if there really was a curse on the McGilchrists, then that it had come about during the construction of Temple House. To discover why this was so, he had delved back into the years prior to its construction in this cleft in the hills, and his findings had been strange indeed.

It had seemed to start in England in 1594 with the advent of foreign refugees. These had been the members of a monkish order originating in the mountains of Romania, whose ranks had nevertheless been filled with many diverse creeds, colours and races. There were Chinamen amongst them, Hungarians, Arabs and Africans, but their leader had been a Romanian priest named Chorazos. As to why they had been hounded out of their own countries, that remained a mystery.

Chorazos and certain of his followers became regular visitors at the Court of Queen Elizabeth I—who had ever held an interest in astrology, alchemy and all similar magics and mysteries—and with her help they founded a temple "somewhere near Finchley." Soon, however, couriers from foreign parts began to bring in accounts of the previous doings of this darkling sect, and so the Queen took advice.

Of all persons, she consulted with Dr John Dee, that more than dubious character whose own dabbling with the occult had brought him so close to disaster in 1555 during the reign of Queen Mary. Dee, at first enamoured of Chorazos and his followers, now turned against them. They were pagans, he said; their women were whores and their ceremonies orgiastic. They had brought with them a "familiar," which would have "needs" of its own, and eventually the public would rise up against them and the "outrage" they must soon bring about in the country. The Queen should therefore sever all connections with the sect—and immediately!

Acting under Dee's guidance, she at once issued orders for the arrest, detention and investigation of Chorazos and his members…but too late, for they had already flown. Their "temple" in Finchley—a "columned pavilion about a central lake"—was destroyed and the pool filled in. That was in late 1595.

In 1596 they turned up in Scotland, this time under the guise of travelling faith-healers and herbalists working out of Edinburgh. As a reward for their work among the poorer folk in the district, they were given a land grant and took up an austere residence in the Pentlands. There, following a pattern established abroad and carried on in England, Chorazos and his followers built their temple; except that this time they had to dam a stream in order to create a pool. The work took them several years; their ground was private property; they kept for the main well out of the limelight, and all was well…for a while.

Then came rumours of orgiastic rites in the hills, of children wandering away from home under the influence of strange, hypnotic music, of a monstrous being conjured up from hell to preside over ceremonial murder and receive its grisly tribute, and at last the truth was out. However covertly Chorazos had organized his perversions, there now existed the gravest suspicions as to what he and the others of his sect were about. And this in the Scotland of James IV, who five years earlier had charged an Edinburgh jury with "an Assize of Error" when they dismissed an action for witchcraft against one of the "notorious" North Berwick Witches. In this present matter, however, any decision of the authorities was pre-empted by persons unknown—possibly the inhabitants of nearby Penicuik, from which town several children had disappeared—and Chorazos's order had been wiped out en masse one night and the temple reduced to ruins and shattered quartz stumps.

Quite obviously, the site of the temple had been here, and the place had been remembered by locals down the centuries; so that when the McGilchrist house was built in the mid-18th Century it automatically acquired the name of Temple House. The name had been retained…but what else had lingered over from those earlier times, and what *exactly* was the nature of the McGilchrist Curse?

I yawned and stretched. It was after eight and the sinking sun had turned the crests of the hills to bronze. A movement, seen in the corner of my eye through the window, attracted my attention. Carl was making his way to the rim of the pool. He paused with his hands on his hips to stand between two of the broken columns, staring out over the silent water. Then he laid back his head and breathed deeply. There was a tired but self-satisfied air about him that set me wondering.

I threw the window wide and leaned out, calling down through air which was still warm and cloying: "Hey, Carl—you look like the cat who got the cream!"

He turned and waved. "Maybe I am. It's that painting of mine. I think I've got it beat. Not finished yet…but coming along."

"Is it good?" I asked.

He shrugged, but it was a shrug of affirmation, not indifference. "Are you busy? Come down and see for yourself. I only came out to clear my head, so that I can view it in fresh perspective. Yours will be a second opinion."

I went downstairs to find him back in his studio. Since the light was poor now, he switched on all of the electric lights and led the way to his easel. I had last looked at the painting some three or four days previously, at a time when it had still been very insubstantial. Now—

Nothing insubstantial about it now. The grass was green, long and wild, rising to nighted hills of grey and purple, silvered a little by a gibbous moon. The temple was almost luminous, its columns shining with an eerie light. Gone the wraithlike dancers; they capered in cassocks now, solid, wild and weird with leering faces. I started as I stared at those faces—yellow, black, and white faces, a half-dozen different races—but I started worse at the sight of the *Thing* rising over the pool within the circle of glowing columns. Still vague, that horror—that leprous grey, tentacled, mushroom-domed monstrosity—and as yet mainly amorphous; but formed enough to show that it was nothing of this good, sane Earth.

"What the hell is it?" I half-gasped, half-whispered.

"Hmm?" Carl turned to me and smiled with pleased surprise at the look of shock on my blanched face. "I'm damned if I know—but I think it's pretty good! It will be when it's finished. I'm going to call it *The Familiar*…"

7. The Face

For a long while I simply stood there taking in the contents of that hideous canvas and feeling the heat of the near-tropical night beating in through the open windows. It was all there: the foreign monks making their weird music, the temple glowing in the darkness, the dam, the pool and the hills as I had always known them, the *Thing* rising up in bloated loathsomeness from dark water, and a sense of realness I had never seen before and probably never again will see in any artist's work.

My first impulse when the shock wore off a little was to turn on Carl in anger. This was too monstrous a joke. But no, his face bore only a look of astonishment now—astonishment at my reaction, which must be quite obvious to him. "Christ!" he said, "is it that good?"

"That—*Thing*—has nothing to do with Christ!" I finally managed to force the words out of a dry-throat. And again I felt myself on the verge of demanding an explanation. Had he been reading my uncle's notes? Had he been secretly following my own line of research? But how could he, secretly or otherwise? The idea was preposterous.

"You really do *feel* it, don't you?" he said, excitedly taking my arm. "I can see it in your face."

"I…I feel it, yes," I answered. "It's a very…powerful piece of work." Then, to fill the gap, I added: "Where did you dream it up?"

"Right first time," he answered. "A dream—I think. Something left over from a nightmare. I haven't been sleeping too well. The heat, I guess."

"You're right," I agreed. "It's too damned hot. Will you be doing any more tonight?"

He shook his head, his eyes still on the painting. "Not in this light. I don't want to foul it up. No, I'm for bed. Besides, I have a headache."

"What?" I said, glad now that I had made no wild accusation. "You?—a strapping great Viking like you, with a headache?"

"Viking?" he frowned. "You've called me that before. My looks must be deceptive. No, my ancestors came out of Hungary—a place called Stregoicavar. And I can tell you they burned more witches there than you ever did in Scotland!"

There was little sleep for me that night, though toward morning I did finally drop off, slumped across the great desk, drowsing fitfully in the soft glow of my desk light. Prior to that, however, in the silence of the night—driven on by a feeling of impending…something—I had delved deeper into the old books and documents amassed by my uncle, slowly but surely fitting together that great jigsaw whose pieces he had spent so many years collecting.

The work was more difficult now, his notes less coherent, his writing barely legible; but at least the material was or should be more familiar to me. Namely, I was studying the long line of McGilchrists gone before me, whose seat had been Temple House since its construction two hundred and forty years ago. And as I worked so my eyes would return again and again, almost involuntarily, to the dark pool with its ring of broken columns. Those stumps were white in the silver moonlight—as white as the columns in Carl's picture—and so my thoughts returned to Carl.

By now he must be well asleep, but this new mystery filled my mind through the small hours. Carl Earlman…It certainly sounded Hungarian, German at any rate, and I wondered what the old family name had been. Ehrlichman, perhaps? Arlmann? And not Carl but Karl.

And his family hailed from Stregoicavar. That was a name I remembered from a glance into Von Junzt's *Unspeakable Cults*, I was sure. Stregoicavar: it had stayed in my mind because of its meaning, which is "witch-town." Certain of Chorazos's order of pagan priests had been Hungarian. Was it possible that some dim ancestral memory lingered over in Carl's mind, and that the pool with its quartz stumps had awakened that in his blood which harkened back to older times? And what of the gypsy music he had sworn to hearing on our first night in this old house? Young and strong he was certainly, but beneath an often brash exterior he had all the sensitivity of an artist born.

According to my uncle's research my own great-grandfather, Robert Allan McGilchrist, had been just such a man. Sensitive, a dreamer, prone to hearing things in the dead of night which no one else could hear. Indeed, his wife had left him for his peculiar ways. She had taken her two sons with her; and so for many years the old man had lived here alone, writing and studying. He had been well known for his paper on the Lambton Worm legend of Northumberland: of a great worm or dragon that lived in a well and emerged at night to devour "bairns and beasties and foolhardy wanderers in the dark." He had also published a pamphlet on the naiads of the lochs of Inverness; and his limited edition book, *Notes on Nessie—the Secrets of Loch Ness* had caused a minor sensation when first it saw print.

It was Robert Allan McGilchrist, too, who restored the old floodgate in the dam, so that the water level in the pool could be controlled; but that had been his last work. A shepherd had found him one morning slumped across the gate, one hand still grasping the wheel which controlled its elevation, his upper body floating face-down in the water. He must have slipped and fallen, and his heart had given out. But the look on his face had been a fearful thing; and since the embalmers had been unable to do anything with him, they had buried him immediately.

And as I studied this or that old record or consulted this or that musty book, so my eyes would return to the dam, the pool with its fanged columns, the old floodgate—rusted now and fixed firmly in place—and the growing sensation of an onrushing doom gnawed inside me until it became a knot of fear in my chest. If only the heat would let up, just for one day, and if only I could finish my research and solve the riddle once and for all.

It was then, as the first flush of dawn showed above the eastern hills, that I determined what I must do. The fact of the matter was that Temple House frightened me, as I suspected it had frightened many people before me. Well, I had neither the stamina nor the dedication of my uncle. He had resolved to track the thing down to the end, and something—sheer hard work, the "curse," failing health, *something*—had killed him.

But his legacy to me had been a choice: continue his work or put an end to the puzzle for all time and blow Temple House to hell. So be it, that was what I would do. A day or two more—only a day or two, to let Carl finish his damnable painting—and then I would do what Gavin McGilchrist had ordered done. And with that resolution uppermost in my mind, relieved that at last I had made the decision, so I fell asleep where I sprawled at the desk.

The sound of splashing aroused me; that and my name called from below. The sun was just up and I felt dreadful, as if suffering from a hang-over. For a long time I simply lay sprawled out. Then I stood up and eased my cramped limbs, and finally I turned to the open window. There was Carl, dressed only in his shorts, stretched out flat on a wide, thick plank, paddling out toward the middle of the pool!

"Carl!" I called down, my voice harsh with my own instinctive fear of the water. "Man, that's dangerous—you can't swim!"

He turned his head, craned his neck and grinned up at me. "Safe as houses," he called, "so long as I hang on to the plank. And it's cool, John, so wonderfully cool. This feels like the first time I've been cool in weeks!"

By now he had reached roughly the pool's centre and there he stopped paddling and simply let his hands trail in green depths. The level of the water had gone down appreciably during the night and the streamlet which fed the pool was now quite dry. The plentiful weed of the pool, becoming concentrated as the water evaporated, seemed thicker than ever I remembered it. So void of life, that water, with never a fish or frog to cause a ripple on the morass-green of its surface.

And suddenly that tight knot of fear was back in my chest, making my voice a croak as I tried to call out: "Carl, get out of there!"

"What?" he faintly called back, but he didn't turn his head. He was staring down into the water, staring intently at something he saw there. His hand brushed aside weed—

"Carl!" I found my voice. "For God's sake get out of it!"

He started then, his head and limbs jerking as if scalded, setting the plank to rocking so that he half slid off it. Then—a scrambling back to safety and a frantic splashing and paddling; and galvanized into activity I sprang from the window and raced breakneck downstairs. And Carl laughing shakily as I stumbled knee-deep in hated water to drag him physically from the plank, both of us trembling despite the burning rays of the new-risen sun and the furnace heat of the air.

"What happened?" I finally asked.

"I thought I saw something," he answered. "In the pool. A reflection, that's all, but it startled me."

"What did you see?" I demanded, my back damp with cold sweat.

"Why, what would I see?" he answered, but his voice trembled for all that he tried to grin. "A face, of course—my own face framed by the weeds. But it didn't look like me, that's all…"

8. The Dweller

Looking back now in the light of what I already knew—certainly of what I should have guessed at that time—it must seem that I was guilty of an almost suicidal negligence in spending the rest of that day upstairs on my bed, tossing in nightmares brought on by the nervous exhaustion which beset me immediately after the incident at the pool. On the other hand, I had had little sleep the night before and Carl's adventure had given me a terrific jolt; and so my failure to recognize the danger—how close it had drawn—may perhaps be forgiven.

In any event, I forced myself to wakefulness in the early evening, went downstairs and had coffee and a frugal meal of biscuits, and briefly visited Carl in his studio. He was busy—frantically busy, dripping with sweat and brushing away at his canvas—working on his loathsome painting, which he did not want me to see. That suited me perfectly for I had already seen more than enough of the thing. I did take time enough to tell him, though, that he should finish his work in the next two days; for on Friday or at the very latest Saturday morning I intended to blow the place sky high.

Then I went back upstairs, washed and shaved, and as the light began to fail so I returned to my uncle's notebook. There were only three or four pages left unread, the first dated only days before his demise, but they were such a hodge-podge of scrambled and near-illegible miscellanea that I had the greatest difficulty making anything of them. Only that feeling of a burgeoning terror drove me on, though by now I had almost completely lost faith in making anything whatever of the puzzle.

As for my uncle's notes: a basically orderly nature had kept me from leafing at random through his book, or perhaps I should have understood earlier. As it is, the notebook is lost forever, but as best I can I shall copy down what I remember of those last few pages. After that—and after I relate the remaining facts of the occurrences of that fateful hideous night—the reader must rely upon his own judgement. The notes then, or what little I remember of them:

"Levi's or Mirandola's invocation: *Dasmass Jeschet Boene Doess Efar Duvema Enit Marous.*" If I could get the pronunciation right, perhaps...But what will the Thing be? And will it succumb to a double-barrelled blast? That remains to be seen. But if what I suspect is firmly founded...Is it a tick-thing, such as Von Junzt states inhabits the globular mantle of Yogg-Sothoth? (*Unaussprechlichen Kulten*, 78/16)—fearful hints—monstrous pantheon...And this merely a parasite to one of Them!

"The Cult of Cthulhu...immemorial horror spanning all the ages. The *Johansen Narrative* and the *Pnakotic Manuscript*. And the Innsmouth Raid of 1928; much was made of that, and yet nothing known for sure. Deep Ones, but...different again from this Thing.

"Entire myth-cycle...So many sources. Pure myth and legend? I think not. Too deep, interconnected, even plausible. According to Carter in SR, (AH '59) p. 250-51, *They* were driven into this part of the universe (or into this time-dimension) by "Elder Gods" as punishment for a rebellion. Hastur the Unspeakable prisoned in Lake of Hali (again the lake or pool motif) in Carcosa; Great Cthulhu in R'lyeh, where he slumbers still in his death-sleep; Ithaqua sealed away behind icy Arctic barriers, and so on. But Yogg-Sothoth was sent *outside*, into a parallel place, conterminous with all space and time. Since YS is everywhere and when, if a man knew the gate he could call Him out...

"Did Chorazos and his acolytes, for some dark reason of their own, attempt thus to call Him out? And did they get this dweller in Him instead? And I believe I understand the reason for the pool. Grandfather knew. His interest in Nessie, the Lambton Worm, the

Kraken of olden legend, naiads, Cthulhu…Wendy Smith's burrowers feared water; and the sheer weight of the mighty Pacific helps keep C. prisoned in his place in R'lyeh—thank God! Water subdues these things…

"But if water confines It, why does It return to the water? And how may It leave the pool if not deliberately called out? No McGilchrist ever called it out, I'm sure, not willingly; though some may have suspected that something was here. No swimmers in the family—not a one—and I think I know why. It is an instinctive, an ancestral fear of the pool! No, of the unknown Thing which lurks beneath the pool's surface…"

The thing which lurks beneath the pool's surface…

Clammy with the heat, and with a debilitating terror springing from these words on the written page—these scribbled thought-fragments which, I was now sure, were anything but demented ravings—I sat at the old desk and read on. And as the house grew dark and quiet, as on the previous night, again I found my eyes drawn to gaze down through the open window to the surface of the still pool.

Except that the surface was no longer still!

Ripples were spreading in concentric rings from the pool's dark centre, tiny mobile wavelets caused by—by what? Some disturbance beneath the surface? The water level was well down now and tendrils of mist drifted from the pool to lie soft, luminous and undulating in the moonlight, curling like the tentacles of some great plastic beast over the dam, across the drive to the foot of the house.

A sort of paralysis settled over me then, a dreadful lassitude, a mental and physical malaise brought on by excessive morbid study, culminating in this latest phenomenon of the old house and the aura of evil which now seemed to saturate its very stones. I should have done something—something to break the spell, anything rather than sit there and merely wait for what was happening to happen—and yet I was incapable of positive action.

Slowly I returned my eyes to the written page; and there I sat shivering and sweating, my skin crawling as I read on by the light of my desk lamp. But so deep my trancelike state that it was as much as I could do to force my eyes from one word to the next. I had no volition, no will of my own with which to fight that fatalistic spell; and the physical heat of the night was that of a furnace as sweat dripped from my forehead onto the pages of the notebook.

"…I have checked my findings and can't believe my previous blindness! It should have been obvious. It happens when the water level falls below a certain point. It *has* happened every time there has been extremely hot weather—when the pool has started to *dry up*! The Thing needn't be called out at all! As to why it returns to the pool after taking a victim: it must return before daylight. It is a fly-the-light. A haunter of the dark. A wampyre!…but not blood..Nowhere can I find mention of blood sacrifices. And no punctures or mutilations. What, then are Its "needs?" Did Dee know? Kelly knew, I'm sure, but his writings are lost…

"Eager now to try the invocation, but I wish that first I might know the true nature of the Thing. It takes the life of Its victim— but what else?"

"I have it!—God, I know—and I wish I did not know! But that *look* on my poor brother's face…Andrew, Andrew…I know now why you looked that way. But if I can free you, you shall be freed. If I wondered at the nature of the Thing, then I wonder no longer. The answers are all there, in the *Cthäat A.* and *Hydrophinnae*, if only I had known exactly where to look. Yibb-Tstll is one such; Bugg-Shash, too. Yes, and the pool-thing is another…

"There have been a number down the centuries—the horror that dwelled in the mirror of Nitocris; the sucking, hunting thing that Count Magnus kept; the red, hairy slime used by Julian Scortz—familiars of the Great Old Ones, parasites that lived on *Them* as lice live on men. Or rather, on their life-force! This one has survived the ages, at least until now. It does not take the blood but the very essence of Its victim. *It is a soul-eater!*

"I can wait no longer. Tonight, when the sun goes down and the hills are in darkness…But if I succeed, and if the Thing comes for me…We'll see how It faces up to my shotgun!"

My eyes were half-closed by the time I had finally scanned all that was written, of which the above is only a small part; and even having read it I had not fully taken it in. Rather, I had absorbed it automatically, without reading any immediate meaning into it. But as I re-read those last few lines, so I heard something which roused me up from my lassitude and snapped me alertly awake in an instant.

It was music: the faint but unmistakable strains of a whirling pagan tune that seemed to reach out to me from a time beyond time, from a hell beyond all known hells…

9. The Horror

Shocked back to mental alertness, still my limbs were stiff as a result of several hours crouched over the desk. Thus, as I sprang or attempted to spring to my feet, a cramp attacked both of my calves and threw me down by the window. I grabbed at the sill…and whatever I had been about to do was at once forgotten.

I gazed out the open window on a scene straight out of madness or nightmare. The broken columns where they now stood up from bases draped with weed seemed to glow with an inner light; and to my straining eyes it appeared that this haze of light extended uniformly upwards, so that I saw a revenant of the temple as it had once been. Through the light-haze I could also see the centre of the pool, from which the ripples spread outward with a rapidly increasing agitation.

There was a shape there now, a dark oblong illuminated both by the clean moonlight and by that supernatural glow; and even as I gazed, so the water slopping above the oblong seemed pushed aside and the slab showed its stained marble surface to the air. The music grew louder then, soaring wildly, and it seemed to me in my shocked and frightened condition that dim figures reeled and writhed around the perimeter of the pool.

Then—horror of horrors!—in one mad moment the slab tilted to reveal a black hole going down under the pool, like the entrance to some sunken tomb. There came an outpouring of miasmal gasps, visible in the eerie glow, and then—

Even before the thing emerged I knew what it would be; how it would look. It was that horror on Carl's canvas, the soft-tentacled, mushroom-domed terror he had painted under the ancient, evil influence of this damned, doomed place. It was the dweller, the familiar, the tick-thing, the star-born wampyre…it was the curse of the McGilchrists. Except I understood now that this was not merely a curse on the McGilchrists but on the entire world. Of course it had seemed to plague the McGilchrists as a personal curse—but only because they had chosen to build Temple House here on the edge of its pool. They had been victims by virtue of their *availability*, for I was sure that the pool-thing was not naturally discriminative.

Then, with an additional thrill of horror, I saw that the thing was on the move, drifting across the surface of the pool, its flaccid tentacles reaching avidly in the direction of the house. The lights downstairs were out, which meant that Carl must be asleep…

Carl!

The thing was across the drive now, entering the porch, the house itself. I forced cramped limbs to agonized activity, lurched across the room, out onto the dark landing and stumbled blindly down the stairs. I slipped, fell, found my feet again—and my voice, too.

"Carl!" I cried, arriving at the door of his studio. "Carl, *for God's sake!*"

The thing straddled him where he lay upon his bed. It glowed with an unearthly, a rotten luminescence which outlined his pale body in a sort of foxfire. Its tentacles writhed over his naked form and his limbs were filled with fitful motion. Then the dweller's mushroom head settled over his face, which disappeared in folds of the thing's gilled mantle.

"Carl!" I screamed yet again, and as I lurched forward in numb horror so my hand found the light switch on the wall. In another moment the room was bathed in sane and wholesome electric light. The thing bulged upward from Carl—rising like some monstrous amoeba, some sentient, poisonous jellyfish from an alien ocean—and turned toward me.

I saw a face, a face I knew across twenty years of time fled, *my uncle's face!* Carved in horror, those well remembered features besought, pleaded with me, that an end be put to this horror and peace restored to this lonely valley; that the souls of countless victims be freed to pass on from this world to their rightful destinations.

The thing left Carl's suddenly still form and moved forward, flowed toward me; and as it came so the face it wore melted and changed. Other faces were there, hidden in the thing, many with McGilchrist features and many without, dozens of them that came and went ceaselessly. There were children there, too, mere babies; but the last face of all, the one I shall remember above all others— *that was the face of Carl Earlman himself!* And it, too, wore that pleading, that imploring look—the look of a soul in hell, which prays only for its release.

Then the light won its unseen, unsung battle. Almost upon me, suddenly the dweller seemed to wilt. It shrank from the light, turned and flowed out of the room, through the porch, back toward the pool. Weak with reaction I watched it go, saw it move out across the now still water, saw the slab tilt down upon its descending shape and heard the music fade into silence. Then I turned to Carl…

I do not think I need mention the look on Carl's lifeless face, or indeed say anything more about him. Except perhaps that it is my fervent prayer that he now rests in peace with the rest of the dweller's many victims, taken down the centuries. That is my prayer, but…

As for the rest of it:

I dragged Carl from the house to the Range Rover, drove him to the crest of the rise, left him there and returned to the house. I took my uncle's prepared charges from his study and set them in the base of the shale cliff where the house backed onto it. Then I lit the fuses, scrambled back into the Range Rover and drove to where Carl's body lay in the cool of night. I tried not to look at his face.

In a little while the fuses were detonated, going off almost simultaneously, and the night was shot with fire and smoke and a rising cloud of dust. When the air cleared the whole scene was changed forever. The cliff had come down on the house, sending it crashing into the pool. The pool itself had disappeared, swallowed up in shale and debris; and it was as if the House of the Temple, the temple itself and the demon-cursed pool had never existed.

All was silence and desolation, where only the moonlight played on jagged stumps of centuried columns, projecting still from the scree- and rubble-filled depression which had been the pool. And now the moon silvered the bed of the old stream, running with water from the ruined pool—

And at last I was able to drive on.

10. The Unending Nightmare

That should have been the end of it, but such has not been the case. Perhaps I alone am to blame. The police in Penicuik listened to my story, locked me in a cell overnight and finally conveyed me to this place, where I have been now for more than a week. In a way I supposed that the actions of the police were understandable; for my wild appearance that night—not to mention the ghastly, naked corpse in the Range Rover and the incredible story I incoherently told—could hardly be expected to solicit their faith or understanding. But I do *not* understand the position of the alienists here at Oakdeene.

Surely they, too, can hear the damnable music?—that music which grows louder hour by hour, more definite and decisive every night—the music which in olden days summoned the pool-thing to its ritual sacrifice. Or is it simply that they disagree with my theory? I have mentioned it to them time and time again and repeat it now: that there are *other* pools in the Pentlands, watery havens to which the thing might have fled from the destruction of its weedy retreat beside the now fallen seat of the McGilchrists. Oh, yes, and I firmly believe that it did so flee. And the days are long and hot and a great drought is on the land…

And perhaps, too, over the years, a very real curse has loomed up large and monstrous over the McGilchrists. Do souls have a flavour, I wonder, a distinctive texture of their own? Is it possible that the pool-thing has developed an appetite, a taste for the souls of McGilchrists? If so, then it will surely seek me out; and yet here I am detained in this institute for the insane.

Or could it be that I am now in all truth mad? Perhaps the things I have experienced and know to be true have driven me mad, and the music I hear exists only in my mind. That is what the nurses tell me and dear God, I pray that it is so! But if not—if not…

For there is that other thing, which I have not mentioned until now. When I carried Carl from his studio after the pool-thing left him, I saw his finished painting. Not the whole painting but merely a part of it, for when it met my eyes they saw only one thing: the finished face which Carl had painted on the dweller.

This is the nightmare which haunts me worse than any other, the question I ask myself over and over in the dead of night, when the moonlight falls upon my high, barred window and the music floods into my padded cell:

If they should bring me my breakfast one morning and find me dead—*will my face really look like that?*